Praise for *Maybe Meant to Be* (formerly titled *If We Were Us*)

"Gripping... Entertainingly depicts mature views on life, friendship, and romance."

—*Kirkus Reviews*

"An excellent choice for most YA collections, this will be welcomed by fans of Becky Albertalli's *Simon vs. the Homo Sapiens Agenda* and Molly Backes's *The Princesses of Iowa*."

—*School Library Journal*

Praise for *The Summer of Broken Rules*

"[It's] a rose-tinted romance that readers will want to toss into a beach tote for some relaxing, enjoyable fun."

—*The Bulletin of the Center for Children's Books*

"The mix of budding romance, competitive hijinks, a close-knit circle, as well as dealing with loss make for a satisfying read."

—*Kirkus Reviews*

"[A]n engaging read... Recommended for larger collections with dedicated romance readers."

—*School Library Journal*

"[I]deally suited for those who enjoy contemporary romance... A perfect summer or beach read!"

—Andrea Reid, *The Nerd Daily*

"Seamlessly weaves in the importance of family, and by the end, I felt like I had joined the Fox family and their traditions... A quick and easy read recommended for anyone who is looking for a lighthearted book sprinkled with elements of reality."

—Sachi Sharma, *Manhattan Book Review*

Praise for
What Happens After Midnight

"An instant hit...carefully plotted [with] delightfully witty banter... The combination of engaging characters and plot successfully entertains while simultaneously asking big questions about legacy, memory, and the high school experience. Growing up is hard, but this book about transitioning from teen to adult makes for a fun book recommendation for a relatable life experience."

—*School Library Connection*

"An engaging story of personal growth and a second-chance romance."

—*Kirkus Reviews*

"Lily and Tag's sparkling second-chance romance is the stuff Taylor Swift songs are made of, their boarding school world as cozy and close-knit as Stars Hollow. I loved the epic senior prank schemes, clandestine kisses, and every other twist and turn in this delightful story!"

—Kaitlyn Hill, author of *Love from Scratch*

"Walther builds romantic tension and develops some genuine nail-biting moments as the pranksters creep around campus, breaking into off-limits buildings, ascending a ropes course, and even hijacking a golf cart, all the while avoiding campus security."

—*Youth Services Book Review*

"Walther (*The Summer of Broken Rules*) fills this edge-of-summer rom-com with mischief and mayhem, delivering swift action and a swoony second-chance romance perfect for soon-to-be grads suffering from senioritis."

—*Publishers Weekly*

"A complete delight! This is a swoony second-chance love story intertwined with a comedy of errors, performed by a lovable, vivid ensemble."

—Samantha Markum, author of *This May End Badly*

"Full of fun and charm…this sweet second-chance romance kept me smiling throughout!"

—Becky Dean, author of *Love & Other Great Expectations*

"Brimming with high stakes hijinks and swoony romantic tension, *What Happens After Midnight* is a laugh-out-loud, perfect page-turner you won't be able to put down. Great fun!"

—Robin Reul, author of *Where the Road Leads Us* and *My Kind of Crazy*

Also by K. L. Walther

Maybe Meant to Be
The Summer of Broken Rules
What Happens After Midnight

A First Time for Everything

A First Time for Everything

K. L. WALTHER

sourcebooks fire

Copyright © 2025 by K. L. Walther
Cover and internal design © 2025 by Sourcebooks
Cover design by Erin Fitzsimmons/Sourcebooks
Cover art © Monique Aimee
Internal design by Laura Boren/Sourcebooks
Emoji art © streptococcus/Adobe Stock

Sourcebooks and the colophon are registered trademarks of Sourcebooks.

All rights reserved. No part of this book may be reproduced in any form or by any electronic or mechanical means, including information storage and retrieval systems—except in the case of brief quotations embodied in critical articles or reviews—without permission in writing from its publisher, Sourcebooks.

No part of this book may be used or reproduced in any manner for the purpose of training artificial intelligence technologies or systems.

The characters and events portrayed in this book are fictitious or are used fictitiously. Any similarity to real persons, living or dead, is purely coincidental and not intended by the author.

Published by Sourcebooks Fire, an imprint of Sourcebooks
P.O. Box 4410, Naperville, Illinois 60567-4410
(630) 961-3900
sourcebooks.com

Cataloging-in-Publication Data is on file with the Library of Congress.

The authorized representative in the EEA is Dorling Kindersley Verlag GmbH. Arnulfstr. 124, 80636 Munich, Germany

Manufactured in the UK by Clays and distributed by
Dorling Kindersley Limited, London
001-351148-Jun/25
10 9 8 7 6 5 4 3 2 1

For Madison:
Thank you for the bridesmaid life,
but thank you even more for almost
two decades of best friendship.
Till death do us part!

And, to Christopher:
I'll save my dedication for June 27, 2025.
Will my words be as beautiful as my dress?
Fingers crossed, because as I might've
mentioned, it's pretty gorgeous.

WINTER

ONE

"How many times are you going to watch that?"

I looked up from my phone, eyes flashing to my dad over at the stove. Lee was thoughtfully stirring a pot of his famous chicken-and-rice soup. "What?" I shrugged as if I had no idea what he was talking about. "I'm just scrolling."

"More like *trolling*," my other dad commented from across the kitchen. Per usual, Harry was wearing his favorite pair of Warby Parkers and sitting with his MacBook at our long oak table, reading and revising contracts for his various property listings.

"Your father's right, Madeline," Lee said. "Watching the same video over and over is more akin to trolling, not scrolling." He paused to comically narrow his eyes. "You haven't posted something snarky, have you?"

"No, Da." I smiled and shook my head. Lee was "Da," because my older brother, Austin, hadn't been able to say the full *dad* when he was little, and by the time he'd finally grasped it, Harry had been holding him. A clear sign, apparently, that Harry was meant to be "Dad" and Lee was officially "Da."

The Fisher-Michaels family rolled with it.

My comment on the aforementioned Instagram Reel had been a short and sweet emoji combination: a starry-eyed smiley face followed by confetti and a popping champagne bottle. It was nothing compared to the seemingly endless stream of comments that kept the online celebration raging.

@amber.kovac: Wowweeee!! Congrats!! <3

Triple fire emojis from @heelyj.
What's the hashtag? asked @nate_the_great.
IM NOT CRYING, my thirteen-year-old cousin had written.
@mfoxw said, The Married Club has jackets!
And from one of Austin's best friends: Way to ruin things for the rest of us, man...

Or, in other words: *Major congratulations, but did you really need to set the bar so high?*

Two days ago, my brother had proposed to his girlfriend. And not only did he propose, but he proposed in freaking *Paris*. He and Katie and her family had spent two weeks there for some relative's wedding, and on their last day...

My parents groaned when I replayed the video. Paris was gorgeous in the winter. Someone's drone had captured the city—the Eiffel Tower, the Musée d'Orsay, and other elegant limestone buildings dusted with snow. Even in the new year, Christmas markets still bustled and people sipped hot chocolate while ice skating. A classic piano riff had been edited in as background music, and we were soon treated to a sweeping shot of the Seine before the camera cut to Katie wandering along the river. Her long blond hair had been curled to beach-wave perfection and she wore a timeless white peacoat. Her choice of high-heeled boots was proof that she didn't exactly have serious plans to go on a walk.

"She *had* to have known!" I exclaimed to no dad in particular.

"She *totally* knew!" they exclaimed back for the millionth time.

And then there, at a turn in the stone pathway, was my brother on a bridge adorned with greenery and twinkle lights. His unkempt brown hair refused to stay combed back, but he looked so handsome with his dimpled grin. Katie ran—or tottered, in those shoes—toward him. The piano still played, so you couldn't hear any words exchanged, but ten heartbeats after Austin had gotten down on one knee, he was back on his feet and spinning Katie around as they kissed.

And they lived happily ever after! anyone would think.

The video ended, but the scene did not—pictures had later been posted of Katie's parents and grandparents and random relatives at a fancy restaurant with the happy couple. They were all laughing and smiling while raising glasses of bubbly.

Objectively, it looked like a fairy-tale engagement.

But subjectively, it sucked that my family hadn't been a part of it. We knew—I mean, of course we knew that it was on the horizon. My brother and his girlfriend had been together five years, and Austin had even come home a couple months ago to ask our parents for advice on how to approach Katie's father for his blessing. (I may or may not have been eavesdropping from the top of the staircase.)

Like I said, we knew it was coming.

Paris, though? That was a blindside. "Wasn't it his plan to propose in the pasture?" Dad said after we'd originally watched the Reel. "Didn't he say he wanted it to be a meaningful place?"

Da and I hadn't responded. Congratulations! I'd texted Austin later, even though I was kind of pissed at him for not telling us. It was his moment, not mine. Get ready for a huge-ass hug when you get home!!!

"I'm going for a walk," I said suddenly, dragging myself up from my spot on the warm kitchen floor. Its radiant heating was forever too tempting to ignore. I loved stretching out on the tile like a starfish and letting my eyes drift shut, especially in the early mornings before school. Arthur and Francine, our two black Newfoundlands, were currently passed out. Francine snored loudly while Arthur twitched, probably in the middle of a dream.

"Alright." Da nodded as he taste tested the soup. He adjusted one of the stovetop's knobs, a signal that dinner was almost ready. A pang of hunger hit me.

Over at the table, Dad's laptop chimed. "Austin messaged they'll be here in ten. Make it a mission, Mads. Not a meander."

"Roger that." I dug in the fridge for some carrots and then caught an apple Da tossed me from the fruit bowl. My brother and Katie had gotten home yesterday and were coming for dinner tonight. They lived forty-five minutes away in Philadelphia; Austin was halfway through his third year of dental school at the University of Pennsylvania. He'd always liked working with his hands and found teeth strangely fascinating, but I never let him forget he was going to someday star in a bunch of children's nightmares. He always retaliated by tickling and teasing me about all the times I'd dreamt about my orthodontist taking a hammer to my teeth.

Despite myself, I smiled at the memory as I pulled on my rusty red-orange-and-black-plaid wool coat and favorite Carhartt beanie. Austin, he was the best. Not only the best brother or my best friend—just *the best*. And it felt like I hadn't seen him in forever. *I'm going to tackle him*, I decided, the mudroom door slamming behind me. *When he gets out of the car, I'm going to tackle him into the snow.*

I could already hear us laughing.

My family and I lived on twenty acres near the Delaware River in Pennsylvania. Our farmhouse had been built in 1774, and while there had certainly been a couple renovations, it still stood tall centuries later. It was white with two brick chimneys, black shutters, a bright red front door, and a wide porch that overlooked the front lawn (that I had more or less turned into a field hockey practice field), the horses' rolling pasture, and beyond that, a small pond. Ducks flocked there in the springtime, and when it froze in the winter, Austin and I skated on it until our cheeks and toes went numb from the cold.

It was frozen now. After a busy Jingle Bells season with our backyard Christmas tree farm, pine and spruce trees planted everywhere, we'd rung in the new year several days ago with a snowstorm. Da had plowed and salted our long driveway enough to come and go, but it was still caked with ice and snow. I tucked my tingling nose into my scarf as I trudged through the snowy dunes, our front barn growing larger with each step. Dad was a Realtor and had the shortest commute ever; he and his partners had gutted and converted the barn into their office space after starting their own firm. THE CHEVAL COLLECTIVE, the snow-frosted masthead over the door read.

Cheval was French for *horse*. Because years ago, horses had been Dad's life. He'd grown up riding and competing, and in his twenties, had been a three-day eventer on the U.S. Equestrian Team. "And then I really wrecked my back and needed serious surgery..." was how he finished when telling the story at dinner parties.

"But it ended up being a total win," Da would chime in,

"because if he hadn't needed that operation, he wouldn't have met me!"

Da was technically Dr. Lee Fisher, orthopedic spine surgeon. He'd done such a fantastic job on Dad's back that he could still ride casually these days. We had three horses. Tally-Ho, our chestnut mare, crossed the paddock when I leaned against the split-rail fence. "Looking good, Tal," I said as she nuzzled me, toasty in her tartan blanket. She knew I had treats.

I fed Tally an apple, and when Chip and Chop wandered over, I gave them the carrots. While they munched, I stared out at the pasture and imagined Austin here four summers ago with Katie. He was twenty, she'd been twenty-one. My brother had taken her horseback riding the first time she'd come to our house. Dad and I'd watched from the porch as Austin expertly saddled up Chip for Katie, and when she hadn't been able to mount the palomino herself, he'd put both hands on her waist and swept her up into the saddle.

"You think that's a *move*?" I'd asked, sipping a glass of Da's homemade lemonade. It hadn't looked like Katie had even tried.

I really thought Austin would've proposed to Katie right here, not in *Paris*. It was so professional-athlete-proposing-to-his-supermodel-girlfriend, so Bachelor Nation and reality TV, so *not* my brother. He was easygoing and low-key. And, I mean, Katie was obsessed with the horses. She was always dragging Austin out of the house and over here for visits. I was pretty sure she liked them more than she liked *me*.

Which is fair, I thought, rubbing Tally's muzzle, *because I like the horses more than I like Katie.*

Tally snorted as if I'd confessed that aloud.

"Oh, shit, I don't mean it," I breathed, my spine straightening. "Of course, I don't mean it! She's Katie… She's nice… She's smart… She's…?" I floundered in front of the horse, who was definitely giving me a capital-*L* look. I sighed. "Austin loves—"

Someone laying on their car horn made me drop off; I whipped around to face the house, just in time to catch my brother bursting out of his blue Mazda. "MADELINE FISHER-MICHAELS!" he called. "WHERE IS MY HUGE-ASS CONGRATULATORY HUG?"

⊢—⊣

We rarely ate in the farmhouse's formal dining room, but tonight was a different story. Tonight, we were celebrating. Earlier I'd set five place settings with Nana's wedding china and silver. "This is interesting," Katie remarked as Austin pulled back her chair for her. She gestured at her plate, white with a thick teal band decorated with silver flowers. The soup bowls matched perfectly. Totally retro. "Very…" She searched for another adjective as she sat down, Austin squeezing her shoulders before taking his own seat. "Interesting," she repeated.

"Thank you," Dad said. "They were my mother's, and

apparently quite fashionable at the time." He smirked. "She wanted them out of her sight the second her divorce was finalized."

Austin laughed. Thanks to our congratulatory hug-turned-snowy-wrestling-match, he was wearing an old gray sweatshirt and faded pajama bottoms while his wet clothes took a spin in the dryer. "Yeah, that's right," he said. "Didn't she leave them outside your apartment one day?"

Dad nodded. "The note said, *For Lee's dinners, because you're marrying him.*"

"And here we are." Da smiled and shook his head, then gestured to the food. Soup and salad with warm crusty bread. "Let's dish up!"

It wasn't until dessert that Austin and Katie's engagement was mentioned. Austin spoke about France all throughout dinner, and I admit, he made me want to visit someday. It sounded extraordinary. Even our parents exchanged a look and simultaneously said, "Anniversary trip?"

"How about a *family vacation*?" I suggested. "I wouldn't mind checking it out myself."

"The wedding was gigantic," Austin added. "Three hundred people."

"It was actually two-fifty." Katie took a sip of water. Her cousin had gotten married in a palatial chateau right outside Paris. "Everything about it was magical."

"Really?" Dad asked. "How so?"

"Oh...well..." Katie began, and I resisted the urge to tilt my head back and sigh. Katie—to use her word, she was *interesting*. I wished I could just stamp her as *shy*, but she was more complex than that. Reserved, maybe? Removed? It felt like whenever you talked to her, you were traveling on a road that led to nowhere. I'd once mentioned to Austin that instead of working in marketing, Katie should consider a career as an audiobook narrator, or start a podcast on the side. "Really?" He'd looked bemused. "What genre are we talking?"

"Bedtime stories," I replied. "She could lull any insomniac to sleep."

"Because of her soft, dulcet tones?" my brother asked.

"Uh-huh," I lied, knowing he was serious. He was head-over-heels for her. He couldn't hear that she spoke with an invisible ellipsis...after ellipsis...after ellipsis...

Meanwhile, when I'd made that joke to Dad, he'd nodded. "She should. That dispassionate, detached voice of hers could be a real moneymaker."

I was being harsh, I know. But I just didn't get it. There was something—or many somethings—about Katie that Austin loved. Why couldn't I see them? It wasn't as if I hadn't been trying.

Honestly, I was grateful when Dad volunteered me to help clear the table. Katie was musing about each and every cocktail hour hors d'oeuvre. "The silver doesn't go in the dishwasher, right?" I asked. "Hand-wash only?"

"Yes, hand-wash only," he answered from our tiny wine cellar. "Even though she claims the opposite, your grandmother still cares *deeply* for that silver." He emerged through the cellar's stone archway, holding a bottle of Katie's favorite prosecco. "We'll clean up later, though." He nodded toward the mudroom, and I caught his drift to grab the raspberry cheesecake from the garage fridge. It was time.

Da made the toast, officially congratulating Austin and Katie on their engagement. My brother couldn't stop sneaking peeks at Katie, and with her champagne flute raised, I assessed the unfamiliar diamond sparkling on her manicured finger. Emphasis on *unfamiliar*, because Austin had chosen to buy Katie a ring rather than propose with the beautiful engagement ring Da's mother had given my brother before she died—a round ruby flanked by two small diamonds. It was unconventional, sure, but it stole my heart every time I saw it. "For the future Mrs. Fisher-Michaels," I remembered Grandma telling sixteen-year-old Austin.

But apparently the family heirloom wasn't Katie's style, and my brother didn't want to propose to her with something she wouldn't like.

There's no way he could afford that himself, I thought now as I looked at Katie's skating-rink ring. The singular diamond was so big. *No way in hell.*

My guess was the ring had not only been from Austin, but also from our parents. Knowing Dad, the jeweler's receipt was probably flagged in his inbox to reference when negotiating a payment plan with my brother.

Even though I was irked, I couldn't ignore the flicker of warmth in my heart. Austin and I were beyond lucky to have parents who loved and supported us so fiercely.

"Do you have any initial ideas?" Da asked while we devoured our cheesecake. Little Sunflower Bakery in town never missed the mark. "Created a Pinterest board yet?"

I couldn't help but laugh. "Da, come on, even *I* have a wedding Pinterest board!"

"Yes." Katie put down her fork. "My mother and I have a few thoughts."

"Christmastime," Austin said. "This Christmas."

Visions of sugarplums suddenly danced in my head when I word-vomited: "Like, *Christmas*-Christmas?"

My brother shook his head while Katie simply wiped her mouth with her napkin. "Early or mid-December in Princeton. Right, Kates?"

Katie had grown up across the river in New Jersey, and it was also where she and my brother met. While on Thanksgiving break in college, Austin and his high school friends had used fake IDs to hit up the bars in Princeton, and apparently after striking out left and right, he'd "triumphed" at Triumph Brewery by charming Katie. After Thanksgiving, they spent the rest of the vacation hanging out before returning to their schools, committed to long distance. It was only in the last year that Katie had moved in with Austin in Philly. Before that, she'd been at business school in Chicago.

"Princeton sounds lovely." Da smiled. "Your engagement celebration in Paris also looked beautiful, although based on the Instagram comments alone, I know you have so many people in your life who would've loved to be a part of it."

Nicely done, Da, I thought as I sliced myself a second piece of cheesecake.

"So," he continued smoothly, "Harry and I"—he reached for Dad's hand—"would be honored to host an engagement party here, for more family and friends."

"Oh, wow," Katie said. "That's really kind of you." She turned to Austin. "We should talk to my parents—"

"What's there to talk about?" My brother grinned and kissed her, then turned to our dads. "Thank you! You guys are the best!"

"We are." Dad nodded stoically. "It can sometimes be a heavy burden to bear, but indeed." He squeezed Da's hand. "We are the best."

"You are, really," Katie said after a moment, but I could tell by her smile she didn't actually mean it. "What number did you have in mind for the guest list?"

⊢—⊣—⊣

"Hey, can I talk to you a sec?" Austin asked, joining me at the sink while I was hard at work doing the dishes. His cheeks were still pink and the tips of his ears red from the cold. Katie had wanted to visit the horses.

"Sure." I dried off a silver dessert fork. "What's up?"

"The wedding," he said.

"Is already off?" I joked. "Did Tally talk you out of it?"

Austin elbowed me. "Mads."

"Why did you propose in Paris?!" I blurted.

Why Paris and not here?

"Because I thought it would be special," Austin said. "Yeah, the City of Love sounds cliché, but it truly is a magical place." A dreamy expression crossed his face. "It was perfect that her whole family was there."

But yours *wasn't*, I thought. *Our family wasn't there.*

I forced myself to bite my tongue, but maybe Austin could read my mind, because the kitchen was quiet until he eventually prompted: "The wedding...?"

"Right." I put down the clean fork and picked up a dirty soupspoon. "I'm listening."

He cleared his throat, like he was nervous or something. "So, I know we didn't mention it at dinner, but Katie and I talked about the wedding party on the plane the other day. You know, who should be in it and stuff."

My pulse quickened. *Oh, god, the wedding party...*

"Katie's sister is going to be her maid of honor."

I nodded, unsurprised. "And your best man?"

Austin smiled, and I wondered if he was about to say my

name. "Be my best man someday?" he'd asked after I'd given a speech at his high school graduation dinner, a speech I had worked on for two months. "No one knows me like you do, Mads."

But this time, Austin said, "Nate the great."

Something in me deflated a bit, even though Nate was our favorite cousin. "Oh, awesome!" I recovered quickly. "How hyped is he?"

"Totally off the charts." Austin chuckled, then tried to cough away the weird awkwardness in the air. "I also, um, wanted to let you know that Katie has a couple really close cousins, and I can't even count her friends, so..." He grimaced. "I don't think you're going to be a bridesmaid, Mads. Even though it's apparently tradition for the bride to ask the groom's sister, she's not going to ask you."

I took a breath, a sudden spike in my pulse.

I don't think you're going to be a bridesmaid, Mads.

She's not going to ask you.

Would it be awful of me to admit I was relieved?

"I'm sorry," Austin said as I exhaled and my blood flow returned to normal. "We don't want to hurt your feelings, but I thought maybe you could do a reading?" He smiled. "Or give another legendary speech?"

"Definitely!" I chirped.

Relax, Mads, the voice in my head warned. *Don't sound too cheerful.*

"Really?" My brother brightened. "You understand?"

"Austin, of course!" I snapped my wet dish towel at him. "Isn't being a bridesmaid a major commitment, anyway? There are a ton of events before the wedding?" I shook my head. "I don't have time for any of that, no offense. I'm a junior this year—I need to keep my high honor roll streak going and get recruited for field hockey."

"True," he said, then ruffled my hair. "You're such a good juggler, though. School, sports, social life…"

I wanted to laugh. *Excuse me,* what *social life?*

"Everything will work out, Mads."

"Well, I did learn some tips and tricks from the master." I grinned at him.

But instead of smiling back, Austin pulled me into a bone-crushing hug and whispered: "I'm so proud of you."

TWO

A few weeks later, after Valentine's Day, Arthur and Francine broke my concentration while I was doing my biology homework and eating leftover chocolate by barking, barking, barking like the guard dogs Dad encouraged them to be. He was currently grabbing coffee with prospective clients while Da had gone for a run on the canal. I was home alone, the dinner hour creeping closer. "Relax!" I called to the dogs, seeing a brown van slow to a stop in the driveway. "It's UPS!"

I waved to the deliveryman through the window, not wanting to risk Arthur barreling through the front door if I opened it. He loved launching himself into delivery trucks, and it always took forever to get him out.

There were three packages. The first was Banana Republic (Dad), the second new sneakers from Allbirds (Da), and the third was for *me*. I hadn't ordered anything recently, but my name was written in metallic Sharpie on the box. And goddammit, it was spelled wrong, too. *Madeleine*, not *Madeline*.

I didn't need to look at the return address to know who the sender was. Only one person, even after half a decade, thought my name was spelled like that.

Crap. My breathing grew shallow as I searched for something to open the box with. *Crappity, crap, crap, crap!*

What was happening? Austin had told me; he'd *told me* she wasn't going to ask. I grabbed my car keys off their brass hook in the mudroom, then waited until my hands stopped trembling—I could never be a surgeon or a dentist—to slice open the box's lid.

I didn't choose the bridesmaid life, I thought to myself, but as soon as I pulled back the key-mangled box's flaps and saw the tufts of Tiffany-blue tissue paper, sprinkled shiny gold confetti, and cutesy note, I knew the bridesmaid life had chosen me.

Katie had chosen me.

It appeared she was a stickler for tradition, after all.

"Look at this!" I squeaked when Da got home from his run. "Da, just look!"

I unpacked everything for him; first, a mini bottle of prosecco with a gold-and-white-striped paper straw attached with a gold ribbon. "How did UPS overlook that?" Da joked. "You can't ship alcohol."

I ignored him to present the gifts—an *abundance* of gifts. There was a silky blue sleeping mask that had SOMETHING BLUE CREW stitched across the eyes in white cursive letters, along with a quartz face roller and a candle whose sandalwood scent was actually SMELLS LIKE YOU'RE A BRIDESMAID. I'd also received a small gold compact mirror engraved with delicate flowers and my name—pardon, *Madeleine*'s name—and a stylish gold bangle that twisted in the center. Its cute little card read: I COULDN'T TIE THE KNOT WITHOUT YOU!

"Well, it looks like Katie is a top shopper on Etsy," Dad said after I'd shown him later that night. He pointed to the bracelet. "This is nice."

"Yeah, it's really pretty." I sighed. "But I don't want to be a bridesmaid. Austin straight up *said* Katie wasn't going to ask me."

My parents exchanged a look. "When did he say this?" Dad asked.

"When they got back from France last month."

"She must've had a change of heart," Da said after a moment, and this time, it was Dad and I who shared a look. Katie? A change of heart? She always seemed to have her mind made up, even if she rarely shared it. "Thinking more about it might have made her realize that including you would make the day more special."

"Okay, sure," I said, "but that doesn't change the fact that I don't *want* to be included. Can I say, *Thanks but no thanks?* I bet she has plenty of backups."

"No, you cannot, Madeline," Da said, his tone surprisingly firm. "This is Austin's wedding."

"What happened to rushing into things?" I asked. "Last year, when he told you he planned to propose to Katie, you guys said he might be jumping the gun."

Austin and Katie had been together five years, yes, but the first four had been entirely long distance. How did they *know* they were each other's perfect match? Shouldn't they live together for a while to really find out?

My parents were quiet for a moment. "Top of the stairs?" Dad asked lightly.

By way of an answer, I felt myself flush. They knew my go-to eavesdropping spot.

"Your brother is an adult, Madeline," Da said. "He can make his own decisions."

"And remember how many times you watched that proposal video?" Dad asked. "Over and over again, because we weren't in Paris to see it for ourselves?"

I sighed; they weren't *wrong*.

And Austin knew how bummed I'd been. I'm sorry, he'd texted me after doing the dishes last month. I don't know why I didn't tell you guys. I know you would've gotten on a plane.

We would've, I'd replied. Provided aisle seats were available.

Then I'd sent a hug emoji.

"You'll regret it," Da now said. "If you say no to Katie, Mads, you'll miss out on what will probably be a lot of fun. Not to mention, damage your relationship with her."

"We barely have a relationship!" I exclaimed.

"This will be the perfect opportunity to develop one," Dad pointed out. He gave me an encouraging smile.

"Excellent parenting," Da whispered to him.

"Thanks, hon," Dad whispered back. "I try."

"I can hear you," I deadpanned.

Da chuckled. "Call Katie—"

"I am *not* calling Katie." I cut him off, extremely self-aware that I was being a total brat.

"Then *text* Katie," Dad said. "Accept her offer."

"You sound like a Realtor," I mumbled before asking him for Katie's phone number.

Because why would I ever have needed it before now?

Did Katie even have *my* number?

Hi, this is Mads! I texted after much contemplation. I got your package and would LOVE to be your bridesmaid, Katie! I'm really honored. <3

She didn't respond for several hours, and when she finally did, the message read: Great! More details soon.

THREE

The night of Austin and Katie's engagement party, I took forever to get ready. Seriously, I was pretty confident that in my whole entire history of being a teenage girl, it had never taken me so long to get dressed. I sang an entire concert set list in the shower, then flopped on my unmade bed and scrolled aimlessly through my phone for a while before mustering the strength to change into something a little more appropriate than my orange-and-pink-checkered bathrobe. I swapped it out for a dusty violet dress; it had a cool metallic sheen to it. And despite blowing my brown hair dry, it ended up in a French braid, which was how I always wore it for field hockey.

But then I did something way out of the ordinary: I searched for a makeup tutorial on YouTube and followed along with my eyeliner pen, hoping to execute the perfect cat eye.

I don't know; I guess I wanted to look older tonight? I would be meeting Katie's other bridesmaids for the first time and didn't want it to be so obvious that I was Austin's younger sister—his *kid* sister.

Downstairs, I could hear my dads debating over the party's mood music. Da wanted smooth jazz while Dad was pitching something called "Hipster Cocktail Party" on Spotify. "Harry, how did you even discover this playlist?" Da asked, chuckling as Lana Del Rey purred through our speakers. "We don't frequent Brooklyn coffee shops…"

Per its invitation, the party began at seven, but the key players had arrived by six-thirty. "Mads?" Austin walked into my room looking dapper in a slate-colored suit. "You ready? Everyone's downstairs."

I finally found the right heels, vintage silver T-straps from the 1960s. They'd been Grandma's and were still in perfect condition. "Yeah, almost!"

"Wait, you haven't drunk this yet?" Austin seemingly teleported from my doorway to my closet, where he pulled out the mini bubbly bottle from my bridesmaid box. "Did Da say no?"

I shrugged. "You know I'm only allowed to drink on super special occasions."

Austin chuckled but didn't pop the prosecco. "Well, I'm sure he'd agree tonight qualifies." He raised the bottle. "To the highly esteemed hosts!"

"Yes." I grinned. "To Dad and Da!"

We pretended to take a sip (that bottle was way too warm to actually drink) right as Katie called up the stairs, "Austin, your nana just got here!"

"Coming, Kates!" my brother called back, then rustled

through my goody bag until he found the bracelet. "Don't forget this," he told me. "Katie mentioned all the bridesmaids are wearing them."

That's news to me, I thought, even though Katie was apparently *thrilled* I was a bridesmaid. She's so happy you said yes, Austin had texted after Katie's curt response. I know you've got a lot of stuff going on, but thanks, Mads! Love you!

I desperately wanted to ask my brother *why* Katie had changed her mind and asked me, but I didn't. Love you, too, I'd written back. I'm pumped!!!

"I'll be right down," I told him now, and after he hurried out of the room, I took a deep breath and stared down my reflection in the mirror over my dresser. *They'll like you*, I reassured myself. *Just because they love Katie doesn't mean they won't like you!*

After all, no one but my parents knew my true feelings about Katie. I could pretend I loved her, too. Who knew? Dad and Da could be right; by the end of this, Katie could be the sister I never had.

Not that I'd ever really dreamt of a sister. Austin was all I needed.

But still.

We had three sets of stairs in the farmhouse; the wide kitchen staircase was the easiest to navigate in heels, so I stomped down only to be greeted by the caterers. We all considered Da a gourmet cook, but with all the people invited, solo cooking wasn't feasible even if it was only drinks and heavy hors d'oeuvres. Ember & Ash in Princeton was at the helm tonight. Dad knew the owners; the Álvarez family had inquired about potentially putting their house on the market this spring.

I inhaled an aroma of deliciousness from the second-floor landing before gliding downstairs to the kitchen. Well, maybe not *gliding*—I spent most of my time in turf shoes or cleats, not high heels—but it wasn't until I tripped over the last couple steps that my cheeks sparked with embarrassment. "And she sticks the landing!" someone shouted when I got my footing at the bottom.

I stood there for a moment, staring at the floor and desperately willing my warm face to cool before looking up and across the kitchen to see a familiar guy smiling at me. He was wearing Ember & Ash's standard light gray and white ombré button-down with black pants, and was busy polishing glassware. "Marco…" a nearby server warned. She was plating one of the appetizers, which I recognized as the cranberry-fig-goat-cheese crostini.

"It's okay, Teresa," Marco replied. "I know her."

"Yeah," I corroborated. "Unfortunately."

Marco Álvarez and I had gone to school together. He'd been two grades ahead of me, the resident soccer player that all the girls swooned over thanks to his naturally tousled dark hair and salted-caramel-colored eyes.

Yes, I realized that description suggested I had a thing for him, too.

Or, far more likely, I had a sweet tooth and constantly craved candy.

"What are you doing here?" I asked now.

Marco inspected a wineglass. "Helping out."

"It's a Saturday night."

"I'm aware," he said lightly. "I own a calendar, believe it or not."

"So don't you have something to do?" I teased as the front doorbell rang. Marco and I were sort of friends. We weirdly used to park next to each other at school and hang out by our cars after sports ended. We'd talk, banter, and sometimes bicker about random stuff until he remembered he was supposed to be somewhere or had someone to meet. A smirk tugged at the corner of my mouth. "There isn't a party at one of the supper clubs?"

Marco sighed. He played soccer at Princeton now. "They're called *eating* clubs," he said, then gave me a look. "And I bet my Tower membership that you *knew* that, Catwoman."

Indeed, I had, since Princeton was recruiting me for field hockey. Their historic "eating clubs" were the exclusive social clubs on campus, absolutely legendary. F. Scott Fitzgerald had been in one when he was a student.

But okay, *Catwoman*?

"Oh, great." I resisted the urge to touch my eye makeup. "Does it look that bad?"

"No." Marco shook his head. "It looks cool, Mads. Goes

with the whole witchy thing you have happening." He winked. "You're missing the pointy hat, though."

"It's at the dry cleaner's," I shot back.

Marco tilted his head, clearly holding back a laugh. "Bummer."

My hands went to my hips. "Okay, you know what," I began, even though I had no idea where I was heading. "I—"

"Madeline!" My grandmother saved me from fumbling. Nana breezed through the swinging kitchen door, with her silver hair in a chic bob and wearing a sophisticated pink tweed-and-sequined blazer-skirt combo. "I've been looking for you," she said. "Katie is with most of the bridesmaids, and I think it would be nice if—" She cut herself off, and a blink later, was unbraiding my braid. "Darling, no," she said. "You have such beautiful hair; you should show it off every once in a while…"

Decades ago, Nana had been a hairstylist. She'd worked at one of those fancy salons that served clients champagne while they got their hair done.

Today, she owned the place.

"Okay, wonderful!" She smiled once she was satisfied with her work. There was no mirror in the kitchen, but I knew we had a half-up, half-down situation on our hands. "Doesn't she look lovely?" she asked Marco.

And dear lord, my face practically burst into flames.

"Yes," he said, nodding robotically. "She is beauty and she is grace."

I flipped him off when Nana took me by the shoulders and directed me toward the door.

Marco gave me a thumbs-up, then went back to work. If Nana hadn't been physically pushing me out of the room, I might've asked for his number so we could keep in better touch. I'd only been a sophomore during his senior year; his popularity had intimidated me.

It didn't now.

The party, Da joked, was popping. There were people *everywhere*. My family, Katie's family, my parents' friends, Katie's parents' friends, and friends of the bride and groom. Ember & Ash servers skillfully weaved in between everyone, offering hors d'oeuvres.

My stomach growled. I'd gotten a sneak peek at the menu last week and had been looking forward to it since then. The stuffed portobello mushrooms could be skipped, but the beef tenderloin bites with caramelized onions and blue cheese?

Even with Nana at my side, I felt like I was approaching my high school's tightest clique as I made my way to the bridal party. They had staked out a spot by the keeping room's crackling fire. "Can we get a drink first?" I whispered to my grandmother. "I don't know what to do with my hands." They flopped lifelessly at my sides.

In response, my grandmother rerouted us to the bar in the

library, where she ordered a chardonnay for herself and a Coke for me. I inwardly sighed, having pictured myself drinking club soda and cranberry juice with a slice of lime; it would look more cosmopolitan.

But Nana knew me too well. I loved an ice-cold Coca-Cola and would definitely need a serious sugar rush for this.

Armed with my emotional-support beverage, I let Nana lead me into Katie's clutches. "You have nothing to worry about," she whispered. "I introduced myself to them earlier—we know Katie's horrible at that—and they seem like nice women."

Women.

I was a *girl*.

Austin, where are you? I thought. He was so good at this stuff.

By the time we reached the bridal circle, my pulse was pounding so hard that I barely heard myself say, "Hey, Katie."

Then I immediately noticed Nana had ghosted me.

Katie, wearing a white halter dress and wineglass in hand, opened her mouth, but someone beat her to the punch. "Oh my god!" a woman exclaimed. "We were just talking about you! You're Mads, right? The sister Austin never shuts up about?"

"Well, to be fair, I'm his only one," I replied.

The bridesmaid laughed. She smiled and stuck out her hand, the gold knot bracelet on her wrist shining as we shook. "I'm Amanda. Katie's *older* sister."

Katie rolled her eyes, like this was an inside and reoccurring joke. "Only by a year."

"Still." Amanda lovingly patted Katie's cheek. "Older, wiser, and whatever else it is they say." She looked back at me. "I'm also the MOH."

My eyebrows knitted together. "The MOH?"

"The maid of honor," another bridesmaid translated. "I'm Reese, and I believe my title is *childhood best friend*."

Then there was Courtney, a cousin.

Paige, another cousin.

Yasmin, a college friend.

"And my college roommate…" Katie began.

"Is finally here," Yasmin finished, waving her arm in the air. "Mer!"

"Hey, guys!" A seventh bridesmaid joined our group. She had bright green eyes and honey-colored hair that cascaded down her back. I was instantly obsessed with her one-shoulder black jumpsuit and chunky gold heels. "I'm so sorry we're late," she said, hugging Katie. "Our flight was delayed, and then we sat forever at the gate in Philly. Stephen also forgot to book our Uber in advance…"

"My oh my, where in the world did the Witrys come from this time?" Reese asked dryly.

"We just did three months in St. Croix," the new bridesmaid answered. "One of the many wonders of remote jobs, Reese." They hugged. "But I know you are married to Manhattan."

"'Til death do us part," Reese quipped, then gestured to me. "This is Mads, Katie's soon-to-be sister-in-law."

"Oh, hello." She grinned and surprised me with a warm side hug. I was a couple inches taller than her. "I'm Meredith. It's so great to finally meet you!"

"Mer, Yaz, and I all roomed together at Hamilton," Katie supplied, and I nodded. Hamilton College in upstate New York, one of the prestigious NESCAC schools. Their field hockey team was pretty good.

"But Reese was like our fourth roommate," Yasmin added. "She was an hour and a half away at Hobart and would visit like every other weekend."

Reese shrugged. "You had better parties."

"More like better *boys*," Katie countered.

"Yeah, I heard about this!" Amanda snapped her fingers. "There was some Italian exchange student you had a crush on sophomore year?"

The bridesmaids giggled, and I silently sipped my soda. Even though Katie had chosen bridesmaids from different chapters of her life, they seemed as thick as thieves. Why couldn't there be a work friend or something? Someone who could be slow on the uptake like me?

"For you, Killer," someone said, and Meredith and I turned to see a cute blond guy holding two glasses. He smiled crookedly at the group as Meredith accepted a copper-colored cup garnished with lime. Moscow mule, I guessed. "Ladies." He toasted us with his bourbon. "Katie."

"Wit..." they singsonged back.

A nickname? I wondered. Hadn't Meredith mentioned someone named Stephen?

In any case, the guy kissed her cheek before melting back into the party. Meredith beamed and took a sip of her cocktail. She wore no engagement ring, but her gold wedding band was inlaid with pale blue gemstones. They looked like aquamarine.

She'd think Grandma's ruby was cool, I thought.

Katie's cousins soon asked if she'd thought about any potential bachelorette weekend destinations, but before she could answer, Marco arrived with hors d'oeuvres. "Would any of you care for tomato soup and grilled cheese?" he asked.

I watched the bridesmaids' eyes narrow at the tray, which held shot glass cups of tomato soup topped with bite-sized grilled cheese sandwiches. They were smaller than a potato chip and totally didn't match tonight's upscale foodie vibe. "This is my dads' idea of a joke," I explained, giggling. "When Austin was in elementary school, all he wanted for dinner was tomato soup with grilled cheese."

"Crusts cut off, too." Katie smiled. "If the crust wasn't cut off, it was a deal-breaker."

I nodded.

"That's adorable," Meredith said, taking one American Girl–sized meal for herself. "Yaz, you want one?"

"Yes, please!" Yasmin smiled, but Marco and I both sucked in a breath before disaster struck. You could tell from the way Meredith was trying to balance her drink that she didn't have a good grip on the little plate, and when Yasmin stretched to take it, her phone started to slip from her hand. She tried to catch it at the same time Meredith passed off the appetizer.

And even though it wasn't remotely my fault, I wanted to click my heels three times to disappear after the soup spilled down the front of Yasmin's red dress.

Shit, I thought, wincing as the other bridesmaids swarmed Yasmin. Was this mess how they'd remember meeting me?

"Napkin?" Reese asked Marco. "Could you get some napkins, please?"

Dad swept in out of nowhere. "Seltzer and a dish towel, Marco," he amended, knowing basically every cleaning hack. "We're going to dab, Yasmin, *not* rub…" He began ushering Yasmin toward the kitchen, with Meredith following and apologizing profusely.

"Mer, stop! It's totally fine," Yasmin said. "It's not like you spilled on *Katie*…"

As if on cue, Katie glanced down at her ivory dress. "I think I'm going to switch to white," she said mildly, passing off her red wine to Amanda. "I'll be—"

"Katie!" Paige half shrieked. "She's coming!"

"Paige, can you ever keep your cool?" Courtney whispered as Katie stole her wine back from her sister. She took a long sip. "Like, just once?"

"Showtime," Katie muttered, but it wasn't until Amanda murmured that Austin and the groomsmen were also heading over that I realized who they were talking about.

Finally, I thought, shoulder muscles unwinding. *Someone I know.*

"Samira!" Katie gushed, stepping forward in her sky-high strappy heels for a hug. "I'm so glad you made it! How've you been?"

Samira Bhatia, a longtime family friend, squeezed Katie back before breaking away with a smile. "I've been great, Katie," she said. "Busy with school, but what else is new?"

Behind her, Austin's groomsmen were practically drooling like a horde of hound dogs. Samira was stunning.

End of sentence.

But she was *especially* stunning tonight, in a deep green dress and her long black hair hanging in a loose fishtail braid. I'd taught her how to do one several years ago.

"Great!" Katie tried to smile, but I caught her shift from one foot to the other right before Samira hugged me hello. It wasn't hard to figure out why. Samira wasn't only a friend; she was also my brother's ex-girlfriend. Best friends since sixth grade, they'd dated all through high school and for their first year of college. My parents and I'd been nothing short of *shocked* when Austin told us they'd broken up. We thought they were endgame, especially since they went to Johns Hopkins together. "We've been together for so long," Austin had said, insisting the breakup was mutual (his sniffling over the phone didn't help his case). "We need freedom to live our own lives for a while."

Everyone was bummed, but we became optimistic when they'd stayed close. We thought it was only a matter of time before they got back together. It was fine when Samira started dating someone new. It was fine, because eventually...

Well, eventually, Austin met Katie.

"Sam and I are *friends*," my brother had said the time Dad had brought up rekindling a romance with Samira (I mean, what exes decided to live together senior year?). "Best friends, but *just* friends. I'm with Katie." He grinned, as if the world were made of ice cream and rainbows. "I *love* Katie."

Now, Samira was at Johns Hopkins Med, and after looping her arm through Austin's, Katie politely asked a few questions about the semester, and Samira answered them self-deprecatingly. Austin's best friend was brilliant, and everyone fell in love with her...

Except Katie.

You really can't make an actual effort? I wanted to ask, because while Katie talked to Samira, she didn't seem genuinely interested. Sometimes, like right now, she even sounded fake. Samira might've been Austin's ex, but she was also like family. She and Austin always took me sledding as a little kid, we watched her high school diving meets, and her desserts were a staple at our summer cookouts. We loved her, and she wasn't going anywhere. It was time Katie truly accepted it.

The bridesmaids and groomsmen soon blended together in conversation, and after Yasmin and Meredith returned, Austin's best man flagged down the professional photographer circulating the party. "Group photo?" he suggested.

"Group photo!" everyone agreed.

I smiled for the camera, but internally started plotting my escape. How was I going to get out of being Katie's bridesmaid?

I'm not, I thought as the flash went off. *This is also Austin's wedding, remember?*

I really was going to have to grin and bear it.

FOUR

"No, no, no." Connor shook his head. "You are not faster than me. Absolutely not."

"Well not right *now*," I said. "Not in these shoes." I gestured to my feet, which were really starting to hurt thanks to my heels. After making the rounds at the party—please don't ask me to recall anyone's name—I was hiding in the kitchen to enjoy a plate of chocolate petits fours for dessert. But instead of stretching out on the heated floor, I'd hopped up on a barstool at the island to stay out of the catering crew's way. Connor McCallister, my oldest friend, had had the same idea. We hadn't been able to hang out yet tonight. He'd tried to extract me from a conversation earlier but ended up trapped in another. "But seriously," I told him, "I *am* faster than you."

Connor's face reddened. He played midfield on the lacrosse team at school and prided himself on being in great shape. We ran eight miles together on the canal during our offseasons.

"Careful, Mads," Marco said from the sink. The party was

winding down, so he'd started the dishes. "McCallister might detonate."

"Lace up your sneakers," Connor said suddenly. "We'll race down the driveway."

"Yes, in the dark." I nodded. "Sounds like a smart idea." I knocked his foot under the island. "May I point out that you're *also* wearing the wrong shoes?"

Connor's mouthful of mini lemon bar made it impossible to understand whatever he said back. It reminded me of Halloweens together as little kids. There was a neighborhood at the end of my house's long driveway, and the McCallisters were the closest thing the Fisher-Michaels family had to next-door neighbors (there weren't many kids in the ten-house neighborhood, so Connor and I became attached at the hip after our first game of cul-de-sac street hockey). We always trick-or-treated together before ending the night at the McCallisters' to sort out our haul, and when we got older, we convinced Austin to drive us to *much bigger* neighborhoods so we could double or triple our treasure. I smiled to myself; it didn't matter if we were six or twelve—if I shut my eyes, I could see Connor trying to shove an entire Milky Way into his mouth.

"I do have my sneakers in the trunk, Connor," Marco said, apparently fluent in Mouthful. "But I know you're gonna ask me to ref, and I'm still working."

Rose Álvarez clucked from Da's built-in kitchen counter desk. "Working hard or hardly working?" she mused. "If you keep chatting..." She glanced up from her laptop to give her son a look. "I'm clocking you out."

Marco flushed, and I watched him scrub the next dish until it shined.

"There's an easy way to settle this," I told Connor. "What was your mile time in gym this week?"

"I haven't run it yet," he said. "Remember my dentist appointment? I missed the last couple periods of the day." He paused. "What was yours?"

"Six minutes flat," I said proudly, but Connor didn't react. His attention had shifted to his girlfriend; Brenna had suddenly reappeared with another dessert plate piled high. She knew the way to Connor's heart.

And listen, I liked Brenna; she was easygoing and knew the answer to any and every *Gilmore Girls* trivia question, but why was she *here* tonight? She and Connor had only been dating a month, and his family's invitation hadn't included a plus-one.

Am I not enough? the most insecure part of me wondered as Connor kissed Brenna's cheek before she claimed the island's third barstool. Connor was always enough for me, but unless it was a casual one-on-one hangout, I didn't seem enough for him. He was a more-the-merrier guy.

"Hey!" someone called, making me blink. "Katie said I might find you in here."

I looked over to see Bridesmaid Meredith pushing through the swinging door. Arthur and Francine jumped up on the mudroom's pony door and began barking and wagging their tails wildly, excited by a new voice. Meredith laughed. "Hello there, guys," she cooed. "I'll introduce myself in a sec…" She turned to me. "Everyone's making their exodus for the night."

"Ah, shoot," I said. "I should say some goodbyes."

"I wouldn't worry," Meredith said before I could hop off my stool. "Katie, Austin, and your parents have it handled."

"Oh, okay." It felt strange not being included, but then again, it wasn't my party. I technically wasn't a host. "Well, it was really nice to meet you." I smiled. "I'm excited for Katie's bridal shower."

Thankfully, that was who-knew-how-many months away.

Under the island, Connor knocked my knee, as if to say, *Liar, liar, pants on fire!*

I was literally complaining to anyone who would listen about being a bridesmaid. Maid of Honor Amanda had shown us some dress ideas from Katie's Pinterest and talked about everyone shopping together since most of us lived on the East Coast.

Now, Meredith waved away my goodbye. "Save it for tomorrow, Mads," she said. "We're all headed back to Katie's house for a slumber party!"

My spine straightened.

A slumber party? Like a sleepover?

I opened my mouth, then closed it, not trusting myself to not say what I wanted to say: *Who is responsible for this invitation?*

Had it been Katie's idea? Or was this Meredith's assumption?

"She's really flattered, but she can't," Connor answered for me. "She has field hockey tomorrow."

"Field hockey?" Bridesmaid Reese said, joining us at the island. Katie's cousins were behind her. "It's February. Isn't field hockey a fall sport?"

"She plays on a club team," Marco and Connor said simultaneously, with Connor adding, "And it's not a sport; it's a lifestyle."

I elbowed him. He was both quoting and mocking me.

"Practice isn't until tomorrow afternoon, though." Austin set a pile of dirty dishes on the counter. "I double-checked with Da," he said, "and Kates really wants you to come."

But can't "Kates" tell me that herself? I thought.

"Plus, I kinda told Sam she could have your bed," he said.

I pretended to groan. "Austin!"

He laughed, seeing right through me. Our parents and I'd missed Samira; her RSVP to the party had been the best news.

Austin slipped off his suit jacket, rolled up his shirtsleeves, and told Marco to take a break and enjoy the leftovers. He'd take over dishwashing duty.

"Come on, Mads!" Meredith called from the mudroom. My family's dogs could not get enough of her. "It'll be so much fun!"

My stomach twisted. "Alright, alright," I agreed, forcing a smile as I slid off my barstool. Because honestly, how could I have said no? "Let me go pack a bag…"

|—+—+—|

Katie's childhood home was twenty-five minutes away, but I'd only been there twice. Once for the Gallants' annual New Year's Eve open house, and once for Katie's business school graduation party. It was walking distance from Nassau Street, Princeton's main drag, and absolutely massive. Limestone with a hulking black front door. "Brand-new," Realtor Dad liked to say, "but built to look like an antique."

It wasn't our style, but damn, was it a gorgeous property, with its pebbled driveway and landscaping. Every box hedge was impeccably trimmed and stood at attention, and I imagined flowers lining the flagstone front walk come spring.

"Welcome, girls!" Katie's mom ushered us inside with a bright smile on her face. "It's so wonderful to have you—oh, Wit." She noticed Meredith's husband among us. Stephen Witry, who I'd picked up was "Wit" to everyone but his wife. "I didn't know you were coming."

"Only to crash on your couch, Mrs. Gallant," he said. "I promise I will have no involvement in whatever mischief these miscreants get up to tonight."

He's charming, I thought. *Charming on top of being very cute.*

"He's married," Yasmin whispered in my ear, making me blush. She'd caught me checking him out.

Katie's mom laughed. "Don't even think about the couch, young man," she said, giving him a tight hug. "We have a full house tonight, but Amanda's room is free." She conferred with her daughters. "Since I assume you'll all be in Katie's room?"

The Bride led the way up the sprawling staircase after Mrs. Gallant told us the pantry was stocked with every type of snack imaginable, freshly washed towels were in the linen closet with extra pillows and blankets, and breakfast would be waiting in the morning.

I forgot Katie's house is literally a five-star hotel, I quickly texted my parents.

Dad responded with how much he would list it for should the Gallants ever decide to put it on the market.

I'd never been in Katie's bedroom before, light blue walls with white bedding and accents. There was a beautiful bulletin board over her white desk, made out of old-fashioned blue toile fabric and spring-green grosgrain ribbon. Family photos, concert tickets, and little doodles that I recognized as Austin's artwork had been tacked to it. "My mom made that for me when I was little." Katie noticed me admiring it. "Amanda has one, too. Somehow they've held up after all these years."

"It's beautiful," I said, then gestured to a doodle. "Austin can't draw to save his life."

"Tell me about it." Katie smiled before turning to her king bed. "Three of us can cuddle in here." She patted the bed's white duvet. "We have air mattresses—"

"In the linen closet!" her bridesmaids chorused back, but once everyone had gotten cozy in their pajamas, we crowded together on Katie's bed with the cheese plate and charcuterie board Mrs. Gallant had delivered. Plus, a couple bottles of Whispering Angel rosé.

"Thank you," I said when Katie's mom handed me a blackberry-cucumber seltzer. "And thank you so much for having us."

"Are you kidding?" She grinned. "Madeline, I *live* for this stuff."

"Good night, Mother!" Amanda chirped.

Hint, hint.

"I feel like I'm back in high school," Yasmin said once Mrs. Gallant left. "Except instead of fancy meats and cheeses, we had greasy pizza and then went to town on popcorn, M&Ms, Twizzlers, and Sour Patch Kids."

"A feast fit for queens," Meredith noted.

"And instead of expensive rosé, my best friend and I used to steal Coronas from the garage fridge," Courtney said.

Paige groaned. "Corona tastes like cat piss."

"Paige!" Amanda feigned shock and clamped her hands over Katie's ears. "We have young minds in the room!"

"Haha, very funny." Katie shook her sister off with a smile. "And, for the record, Corona *does* taste like cat piss. Even when you add lime."

"What was your go-to sleepover activity?" Meredith asked. "My friends and I'd binge old seasons of *The Bachelorette*."

"Oh, I did that too!" I exclaimed, the forgotten young mind

in the room. My friends and I'd been middle schoolers on a mission; the Bachelorette and her suitors had to at least fly to Europe before we'd go to bed.

That feels like ages ago, I thought, and after a beat, realized it *was* ages ago. This was my first sleepover in *ages*. Because once I'd started taking field hockey so seriously...well, my life had gotten very busy very fast. With all my practices, games, and tournaments, I didn't have much time for a weekend social life. I still had a good group of friends, but the majority of them were on my team and weren't local. The school friends I used to have slumber parties with? We'd drifted apart once hitting high school. My constant was Connor. Between his lacrosse and hanging out with his girlfriend and my field hockey, we still managed to grab dinner and binge some Netflix every week.

"Katie, Amanda, and my sleepovers were exactly how Hollywood makes them out to be," Reese said. "We gave each other makeovers, gushed over boys, and obviously someone always had a Ouija board..."

"And we always, *always* played truth or dare," Amanda said, giving her sister's sleek ponytail a tug. "Katie here was our little daredevil."

I almost choked on my seltzer. *Excusez-moi?* Katie chose *dare* over *truth*? I never would've expected that from her. She seemed so prim, proper, and play-it-safe.

Reese laughed. "Oh, yeah, the time she walked to Wawa at midnight and brought us each back an Icee is *iconic!*"

"She was only thirteen," Amanda said.

What?! I thought, ears almost ringing.

"Respect, Katie." Meredith offered her a fist bump, and then it only took three seconds after their knuckles knocked for someone to squeal, "Let's play!"

The bed full of bridesmaids cheered, and I heard myself cheering right along with them. Was I nervous? Yes, my pulse was pumping, but with both nerves and excitement. I hadn't realized how much I'd missed games like this.

"Truth or dare?" Amanda asked Yasmin.

Yasmin considered, then said, "Truth."

"Booooo," Katie and Meredith crowed.

Amanda shushed them, then returned to Yasmin. "Hmm… who was the last person you searched on Instagram?"

"Oh my god, that's *such* a softball," Courtney said.

But nevertheless, Yasmin blushed and answered so quietly that everyone went, "Huh?"

"Bieber," she spoke up. "Justin Bieber."

Meredith promptly whacked her with a pillow.

"I'm not going to apologize," Yasmin said through giggles. "Call me a Belieber, his concerts are life-changing!"

"Sorry, but Justin Bieber is *no* Harry Styles," I said as I helped myself to a slice of Brie. "Harryween at Madison Square Garden will go down in history as the most mind-blowing concert of all time. My thirteen-year-old-self lost her voice for two days."

"And I lost mine for three," Reese said. "So I completely cosign that." She mimed dashing off her signature.

"Truth or dare?" Courtney asked Paige.

"Dare."

"I dare you to go rearrange Aunt Stacy's spice cabinet."

Katie cracked up and fell back against her pillows.

"You two are *evil*," Amanda breathed. "She is going to lose her shit…"

Paige smirked. "It's done!" she announced after disappearing downstairs for five minutes. "Everything is officially *un*-alphabetized."

"Katie!" Meredith said brightly. "Truth or dare?"

"Dare," Amanda answered for her.

Meredith took a sip of her rosé and then scratched her chin, pretending to think. "Okay, I dare you…" She paused to build the suspense. (Admittedly, I barely took a breath.) "To put Stephen's hand in a bowl of warm water."

Katie blinked. "What?"

"You heard me," Meredith said, lips curling into a smile.

"You want me to make your husband wet himself?"

Meredith nodded. "I do."

The rest of us took that as permission to cackle, and we cackled harder when Katie gingerly got off the bed and moved at snail speed toward her bedroom door.

Austin is going to die, I thought as I filmed her slo-mo exit. Maybe *this* was one of the things he loved about Katie. Her willingness—or, in this case, unwilling willingness—to step up to a challenge.

"Oh my god," Yasmin said a few minutes later, still wiping tears of laughter from her eyes. "Meredith—"

Whatever she was about to say got cut off; suddenly the door flew open and Katie ran through it, water sloshing out of the bowl she held. "I didn't even make it to the bed," she told us. "Let alone pick up his hand." She looked at her friend. "He knew it wasn't you based on my footsteps alone; he knows yours by heart."

Meredith smirked. "Did I not mention that?"

Katie rolled her eyes. "He *also* knew you were going to pull something like this." She whipped around and locked eyes with none other than *me*. "Madeline!"

My smile slipped off my face right as my heart slipped into my stomach. "Yes?"

"Truth or dare?"

Blood pounded, pounded, pounded in my ears. I liked a good dare, but there was no way I was going to risk Katie and her embarrassment countering Meredith's dare by instructing me to draw on her grandfather's face with lipstick or send me over to Wawa for snacks. (That walk didn't scare me, but it was past 1 a.m. and I hadn't packed my pepper spray.)

"Truth!" I basically shouted. "I pick truth."

Katie's shoulders slumped; she'd definitely had a dare planned. "Um…"

"I have one," Reese said when Katie couldn't come up with a question. "Mads, which guy are you hooking up with?"

My mind went blank. I had zero clue what she was talking about, even though Katie's cousins both exclaimed, "I was wondering that too!"

Reese could tell. "You were hanging with two guys in the kitchen earlier," she said as if I had amnesia. "The dude washing dishes, and the lax bro stuffing his face at the island. Which one are you with?"

It clicked.

Oh.

My.

God.

Too much cheese curdled in my stomach. "Neither!" I all but vomited. "Ew, neither. Connor and I have been friends forever, and his *girlfriend* was also there tonight."

"Is that why you aren't with him?" Reese asked. Her voice somehow poked me. "Because he's taken?"

I ignored her. "And we went to high school with Marco. He goes to Princeton now."

"Ooh…" Amanda raised an eyebrow. "A *Princeton* man."

"Never in a million bazillion years!" I exclaimed.

"Okay, okay, we get it." Courtney gestured for me to lower the volume. "You are not romantically linked to either of them."

"But are you romantically linked to someone?" Yasmin asked.

Meredith chuckled. "Yaz, she's seventeen!"

"Says the person who started dating her high school boyfriend at *fourteen*!"

"Yeah, and he turned out to be a total shithead," Meredith said, shrugging. "I'm just saying that you have a lot on your plate at seventeen, and maybe Mads doesn't have time for a love life." She glanced at me. "Please tell me to shut up if I'm off base."

I shook my head. I liked Meredith—I actually liked her *a lot* but couldn't help wondering why she was the one sticking up for me rather than Katie. Because *Katie* was the one who'd known me for more than several hours. "You're not."

She nodded in confirmation, but just when I thought that was the end of *that*, Katie cleared her throat. "Mads," she said. "Have you ever kissed anyone?"

Have you ever kissed anyone?

The question felt like someone was tugging my heart up from my guts, back to my chest where it belonged and could rattle around in my rib cage.

The answer, of course, was now obvious.

No, I hadn't had my first kiss. I was seventeen yet hadn't done more than hug a guy. Which barely counted because the only guy I'd hugged besides my brother was Connor, and hugs with Connor were more like football tackles.

Katie tilted her head, as if she suddenly found me the most fascinating creature alive—an absolute alien. "Have you ever gone on a date?"

Blood began pulsing through my ears again. This was, officially, the most embarrassing moment of my life. How had the weight of everyone's judgment not broken the bed yet?

"Mads, come on!" Katie lobbed a grape at me. "You seriously haven't been on a date?"

My hands balled into fists, wanting to scream at her. Why was she doing this?

"Katie," Meredith murmured as my eyes smarted with tears. "Stop."

Everyone was looking at me. I so very desperately wanted to go home, but I couldn't. And even if I could, I still had an abundance of quality time to spend with these people in the coming months.

You need to own this, I told myself. *Just own this, Mads.*

"No, I haven't been on a date," I said, trying to keep my voice level. "And I've never been kissed." I reached for our Whispering Angel rosé, and no one protested when I took a sip straight from the bottle. One dose of liquid courage. "It's not that I don't want to fit someone onto my metaphorical plate, and it's not that there haven't been opportunities…but those opportunities usually present themselves at field hockey camps."

I waited for them to put it together.

They did not.

Alright, I thought. *None of you played sports.*

"I was flattered by the attention," I said slowly. "And love is love—"

"But you aren't into girls," Meredith said, nodding as the other bridesmaids' eyes blinked with enlightenment. "Got it."

"And I have no social life," I went on. "I'm away almost every weekend for field hockey, so I've only been to three—maybe four—parties since I started high school. And when I'm not gone, I really want to spend time with Connor and my family. I just…" I raised my arms. "I don't know."

A knot twisted when no one responded, and I took another sip of rosé to hide how uncomfortable I was from the silence. Then, a third sip.

But before I could take a full-on pull, Meredith confiscated the bottle and said, "I have an idea." She nudged Yasmin.

"What's your idea, Mer?" Yasmin asked in an obvious stage voice.

I laughed, letting a few tears loose. "You two are terrible actors."

"They are," Reese agreed. "Hamilton once put on an amateur production of *Twelfth Night*, and they were—"

"A travesty!" Meredith interrupted like she still wasn't over her flop as a thespian. "We were a travesty, okay? *Twelfth Night* is a comedy, but Yaz and I turned it into a *tragedy*." She exhaled. "Moving on."

"To your idea," Yasmin prompted (much more naturally this time).

"Yes, my idea." Meredith smiled at me. "Remember how you said you and your friends would go on Bachelor Nation benders during your sleepovers?"

I nodded.

"Well, I think *you* should be the Bachelorette!"

A little part of me deflated. Aspiring to Bachelor Nation? *That* was her idea? "Sure, maybe someday," I said gently. "But I'm underage right now, and even if I weren't, that audition process is pretty much a science. I heard if you make the top hundred, there's a mock cocktail party with producers, and psych tests are involved…"

Katie laughed and shook her head. "Mads, I don't think she's talking about you *actually* going out for the show."

The snark was out before I could stop it: "Then what *is* she talking about, Katie?"

"Making you *our* Bachelorette," she replied, taking it in stride. In fact, her eyes had lit up with what resembled delight. "You have no romance in your life. Let *us* help you change that."

"Exactly," Meredith said. "We're Katie's hype squad for the next ten months, and we can be your hype squad, too. The seven of us can totally help boost your confidence to put yourself out there with guys." She squeezed my shoulder. "We'll put our brains together and orchestrate different dates to help you find your dude."

"Absolutely!" Amanda nodded enthusiastically. "The goal will be for you to have a plus-one for Katie and Austin's wedding."

"Well, no," Meredith said, "I didn't mean for the wedding to be the motivating factor. Maybe she has a plus-one; maybe she doesn't. She'll have an amazing time at the wedding either way. I think the overarching goal should be for Mads to gain some valuable experience and have some fun as she searches for—"

"That message does not translate well into an Instagram story series, Meredith," Reese interrupted. "Amanda's is much catchier." She tipped her rosé at me. "Let's get you a wedding date, yes?"

Hesitating, I glanced around at the other bridesmaids.

Yasmin winked at me. "I'm in."

"Me too." Courtney nodded. "Definitely."

My mind swirled. Was I in? Was I actually going to do this?

"Me three," Paige said, and then there was only the Bride. Her eyes still shone, but I couldn't read Katie's expression; unlike her college roommates, she had some acting chops. Or a poker face, at least. My heart hammered.

I'll say yes, I thought. *If she wants me to do it, I'll say yes.*

Because then we would *really* have the chance to bond, and if we finally clicked, maybe she wouldn't be so dead set on keeping her distance from my family anymore—or worse, so dead set on taking Austin away from us.

And I wanted Katie to like me. I admit, I did.

"How about it, bride-to-be?" Meredith asked. "Is there room in this party for another journey to love?"

One heartbeat.

Two heartbeats.

Three.

And then Katie smiled and raised her rosé to me. "Yes," she said, "as long as she's doing it for the right reasons."

FIVE

Katie drove me home late the next morning. As promised by Mrs. Gallant, our slumber party had woken up to a breakfast spread of French toast, bacon, fruit salad, yogurt, and bagels with various spreads. The coffee smelled delicious, and two big carafes of fresh orange juice sat on the kitchen table. Katie's dad was even running an omelet bar at the eight-burner stove. Again, the place was like a boutique hotel.

After breakfast, the bridesmaids hit the road. Amanda, who lived in Princeton, drove the rest of the group to the train station. Reese would return to New York with Courtney and Paige while Yasmin trained down to DC. Meredith and Wit were airport bound.

"What do they do?" I asked Katie as we crossed the bridge over into Pennsylvania.

She turned down the music. We hadn't been talking; the only sound in the car up until now had been Spotify. Katie was a country fan. "Who does what?" she said.

"Meredith and Wit," I clarified. "What do they do that allows them to travel and live wherever?"

"They're computer nerds," Katie said, not unkindly. "Mer does something for Netflix; Wit does something for Apple." She smiled a bit, like she knew what I was going to ask next. "They got married three years ago but have been together for as long as I've known them."

"Did you go to their wedding?"

Katie nodded. "They eloped like a week after we graduated college. Only their best friends and families were there."

"That's cool," I said, and Katie *mm-hmm*-ed before turning the music back up to Carrie Underwood midchorus. I turned and looked out the window. Country was not my favorite.

Arthur and Francine were the first to greet us when we got back to the farmhouse. "Just knee him down," I said when Arthur jumped up on Katie. She always said *No!* or *Stop!* but never in a firm enough voice. I guess it was hard when you hadn't grown up with dogs.

Arthur finally let up when Da whistled sharply from the porch. "How was the slumber party?" he called, Arthur bounding toward him. He scratched the Newfoundland's head before descending the porch steps and walking over to meet us on the driveway.

"Lots of fun," Katie replied as I said, "An experience."

Katie wordlessly folded her arms over her chest, and my father gave me a familiar raise of the eyebrow. *I didn't mean to be sarcastic,* I wanted to say.

It *had* been an experience!

"Katie's mom hosts the sleepover of all sleepovers," I backtracked, trying to share a smile with Katie. But she didn't look at me; instead, she gave a calm Francine a few pets before asking where Austin and Samira were.

"Sam caught an early train back to Baltimore this morning," Da said, then gestured out past the barn to the far fields. "Austin went out an hour ago with Harry."

"Surprise, surprise!" Katie laughed, cheerfully enough that Da and I exchanged a look. She seemed relieved Samira was gone.

I certainly wasn't; I was confused. Last night, Samira had mentioned coming to watch my practice today. It had been a while since she'd seen me play.

Katie set off for the fields, knowing Austin was skeet shooting. I wished I could join him; skeet shooting was our thing. My brother and I loved obnoxiously sporting muddied Wellington boots with green wool hunting coats and matching caps, cosplaying *The Crown* or *Downton Abbey*. Dad always manned the machine that released the circular bright orange clay targets at lightning speed while Austin and I stood ready with our shotguns.

Da touched my shoulder, a reminder that we needed to leave for practice. "You want to get your stuff together?"

I nodded and headed toward the house, only to discover that my bedroom was messier than I'd left it last night; the covers on my bed were twisted and tangled like someone had slept restlessly with my pillows at the foot instead of the head. I also noticed couch cushions from our upstairs den's sectional arranged on my rug with another pillow and Austin's familiar pinstriped comforter.

He slept in here, I realized. My brother and Sam had probably stayed up all night talking. They hadn't seen each other for six months, at least.

I deduced they'd also been drinking when I noticed a collection of empty bottles on my desk. Next to the stash was a piece of loose-leaf paper covered in Samira's hurried handwriting. *It was so good to see you, Mads*, the note said. *Sorry to leave so early, but something came up! Thank you for letting me crash here! Austin insisted he'd clean up, so if your room's still a raging dumpster fire when you read this, BLAME HIM. XO, Sam*

Hmm, I thought, then texted Samira a photo of my disastrous room.

He's the worst! she responded while I was changing for field hockey. I'll punch him next time I'm back.

Which will be...? I asked.

Soon, she replied. Now go kick ass at practice!

I smiled and sent her a stream of pink hearts. Part of me wanted to fill her in on last night's slumber party, but there wasn't time.

"So, how was your experience last night?" Da asked on the way to practice. He was almost always my chauffeur, having retired when I started playing club field hockey in seventh grade. Driving me all over the place for games and tournaments appealed to him more than scrubbing up in the OR.

Winter was spent playing indoors, but the National Indoor Tournament earlier this month had brought that season to a close. After the championship game, I'd met and caught up with a few college coaches. All conversations had ended with me getting their cards.

I couldn't wait until spring sprung so we could start training outdoors. Indoor field hockey got tedious; outdoors allowed you to stretch your legs and get creative.

"Mads?" Da prompted. "Last night?"

I swallowed hard, struggling with how much to tell Da, who would tell Dad. They would then talk, and depending on that talk, we *all* would have a talk. I loved being so close to my parents—I couldn't imagine us operating any other way—but did I seriously want to explain why I was about to start going on all these silly dates? "Ready-Set-Date" Katie had nicknamed my quest, because I wouldn't *really* be like the Bachelorette, dressing up in evening gowns and flirting with multiple men at once.

"I had some rosé," I admitted. "I hope that's okay."

I was very open with my dads about alcohol, because Austin had been…well, out of control when he was in high school. They knew what he was doing, of course, because he went to parties every weekend and even dared to throw one or two. He took his groundings nobly, but the last straw had been when he literally woke up face down on our front lawn the morning after his senior prom. He'd blacked out and couldn't remember where he'd gone after the dance, how he'd gotten home, or whose puke was all over his tux. Instead of spending one last summer in Pennsylvania before college, our parents had sent him on an Outward Bound trip in the Rocky Mountains. It was how he'd fallen in love with the outdoors.

And cleaned up his act. The beer bottles littering my desk? They were all empty root beers. Austin rarely drank now, not even socially. He called himself a "celebration drinker."

I only drank with my parents' permission under my own roof. Some might say I needed to loosen up, that I was a goody-goody, but I didn't want to betray their trust.

"That's fine," Da said. "It's against the law, but that's fine. What vintage?"

"*Whispering Angel...*" I stage-whispered.

He chuckled. "I expect Katie's mother had plenty of snacks on hand?"

"Oh, you have *no* idea!" I laughed too, then told him about truth or dare. Or I told him we'd *played* truth or dare. No specifics.

He didn't ask for them, but he did ask if it had been fun to spend more time with Katie.

"Sure," I said, a hitch in my throat at the thought of Katie asking me if I'd ever been kissed or gone on a date with anyone.

Her voice had been slow and so sweet. It was like she *knew* she was on the cusp of epically embarrassing me.

But I'd handled it, and thanks to Ready-Set-Date, she was excited and we were going to bond! "She was with her friends, Da," I added nonchalantly. "She was happy."

"Good." He nodded. "Dad and I are glad you went."

"Yes, you're welcome," I deadpanned; then I asked how things had gone at home. He started telling me about Nana and Dad arguing over when she was going to retire (the salon *could* survive without her!), but my mind began to drift after my phone buzzed on my lap.

Already?! I thought, because Amanda had created a bridal party group chat during breakfast this morning. "Who has the goddamn Android?" she'd said, the Whispering Angel no longer so angelic. "I can't name the chat because we're not all iPhones."

Yasmin held up her phone. "It's a Samsung Galaxy, not an Android!"

My notification turned out to be an email, though. It wasn't even a good email, either. Just a promotion from Athleta. Disappointed, I found myself wishing for a text from the bridesmaids. I was curious how long it would take them to brainstorm my first suitor, if it would be as easy as they thought. "What's your type?" Amanda had asked last night, and when I said I didn't think I had one, the question was broken down into so many subquestions. *Brunette or blond? Blue eyes or brown? Built* or skinny? Extrovert or introvert? More Tom Holland or more Timothée Chalamet?

It had gone on...and...on...and *on*. Lawyer Yasmin had recorded a voice memo of the entire interrogation to reference later.

Once Da parked our Ford Explorer outside the bubble, we left each other in the dust. He was just as excited to join the parents—they were pretty much a cult—as I was to join my teammates. "Mads!" they called, and I grinned and hustled over to the sideline, where everyone was tugging on their shin guards before tying their turf shoes.

They *all* wanted to know how the party had gone. "This discussion ends the *second* we start warm-ups!" Coach Webber warned.

"Was it terrible?" our captain asked when I mentioned Katie's sleepover. "Or are the other bridesmaids cool?"

"One definitely is," I said. "Her name's Mer—"

Coach Webber blew her whistle, and then like the snap of a finger, practice began. We started with ladder drills to work on our quick feet, partner passing, and then three-on-three mini games. It wasn't until we were dripping with sweat, and our breathing became all over the place that we got a water break.

Thank god I'm back where I belong, I thought. Here I was confident and on fire, not constantly wondering if I said the wrong thing or was somehow being judged. Up in the stands,

Da gave me a thumbs-up while my teammate's mom called out that Amy needed to stop telegraphing her passes.

After chugging some water, I unzipped my backpack and rooted around for my prewrap and some tape. My left ankle was bothering me, so I needed to call in reinforcements. I'd have Da look at it later.

My phone slipped out while I dug around for my tape, and as if it were fate, my screen lit up to show a missed text from the unnamed bridesmaid chat. It was from Reese.

Don't, part of me thought. *You're at practice.*

Do, the other part said. *You don't need to respond right now.*

"Hustle, ladies!" Coach Webber called as the back of my neck sizzled from the temptation to read the text.

I took a deep breath and bit back a smile before quickly unlocking my phone. I didn't want to wonder for the rest of practice. For some reason, I *had* to know.

But of course, Reese's message only sparked *more* wonder, reading:

> So I just heard my cousin needs a date for his junior prom...

SIX

Believe it or not, curiosity about my date did *not* get the better of me; the bridesmaids would have to wait. Da and I discussed how practice went on the way home, and then I needed to make a quick turnaround to meet Connor. We always had dinner together on Sunday. Tonight was Mexican. "New shampoo?" he asked after I climbed into his Jeep, my hair still wet from the shower. He must've caught a whiff.

"Why, yes." I dramatically flipped my long locks over my shoulder. "Herbal Essences with rose hip extract. Thank you for noticing!"

Connor leaned over the center console to take an obnoxious sniff, crooking an arm around my neck. "I like the coconut one better."

I felt my phone burning a hole in my pocket while we debated whether or not to order Bomba's specialty guacamole again (it was delicious, but Connor had spent a while in the restroom last time). "Wait," I said when Connor flipped his left blinker instead of his right, heading away from town. "Where are we going?"

"Kevin's house," he replied. "He invited me and some other people over, and when I mentioned you and I were grabbing dinner, he asked if they could join..." He glanced at me with a guilty look.

"It's cool," I assured him, wondering how many of his friends would soon squeeze into the back seat. Beyond being way more social than me, Connor was one of the nicest people I knew. If someone dropped even the slightest hint that they wanted to hang out, he extended an invite. I liked his other friends...for the most part.

"Mads, hey!" Lauren Bitterman said when she and a friend got into the car with Kevin and another guy. She wore her fitted blue COUNCIL ROCK NORTH LACROSSE jacket, and as usual, her makeup looked flawless. "How are you?" She giggled. "We aren't crashing date night, are we?"

Date night.

That's it, I thought, heart racing when Connor mentioned Brenna being sick this weekend. *I'm texting them back!*

After Connor backed out of Kevin's driveway, I casually unlocked my phone and went to the bridesmaid chat to read Reese's text again.

> So I just heard my cousin needs a date for his junior prom...

The other bridesmaids had acknowledged the message with an array of hearts and smiley emojis, but now there was a new text from Katie: She's in, set her up!

My stomach squirmed, suddenly so not in the mood for guacamole with questionable ingredients. Maybe Katie was excited, but had she *really* just accepted on my behalf? What if I thought someone's junior prom was too serious for a first date?

Because, funny story, I did.

THERE IS NO WAY, I typed now, fingers flying across my screen. I'm not showing up in a ball gown to dance the night away with some stranger!!!

Oh, you make it sound so romantic...Yasmin wrote with a winky face.

Amanda quickly pointed out that he wouldn't be a total stranger. He was Reese's cousin; she could vouch for him.

True, I realized, but that didn't make me feel much better. I didn't know Reese that well yet.

Why don't you grab coffee together first? Meredith suggested. Get to know each other.

Yasmin, Reese, and one of Katie's cousins agreed with Meredith. I did too, feeling bolstered by the bridesmaids. Coffee—coffee wasn't a huge commitment. I could totally walk out if I wanted.

That sounds good, I typed, but a message from Katie appeared before I hit send.

It wouldn't count as a date, though, she'd texted.

"Alright, who's irking you now?" Connor asked from the driver's seat, which was a dead giveaway that he'd caught me rolling my eyes.

"Just the bridesmaid chat," I told Connor, then lied, "They're talking dates to go dress shopping."

I loved Connor, but I didn't want to tell him about Ready-Set-Date yet. I wasn't sure why.

"Bleh," he said as Lauren Bitterman stretched forward in the middle seat, desperate to be part of our conversation—or, more likely, in Connor's orbit.

He has a girlfriend, I almost grumbled.

"Oh, right!" she exclaimed. "Connor mentioned the wedding. Where's the bachelorette weekend gonna be?"

"I don't know." I shrugged. As the maid of honor, Amanda was in charge of planning it, but I suspected Katie would sign off on everything ahead of time. And would I be invited—or even *allowed*—to go? I'd be eighteen in September, but *legal* didn't equate to *drinking age*.

"I hope not Nashville," Lauren said. "It's so overdone, don't you think?"

"Mmm-hmm," I agreed, skimming the chat's newest text.

No one said it was a date, Katie, Meredith had messaged. We just want Mads to be comfortable! ☺

Once Katie and the others gave the message a thumbs-up, Reese wrote, Send me some times that work for you, Mads, and I will coordinate with Davis.

Davis, I thought, letting out a slow breath. Lauren was too busy trying to flirt with Connor while Connor was too busy driving for either of them to notice. *Davis*. He had a name. Knowing his name brought on some relief.

But then I learned nothing about Davis *beyond* his name. Katie and the bridesmaids didn't want me stalking his social media ahead of time. Remember, the Bachelorette is our inspiration! Amanda told me. Meeting someone for the first time and knowing nothing about them...

I responded that, as much as Bachelor Nation liked to pretend otherwise, the lead and contestants totally stalked one another on Instagram before production.

Everyone disliked that text.

Please? I started to type, but then someone lightly tugged on my damp hair. I realized Connor had parked. Lauren and their friends had already spilled out of the Jeep, but Connor hadn't moved from his seat. His steady blue eyes caught mine, and I felt my blood pressure calm. I was always comfortable with Connor—*content* with Connor.

"We never made a final call on the guac," he said. "Should we give it another chance?"

"It *was* addicting..." I admitted. "But, Con, you were in the bathroom for twenty minutes. Your tacos were cold and congealed by the time you made it back."

He ran a hand through his fair hair. Sometimes it looked blond, sometimes red. It all depended on the light. "You make a good point." He thought for a moment, then shrugged. "Eh, who cares? It'll flush out my system."

I snorted. "Connor!"

He grinned. "What?"

"That's—" I started, but giggles got the better of me. Connor cracked up, too.

We sat there laughing until Lauren texted him that they'd gotten a table.

SPRING

SEVEN

A couple weeks later, we were well into March, and I found myself gritting my teeth one Friday after school as I drove into Princeton. Davis and I'd both had packed schedules, so it had taken some time for them to align. I was nervous about finally meeting him, but I was even more nervous about *parking*. My dads liked to call me a *capable but cautious driver*.

Princeton was an idyllic town with historic Gothic architecture and high-end stores and restaurants, but at its core, it was also a college town. Gripping the steering wheel with both hands, I had a hard time knowing where to look. There were so many pedestrians. Shoppers congested the sidewalks, and students seemed to have no patience for the crosswalks, choosing to ignore the laws of traffic to jaywalk.

And, oh god, parking. I spotted a few open street-side spaces here and there, but I wasn't confident in my parallel-parking abilities. While Austin's car had an awesome rear backup camera, I had to rely on my own skills, driving my late grandfather's 1990 Land Rover Defender. It was the coolest car ever, and I felt a huge rush of pride every time someone complimented it. A few people had even offered to buy it from me, right on the spot.

But yes, I couldn't parallel park.

I wasn't especially proud of what I ended up doing. Both parking garages were full, so I swung into the spacious lot behind St. Paul's Church and its school. Only ten or so cars were there. PARISH MEMBERS ONLY, the sign read, and I cringed after cutting the ignition.

But you know *parish members*, I reassured myself. *The Gallants attend mass here, Katie went to elementary school here, and now Austin comes here every Christmas Eve…*

Once I'd locked the car, I not-so-subtly speed walked across the parking lot, only stopping to smooth my shirt after I turned left on Moore Street. Do you need advice on what to wear? Katie had texted last night, and even though I *knew* what to wear (fun pants and a white top, an outfit ingrained in a girl's brain), I said yes.

Fun pants and a white top, she told me. Hair down with casual makeup.

I wore a pair of high-waisted black jacquard pants embroidered with silver flowers and a cropped off-the-shoulder sweater. I'd weaved my hair into a side braid, and I didn't need a guide for casual makeup. To me, that was light eyeshadow with mascara, a dusting of blush, and a swipe or two of lip gloss.

You look adorable, Katie's cousin Paige wrote after I texted the promised selfie to the group. *Good luck!*

Davis and I were supposed to meet at Crescent Moon Coffee, an artsy café right off Nassau Street. I'd learned he was a junior at a nearby private day school (the bridesmaids wouldn't tell me which one, for fear I would use that as a stalking tool). Reese also told me she'd sent him a photo of me for recognition purposes. *The suitors always know what the Bachelorette looks like before she knows what they look like*, Meredith had reminded me. *It's all good!*

I told myself I could do this all the way to the coffee shop, but the second I stepped inside, my heart began to quake with nerves and I straight up forgot how to "people."

My eyes flicked around as I stood frozen in the entrance, taking in the clusters of customers chatting at tables and the assortment of eclectic armchairs and couches. Laptop users occupied the windowfront bar, their oversized mugs long drained but not ready to say goodbye to the free Wi-Fi. *He's not here*, I surmised. He'd know if I were here. He would've noticed me the moment I walked in...

Madeline Fisher-Michaels, you are so delusional, the host in my head said. *It's a busy-ass coffee shop.* Nobody *noticed you walk in, and you better move it before someone opens the door and slams into you!*

Sure enough, I heard the bell above the door chime behind me several seconds later, so I quickly stepped out of the way and into line to order. I had to do something, right? I didn't want to stand around and wait for Reese's cousin to recognize me. How awkward would that be?

Katie had pointed out that today wouldn't count as a date, but who was she kidding? My palms were starting to sweat. This already felt like a date because this was the closest thing I'd ever had to a date!

There was a handwritten menu on the big blackboard above the coffee bar, and pastries upon pastries tempted everyone behind a glass case. "Hello!" the barista said brightly. "What can I get you?"

"Um…" I quickly scanned the endless menu before settling on their seasonal drink. "A lavender latte, please."

"Hot or iced?"

"Hot."

The barista nodded. "What size?"

"Tall," I said, used to Starbucks lingo. "I mean, small."

"Great!" The barista input my order into the iPad-resembling register. "That'll be eight oh five."

Sadly, I didn't even blink. Everything was so expensive these days.

"Put it on my tab," someone said before I could dig out my wallet, and I whipped around to see Marco Álvarez standing behind me. One corner of his mouth tipped up in a smile, like we shared some kind of secret. "I'll have a medium chai," he added. "Iced, and we'll also take two chocolate chip muffins."

He dropped his voice to a whisper while tapping his debit card against the register PIN pad. "They aren't the *best* pastries in town, but they're good enough."

Speechless, I couldn't find my words until he'd guided me over to the pickup area, a gentle hand on my back until I not-so-subtly elbowed him. "What are you doing here?" I finally asked.

"I like to study here," Marco answered, and it was then I realized that I was looking at a Marco I hadn't met before. I was used to him walking our school hallways in track pants and soccer hoodies or his soccer uniform. His Ember & Ash attire, even. But no, today, right in front of me, he wore an army-green jacket and white Converse high-tops with what I *knew* were Lululemon pants. Austin had the same pair.

They looked nice on Marco.

You know, objectively speaking.

"And since when do you wear glasses?" I asked, my brow wrinkling at his rounded tortoiseshell frames.

"Technically since fourth grade," he said, annoyingly amused. "But I only wore them at home; contacts were much better for soccer." He stepped forward to grab our order. I hadn't even noticed his name had been called.

"Ah," I said.

"It's true." His lips twisted into a smile, and he handed me my million-dollar coffee. It was in a takeout cup, and our pastries were in the same brown paper bag. "Anyway." He took out one of the muffins. "What are you doing in town?"

"Oh, well, I'm…" I started, but drifted off, somehow noticing Crescent Moon's bell ring amid all the chaos. A cute Black guy walked through, wearing a blazer with a white button-down and a loosened striped tie. A private school uniform if there ever was one.

That had to be Davis.

"I have to go," I abruptly told Marco. "I'm meeting someone."

He raised an intrigued brow. "Okay," he said and handed me the pastry bag. "It was good seeing you, Mads."

Instead of grabbing a table and waiting around for Reese's cousin to track me down, I went straight up and greeted him like he'd just gotten out of a limo at the famous Bachelor Mansion. "Davis?"

From the flash of light in his eyes, I could tell he recognized me. "Hey, Madeline!"

"Mads," I said back. "It's just Mads."

Crap. I wanted to backtrack. *I couldn't have said hello first?*

"It's nice to meet you," I added quickly, smiling.

"It's nice to meet you, too." He smiled back, and then it was clear that neither of us knew what to do next. A hug seemed like too much, and we couldn't shake hands because I was double-fisting it with my latte in one and my muffin in the other.

Also, was shaking hands even a thing anymore?

"I'm sorry I already ordered," I blurted. "I, um, wasn't sure…"

"No, no, it's fine," Davis said. He was cute, looking more like Reese's younger brother than her cousin. Tall and lean with what Austin and I called the "*Peaky Blinders* haircut." Shaved on the sides and longer on top. His ears adorably stuck out a little. "How about you find us a spot," he suggested, "while I go grab a drink?"

I managed to snag two cushy armchairs the second two people vacated them, and Davis joined me several minutes later with what looked like a swirled caramel Frappuccino. "School was really draining today," he said when he caught my amused look. "I'm treating myself."

"Where do you go to school?" I asked. "Reese wouldn't tell me anything beyond your first name."

Davis chuckled. "That sounds like her." He took a sip of his drink. "I go to Hun. It's right down the road."

"I know Hun," I said. "They tried to recruit me for field hockey."

"Oh, yeah, Reese mentioned you're really into field hockey," Davis said. "Have you committed anywhere yet?"

I shook my head. I didn't really discuss my college prospects with anyone except my family and Coach Webber. Well, and my high school guidance counselor because it was encouraged that she be in the loop. "Not yet," I told Davis. "Hopefully by the end of the school year, though."

Because *that* was when the Ivy League schools made the last of their offers. April through June of a player's junior year was their sweet spot, and I knew I would be holding my breath for those three months. The University of Pennsylvania—Penn— was my *dream* school. The Quakers were my dream *team*. I loved their city campus and the team's style of play. I'd gone to their annual summer camp for the last several years, and nearly screamed when I got my first invite to their smaller, more exclusive clinics.

What I was now hoping for was an invitation for an official visit to campus. If a coach wanted you to spend a weekend getting to know the girls on the team?

It was a big deal.

"Do you play any sports?" I asked Davis before taking an anxious sip of my coffee. Was I talking about myself too much? And even if I wasn't, we needed to shift the conversation away from field hockey. I could go on about it forever, but the bridesmaids had told me it was important to find out if Davis and I had anything in common.

"I played a bunch when I was a little kid," he said as I chewed and swallowed a bite of muffin. It was a little dry, but still good. "But I wasn't very good at them, so my parents thought maybe art or music would be more my thing."

I smiled a little. "And? Are you an artist or musician?"

"I'm the saxophonist in Hun's band and in their choir. I'm also in a local chamber choir."

"That's really cool," I said. "I like to sing too, but my school's choral director cut me for my extreme pitchiness." I shrugged. "So instead, I perform in the comfort of the car."

"Oh, yeah?" Davis's eyes shined. "Let me guess—"

I cut him off. "If you say Taylor Swift, I'm going to punch you."

He chuckled. "You don't like Taylor Swift?"

"No, no, I do," I said. "I just think it's stereotyping to assume every girl on earth is a Swiftie."

"Fair enough." Davis smiled, then after a beat added, "Although, as a guy, I am not ashamed to say she's incredible. I skipped school to get tickets for the Eras Tour two years ago."

"Are you kidding me?"

"Nope," he said. "I suffered for seven hours, but then *finally* triumphed with two tickets. New Orleans, night one. We had to fly down and stay with my cousin, but it was so worth it. My girlfriend lost her mind."

My spine straightened. Girlfriend? He had a *girlfriend*? How had Reese not mentioned that?

"Oh." Davis read the confusion on my face. "No, Mads, I meant *ex*-girlfriend. It's sort of"—he searched for the right word—"*new*. I haven't totally broken the habit yet."

I bit the inside of my cheek. "Is that why you need a date to JProm?"

Davis sighed. "Yeah," he said. "I really want to go, but all my friends have girlfriends or are, you know, *talking* with someone, so I'd be the only one going stag." He paused to sip his drink. "And I know I could just ask one of my friends, but they're also friends with my ex…" He shook his head. "Hun feels too small sometimes, and everybody knows everybody, and that can get old when it comes to dances. So yes, when Reese texted me about you, I didn't hesitate."

My heart flipped. *He's sweet*, I thought. *He's really adorable and really sweet.*

Maybe the ex-girlfriend thing was a bit uncomfortable, but besides me, who *didn't* have an ex? I liked talking to him. It was fun and easy.

I didn't realize my lack of response until Davis grimaced and asked, "Did I blow it?"

"Oh my god, no!" I exclaimed. "No way! I was literally thinking about what a great time we're going to have together."

Davis grinned. "You'll be my date?"

I found myself grinning back. "I'd love to."

Then, I internally screamed. *I HAVE A DATE!*

Davis and I talked for another hour, mostly about music. "You *have* to check out Maisie Peters," I told him. "I guess she's technically pop, but definitely has this British rock edge to her music, and she writes all her own songs…"

"Wait, I've *seen* Maisie Peters!" he said. "Years ago, when she opened for Ed Sheeran in Philly. I supervised my little sister and her two friends while the parents peaced out for dinner. It was a great concert!"

Later, we exchanged numbers. I internally rolled my eyes at myself when I saw Davis Adams in my phone, since *Adams* was also Reese's last name. I should've been able to guess that for social media reconnaissance.

Maybe I'd liked going in blind, though; it stopped me from wondering if the person I saw on Instagram would live up to their profile's hype.

Davis said he would text me details for the dance, plus some songs he thought I would like. I had some in mind for him, too, which made my stomach spin a little. He hugged me before saying goodbye; we'd parked in opposite directions. It wasn't until I turned off Witherspoon Street and started up Nassau that I realized I'd forgotten my purse-that-I-literally-never-used back at the coffee shop.

I sighed, and then back to Crescent Moon I went. The sun was starting to sink in the sky, and even though I'd only been gone for ten minutes, the café had calmed—calmed enough that I could clearly see Marco through the front window; he had an entire couch to himself and was focused on his laptop. A few books and a couple of binders were splayed open on the cushions next to him.

Along with my purse!

"I tried calling after you," he said by way of greeting when I marched up to him. He closed his laptop. "But you were definitely surfing some other galaxy."

"Space cadet reporting for duty." I sarcastically saluted him, then dropped the act. "I had my AirPods in. I couldn't hear you."

And I might've been in the middle of sending a text to Katie and the bridesmaids: It went well!!

As if on cue, my phone buzzed; I pulled it out of my pocket and placed it on the nearby coffee table, not yet ready to read the flood of messages. It vibrated again on the tabletop, the screen lighting up to show there were six new texts in the chat.

Once six became eight and eight became ten, Marco gave me a look. "Care to share what that was earlier?"

Not particularly, I almost said.

But those *eyes*.

Those damn honey-dipped eyes of his.

They looked dangerous.

Anyway.

"Earlier?" I asked, trying to play it cool.

"Yeah." Marco moved his school stuff to make room for me on the half-moon-shaped couch. I waited a beat before sitting down; he and I hadn't hung out like this in a while. "You and Davis." He held up his hands before I could call him on it. "I swear I wasn't eavesdropping. You just turn up the volume when you're nervous."

I glared at him. "I *wasn't* nervous."

He ignored me. "Were you two on a date?"

I opened my mouth, then closed it. His voice was teasing, but I swallowed my snark. "More of a predate," I said eventually. "He goes to Hun and asked me to be his date to their junior prom. We wanted to meet in person first."

"Mmm," Marco hummed, which I somehow knew translated to, *Someone set you up?*

"Marco." I sighed. "Don't ask."

"Okay." He shrugged. "Don't tell."

He opened his laptop again and went back to whatever he'd been doing earlier. I tried not to fidget next to him, but my thudding heart made that difficult. Because what if I *did* want to tell him about the bridesmaids' Ready-Set-Date scheme? Ever since agreeing, I had felt the urge to talk to someone uninvolved about it, but I hadn't been able to figure out who that uninvolved someone was. Because for once in my life I didn't want to share with Austin. How confused would he be when I told him this game was my make-or-break moment with Katie? I also definitely didn't want to tell my dads, and Connor would think the whole thing was ridiculous.

Marco glanced up at me after a few moments. "You alright, Mads?"

I flopped back against the couch cushions. "Marco, I never wanted to be one of Katie's bridesmaids."

"Ah, so you *are* telling." He closed his computer and folded his arms across his chest; I had his full and undivided attention. "Am I allowed to ask now?"

I waved my hand. *Be my guest!*

He smirked. "Did someone set up you and Davis?"

"Yes," I said, and then let the whole saga spill out. Everything from my parents and me being excluded from Austin's Parisian proposal to Katie asking me to be a bridesmaid, to the engagement party, to the bridesmaid slumber party (and with plenty of tangents along the journey). By the time I finished, we'd left Crescent Moon behind and were crossing St. Paul's parking lot. My lungs wouldn't stop fluttering. It had been such a relief to tell someone that I hadn't been able to get the words out fast enough. "What do you think?" I asked when Marco didn't offer an opinion. "Am I nuts?"

Marco took off his glasses. "No, I wouldn't say so," he said, using his T-shirt's hemline to methodically wipe their lenses. He didn't speak again until they were clean. "It more sounds like you want to connect with Katie, and you're willing to go a very long—and slightly silly—way to do so. I admire that; I can tell how important family is to you."

"Family is everything to me," I said with a delayed and dazed nod. Because, *excuse me*? I'd just told him that I was trying to make the world's most famous reality dating show a genuine reality, by being set up on who-knew-how-many dates. I was expecting Marco's reaction to be something more along the lines of an amused, *Wow, you're* that *desperate for a wedding plus-one?*

But no, he'd seen right through the plan; he'd discerned my motivation as if it were tattooed on my forehead. "I would..." I started but kept the rest to myself.

I would like a boyfriend, though. I don't think a boyfriend would be so bad.

Maybe a boyfriend would be a bonus of bonding with Katie.

Instead, I asked where Marco was parked. The only other car in the lot was a Mom-mobile minivan, and bless me, I hadn't been served with a ticket! "Back home in Pennsylvania," he answered. "Students aren't allowed to keep cars on campus."

"Oh," I said. "Would you, um, like me to drive you back to your dorm?"

Marco shook his head. "Thanks, but I'm meeting friends for a late dinner at Winberie's."

My eyebrows knitted together. "Didn't we pass Winberie's on the walk back here?"

"Yes," he said. "But I wanted to make sure you got back to your car okay."

"You didn't have to," I replied. "I know my way around. Plus, I have pepper spray. You know, in case it ever comes to that."

Marco opened the driver's-side door. "I *know* you know your way around." He gestured for me to get inside, really committing to this bit we were doing. "And I would be shocked if Mads Fisher-Michaels *didn't* own pepper spray." He winked. "But that doesn't mean she should use it. Princeton might never recover."

"Correct," I said, hopping into the Defender. "My aim is impeccable."

Once I'd closed the door with a sweet and satisfying slam, I expected Marco to take off across the lot to meet his friends, but he barely moved. He only took two steps backward to wait under a lamppost. I felt almost awkward buckling my seat belt before queuing up Waze (I knew my way home, but assistance from my Australian-accented guide never hurt). Marco waved when the Defender rumbled to life, and I did my best Queen-of-England wave back.

He didn't leave his post until I'd flicked my left-hand blinker to leave the church; in my rearview mirror, I watched him start across the lot to take some shortcut I didn't know about. It must've been a Princeton thing.

EIGHT

Connor almost choked on his root beer when he heard the news. "What do you mean you're going to the Hun School's junior prom?" he asked from the couch, leg casually draped over the arm. He'd made himself at home here years ago. "Since when do you even *know* anyone from Hun?"

"Since yesterday," Dad answered before I could, failing miserably at masking a small smile. "She went on a coffee date."

I groaned. "It *wasn't* a date!"

"Then what was it?"

"I don't know, Dad," I said. "I guess whatever you call coffee dates with your clients."

"A war room meeting?"

Connor chuckled, but it was all too quickly drowned out by the NHL game on TV. The New York Rangers versus their cross-river rival, the New Jersey Devils. "AND HE SCORES!" the commentator exclaimed. "NICK CARMICHAEL ON A POWER PLAY GOAL!"

Across the room in his designated armchair—we were a tad superstitious and all had "lucky spots" for Rangers games—Da pumped a fist in the air before unlocking his phone and furiously texting Austin. Professional hockey had always been their thing. Katie apparently loved it too, but she was a Devils fan. "Only Rangers fans are welcome around here!" Da had joked when Katie first told us, but you could tell from her flushed face that she hadn't taken it as one.

Ironically, Mr. Gallant had made the same crack to Austin, but now they made absurd bets before every game. The last time the Rangers had beaten the Devils, Katie's dad had to wear Austin's Rangers tie to work for an entire week.

Marc Gallant, it turned out, was the Devils' general manager.

"Connor's right, though," Da said after the second period had ended. "How did you originally meet this kid?"

"He's cousins with Reese, one of Katie's bridesmaids," I said. "He needs a date for JProm, and she thought we might hit it off."

"Did you?" Connor asked while I felt my parents both eyeing me. Dad seemed amused and Da a little suspicious. He definitely wanted more of the story.

Not yet, I thought. This was between Katie, the bridesmaids, and me (and Marco, but unofficially). *Just trust me.*

Katie's girl gang had been *thrilled* that Davis and I clicked. Amanda had sent a spree of enthusiastic emojis while Courtney and Paige had both texted some version of, You go, Mads!

I just got off the phone with him, Reese had messaged. *He thinks you're cute and says you have a ton in common!*

That made me blush; no guy had ever called me cute before. I reread her text before Katie chimed in: *Ooh, details please...*

I'd been happy to provide them.

Now, Connor asked if Davis played a sport.

"No." I shook my head. "He's a musician—"

"A *musician*?" Dad sucked in a sharp breath. "Are we talking rock band or boy band?"

"Does it matter, Harry?" Da asked. "Both have a long and complicated history with substance abuse."

"Wedding band, actually," I reported. "Besides playing saxophone in his school band and singing in two choirs, he and his friends have formed a wedding band. I can show you their Instagram page."

My dads looked genuinely impressed.

"And," I added, "he has been appointed official concert chaperone for his younger sister and her fellow tweens."

I expected Connor to roll his eyes. When his parents had asked him to take his thirteen-year-old brother and his buddy to Olivia Rodrigo last year, he had outright refused. Instead, it was me who screamed and sang along with Liam and Noah at the Wells Fargo Center in Philly. Austin had plenty of yummy greasy takeout waiting for us afterward; he'd insisted we crash at his apartment. Katie hadn't moved in yet.

Whenever Liam McCallister referenced it as "the best night

ever," Connor looked like a dog with his tail curled between his legs. "There's always Shawn Mendes next July…" I liked reminding him.

"He sounds like a good guy," Connor eventually said, and my parents nodded in agreement. Dad—who now had his laptop out, probably doing a background check on Davis—also gave me an emphatic thumbs-up. "But"—Connor cleared his throat—"if you have a good time, does that mean he'll be coming to *our* JProm?"

Shoot, I thought. Our high school's junior prom was a week after Hun's, and technically, I already had a date. Well, not exactly a date, because said date was Connor. He and Brenna had broken up at the end of February (and Lauren Bitterman hadn't wormed her way into his heart yet). Do you want to go to JProm together? he'd texted while I was playing a showcase down in Florida. I really want to have fun, and I always have the most fun with you.

Yes, I'd replied. Because I have the most fun with you, too.

Then I took a screenshot of those two messages and saved them to my camera roll, rereading them every now and again. They made my heart twist for different reasons. I loved knowing that our friendship was solid, strong, and true…but it also made me think of Austin and Samira, best friends who'd fallen so hard for each other in high school.

Sometimes I spiraled, wondering why Connor and I weren't like them. If he could just stay single for five seconds, would something happen between us?

"I mean, I hope Davis and I have a great time together," I told Connor now, a lump in my throat. "But I'm already locked down for JProm." I shrugged. "Some lax bro asked me via text."

"Lame!" my parents chorused. They still wouldn't let Connor live down the fact that he hadn't asked me in person.

Connor's lips twitched up in a smile. I shook my head and smiled back before Face-IDing into my phone, which was blowing up thanks to the bridesmaids. Now that Davis and I were officially going to JProm together, they were hell-bent on finding me the perfect dress. I'd been immediately bombarded with links to potential dress options before Meredith had quelled the madness. Everyone cease! she'd texted, and then: Mads, would you like ideas? Or do you have it covered?

Ideas welcome! I wrote, even though I could literally just wear the violet cocktail dress I'd worn to Katie and Austin's engagement party. Davis had said the dress code was semiformal.

But the truth was, this was so unexpectedly fun that I'd consider all input offered—and hoped for some from Katie. Maybe I wasn't looking forward to browsing bridesmaid dresses for hours together, but a link or two from Lulus or Reformation would be nice. She knew my style best.

Cool! Meredith texted. Please describe your personal style so Amanda doesn't waste time scouring the White House Black Market website.

I giggled a little. WHBM tried to be cool and sophisticated but was on the preppier side. Not to mention, way too old for me.

Nana still shopped there.

"How would you describe my style?" I asked the family room.

"Fun pants and a white top," Connor said automatically, unaware how well he'd been trained.

"That's an *outfit*," I said. "Not an aesthetic."

"Fine. Purple, then."

"And that's a color." I sighed, though from the mischievous look on his face, he was clearly just teasing me. "We need a *vibe*, Con."

Connor's next contribution was a shrug.

"Mmm, how about classic…" Da started.

"With a bohemian twist," Dad finished.

I gave him a blank look. "You used that description for a listing in Lambertville."

My Realtor father smirked. "Did I?"

"Yes." I laughed, but then my fingers flew across my touchscreen. "And it's totally perfect!"

"What do you mean he's not picking you up?" Da asked on the drive home from a Saturday field hockey game. Here we were in mid-April, finally playing outdoors. We'd won, but it had been a close one: 5–4. Half my mind was still back on the turf, visualizing Amy and me playing tic-tac-toe up the field before she faked out the other team's goalie and passed the ball to me…

But still no invitation to visit Penn, I thought. *Why hasn't it happened yet?*

I was doing everything right. Wasn't I?

"Mads?" Dad's voice brought me back to reality. "Davis isn't picking you up for the dance?"

"Oh, no." I shook my head. Hun's JProm was tonight. "He's not."

Dad turned in the front seat to give me a look while Da shot me one in the rearview mirror. *Why not?*

"It doesn't make sense," I told them. "He lives in Princeton, we're having dinner in Princeton, and the dance is in Princeton…" I shrugged. "Why should he have to drive to Pennsylvania only to go back to New Jersey?"

"Because it's the chivalrous thing to do," Dad said.

"Well, chivalry might be dead," I replied. "I don't know if picking up your date is even a thing anymore." At least, not according to my goalie. When she and her boyfriend had first started going out, they always met up places. It wasn't until they were official that she started riding shotgun in his car.

"Perhaps," Da said. "But that doesn't change the fact that we'd like to meet the young man taking our daughter out tonight."

I tried not to roll my eyes. *This will be so much easier with Connor next weekend,* I thought. *They know Connor, and they love Connor. We'll laugh while Dad takes photos on the porch before we take off in the Jeep.*

Something in me twinged.

It wasn't that I *didn't* want my parents to meet Davis. I liked him a lot. We'd been texting pretty regularly, sending music recommendations back and forth, and then talking about school and stuff. Part of me had been wondering why he hadn't suggested we hang out again before JProm. You could always suggest it, Meredith had said when I asked her opinion, which was fair. I could. But I didn't.

I'd been busy.

My dads dropped the subject of meeting Davis. They weren't going to push too hard on it, knowing that the last thing I'd do was text Davis to change our plans. I didn't want it to seem like I was bumming a ride. I had the Defender and would make it to Princeton on my own.

Only I planned to leave the house wearing sneakers with my dress. Driving stick in heels? Hard pass. I'd change into them once I parked.

I checked my phone, wishing Da would speed up a little. There was still plenty of time before I needed to get ready, but I always preferred having more time to less. How are you doing your hair? Amanda had texted in the bridesmaid chat. Because I'm thinking Old Hollywood curls.

Or a classic chignon, Courtney wrote, which Paige immediately hearted. (For whatever reason, I was beginning to think of Katie's cousins as a set of twins. Courtney-and-Paige.)

Just no braids, Mads, Reese texted.

Ladies, you do know she's not your Barbie, Meredith said. Right?

I smiled; Meredith hadn't sent that message. Her husband hijacked her phone every now and again.

I was actually more into American Girl dolls, Wit, Katie wrote, and ironically, a few beats after her text appeared, our car's Bluetooth alerted us that we had an incoming call from Austin. Dad tapped accept. "Hey, kid. What's up?"

"Not much," Austin said through the speakers. "Just calling to see how the game went. Mads mentioned it was going to be a tough one…"

"Where are you?" I asked after recapping my game for him. He'd whistled when I described my goal. "I heard some police sirens."

"Yeah, some moron in a Mustang has been driving like he's in a car chase in downtown LA," my brother said. "Katie and I are on our way to spend the night at her house."

My spine straightened. Katie was *with* Austin? Currently riding shotgun and listening to this call? Without feeling the need to say hello?

"Her parents are making dinner and breaking out the board games," Austin continued while Dad leaned over and whispered something to Da. "I think Amanda's bringing the guy she's been seeing, too."

His name was out of my mouth before I could stop it. "Neil, right?" I said, trying to keep my tone light but not *too* light.

Everyone knew any airiness in my voice was code for sarcasm. "Isn't it Neil, Katie?"

There was a beat of silence, and then—miraculously—she spoke! "Yes, it's Neil."

"Oh, Katie, hello!" Da exclaimed warmly, but Dad covered his mouth to keep from laughing. "We didn't know Austin had you on speaker!"

"He does," she confirmed, and that was literally it. She sounded like she was too busy searching for split ends to really talk to us.

I shifted in the back seat, uncomfortable and a little upset. Things between Katie and me…well, I guess they hadn't really improved. Her enthusiasm for Ready-Set-Date wasn't translating to real life.

Austin didn't seem to notice her disinterest. "So, Mads," he said, "what time is Reese's cousin swinging by to get you later?"

"He isn't," Dad said before I could. "They're 'meeting up.'"

"Mmm," Austin said, the flip of his blinker audible. "Well, that *is* sort of how things are done now, Dad. Amanda has been going out with this Neil guy for"—he dropped off to consult with Katie (why couldn't she just participate in the conversation?!)—"three months, and he never picks her up. They always rendezvous."

"That's unfortunate," Da said.

"Not to mention, a waste of gas," Dad joked.

Austin chuckled. "Last time I checked, Dad, you weren't exactly the paragon of environmental sustainability," he said. "Does Da still double-check that you recycle correctly?"

I groaned. Dad's recycling was never going to be up to par, but in his defense, Da had an absurdly specific system. "Can we go back to talking about me, please?" I asked, ever the melodramatic me-me-*me* little sister.

"Of course," Austin said. "Because Dad and Da should be meeting your date, Mads. I get the whole not-picking-you-up thing, but—"

"Well, what do you want them to do?" I asked. "Davis said our group got the last table at Ember & Ash tonight, so it's not like they can crash our dinner with their own reservation."

"You never know," Dad said dryly. "Rose Álvarez and I text regularly now."

I threw him the sharpest of dagger eyes. "I will *murder* you."

"Hey, I have an idea!" Austin exclaimed, and I swear it was one second later that his idea chimed like an email in my head. *Why don't you come to the Gallants' house? Mads can get ready there, ask Davis for a last-minute ride, no big deal, and then you can meet him before spending the evening with us!*

Because my parents liked Marc and Stacy Gallant. The only issue was that neither couple could fully commit to getting to know the other better. "He's a huge sports guy and she has impeccable taste," Dad said after having dinner at their house for the very first time. "They're nice people."

That dinner had been four years ago. The Gallants were still just "nice people."

Austin, you're a genius, I thought. *I'll go out with Davis, and Dad and Da will have a great time with you guys—*

"What was that idea, kid?" Dad asked. "You mumbled. We couldn't quite hear you."

The balloon of hope in my chest deflated when we heard unintelligible whispers. Katie had also read Austin's mind, but unlike me, she wasn't on board. My stomach soured; now that they were engaged, it felt like Katie was yanking my brother away from us instead of gently tugging.

"Oh…well…" Austin said, obviously trying to pull something out of his ass. "Just that Mads could probably ask Davis for a last-minute ride. He likes you, sis. He won't say no."

"Thanks," I said, irked. "But I'd like to have my own car, so I can come home when I want. I'll introduce him to Dad and Da if it goes well."

Then I leaned forward and disconnected the call.

Neither of my parents said anything.

"We know Davis is a great kid," Dad said. "I had lunch with Jim Dougherty on Tuesday. He wants to downsize to a townhouse."

"And let me guess," I said. "Jim Dougherty is what? Their next-door neighbor?"

"Three houses down, actually," he replied.

"What are the freaking odds," I muttered.

"The point of preferring Davis to pick you up is *not* so we can turn into intimidating dads and ask about his intentions," Dad said. "We trust you."

"I know you do," I said, sighing. "What *is* the point?"

"For you to be wooed, Madeline," Da said. "The point is for you to be *wooed*."

I napped the rest of the way home (something told me freshly charged batteries were best for the dance floor) but woke up to a text from Austin: Hey, sorry about earlier. I know you knew what I was going to propose (because you're a certified genius)... but so did Kates...and I had to go with her this time. Tonight is supposed to be about Amanda introducing Neil to their parents. She didn't want hosting our family to steal her sister's thunder. I hope you get that.

Yeah, no worries, I said. Have fun tonight.

No exclamations, he immediately wrote back. You're Mad Mads.

No, I'm not, I lied. HAVE FUN TONIGHT!!!!!!!!!!

YOU TOO!!!!!!! he replied, and even though I *was* "Mad Mads" and still a little annoyed with him, I couldn't help but laugh.

NINE

I was relieved when Davis suggested that we meet at Hun before heading into Princeton for dinner; it meant I wouldn't need to navigate town on a Saturday night. "Cool car!" a guy in a black suit called after I'd parked the Defender and quickly swapped out my Stan Smiths for heels. He stood next to Davis, who greeted me with a hug.

"You look beautiful." He smiled.

"Thank you." I smiled back. The bridesmaids had let me make the executive decision, but Katie highly encouraged me to pick a strapless navy silk dress covered with light blue and yellow roses. "You look great, too," I added, touching the lapel of Davis's burgundy suit.

"Thanks," he said, then put a hand on my back. A thrill sparked up my spine. This was my first date! "Let me introduce you to everyone." We walked over to the group hanging out by a blue Tesla. "Guys, this is Mads!"

"Hey, I'm Evan," the guy in the black suit said. Davis had

mentioned Evan in his texts. They were best friends. "And that seriously is a *sweet* ride. What year is it?"

"Nineteen ninety," I said proudly. "My grandfather taught me to drive in it."

Evan's date was named Rebecca, and then there were two other couples. One girl—Natalie—seemed to be giving off a strange vibe, but when *she* noticed that *I* noticed, she dropped her pout. "I like your earrings," she said, pointing to my wavy gold hoops. The bridesmaids couldn't be thanked for my accessories. All me.

Hun's JProm apparently wasn't as much of a big deal as it was at my school. I was a little surprised that we weren't taking any pre-prom pictures like Connor and I would next weekend poolside in Erin Magee's backyard.

Tonight's dance also wasn't at an off-campus venue. "It's always in the senior dining hall," Rebecca informed me as we piled into Natalie's white Range Rover, but with Davis behind the wheel. "They closed it for lunch today so they could transform the place…"

No one really spoke to me on the way to Princeton proper; instead, they fought over who should DJ, and once Rebecca was chosen, it became all about booing her playlist. She was, it seemed, pro-Pitbull.

I felt my phone buzz while Davis circled town for parking— I'd silenced all alerts from the bridesmaid chat, but was happy to see a text from Connor: How's it going so far?

Fine, I typed back. They seem nice, but nobody's really talked to me yet.

Bet that's because they're close friends and aren't used to newcomers, he wrote. It'll get better at dinner. Just be yourself!

Such original advice, I messaged, resisting the urge to ask what he was up to tonight. Texting with Connor always made me feel less nervous about things, but it also distracted me. I had to be present; I had to be here. I didn't want Davis to think I wasn't interested.

Ember & Ash was unsurprisingly flooded when we arrived, but I smiled to myself. It wasn't the only restaurant the Álvarez family owned, but Marco once told me it was their favorite, and I understood why. I loved the restaurant's moody vibe. Low lighting with custom plastered ombré walls—white that gradually darkened into gray that deepened into black. There was an elegant stone firepit in the center of the space—only lit for dinner, I knew—and surrounding it were reclaimed wood tables. Some were large enough to seat ten, while much more intimate tables were arranged near the mile-long banquette against the wall. Its cushions were inky velvet. *Date night central*, I surmised upon noticing all the couples. A bespectacled blond man and a pretty brunette held hands across their small table and wouldn't stop smiling at each other. He raised their entwined fingers and kissed her knuckles when she laughed at something he'd said. It was a little nauseating, but a lot adorable. It was as if they were off in their own orbit, one where only the two of them existed.

Were Austin and Katie ever like that?

"Adams for eight," Natalie said breezily once we finally reached Ember & Ash's base of operations, the limestone hostess podium.

My nose crinkled. "Is Natalie's last name Adams, too?" I whispered to Davis. He was standing right next to me, and I was very aware of his hand dangling only inches from mine.

"Oh, no," he replied. "It's Alexakos." He shifted from one foot to the other, and my arm tingled when our fingers brushed. "She just, um, always used my last name for reservations."

Used? I thought. *Why past tense?*

"Yes, I see your reservation right here," the hostess said, her face familiar when she looked up from her iPad to assess our group. "Your table should be ready in..." She trailed off, her neutral but warm expression slipping into a surprised smile when she noticed me. "No way! Mads Fisher-Michaels?"

"Hey, Carina." I waved. Carina was Marco's older sister; she'd graduated from Cornell a couple years ago with a degree in hospitality. According to Dad, she'd spent a year proving her skills at Two Fish, one of the Álvarez family's smaller restaurants—they had the *best* brunch—before her parents promoted her to front of house at Ember & Ash.

"It's great to see you!" she exclaimed, efficiently grabbing eight menus and gesturing for our group to follow her. "Marco mentioned..."

What? I thought, spine straightening. *Marco mentioned what?*

"Who's Marco?" Davis and Natalie asked, but in very different tones. Davis was casually curious while his friend sounded like she'd discovered a juicy secret.

My clandestine lover, I thought about telling Natalie. *He's older; he's worldly; he buys me expensive jewelry and top-of-the-line field hockey sticks…*

"Her brother," I said. "We went to school together. He was a couple years ahead of me."

Carina seated us and menus were circulated. "Your server will be over momentarily," she said, then to me: "Please tell Austin and Katie congratulations!"

"Who are Austin and Katie?" Natalie asked once Carina had disappeared. She and her date—Ben? Brett? Brent?—were sitting directly across from Davis and me. Ben/Brett/Brent was studying the menu like the rest of our table, but Natalie hadn't picked hers up yet.

Learning my life story had apparently skyrocketed on her priority list.

"Austin's my older brother and Katie is his fiancée," I said. "Ember & Ash catered their engagement party two months ago."

Every girl at the table's head snapped toward me. If I had to wager a guess, their wedding Pinterest boards were plenty populated. "Ooh, how did he propose?" Rebecca asked.

"Paris." I knew that one word would provide enough description. Whatever scene the girls conjured in their heads would not be *unlike* the overproduced Instagram Reel. I mean, it's Paris!

"And when are they getting married?" Natalie asked.

"December fourteenth," I answered, then elaborated because I knew the questions that would come next. "The ceremony's going to be at St. Paul's here in town, with the reception at the Bedens Brook Club."

Dad and Da had been quiet when Austin told us last month, but *I* hadn't. We were all in the kitchen, Da making dinner, Dad uncorking a bottle of wine, and Austin's face filling the screen of my MacBook. Katie had gone out to dinner with friends, so he'd FaceTimed to catch up and say hello to Arthur and Francine. "Wait, you're doing a country club wedding?" I'd asked. "Golf course ceremony and ballroom reception?"

"Not exactly," he said. "I know we're lapsed in the religion department, but Katie wants St. Paul's. And then, yes, we'll party in Bedens Brook's ballroom. It's nice."

"But does it have character?" I asked, catching the corner of Dad's mouth tip up. "Austin, I thought you guys would do something *cool*. I know you said it'd be in Princeton, but I thought maybe you'd change your mind and do something in Philly. I heard you can rent out the Reading Terminal Market." I glanced at our parents. "Who told me that?"

"Probably Sam," Austin said. "She's determined to try every vendor, remember?"

Right, I thought, recalling last summer. Samira, Austin, and

I'd spent a Saturday in Philly together. Reading Terminal Market had been lunch, where we'd eaten tacos upon tacos, devoured dumplings, and gotten about a dozen cannoli to bring home.

"It would be an awesome venue, Mads," Austin said, "but Katie wants Bedens Brook."

Dad cleared his throat. "I hope this doesn't come to you as a shock, Austin," he said, "but there's no bride without a groom. This wedding is technically half yours. Do *you* want Bedens Brook?"

Onscreen, Austin shrugged. "I want Kates to have exactly what she wants."

I looked away to roll my eyes while Da diplomatically said, "Well, since we're adhering to tradition, it is the parents of the groom's responsibility to host the rehearsal dinner."

"Yeah." Austin nodded. "The Gallants actually suggested—"

"That we should do something cool, classy, and not remotely country club–related?" Dad cut in, not giving time for Austin to answer. "Excellent, because that's exactly what your father and I were envisioning."

Austin was silent for a beat, his mouth twisting in thought before he smiled sheepishly and said, "Please make it cooler than cool."

Connor had been right; Davis's friend group started getting to know me after we ordered. Evan opened with, "So Davis told us you're a field hockey superstar?"

It turned out Rebecca played lacrosse, so we talked all about the college recruiting process before I answered questions about school and hobbies and stuff. "I can't believe you don't play an instrument." Ben/Brett/Brent shook his head, chuckling. "Davis has never dated anyone who wasn't musical."

I laughed a little, but before I could say anything, Natalie snorted. "Oh, come on. They aren't *dating*. This"—she gestured between Davis and me—"is a cute little stunt."

"Uh, excuse me?" My brows knitted together as the table fell silent. "Stunt?"

Natalie waited until after our appetizers were served to explain. "Yeah, a stunt. Davis isn't really interested in you, Madeline. The only reason you're here tonight is so he can make his ex jealous."

Something in my stomach curdled even though the only milk I'd had today was in my cereal for breakfast. *That's right*, I remembered. Davis had a somewhat still recent ex-girlfriend. He'd told me at Crescent Moon Coffee, but it hadn't come up since. I had forgotten about her.

Her, who was so clearly *Natalie*. It all made sense now. Natalie not being thrilled to meet me earlier, and then Davis driving Natalie's car into town and Natalie using Davis's name for our reservation—they were probably old habits that they couldn't yet kick.

The realization felt like a field hockey ball to the ankle, sudden and sharp.

Under the table, Davis put a hand on my knee. "It's not..." he murmured, but I ignored him. Instead, I leaned forward in my chair and eyed Natalie.

"Well, is it working? Are you jealous?"

Next to her, Ben/Brett/Brent was probably comprehending that he too was here to make someone jealous.

"Damn, girl..." Evan said from farther down the table, as I kept staring Natalie down. My heart was hammering in my chest, but no one needed to know that. It wasn't until I caught her lip just barely tremble and she blinked that I pushed back my chair.

"If you'll excuse me, I'm going to the bathroom," I said, and patted Davis's shoulder—a gesture that I hoped conveyed something along the lines of *We need to talk*, but also *Don't follow me*.

I didn't want to think about what the table was saying about me once I'd weaved my way to the back of the restaurant (because I sure as hell knew they were saying *something*). "Sorry!" I exclaimed when I almost bumped into a server carrying a tray of cocktails, and then immediately afterward dodged a pair of busboys with full bins. They pushed through the kitchen doors together without so much as a glance at me.

The doors not only swept open wide enough for me to see all the behind-the-scenes action, but also what I thought was a total hallucination: Marco Álvarez and three other guys enjoying a steak dinner at a fully set table. White linens, silverware, glassware, everything. They were even wearing blue blazers.

What the fuck? I wondered, and because I knew no boundaries and didn't actually need to go to the bathroom, my high heels and I marched into the kitchen to see what was happening.

"Hey, miss, you can't—" someone started, but all the clanging, clattering, and bellowed kitchen jargon (with plenty of profanity peppered in) made it impossible to hear. Especially when I was still stalking toward Marco's table, trying not to laugh.

"Well, well, well, what do we have here?" I asked.

Marco swallowed a bite of his filet. "Did Carina put you up to this?" He took a sip of his water and smiled. "Because I *did* promise I would come out and say hi…"

"Why are you eating dinner in the kitchen?" I asked.

He gave me a confused look. "Because the kitchen is where one eats dinner?"

"Not at restaurants." I shook my head. "At restaurants, you eat in the *dining room*. Only the Mafia eats in the…" I trailed off and gave his buddies a look. "Don't tell me you guys are cosplaying mobsters?"

It turned out I possessed the power to make Princeton men blush.

"Of course not," one said. "We're not properly outfitted in pinstripes."

"But the food at Tower sucked tonight," a second one confessed.

"And the line for Hoagie Haven was going on two blocks," the third sighed.

"Plus, the dining room is fully booked," Marco said, then shrugged. "Although the ambiance in here is much more pleasing." He gestured around at all the kitchen excitement. "As you can clearly deduce—"

"Are you fucking serious?!" someone somewhere shouted. "The tab clearly says Table Eight has a shellfish allergy! In all capitals!"

"Yes," I said dryly as his friends chuckled. "Nothing beats dinner and a show."

Marco's lips twitched in amusement. "How's it going out there?"

"Well, I'm currently in *here*," I told him. "So how do you think?"

"I thought you maybe wanted to briefly exchange pleasantries," he said, keeping his voice light.

I rolled my eyes.

In response, Marco tugged one of the empty chairs away from the table and gestured for me to sit. I did, less than gracefully because of my semi-formalwear. "What's happening?"

"Um..." I hesitated, glancing at his friends. They didn't look fazed in the least. What did they know? Nothing? Something? *Everything?*

"Carina said you looked excited earlier," one of the guys said. "You wouldn't stop smiling at..." He paused. "David?"

"Davis," I corrected, turning to include the whole table in the conversation. They obviously knew I was here on a date. "And I *was* excited—super excited—but that was before I found out that his *ex-girlfriend* was dining with us!"

If I were with the bridesmaids, they would've gasped, but the Princetonians simply absorbed tonight's plot twist with calm and casual nods.

It was a bit disappointing, to be honest.

"What are your names?" I asked.

"Simon," said one.

"Zach," the second answered.

"Timothy Hobson-Kirby the fourth," proclaimed the third.

Marco chuckled. "Tim, you're such a pretentious prick."

"Make sure that goes on my headstone, Marco," Timothy Hobson-Kirby IV joked.

I smiled. "It's nice to meet you. I'm Mads."

"We know," Simon and Zach said simultaneously, so I assumed Carina had mentioned my name.

"Okay, so his ex?" Timothy Hobson-Kirby IV looked unimpressed. "Really?"

"Yes," I said. "He mentioned her when we first met, but it sounded like he was pretty much over it, so I completely spaced."

"It doesn't matter if you spaced," Marco said as a Coke was set down in front of me. I took a grateful sip, wondering how and when he'd ordered it. "What matters is that Davis didn't tell you she was part of tonight's group. You deserved to know that."

"*Especially* if there's still shit between them," Timothy Hobson-Kirby IV added. "How'd you find out?"

I told them.

"Ah, I've encountered several Natalies in my day," Zach wistfully said, Simon elbowing him in the ribs. "I'm sorry, Mads."

"She's probably not a raging bitch," I backtracked (because I had called Natalie one). "Davis is a nice guy. He wouldn't have dated someone like that."

"He might've," Zach said while a server delivered five ramekins of crème brûlée, caramelized to perfection. "Nice guys can still have questionable taste."

Yeah, I thought. *Like my brother…*

Marco cracked his dessert's burnt-sugar shell with a spoon. "I don't like that he didn't give you a heads-up, Mads. It kind of proves Natalie's point that you're a prop, not a date. He might like you, but…" He shook his head.

A lump formed in my throat. "They took pre-prom pictures without me," I said, it suddenly dawning on me. "I met them in Hun's student parking lot, but we took approximately *zero* pictures together. I bet they did it earlier, at Natalie's house or something. That way there would be no record of me."

The Princetonians considered. "Well, your generation *does* document everything on social media," Simon mused.

My eyebrows knitted together. *My* generation? These guys were only two years older than me.

"Simon has read *This Side of Paradise* too many times,"

Marco whispered to me. "He acts like it's 1914 and we're in the same English class as F. Scott Fitzgerald."

Simon continued. "And Natalie's house *does* fit the narrative…"

Zach swallowed some crème brûlée. "Si, shut up."

I sighed. "I guess I should get back out there."

"Do you *want* to get back out there?" Marco asked as I heaved myself out of my chair. I'd let myself sulk until I left the kitchen. "I saw you ordered the swordfish, Mads, and while it's *spectacular*, I'm not sure it's really worth it."

No, I thought a couple minutes later, when I awkwardly rejoined the table. Everyone went silent. *If this is going to be the rest of my night, it's not worth it.*

Ben/Brett/Brent agreed, as he'd seemingly bailed while I'd been gone. His chair was empty. But I put on a face for the rest of dinner and pretended like everything was fine. Nobody spoke directly to me, but I listened along to the conversation and laughed at jokes cracked. "Can we talk?" Davis asked more than once, his leg bouncing under the table. The frantic movement heightened my heart rate.

"You bet," I whispered. "Just not now."

"When?" he whispered back.

"Later," I swallowed, having an uncomfortable inkling that Natalie was doing her damnedest to eavesdrop on us. "Before the dance."

You could see lights flashing from the senior dining hall's floor-to-ceiling windows as soon as Davis pulled Natalie's car back into the now-packed parking lot. There were no open spots to be had, so he created his own, pulling onto the grassy field near a few other creatively thinking drivers. "We'll see you in there!" Evan and Rebecca called, fingers lacing together as they speed walked toward the dance. The other couple followed suit, and Natalie after them. Reluctantly, I could tell, but still. She was generous enough to leave Davis and me alone to chat.

"I'm so sorry, Mads," he blurted. "I should've told you that Natalie would be part of the group tonight. Evan said I shouldn't have kept you in the dark, but I didn't listen. I thought everything would be chill; I *never* thought she would call you out like that."

"Well, she did," I said, folding my arms over my chest. A breeze had swept up, and I didn't have a jacket. I felt stupid for thinking Davis might offer me his later. "I don't know how long you were together or who broke up with who, but she still loves you, Davis." I took a breath. "She's still *in* love with you, and you brought another girl to an event she always imagined you'd be attending together. How could she not act like a witch?"

Davis tucked his hands into his pockets, then muttered, "I think she was a little worse than a witch."

I tilted my head as if to say, *Of course she was worse than a witch!*

"But I think she's right," I forced myself to say, a sharp

sting in my chest. Tonight had totally unraveled—I wished I could trick myself into thinking coffee with Davis *had* been a real date. I wanted to look back on my first date fondly, and tonight had been terrible. "I think you invited me to shake her," I continued. "To either shake her off for good or to shake some sense into her."

Davis was quiet, and when he did speak, I barely heard him over my thudding heart. "I do like you, Mads. I really like you."

"I like you, too." My voice wavered. "Way more than I thought I would, but you're still in love with somebody else, and I'm not cool with being used as a strategy to get that somebody back. You should've been honest with me from the start."

"Yes, I should've." He exhaled deeply. "I'm sorry. Fuck, I'm such an asshole."

I tried rubbing the goose bumps from my arms. It was really getting chilly. "It's okay."

Davis nodded, then gestured to the dining hall. "Do you want to head in?"

"You should, yeah," I said before pointing in the opposite direction, toward my car. "I'm gonna take off."

"Mads, don't," he protested once I started walking. He took three large steps to catch up with me. "I know I messed up, but we'll still have a great time as friends. I'd *really* like to be friends."

"I would, too," I told him truthfully, because we did have so much in common and I liked talking to him. "Just not on this particular night." I clapped him on the shoulder and gave it a squeeze. "Get in there, have fun with your friends, and ask Natalie to dance if that's what you want to do. But I'm going home."

I smiled a goodbye.

|—+—+—|

By midnight, I was under my covers with Francine sprawled out across my bed. Almost all the bridesmaids had texted to ask how the night went. She's not gonna answer you, Yaz, Reese wrote. JProm always has an after-party!

Davis must not have texted her, I thought as I tapped out of the chat and into my chat with Austin. He'd asked how the evening had gone, too.

Private school is overrated, I typed in response.

Not even ten seconds later, the bridesmaid chat buzzed with a new message from freaking Katie: Sources suggest Davis did not receive a rose.

"Oh, how you irk me, Katherine Marie Gallant," I muttered, though I was fighting a slight smile. Katie was pretty witty in this group chat. "How you irk me so…"

Text bubble after text bubble soon popped, including one from Meredith. It was funny like Katie's: Mads Fisher-Michaels's rep has yet to confirm.

I giggled and snuggled deeper into my pillows. But before Francine's even breathing lulled me to sleep, I circled back to one more text thread.

You want to watch a movie later? I'd texted Connor before pulling out of Hun's parking lot. I'll bring snacks!

Tempting... he'd replied. Is Hun's JProm THAT bad?

Eyes welling up with tears, I called him instead of texting back. "I'm bailing on the dance," I said as soon as Connor answered. Music and voices mingled in the background. He was out somewhere. "Ready for a rant?"

"Popcorn's already popped," Connor said.

I told him everything but made sure to add that Davis wasn't really a bad guy, that he apologized, and that I even thought we'd be friends someday. "But this night *sucks*," I concluded. "A raging dumpster fire..."

Drive safely, he messaged after we'd hung up. Text me when you get home.

Twenty-five minutes later, I wrote, Home!

Connor had immediately hearted the message, but I didn't expect him to respond beyond that—he was hanging with friends at Lauren Bitterman's house.

So it'd been a surprise when he texted: Same! I'll be over with a fire extinguisher in five. Let's save the night with Top Gun?

Now, after a *Top Gun* and *Top Gun: Maverick* double feature, I read our messages one more time before locking my phone and closing my eyes. My heart warmed. Connor had showed up for me before, but tonight had been different.

Hadn't it?

TEN

On April twenty-something, it was time to go bridesmaid dress shopping. Bridesmaids assemble! Amanda had texted, even though the wedding wasn't until freaking Christmas.

Katie had chosen a store in Philly to start the search, and everyone except Meredith—still living on St. Croix—was coming into town for the festivities. Mrs. Gallant and Amanda had offered to pick me up on their way into the city. Samira had surprised me with a visit, and we were hanging out on the front porch when a silver Audi pulled up my driveway. Samira waved to Amanda and Mrs. Gallant before hugging me and disappearing into the house. I guess she wasn't in the mood for small talk. "Have fun," she whispered as a goodbye.

"Was that Samira?" Mrs. Gallant asked once I'd buckled my seat belt. "What's she doing here?"

"Visiting," I said. "She got here late last night."

"That's nice," Katie's mom said lightly, but I caught Amanda purse her lips and take her phone out of the car's cupholder. Part of me worried she was about to text her sister, since Austin had come home for dinner last night. Katie had a work event.

But Luke Bryan soon sang through the Audi's speakers, so she must've been on Spotify. After the second song, Mrs. Gallant turned down the music and brought up Katie and Austin's save-the-dates. They'd just been mailed, and I remembered last month: Dad had compiled a comprehensive list of family and friends from the groom's camp and we'd sat at the kitchen table long after we finished dinner, going through it together. It had started out easy and fun with Nana, Austin's godparents, and the McCallisters, but then we'd hit Dad's clients. "Harry, I don't know why some of these people are even on the list," Da said. "You haven't seen Ron and Lisa Bierman in at least five years…"

I'm not shooting the messenger, Austin had texted after I'd emailed him our finalists, but you guys need to seriously cut this down.

We DID cut it down, I said. Twice!

Third time's the charm? he joked, and when I relayed the request to our parents, they sighed but nodded. The Gallants must've had a tally as long as Santa's naughty-or-nice list, and apparently, the bride's side had the upper hand on invites.

"I know they aren't your style, Mom," Amanda said as Mrs. Gallant merged onto the highway. We'd moved on to formal invitations. "But the standard white card stock with a navy-blue border and typeface isn't really fashionable anymore."

Mrs. Gallant shook her head. "I disagree, darling. Those

are classic." She flipped her blinker to shift into the left lane. "Traditional."

"Okay, sure," Amanda conceded. "But Katie doesn't want traditional."

Huh? I thought. *Katie, who is forcing my brother to have a black-tie country club wedding, doesn't want traditional?*

Maybe Amanda was too tactful to say *boring*. Because that's exactly what vibe *white card stock* gave off to me.

"I'll show you the artist's Instagram later," Amanda told her mother. "Lily's work is on trend but tasteful. You'll like—"

"What's so interesting back there?" she cut her daughter off, shifting her focus to me. I'd been listening to their conversation, but also scrolling through several field hockey commitments on my phone. My club team and I'd congratulated a teammate at practice the other night; she'd pledged her allegiance to Boston College.

While I had an unofficial visit scheduled with Princeton next weekend—"Nothing to take for granted," Coach Webber had told me—I still hadn't heard from Penn.

"Just field hockey stuff," I told Mrs. Gallant, even though field hockey was never "just" anything for me.

She laughed as I locked my phone. "Oh, field hockey… I think we still have Katie's old stick somewhere."

I almost laughed, thinking she was kidding. Because Katie playing field hockey? There was no way. Beyond cheering for the Devils, she was probably the least sporty person I knew.

"Amanda was our natural athlete," Mrs. Gallant continued, and I nodded, knowing Amanda had played basketball in college. "But Katie worked so hard, always practicing in the backyard. I remember she was crushed when her high school coach told her she wasn't good enough to play in college."

"That guy was such a dick," Amanda said, but I barely heard her. My mind was whirring. Katie had *really* played field hockey when she was my age? Why had she never mentioned it to me? Did Austin even know? He would've told me.

I sat quiet and confused in the car for the rest of the ride. For the last five years, it had felt like I'd barely gotten to know Katie. She kept herself and most of her life closed off from my family, like she didn't want us peeking in on it.

For the millionth time, I wondered why.

Did she truly not like us?

―――・―――・―――

Katie looked livid when her mother, maid of honor, and I pushed through the doors of Petal & Lace Bridal. A storm swirled in her eyes, her lips were in a sharp line, and I suspected her hands weren't far from balling into fists. "What's wrong?" Mrs. Gallant and Amanda asked, and by way of a response, Katie gestured to my fellow bridesmaids. They were all hanging out on the pale pink velvet couch that ran the length of the waiting area. But upon further observation, they weren't "hanging out."

They were *working*.

Yasmin, a lawyer: clickety-clack typing on her laptop.

Courtney, a therapist: speaking into her phone in soft and controlled tones, presumably to a patient.

Paige, an assistant art director at Penguin Random House: drawing something on her tablet.

Reese, a private equity associate: looking over a monstrous Excel spreadsheet taking over her computer screen, visible even from the bridal salon's doorway.

(Dad and I'd checked out all their profiles on LinkedIn.)

"Okay, no," Amanda said. "Nope, not happening." She clapped her hands in a pattern she probably used to get her fifth graders' attention. *Da, da, da-da-da!* "Squad!"

Four heads snapped up and over at us.

Amanda smiled. "Thank you for coming," she said with a tiny hint of passive-aggression. "If you'll now please put away your devices—and wrap up your call, Court—Katie and I are going to make sure we're all checked in so we can get this party going."

Hell, yeah, I thought, certainly hoping today would be a party; I was missing practice for this!

A receptionist led our group through an archway into a spacious room lined with racks of gowns. Svelte mannequins modeled various colors and styles, and mirrors sparkled in the bright light. We were officially in bridesmaid heaven (or hell), no wedding dresses in sight. Katie hadn't mentioned if she'd already said yes to her dress. "Please relax and feel free to enjoy some complimentary champagne," the receptionist said, gesturing to a white chesterfield couch. A bottle of bubbly and empty flutes sat on the nearby glass coffee table. "Viv, our stylist, will be out shortly to assist you."

"Pop it, Katie!" Meredith shouted several minutes later, over FaceTime on Yasmin's phone. We cheered after the cork flew through the air, and Katie grinned as her mom took over to pour glasses for everyone.

"No, thank you," I said when Mrs. Gallant offered me a fizzy flute. "I'll stick with water." I pointed to the Poland Spring bottles.

She smiled. "You are so responsible, just like your brother."

"Not to mention, I'm very underage," I quipped, though I was glad she respected Austin's sobriety. Special occasions only!

I'll be honest: I lost interest in dress shopping almost as soon as it began. My preferred shopping style was online from the comfort of my bed, and it turned out others felt that way, too. Three bridesmaids were elected to model the gowns while the rest of us squeezed together on the cushy couch, happy to assess like we were at New York Fashion Week. Reese, tall and slender, stood on the runway with petite Yasmin, along with Courtney, who winked at us and said, "In your dreams do you have my curves!"

The trio modeled off-the-shoulder sage green chiffon

gowns, as well as some type of violet stretch fabric (whose high slit Mrs. Gallant immediately deemed too sexy), and a red wine–colored velvet dress with a deep V neckline and fluttery cap sleeves. "This is stunning," Courtney said about the latter. She laughed. "But my boobs are totally in your face…"

"We can of course make alterations as needed," stylist Viv said. "Velvet dresses are best suited for autumn or winter weddings. You're having a December wedding, correct?"

"No offense, Katie," Reese said from the runway, "but have you chosen your colors yet? These are a little all over the place."

My thoughts exactly, I agreed. Maybe Katie did have a color in mind, but we were searching for a style first?

Katie looked uncomfortable, shifting in her seat. I caught her eyes flitting to her mom before they locked with Amanda to have what looked like a silent sister sidebar.

After a few beats, Amanda rose from her spot on the couch. "Mom, Katie and I are going to take another loop." She turned to the stylist. "We could use your expertise, Viv. The velvet is gorgeous, but I think Katie is looking for something a little more unique style-wise."

Mrs. Gallant's brow crinkled. "Unique?"

Stylist Viv sensed the tension brewing. "Have you found your mother-of-the-bride dress yet, Stacy?" she asked. "Because if not, we have a lovely selection in the other room…"

Reese, Yasmin, and Courtney—still in their dresses—joined

us on the couch after Mrs. Gallant and her glass of champagne wandered away with another stylist to browse.

"Paige, put your tablet away!" Courtney nudged her cousin. "Did you *see* Katie's face earlier?"

"But I have a deadline," Paige protested. "This YA cover is a trainwreck..." Then she added under her breath, "And you're one to talk. You were *on the phone*."

Courtney straightened up in her seat. "It was an emergency."

Reese changed the subject. "So, Mads, why didn't you tell us about last weekend?"

"Last weekend?" I asked, not really paying attention. Ever since Katie and Amanda had been swallowed up by the sea of dress racks, I'd been refreshing my Gmail account—hoping, wishing, praying that a new email would magically pop up from Penn's coach. Austin said I'd been obsessing, and obviously he was right, but I was nervous about visiting Princeton next weekend without a sign from their rival. Because unofficial visits... they usually ended with an offer to commit. I didn't want to commit to Princeton if Penn was still considering me.

"Yes, last weekend..." Reese said coyly.

"Specifically," Paige picked up, tablet now tucked in her tote bag. "Your junior prom."

Oh, I realized.

"Who was that guy in your Instagram post?" Yasmin asked. "He was hot!"

"It was the lax bro from Katie and Austin's engagement

party," Reese answered before I could, that encounter apparently living in her head rent-free. "The one Mads insisted she didn't have feelings for…" She raised a brow at me.

"Because it's *true*." I felt myself flush. Why did we have to talk about this again? It was embarrassing. "I don't have feelings for Connor."

"That picture totally says otherwise," Paige said. "His hand on your waist while you're smoothing down his hair, him smiling and you laughing…" She sighed. "Gah! If there weren't a pool with a fake grotto and waterslide in the background, it would make an *amazing* book cover." She Face-IDed into her phone. "Actually, I'm going to take a screenshot for inspiration."

"We were just goofing around," I mumbled, the bridal salon's lights suddenly seeming ten times brighter.

Reese shook her head. "It looked pretty candid to me."

I rolled my eyes. Ever since I'd debriefed the bridesmaids on the Davis disaster, they'd been on a quest for my next suitor. Reese, surprisingly, had taken me ditching her cousin in stride. It sounds like you handled it with major badassery, she said. You go, girl.

"I think Connor should be your next date," Yasmin declared. "I know you say you don't feel that way—"

"But friends-to-lovers…" Paige said. "It's a fan-favorite book trope for a reason!"

I sighed as Courtney also sighed, but for entirely different reasons. "I've always preferred enemies-to-lovers," she said. "The bicker, the banter, the bicker, the banter…the sexual tension almost sizzles on the page."

"You know, I'm not a big reader," I said casually, then rose from my seat. I was finished with this conversation.

Or maybe I wanted to continue it with someone else.

"Hey, what's up?" Samira answered on the second ring, after I'd locked myself in the bathroom. "I'm walking Arthur and Francine on the canal."

"The bridesmaids think I should go out with Connor!" I blurted. "How absurd is that?"

The line was silent, so silent that I felt my cheeks warm. "I don't know…" Samira eventually said. "*Absurd* wouldn't be the word I'd use."

Me either, I thought. *But it would've happened by now if we were* fated, *right?*

I swallowed. "Samira, Connor is my best friend."

"Exactly," she said. "It could be *nice* to be with your best friend. The person you never stop laughing with, the person who always has your back, the person who knows you inside and out." She paused, then said: "Isn't he your favorite person?"

Goose bumps bloomed on my arms. *Favorite person* was the Austin Fisher-Michaels equivalent of *soulmate*. He liked to say he had his *people*, but only *one* of us was his favorite.

What happened? I suddenly wanted to ask Samira. *Why is Katie his favorite and not you?*

"Mads?" Her voice was now breathy. It sounded like the dogs were now taking *her* for a walk. "You still there?"

"Yeah, but I should go," I whispered. "We still have more dresses to try."

"Okay," she said. "I'll see you at home."

"Uh-huh." I nodded. "See you at home."

Connor and Mads, I thought once Samira and I hung up. *Mads and Connor.*

I admit, there had always been a part of me that wondered what it'd be like if Connor and I were more than friends—and it was growing harder to ignore. Sometimes, when we watched movies in the McCallisters' basement, sprawled out together and sharing a blanket, I would think, *Kiss me.*

And I don't think it was because he was right there and I wanted to cross my first kiss off my list. If I wanted to get it over and done with, I suspected it was because he was right there and he was *Connor.*

Ugh.

I walked aimlessly along dress racks, stuck in my head until hushed voices stopped me in my tracks. A conversation was happening just around the corner, in a smaller room (how big *was* this bridal place?). "I know Mom wants them to be uniform," I heard Katie say. "No mix and matching. Same color, same style, stuck in the same century as those invitations she suggested."

"Don't worry about Mom," Amanda told her. "I'll have her obsessed with Lily Hopper's portfolio by dinnertime."

"Oh, you work wonders, Ms. Gallant," a third voice said, one that sounded a lot like Meredith. I peeked around the corner to see that the Gallant sisters were indeed huddled together and holding up Katie's phone. "Because those mockups your mom sent you were an absolute snoozefest."

Amanda snorted. "Go ahead, Meredith. Tell us how you *really* feel."

"Reese asked if Austin and I've even chosen a color scheme," Katie rambled, like she was nervous. "I feel like everyone secretly thinks I have no clue what I'm doing."

"Well of course you have no clue what you're doing," Meredith said. "It's a wedding, Katie, and as far as I know, you have no prior experience in planning one."

The sisters laughed. "Neither do you," Katie quipped. "You eloped."

"Yes, but I still had to pick a time, place, and a white dress," she protested. "That has to count for something!"

The three of them giggled for a few seconds before Katie brought things back to the bridesmaid dresses. "Would it be terrible if we left today without making a decision?"

"No," Meredith said. "Because you already made your decision by sending Amanda and me all those links to various

Anthropologie gowns."

"I agree," Amanda said when Katie was quiet. "I mean, you literally assigned one to each person."

I did my best to translate Katie's mumble. "I know, but they're just so…"

"Unique," Meredith said. "They're *fun*, Katie. Just like you."

Katie? I thought. *Fun?*

My interest was piqued about these dresses, though.

"Let's pack up our stuff and grab lunch," Amanda said with maid-of-honor confidence. "I'll email everyone their dress tonight and run any aftermath interference with Mom."

I watched Katie give her older sister a side hug, and suddenly felt a pang of something in my chest. What was it? It was a type of bittersweetness, but before I could dig deeper, my phone pinged in my pocket.

It was an email from Lizzy Hart.

My hand shook. Lizzy Hart was Penn's head field hockey coach.

And her email's subject line read: Visit to campus.

I texted Marco before bed that night. Penn invited me to visit! I wrote, unsurprised when he didn't respond. It was a Saturday night. He was probably at a party or, as Austin had once upon a time, used a fake ID to get into Princeton's bars.

My parents and Samira had been so happy when I'd gotten home from the bridal salon. On the one hand, it was only a visit, but on the other, you had to work so fucking hard for a visit. "My girl!" Da had swept me into a hug and spun me around before Dad squeezed me so tightly that my back cracked. Then, the McCallisters came over for an impromptu cookout. Connor brought me a six-pack of bottled Cokes, the perfect congratulatory gift.

Although, I wasn't sure how "impromptu" it was because Austin arrived just as the hot dogs and burgers hit the grill, equipped with a trunk full of s'more supplies. "Where's Katie?" Connor asked, to which my brother responded, "Probably falling asleep to a true crime documentary. She's wiped from the day." He turned to me. "But she says congrats again, Mads."

"Thanks," I said. All the bridesmaids, along with Mrs. Gallant, had cheered when I announced the news at lunch…but not Katie. She simply smiled and said, "That's amazing!"

In, like, a totally fake voice.

You loved field hockey once! I'd wanted to shake her. *Why can't you actually celebrate?!*

Ironically, I was scrolling through Netflix when Marco did respond. Congrats! he'd written. But nevertheless: puck Fenn.

Brows furrowing, I sent him a question mark.

Puck Fenn, he said. Campus store even sells bumper stickers!

"Okay," I said aloud, "but what does that—"

It clicked.

Puck Fenn translated to *Fuck Penn*.

Because Penn and Princeton?

Bitter rivals.

Puck Frinceton, I wrote.

Eh, doesn't have the same ring to it, Marco wrote back.

I smirked, shook my head, and typed: How are you?

Good, he said, and that was it. I stared at my phone screen until my eyes watered, desperate to blink.

He's busy, I told myself, so I gave the message a thumbs-up and then refocused on Netflix. A new text popped onto my screen five minutes later, when I'd finally settled on a show.

How are you?

I hesitated, extremely tempted to type *G-O-O-D* and hit send, but instead I recapped the day's unsuccessful bridesmaid dress search. Also, I said, they want to set me up with Connor!!!

Again, Marco didn't respond until I was halfway through an episode of *New Girl*. Well, the point of this scheme is to make a successful match, isn't it?

My fingers flew across my phone screen, keeping pace with my heart. Um...you think Connor and I'd be good together?

It doesn't matter what I think, Marco said, dodging the question and thus eliciting an eye roll. What matters is what YOU think.

You're super wise, I joked. Anyone ever tell you that?

All the time, he said. Yesterday, actually. My philosophy professor.

I snorted, then bit my tongue as I wrote. Sometimes I do think about Connor that way... I worry that I won't know about anyone else until I know about Connor and me.

I inhaled as three typing dots appeared.

But before Marco actually responded, a bridesmaid chat message from Amanda announced itself at the top of my screen. I tapped on it.

Davis who? she'd written. Mads, do I have someone for YOU.

ELEVEN

Unable to truly untangle my potential feelings for Connor, I wanted to go on my next date as soon as possible so I could at least move on from my disastrous date with Davis. But Amanda had yet to set a time and place. She'd told me that my next suitor was my age, although he'd skipped a couple grades and was finishing up his freshman year at Princeton. He's excited, she reassured me, but asked to wait until the semester ends. He has a mountain of essays and exams.

So, I had to wait a couple weeks, already knowing from Marco that Princeton's finals didn't end until mid-May. Ironically, there was a chance I'd unknowingly run into my date before then, because my Princeton visit was upon us.

I skipped school on a Thursday in late April, excited to be an unofficial member of Princeton's field hockey team for the next couple days. "Now, Mads, we know where your loyalties lie," Da said when we were about five minutes away from campus. "This family loves Penn, but please go into this weekend with a wide-open mind. Consider Princeton for *Princeton*."

Princeton's head coach, despite not using any exclamation points in her emails, seemed nice. She greeted us in the athletic department's lobby, smiling warmly as handshakes were exchanged before leading us to her office to go over the weekend's agenda. A girl with a blond ponytail sat in one of the chairs. I recognized her right away: Shelly Freeman. She had been Princeton's standout freshman this past season and would be my host for the next couple days.

After we left the office, Shelly walked at a fast clip, and I kept my head on a swivel while trying to keep up with her. Spring had officially sprung on the Princeton campus; its dramatic Gothic architecture spiraled into the blue sky, far above the trees that burst green, white, and pink. Students had spread blankets out on one of the lush lawns, and there wasn't a free spot to be had on any of the benches.

We speed walked across campus until we reached Shelly's dormitory. It was gorgeous, looking like an old estate house—or a vintage hotel, even. Three stories tall, the entrance was white clapboard with soaring white columns and black-shuttered windows, and on each side of this already-incredible entrance were two stone wings, windows flung open to the fresh air. Dormer windows popped out of the roof, as well as four sturdy brick chimneys. A red and white FORBES COLLEGE banner hung from the third-floor balcony. "Wow," I whispered.

Shelly hummed, the polite equivalent of clearing her throat. "Would you like me to turn all tour guide on you and recount its history?" she asked. "Or should we both say it's beautiful and head up to my room?"

"Oh, um…" I said, a little taken aback. She hadn't sounded rude, just unexpectedly direct. "I'm cool with seeing your room."

Truthfully, I did want to know about Forbes's origin story. But I could tell Shelly had no genuine interest in telling me, and it probably would be more informative (and amusing) hearing it from Simon, Marco's friend who spoke like he was from a distant era.

"Get ready for two flights of stairs," Shelly warned as I unlocked my phone and texted a group chat I'd dubbed The Princetonians. Marco had set it up for whatever reason after I'd crashed their dinner at Ember & Ash.

Forbes College? I wrote, and by the time Shelly and I'd made it to the first-floor landing, I had some answers.

Timothy Hobson-Kirby IV: best freshman residential college.

Zach Danzig: Are you staying there this weekend?

And then, Simon Fielding: Built in 1927, FC was originally christened the Princeton Inn. It was a hotel until 1970, when the university bought the property and converted it into student housing to accommodate a growing population. Women were being admitted—

"Okay, here we are!" Shelly chirped. I'd mindlessly followed her to a dorm room midway down the third floor's hallway. Two construction-paper-cutout tigers were posted on the door—one said *Shelly*, the other read *Lois*—and a mini whiteboard had been tacked up in between them. **Return my leopard leggings, Seashell!!!** the message read. Shelly pointed to Lois's tiger while swiping her student ID over the door's sensor. "Lois is another freshman on the team," she said. "She's from the Netherlands."

I nodded, already well aware. Lois Hansen, number six, forward. She'd racked up almost thirty goals this season. Da and I watched a lot of college field hockey.

Shelly and Lois's room was tidy, but I sensed it had been cleaned up for my visit rather than kept clean regularly. There was a standard dormitory-issued twin bed tucked in each corner, and while the wardrobes were shut, I could tell they wanted to burst open from all the clothes inside. The walls were decorated with Princeton field hockey posters, cute art prints, and so many strands of twinkly lights that I questioned the fire marshal's judgment.

An air mattress floated like a life raft in the middle of the room, equipped with lavender-colored sheets, a fuzzy turquoise blanket, and a fluffy pillow. "You can dump your stuff and unpack later," Shelly said. "We have econ in twenty minutes. It's held in McCosh."

McCosh, I soon learned, was the English building. Its lecture hall was all warm wood and sunlight streaming in through its monstrous cathedral windows. Instead of velvet theater seats, hundreds of classic chair-desktop combinations sprawled in a semicircle around the professor's podium and projection screen.

I looked up to see a dark wood-paneled ceiling finished with arched mahogany beams. Two medieval-inspired chandeliers hung above us.

"Follow me." Shelly pointed toward a staircase. "I usually sit up in the balcony."

The room was rapidly filling up, so we hurried up the stairs and into the first row. Our view of the projection screen was crystal clear, but instead of unpacking her backpack like her classmates, Shelly put it on the desk next to hers. "Saving a seat for someone?" I guessed.

"Yeah." She nodded. "My friend—or kind of more than a friend." Her cheeks pinkened a bit. "We're not in a relationship yet. Right now, it's just a situationship."

I looked at her blankly. "What is a situationship?"

Shelly shrugged. "It's like a casual, commitment-free relationship. We're hanging out but not thinking too much about it."

So you're hooking up, I almost said. *Literally just hooking up.*

"It's pretty much the end of the semester," she added. "No point getting into something serious."

Oh, but you want *to get serious*, I suspected, because her thoughtless words did not match the thoughtfulness in her voice. *You are head over heels for this—*

"Shelly, hey," someone said, and I turned to see Marco walking toward us. He smiled. "I see you brought a friend today!"

No way, I thought while at the same time also thinking, *Of course.*

Because who wouldn't want to be in a relationship with Marco Álvarez? And who wouldn't settle for a "situationship" when he avoided agreeing to be in a relationship?

(From Shelly's tone, I was assuming Marco was the one dodging commitment.)

"Yeah," Shelly said as she moved her backpack so Marco could sit down, "this is my shadow for the weekend. Her name is…"

She trailed off when Marco dropped into the desk next to mine. His hair was rumpled like he'd just woken up from a nap. "Mads," he finished for his not-girlfriend. "Madeline Fisher-Michaels. She and I go *way* back."

Shelly's brow pinched in confusion.

"We went to school together," I explained.

"Elementary, middle, and high school," Marco said with a winning grin. "I was always two steps ahead of her."

I rolled my eyes. "Why do you act like that's something to brag about? You're two years older than me." I shrugged. "No one cares."

I mean, Shelly sort of did. About our seating arrangement, at least. She looked like a mix between an angry cat and a wounded kitten. Marco caught on quickly, giving me an on-purpose-or-maybe-not-on-purpose shoulder bump before switching to the spot Shelly had saved for him.

She lit up like an angel atop a Christmas tree.

"My dad is also his family's maybe Realtor," I said (Marco's parents still hadn't decided to list their house), "and we're obsessed with Álvarez dining establishments."

"Oh, I know!" Shelly exclaimed. "Ember & Ash is amazing, right?"

"*Amazing*," I agreed. "Two Fish—their brunch place in Pennsylvania—is also incredible."

"Then you must be over the moon we're hosting the bridal shower there," Marco said.

"Wait, what?" I leaned forward so I could see Marco across Shelly's desk. "*Katie's* bridal shower?"

He leaned forward, too. "Yes, *Katie's* bridal shower. My mom's worried that unless they rent out the entire space, Two Fish will be too small to accommodate the guest list."

"Oh, don't worry, they will." I crossed my arms over my chest, and mumbled, "Seems like a present grab to me."

Marco's lips twitched. "I *did* look at their registry. It's certainly not for the faint of heart."

"Crate and Barrel?" Shelly guessed, trying to rejoin the conversation. For all I knew, she thought Katie was my sister. "Williams Sonoma?"

"Yes," Marco and I said in tandem, right as the lights flickered. Introduction to Microeconomics was about to begin. "Plus Amazon."

Katie had made sure to cover all the bases.

The Princeton field hockey team congregated in Forbes's dining hall for dinner. Shelly had introduced me to everyone, and it felt amazing to be with people who cared about the sport as much as I did. Eventually, the girls started asking about me, myself, and I, and I couldn't help but smile as I talked about my family and where we lived. "She's also going to have a sister soon," Shelly added when I said I just had one brother. "Austin is getting married this December."

There was a moment of silence before an electric current seemingly zipped through the room, everyone bursting with questions. *What is it about girls and weddings?* I wondered.

"Do we like Katie?" Lois Hansen, the player from the Netherlands, asked. Her English was accented, but nearly perfect. "I sense there's a *vibe* there."

I sighed, not very eager to talk about Katie. Lately, she'd been working her way into everything, but I didn't feel closer to her at all. "She's Katie. My brother loves her." I shrugged. "I'm a bridesmaid."

More enthusiastic squeals. "That's so sweet!" a junior said. "Has she picked your dresses yet?"

"Actually, yeah," I said, perking up. "I have a photo."

When Amanda had emailed me my bridesmaid dress, I'd been shocked at first. Our dress was, in fact, the gown Courtney had modeled at the bridal salon: cranberry velvet with a tastefully lowcut neckline and ruffled sleeves. Katie has decided she wants us all in a uniform style, her sister had written. Please see the attached document with more information about sizing, ordering, etc. Let me know if you have any questions!

Mrs. Gallant must be thrilled, I thought. She'd loved that gown.

And it *was* pretty, but I wondered what happened to the dresses it seemed Katie had actually wanted.

The conversation shifted after I said I knew nothing about Katie's wedding dress.

It shifted to the famous eating clubs' *parties.*

My stomach started to squirm as the girls talked. Were we going to a party?

"It's Tiger Inn tonight," Shelly told me, sipping the last of her chocolate milk. "The theme is State Night."

My eyebrows knitted together. "What does that mean?"

"Party like a state school," someone said. "Which roughly translates to *go as wild as you possibly can.*"

I stayed quiet, on the brink of having an internal panic attack. Even though Princeton's coach hadn't explicitly said anything, I knew Shelly and the team weren't supposed to take me to a party. There were rumors in the recruiting circuit that unofficial visits involved parties, but no one on my club team had ever proven them true. Plus, we were going to be playing field hockey tomorrow! Right after classes!

Lois nudged me out of my spiral. "Were you imagining a night in?" she whispered.

"Sort of," I whispered back.

She smiled. "Trust me, it's going to be fun."

"Okay." I tried to smile back. "If you say so."

―――――

Princeton's eating clubs were all grand old mansions lining idyllic Prospect Street, no two looking alike. The sun had set, but thanks to the streetlights, I still recognized Tower Club's imposing brick exterior and limestone arch over the hulking mahogany front door. Its tower reminded me of a medieval castle, and I wondered if Marco was there. The lights were on inside, but otherwise, all was calm.

But at the Tudor down the street, things were decidedly not. An American flag and Tiger Inn's orange club flag rippled in the evening breeze, and music pulsed from the house. Some students had clustered on the front lawn, all in various state school apparel. I spotted a few guys in mesh gym shorts and hideous muscle tees. PENN STATE, a blue and white one read.

And us field hockey girls?

Well, I supposed we had come dressed to impress. Everyone on Tiger Inn's guest list had congregated in Shelly and Lois's room to get ready and pregame. "Don't worry, we've got an outfit for you," Lois had told me after taking a pull of strawberry Smirnoff. She'd opened their wardrobe, and sure enough, clothes came spilling out. We'd all ended up more or less wearing the same outfit: crop tops, neon blue biker shorts, Converse, and high ponytails. My orange FLORIDA GATORS T-shirt had been cut so high that if I raised my arms even a little, you'd see my bralette. I admit I *was* a little envious of Shelly's makeup collection—it looked like she'd robbed Sephora—but I'd wrinkled my nose when she pulled out tubes of body glitter. It was called "Unicorn Snot."

Now, Shelly peeled off Prospect and confidently sauntered up to Tiger Inn's bouncer to confirm we were on tonight's list—everyone got a thumbs-up. The mansion's front door had been propped open, and the foyer's old wood floors creaked under our feet. Its sconces had been dimmed, but I made out the grand staircase ahead of us. A couple people were sneaking up its steps. Whatever was happening up there probably wasn't good.

We turned neither left nor right into the house. Instead, Shelly led us toward the music, which turned out to be banging in the basement. I tucked my arms across my chest, immediately uncomfortable. The lighting was even worse than the foyer, nearly nonexistent unless you counted the flashing multicolored lights from the dance floor, and the whole room was steamy from all the body heat. "Drink, Mads?" Shelly called, but it sounded less like a question and more like a command. *Drink, Mads!*

She pointed over to the bar, where two burly upperclassmen manned legitimate beer taps. "Uh, sure," I stuttered, if only because I desperately wanted something to do with my hands.

"And until then…" Lois winked before she magically produced a small silver flask from her bra. She took the first pull.

"If that's more of your Smirnoff, no thanks," a sophomore teammate said. "Even a whiff of that stuff makes me want to vomit."

Lois shook her head. "Bacardi."

"Is it flavored?"

A nod. "Mango."

The sophomore sighed. "God, Lois, you have the worst taste in booze."

But she took a sip anyway.

Shelly and a teammate returned with beers in hand, and some of mine sloshed over the plastic cup's rim when I felt a hand on my bare back. "Relax, it's me!" a voice called over the EDM beats and I turned to see Marco slip in between Shelly and me. She planted a kiss on his cheek, but he didn't seem to notice. "This sure is a statement." He gestured to my ensemble and discreetly confiscated my drink. "Did you save any glitter for elementary school art projects?"

"Okay, make no mistake, Álvarez," I said as he gulped some beer. "This is *not* glitter." I made a muscle for him to admire. "It's *unicorn* snot."

One side of Marco's mouth curved up in amusement. "Unicorn snot?"

"Yes." I tried to keep a straight face. "But no unicorns were harmed—"

"Did you hear me, Marco?" Shelly interrupted. "Let's dance!"

"Yeah, alright," he agreed as she began tugging him toward

the dance floor. Something in me sinking, I watched him drain the rest of my drink before looking at me. "Come dance."

With you and Shelly? I thought. *No, thanks.*

Marco tipped his head, like he knew what I was thinking. "You love to dance. I've seen the TikToks."

My stomach swirled. My teammates had made so many videos of me shaking it on the sidelines during water breaks at practice, and it didn't help that Dad contributed footage of my *Angelina Ballerina* moves after I scored a goal in games. My pirouettes were amazing.

I loved to dance, and to be honest, I really did *want* to dance. If I was going to be subjected to this party, I wanted to try to have fun. And to me, fun wasn't standing around sipping beer with an already tipsy Lois and the other field hockey girls.

Who, I suddenly noticed, had all dispersed in different directions.

"Okay," I told Marco, not wanting to be alone. "Let's dance."

At first, it felt good. The dance floor, even if it was in a dark basement with slitted windows that may or may not have made it look like a prison, felt familiar. If I shut my eyes, it was kind of like I was dancing with Connor at our JProm after-party, where everyone had changed into casual clothes. I moved to the music, and every now and again, I reopened my eyes and caught

Marco's. He shook his head and smiled, seemingly oblivious to Shelly grinding against him. I smiled back, a strange thrill twirling in my chest.

But Marco excused himself to go to the bathroom once the song ended, and as soon as he disappeared, I heard Shelly call: "Derek, over here!"

The guy in a PENN STATE muscle tee weaved his way toward us; his blond hair was plastered to his forehead from sweat, but he was cute. Warm brown eyes and dimples in both cheeks. "Hey, Shelly," he said, beer in hand. "What's up?"

Shelly introduced me, and Derek drained his drink so he could ask me to dance. "Stay away from Marco," Shelly hissed in my ear before I took Derek's hand.

Huh? I thought, blinking to make sure this wasn't a dream—or a *nightmare*. This night was becoming so twisted; the field hockey girls had scattered, and now, Shelly was telling me to back off from Marco? *Marco?* "Shelly, no," I started. "Marco and I, we're—"

Her next words were like knives. "Fuck off, Madeline. Fuck the hell off."

Derek overheard us. "Yikes," he said, then slipped his arms around my waist as if to hold me back from Shelly. "I know we're in TI, but there's no need for a cat fight, ladies."

"Stay out of it, Derek," Shelly grumbled.

"Gladly!" he chirped, then leaned down and whispered, "Do you still wanna dance?"

By way of an answer, I shook and shimmied myself out of his arms so I could take his hand and tug him deeper into the haze of people.

Maybe Marco would ask where I'd gone; maybe he wouldn't. But I didn't want to be anywhere near Shelly while they figured out their shitty situationship—or, even better, their "shituationship."

We'll find each other later, I assured myself. *I'll find the others later.*

I ignored the prickling at the back of my neck, telling me that I should find them *now*. Instead, I closed my eyes, felt my heart flicker at Derek's warm hands on my hips, and started to dance.

Please pick up, I thought, shivering in the chilly night air. Tiger Inn's tropical weather had worn off entirely. *Please pick up, please pick up, please—*

"Hello?" Austin said groggily. "Mads?"

At the sound of his voice, hot and heavy tears spilled down my cheeks. "Austin," I croaked. "Austin, hey. I need to talk to you. I know it's really late, but…" I swallowed, then repeated, "I know it's really late."

"Really late?" My brother laughed softly, still half asleep. "Try almost two a.m." He yawned. "Just be quiet, okay? Katie's a light sleeper."

"Okay," I agreed, but then did the complete opposite of staying quiet. I openly started sobbing. Sobbing in my stupid excuse for a shirt and drenched in sweat and Unicorn Snot and wearing enough eye makeup that it was probably running in rivulets down my face right about now.

This girl, passersby would think, *is having* a night.

I could tell Austin's spine straightened from the sound of his voice. "Mads, what's going on? Where are you? Princeton, right? This is your Princeton weekend?"

I nodded, even though he couldn't see, and then word-vomited up the whole night. "The field hockey girls totally ditched me, and Shelly won't answer my calls or texts," I said over the lump in my throat. "And I can't go back to her room..."

"You *have* to go back to her room," Austin said firmly. "Right now."

"But she hates me!" I wailed at the same time a muffled voice went, "Austin, is everything alright?"

"Not really," he told Katie. Freaking Katie. "Mads is at Princeton..."

"Oh my *god*," I heard her groan, loud and clear, after he recapped my recap. "Are you *kidding* me? She didn't call your parents?"

My blood burned. *I wanted to call my brother*, I thought. *I wanted to call my best friend, the person I can always count on for help.*

I doubted I would *ever* say that about Katie.

Whatever Austin said was hushed, definitely drowned out by him pressing his phone against his chest.

And then, a beat later, Katie's voice came over the line: "Where exactly are you?"

"Wawa," I answered. "I didn't know where to go after leaving the party, but I knew Wawa would be open—"

"Okay," she cut me off. "Here's Austin."

"Do you have your pepper spray?" he asked.

"No," I said, goose bumps creeping up my arms. "I dropped it at the party." My voice quavered. "I, um, *used* it at the party—"

"What?!" Austin and Katie both shouted.

I was, it appeared, on speakerphone.

"I was dancing with this guy," I explained. "It was fun at first…" I remembered how good Derek's hands felt on me, how his warm breath tickled the tip of my ear. My body was humming, a sensation that made it easy to ignore his slurred words or running his hands over places I didn't quite want them. "But then things took a turn when he told me he hoped I'd be his number three."

"He *didn't*," Austin ground out as Katie said, "What does that mean?"

"Three girls in one night." I couldn't help but blubber again. "You kiss one, kiss another, and then take the third *home*."

"Ah," was Katie's only comment.

"And then," I told Austin, "I stopped dancing, and he asked what was wrong, so I said I didn't want to go home with him.

He tried to kiss me, and I pushed him away, but he followed me off the dance floor and wouldn't leave me alone. Shelly and the other girls were nowhere. He offered to walk me back to the dorm, but once he put his hands on me again... I sprayed him when he tried to stop me on the stairs." I reached up to rub my eyes. "Then I made a run for it."

My brother's voice was almost cold. "Call Da and Dad, Mads. Call them while you walk back to Shelly's dorm."

"Austin, I—"

"Mads?"

I spun around to see Marco longboarding across the parking lot. He wasn't in his State Night spirit wear anymore, just wearing a pair of sweats and a PRINCETON SOCCER pullover with cheeks pink from the cold. I gritted my teeth. Half of me wanted to hug him, so relieved he was here, but the other half wanted to punch him. "Marco?"

"Wait, Álvarez?" Austin asked. "Put Marco on the phone."

They didn't speak for long. I could hear Austin yelling, but I couldn't decipher *what* he was yelling. Marco did a lot of solemn nodding. "I'm going to walk you back to Forbes," he said after hanging up and handing my phone back to me. He jerked his head to Wawa. "We can get an Icee first?"

"An Icee sounds good," I said. "But Forbes doesn't."

Marco sighed. "Mads..."

"They left me there, Marco." My voice jumped an octave. "*Everyone* left me there, but Shelly also *abandoned* me. Your whatever-you-call-her is supposed to watch out for me while I'm here, but instead decided to blow off all my calls and texts when I needed help. I'm not going to go have a slumber party with her after that."

"You won't need to," he said. "She's not…" He trailed off and ran his hand through his hair. Awkwardly.

"Mmm," I said. "Got it."

Shelly was not in her room. She was in Marco's room, probably all snuggled up in his toasty-warm bed waiting for him to return with the late-night goodies he'd clearly come here to collect.

Whatever, I thought, feeling pinpricks at the corners of my eyes. *If Marco wants to be with a girl like Shelly, what-fucking-ever.*

Marco gently mentioned Forbes again, but I barely heard him, busy texting someone. I'll call my parents now, Katie wrote back. Austin wants Marco to walk you there.

Not necessary, I said, Katie's childhood truth or dare game on my mind. Sneaking out of her house at midnight and walking to Wawa when she was only thirteen. I was seventeen; it would be a piece of cake. You were alone when you did it.

But I was still scared, she wrote. Have Marco walk you.

I sighed, then looked at Marco. "You can take me somewhere," I said miserably. "But it's not Forbes."

SUMMER

TWELVE

JOIN US FOR A
Bridal Shower
IN HONOR OF
Catherine Gallant

Saturday, June 16th at noon
1989 Archer Way
Ardmore, PA 19003

rsvp to cpcavanaugh@comcast.net
registered at theknot.com/allinwithaustin

I stared at the invitation while Nana drove. It was beautiful, the card stock thick and cream-colored with a light blue watercolor bow, white hydrangeas springing from the bow's ribbon. The gold script underneath looked effortless. "I never knew she spelled Catherine with a *C*," I remarked. "I always thought it was with a *K*."

"I didn't either," Nana replied as she flipped her blinker and merged into the right lane. "It's very Kate Middleton of her."

I laughed when she reached over and ruffled my hair. Ever the stylist, Nana had given me a "Kate Middleton" blowout.

In a surprising turn of events, today's bridal shower was not being held at the Álvarez family's Two Fish, but at Katie's aunt's house. Austin had given me all the tea. "Yeah, according to Kates, Aunt Celeste *really* wanted to give Katie a shower," he'd said during our camping trip. Every summer, we "camped" in our Christmas tree farm for a weekend. Tent, sleeping bags, lanterns, campfire—the whole enchilada. "She wouldn't take no for an answer."

"Mmm," had been my diplomatic reaction. It was clear that Mrs. Gallant, as kind and caring as she was, was type A and wanted to be in control. Everything needed to be perfect.

Katie's aunt Celeste—otherwise known as "Cousin Paige's mom"—lived in Ardmore, a cute town on Philadelphia's Main Line. "Didn't you play in several tournaments around here?" Nana asked once we'd exited the highway and slowed to a stop at a red light.

"Yes," I answered. "I did a couple camps, too."

She glanced over and smiled at me. "I'm so happy everything is finally settled. And I'm so, so proud of you, honey."

I grinned back. Three weeks ago, I'd officially committed to Penn for field hockey. My visit there had been the complete opposite of my Princeton visit. Unlike awful Shelly, the freshman midfielder they'd paired me with barely let me out of her sight. The team organized a throwback murder mystery dinner instead of taking me to a wild party, and Coach Hart let me play in their scrimmage instead of watching from the bleachers. Not only was there serious chemistry on the field, but I felt like I'd fit in off the field, too. Almost every player had hugged me goodbye and given me their phone number. Honestly, it felt like gigantic knot had untangled itself in my chest.

Out of nowhere, I thought about Marco. Congratulations! he'd texted after the news hit social media (i.e., after Da wrote the ultimate proud-parent post on Instagram), but I hadn't responded for a couple days. I wasn't *mad* at him, but I also wasn't *happy* with him, either. I guess I was just pissed. We hadn't seen each other since he'd walked me to the Gallants' house, only making it halfway before Katie's dad found us in his car. Our goodbye had been super awkward. He'd gone in for a hug while I stepped away and gave him a half wave.

Thanks, I'd messaged back, and after he sent a long apology on Shelly's behalf (I doubted she had any clue he'd written it), I thought, *Fuck it*, and wrote: Get out of that situationship, Marco. She's the worst.

He had yet to respond.

Nana turned onto a leafy green tree-lined street, and we pulled into the driveway whose mailbox had white and gold balloons tied to it. "Here we are!" my grandmother said cheerfully once we'd parked near a long row of cars. "Grab the gifts!"

The gifts, neither of which were on Austin and Katie's registry, were quintessential Nana gifts. She had gotten them a complete set of Barefoot Contessa cookbooks—"Ina's recipes will never go out of style"—and I'd dragged Connor to Anthropologie the other day to help me pick out a cute pair of oversized mugs. One with an *A* and another with a *K* (or maybe I should've gotten a *C*?). In any case, they were more of a rib against Austin than anything else. He always complained about how many mugs Katie owned. "We don't have enough storage space for an entire mug cabinet, yet we somehow have an entire mug cabinet."

Aunt Celeste's house was pretty; Dad would describe it as a stately 1911 Georgian Revival adorned with brick and huge white multipaned windows. Big pots of flowers and herbs sat on the front stoop, and dried lavender wreaths hung on the front double doors. Despite the chorus of voices inside, I rang the doorbell. Nana pretended to cough, and when I looked at her, she pointed to a chalkboard that had been propped up on the stoop's rocking chair. *Welcome to Katie's Shower*, it read. *Door is open!*

Five minutes later, Nana and I introduced ourselves to Katie's aunt before Mrs. Gallant poached us from her sister and took us on a promenade around the house. We met everyone from Katie's grandmother to a few work friends to her childhood babysitter. Eventually, my fellow bridesmaids and I congregated at a white cloth-covered table on the deck. The centerpiece was a small vase of blue hydrangeas. "Mads!" Meredith, her tan glowing and hair sun-streaked from St. Croix, had wrapped me in a huge hug. "How's everything? How's your family? Congratulations on Penn!"

I learned that she and Wit had moved back to the States temporarily. They were in Boston with friends now but planned to spend the summer on Martha's Vineyard with her family.

I should get a remote job someday, I thought to myself.

Lunch was delicious. As the artist in her family, Paige had hand painted a beautiful menu: sweet chili salmon and a tomato, peach, and burrata kale salad, along with brioche rolls and a variety of gourmet quiches, lorraine, mushroom, and caprese. There also was a mimosa bar. "Okay, Mads," Reese said while sipping on her second one. "We're all here—"

"Katie isn't here," Courtney pointed out through a mouthful of quiche lorraine.

"Court, Katie's *never* gonna be here," Amanda said. "She's too busy being *showered*."

The table giggled. Katie had been swirling from circle to circle today, accepting guests' congratulations and thanking them for coming. She was also showing off the glacier-sized engagement ring Austin had bought her. I thought I'd be used to it by now, but I wasn't. It just looked *wrong*.

"True," Reese agreed with the maid of honor. "All of us who can be here are here, so as I was saying…" She gave me a look. "How was the date, Mads?"

"Yes!" Yasmin said. "How'd it go?"

Amanda playfully wiggled her eyebrows. Even though my most recent admirer had been her suggestion, she promised she'd do no digging on how the date had gone. Based on her excitement level, I knew she'd kept her word.

I inwardly groaned, knowing I had to share—or *finally* share. The most recent installment of Ready-Set-Date had been a couple weeks ago, and all the bridesmaids had texted me the next morning asking how it went. I hadn't wanted to relive it, so I said I'd tell them at Katie's shower.

And surprise! Now here we were!

My opening line was tantalizing. "I saw Davis there with his girlfriend."

Reese rolled her eyes as the others booed. "He got back with Natalie?"

I nodded. "She seems cool. She apologized to me for being such a bitch that night. She was already regretting the breakup, and seeing me with Davis made her *really* regret it. She said she could've handled it way better." I shrugged. "I'm going to go with them to a concert this summer."

"That's great, Mads," Paige said. "But this has nothing to do with your date."

"Yes, it does," I lightly countered. "They were at the ice rink, too."

"Oh, cute!" Meredith exclaimed. "You guys went ice skating?"

"We did," I said. "I wouldn't categorize it as *cute*, though."

Brows furrowed, heads cocked, and noses wrinkled. "Why not?" Courtney asked.

"Because," I didn't mean to sputter but totally did, "the guy has an evil twin!"

And then I rewound the tape back to May.

"Who are you going with again?" Da asked as I dug through the mudroom parson's bench for my ice skates. Their blades were dull from the winter, so I planned to arrive at the rink early to get them sharpened. "Connor?"

I shook my head. Connor actually *had* asked if he could come with me. He had been less than impressed by Davis and didn't like the idea of me not having a wingman today. "Come on, we can make it a double date," he'd said. "I'll text…"

No, I'd thought, feeling a little ache. *No, thanks.*

I was torn with Connor. If he was in the picture, I knew I'd wish our dates would disappear—only wanting it to be the two of us. The idea of seeing Connor on a date made me nauseous.

But ever since Samira had planted the seed for a true crush on him, I'd still tried to discourage it from growing. Friends-to-lovers didn't always end in a happily ever after. Connor and I could be perfect for each other, but what if we weren't? What happened then?

"No," I told my dads. "It's someone from Princeton."

"Town or school?" Dad inquired, because at the moment, no one was a fan of the latter; I'd told them all about what had happened during my visit, right down to spending the night at Hotel Gallant instead of Forbes College. I'd burst into tears when I'd walked into the kitchen and saw Katie's mom pulling a sheet of warm chocolate chip cookies out of the oven. She wore a ruffled apron over her pajamas. "Do you want a glass of milk, Mads?"

Now, I felt my stomach spin. "School."

My parents gave me a joint *Are you for real, Madeline?* look.

"Amanda knows him, though," I said calmly. "She tutored his older sister in algebra, but Chad's a genius and *my* age. He skipped a couple grades."

"But his name's *Chad*," Dad deadpanned.

I tried not to giggle.

Da hummed. "Does Marco know him?"

"What does it matter?" I asked, feeling myself flush. "We know Marco isn't the greatest judge of character."

Yes, I'd even told them about Marco and Shelly.

"Tell us you at least know this kid's last name," Dad said.

I shook my head. "I'll find out as soon as we shake hands."

I'd texted the Princetonians to see if they knew a Chad, but the results had been negative. Each Chad they knew was an athlete, and I somehow knew this guy wasn't one.

"Oh, no, don't shake his hand," Da said. "If this is a date, go in for a hug."

"Da, you know I'm not a hello hugger." I folded my arms over my chest for emphasis. "You gotta earn it."

My parents both laughed, and once I found my skates, I hugged them goodbye and drove off in the Defender. Amanda had given me Chad's number, and I'd suggested we go ice skating rather than grab dinner. If skating went well, perhaps there was "dinner potential" afterward, but I didn't want to be committed to at least two hours of small talk if things immediately took a nosedive. Plus, a heat wave hit us this week.

I wanted to cool off somewhere.

I'd run into Davis and Natalie in Ice Land's pro shop, while my skates were being sharpened. She was browsing the rack of hockey sticks, Davis meandering behind her. "Do you play hockey?" was my greetingless greeting.

Natalie looked up and over at me, and her eyes widened before her shoulders curved in from embarrassment. "Yeah," she said. "I do."

"That's awesome!" I smiled. Because I didn't care anymore. I really, really didn't. "I'd try ice hockey in another life."

Natalie smiled back a little. "I played field hockey freshman year, but only lasted a season." She dropped her voice. "I *really* hate running."

I laughed, and without a word, Davis knew to walk away, and by the time he returned, Natalie had apologized and we were talking about music. Phoebe Bridgers, specifically.

"Are you ready to go?" he asked politely.

"Yeah." She turned back to me. "We'll talk details later?"

"Definitely." I nodded, and after we exchanged numbers, she unexpectedly hugged me.

"I'm sorry," she whispered. "I thought you were cool the moment we met, but Davis…"

"Don't worry about it," I said, breaking out of the hug. "I totally get it."

Because, hey, I did.

Skates freshly sharpened, I sat in one of the snack bar's booths to wait for Chad. I'd unlocked my phone and opened my dead-end conversation with Marco, tempted to text him. According to a field hockey teammate, I should never "double-text" a guy, but I wasn't interested in Marco; he was just a friend—or, a pseudofriend.

Hey, I'm sorry, I typed. I was way out of line. If you like Shelly—

"Madeline?"

I looked up from my phone and felt invisible insects skitter and scatter all over my skin before my heart began to hammer. *Penn State*, I thought, mind flashing back to State Night at Tiger Inn. The guy in the PENN STATE shirt who wouldn't let me leave that basement until I'd pepper sprayed the shit out of him. Here he was, right in front of me. Blond hair, brown eyes, dimpled smile.

"Get away." It took a hell of a lot to keep my voice level. "Get away from me."

Penn State furrowed his brow, as if confused. "What?"

"You heard me," I said, suddenly feeling trapped in my booth. "*Away.*" I raised one of my skates, as if to threaten him.

"Okay…" he said slowly. "I really don't know what's going on here."

Liar, I thought. *He remembers my name, so he remembers what he did.*

"Two words," I still reminded him. "*Pepper spray.*"

Penn State backed off, taking several giant steps away from me. I seized the opportunity to scramble out of the booth and toward the rink's automatic doors.

"Wait, where are you going?" he called after me. "I don't understand!"

I stopped for a second. "We didn't have much fun the first time around, *Derek*," I told him dryly. "Which means I *highly* doubt today—"

"Derek?" The guy cocked his head. "You think I'm Derek?"

Now I was the one confused. "Well, aren't you?"

"No." He shook his head. "No, no, no. I'm Chad. Derek is my brother."

Brother?

I didn't believe him.

I might've asked to see his driver's license.

Whelan, Chadwick, it read, along with a birth year the same as mine.

"You look like identical twins," I said weakly when returning his ID. My heart rate had slowed down, almost back to normal.

But not quite.

"Yeah, we get that a lot," Chad muttered, then cleared his throat. "How, uh, do you know Derek?"

I told him.

And, somewhat surprisingly, Chad did not apologize for his brother. "I'm nothing like Derek," he said instead. "I *promise*." He shifted from one foot to the other, and it was then that I noticed he wasn't as tall as Derek and wasn't carrying any beer weight. "And I've been really looking forward to this." He half smiled, dimples appearing—my pulse spiked, wishing they weren't so eerily like his brother's—as he gestured to the rink. "Do you still want to skate?"

I took a breath, then nodded. "Sure," I said. "Let's do it."

But all I could think while tying my skates was: *Why didn't I bring Connor?*

⊢—⊣

"Is there going to be a second date?" Yasmin asked after I finished speaking. "It sounds like it went well overall!"

"No," Courtney, the therapist, said firmly at the same time Meredith, who clearly had impressive intuition, went, "Are you kidding, Yaz?"

Yasmin shrugged. "What? It seems like they had a good time after getting over the whole Douchebag Derek thing."

"*Chad* had a nice time," I said, my quiche now cold. "But

I only pretended to; I didn't—*couldn't*—get over the connection." I chewed and swallowed a bite. "I knew he wanted to hold my hand, but I kept outmaneuvering him. They look so much alike—*too* much alike. I can't..." I trailed off, uncomfortable all over again. "I just can't."

Courtney nodded as Meredith squeezed my shoulder in support. Even though I thought it'd been beyond obvious I hadn't wanted to hold Chad's hand, he kept up our lighthearted conversation and had asked me to dinner after the free skate ended. But I'd declined, and he guessed why. It had put me on edge even letting him hug me goodbye.

"I'm sorry, Mads," Amanda said. "Katie mentioned you visiting Princeton, but all she said was it wasn't the right fit. I didn't know about that guy."

"This isn't the end of the world," Reese said after a few beats. "For your next date, I think you should pick an app—Bumble, maybe—and set up a profile. What do you think?"

"I think we should stop playing this stupid game," I muttered, and when all the bridesmaids blinked at me, I added, "It hasn't worked and hasn't been that fun."

Reese arched an eyebrow. "Oh, really?"

"Reese," Meredith warned. "Don't."

The bridesmaid ignored her. "Well, I hate to break it to you, Mads, but that's what dating's like. You've only been on two dates! Of course it hasn't *worked*. I sometimes go on three dates a week, and still, nothing has truly stuck or been particularly fun. It's not"—she made air quotes—"*magic* like every garbage Bachelor Nation show makes it out to be."

Amanda grimaced in agreement.

My cheeks flamed. "I know that," I fired back. "Those shows are beyond overproduced, and the couples almost always break up once the bubble breaks. I get it." I glanced around for the bride, of all people, but Katie was eternally lost to the shower guests. "I guess I thought you'd all be more like Chris Harrison—yes, I know he no longer hosts the show—and support me." I shrugged. "I feel alone. You set me up with these guys and then I feel alone."

"That's how you feel while dating," Reese said matter-of-factly.

Courtney sighed. "Reese, I know I'm not your therapist, but maybe we should talk about your romantic life…"

"Mads, you could've texted us after Douchebag Derek," Meredith said. "Or FaceTimed after skating with Chad. You didn't need to wait until today to share." She offered me a smile. "We really are here for you."

But I don't want to talk to you about it, I thought, as kind as Meredith and the others (except for Reese right now) were.

"Yeah," Yasmin echoed. "If you want us to be Chris Harrison, all you need to do is ask."

I was silent for several moments, then rose from my chair. I wanted to find Nana. "I have a busy summer," I said. "Can we postpone the setups until further notice?"

"Of course," Amanda said before the others could. "I take dating breaks all the time. It's healthy. Let us know when you're ready again."

"Or *if* you're ready again," Meredith amended. "There's no pressure, Mads." She pushed back her chair too, a signal that she was going to mingle. "And despite what Ice Queen Reese says," she said when we were far enough away from the bridesmaids, "this *is* meant to be fun."

The corners of my eyes prickled. "I want a boyfriend," I said, because after seeing how happy Katie (somehow) made Austin, getting a glimpse of Meredith and Wit's relationship, and running into Davis and Natalie, I realized I did. I wanted that someone that I could share endless inside jokes with and hug after a long day. Someone that would love me even when I was fired up and hangry. "But I don't know how to find one," I told Meredith. "I can talk to guys"—I thought of Connor—"but I can't *talk* to guys."

Meredith smiled faintly. "Katie used to say that all the time in college. People would hit on her whenever we went out, but she said her brain would short-circuit and she couldn't ever generate a snappy response." She laughed. "She once begged me to teach her how to flirt, but it turned out I didn't need to. When she met Austin, she knew exactly what to say." She squeezed my arm. "You'll know what to say when you meet the right person, whether through one of these blind dates or a chance encounter. Who knows…?" She gave me a look. "You might have already met him." A pause, then a slight smile. "You might have met him a long time ago."

After she walked away, I felt a pang of longing for Halloween candy. I closed my eyes and saw Connor trying to shove an entire Snickers bar into his mouth.

Is Meredith right? I wondered. *Have I already met him?*

THIRTEEN

By early July, the sun was blazing, but I was out in our front field doing stickwork drills. Arthur and Francine were keeping to the shade, the two dogs sprawled out on the porch. The Cheval Collective didn't have any meetings in the barn office today; otherwise, I knew Dad would insist I put on actual clothes. The last thing he would've wanted was for prospective clients to drive up and see me in nothing but a sports bra and spandex.

Although I thought my white PENN FIELD HOCKEY baseball hat was an especially nice touch. It had been included in my WELCOME TO THE QUAKERS! gift basket I'd received several weeks after committing. The card had been signed by everyone on the team.

I just have to get in, I kept telling myself like an incantation. *Straight As, awesome application, early acceptance letter.*

But it was also summer, and I was having a lot of fun. Last night, I'd gone into Philadelphia with Davis and Natalie to see

Phoebe Bridgers. "I'm a third wheel!" Davis announced after the concert. "I'm officially a third wheel."

"Yes." Natalie playfully kissed his cheek. He was giving her a piggyback ride while she and I sang "Moon Song" in our raspy, worn-out voices. I couldn't stop laughing, amazed that she and I had become such fast friends. "You are." She turned to me. "Now we need to find a fourth."

"I know, I know," I told her. "I'm working on it."

"But *are* you?" she teased. "*Actually?*"

I comically threw up my arms. Natalie was hardcore shipping Connor and me; I'd brought him as my plus-one to her birthday party a few weeks ago, because I'd been nervous about not knowing anyone. "I can feel the sparks between you two," she'd said that night (slightly sloshed). "Go for it, Mads!"

I admit I now wanted to, but I wasn't sure *how* to go for it. How did one ask their best friend out? And what would happen to our relationship if Connor said no? "He won't," Austin kept telling me. "Trust me, Mads, I've known him since he was a toddler."

"Same here," I pointed out.

"Nope, this is different," my brother said. "I'm older, and a guy."

I'd rolled my eyes. "So what, are you saying he's always been secretly pining for me?"

"No." Austin was blunt. "Definitely not."

He cracked up at the way my face dropped over FaceTime. I

hadn't wanted the answer to be *yes*, per se, but doesn't every girl fantasize—even just briefly—that someone is secretly in love with her? At some point?

"But I *am* saying that I think there's always been something *there*," he continued. "You two have been tight for over a decade, but you're also both complete knuckleheads who won't quit goofing around to see it. If one of you finally opens your eyes and makes a move, the other will get quickly with the program."

"How romantic," I said, straight-faced.

"C'mon, it is!" Austin chuckled again. "Mads, he's your best friend. Wouldn't it be awesome if your best friend became your favorite person?"

His last two words made something twist in my chest. *Favorite person*, Austin Fisher-Michaels's synonym for *soulmate*. I suddenly remembered talking to Samira back in April, while hiding in the bridal salon's bathroom. "It could be nice to be with your best friend," she'd mused. "The person you never stop laughing with, the person who always has your back, the person who knows you inside and out…"

But what happens if we end up like you and Samira, Austin? I thought. *You were best friends before you became more, and look what happened after you did. She wasn't your favorite person forever.*

And I felt like Austin and Samira were the exception to the rule. Most exes never stayed friends afterward. I couldn't bear to lose Connor entirely.

I'd almost mentioned that during Austin's and my FaceTime

call, but I ended up keeping my lips zipped after Austin told me that I'd never know with Connor unless I tried. It was amazing how he could read my mind sometimes. We hung up after he added that texting Connor some version of *Do you want to start going out?* was lazy.

(And *last resort–sounding*, per Katie's unsolicited opinion.)

I had to make a flashy move.

God, what should that be? I wondered as I hit a reverse shot. Embarrassingly, I missed the net and the ball flew far into the meadow. "Dammit," I muttered, grabbing another neon yellow sphere from my ball bucket. A line of fiery sweat trickled down my back.

But it turned ice-cold when I heard the hum of a car coming up the driveway. Arthur and Francine started barking, but I hesitated to turn around, suddenly wishing I'd listened to Dad and put on his definition of *actual clothes*. My workout gear...

Well, I suddenly felt flat-out naked.

The dogs' upbeat woofs meant the arrival was someone they knew. I internally counted to three before turning to see a slate-colored Acura that I knew Marco had affectionately nicknamed the "Bumper Car" due to its various dents.

Sure enough, there was the bright orange PRINCETON decal on the rear window, and I felt my ribs twinge when the driver door opened and Marco slid out; we hadn't seen each other since my campus visit over two months ago.

He looked like summer in a blue EVERTON Premier League

T-shirt and fraying green shorts with flip-flops and a deep tan from soccer training. But he wasn't wearing his glasses, and I wondered why. I liked them.

"Hey!" he called out, raising his arm in a wave.

I waved back with my field hockey stick.

He took that as permission to approach the field.

"Hi," I said, avoiding eye contact when he reached me. I spoke to his favorite soccer team's crest on his chest.

"Are you okay?" Marco asked.

My pulse thudded, but I forced my chin upward and we locked eyes. His irises could only be described as perfectly toasted marshmallows, a sweet golden-brown color. "Hi," I heard myself repeat.

"Hi," he repeated back. "It's been a while."

"Yeah," I said lamely, then straightened my shoulders. "Two months."

Marco's lips curved up in a sly smile. "I know. I also counted."

"You didn't answer my text," I added as if he weren't already aware.

"Not true." He shook his head. "I didn't answer *right away*. The end of the semester was ruthless, and you also made a pretty"—he searched for the right word—"*bold* suggestion."

I didn't answer.

Get out of that situationship, Marco. She's the worst.

An anxious ripple went up my spine, wondering if they were still together.

"I've been trying to text you for weeks," Marco continued, "but all my messages weren't delivered." He hummed. "Am I having technical issues?"

I shook my head. "No."

He raised an eyebrow. "No?"

"No." I rolled my eyes. "I deleted your number."

"Huh." He folded his arms over his chest. "You did, did you?"

"Yes," I lied.

"Well, that doesn't *exactly* explain why the messages failed to send. You'd just receive them from an unknown contact." He paused for a beat. "You blocked me."

"You flatter yourself." I tried to keep casual, but my voice told the truth, its octave skyrocketing up into the heavens.

Marco gave me a crooked, almost amused look. "Was it really necessary to jump to that extreme?"

Yes, it was. Because for some reason, I hadn't been able to deal with his radio silence in our chat. It gave me agita whenever I looked at it, which was weirdly a lot. And so I'd deleted our thread, but that hadn't been enough, either. I didn't trust myself not to open a new message and apologize to him. Because in all honesty, even if it made me sound immature, I still believed *I* deserved the apology.

We stood there in silence for a few moments before Marco let me get away with silently pleading the fifth. "I had some free time today," he said, "and since I had no way of contacting you, I thought I'd stop over."

"I'm touched." I put my hand to my heart. "You could've slid into my DMs. I didn't block you on Instagram."

"I'm not sure I follow you on Instagram," he replied just as dryly. I knew he was kidding; his lips were twitching in a smile. "And that's not my style anyway."

"Seriously?" I started dribbling the field hockey ball at my foot with my stick. "You're telling me you didn't DM"—a sour taste filled my mouth before I said her name—"Shelly after hooking up with her at some party or whatever?"

"No," Marco said lightly. "I met her at an athletic department event and asked for her number." He paused. "You really think I'm an asshole, don't you?"

I shrugged. "More of a dickhead."

"What's the difference?"

"Assholes are aware they're jerks," I said. "Dickheads mostly have no idea how they come off; they're dumb."

Marco chuckled. "Okay, I'll accept the title."

"You might aspire to rid yourself of it," I mumbled.

It went silent between us for a few moments before Marco spoke. "We're not together anymore. Things ended during exams. Shelly wanted to be more than what we were, but I'm not in the right headspace for a serious girlfriend."

All I did was nod, heart quickening.

"She ultimatum-ed me," he added.

"*Ultimatum-ed* is not a verb," I said. "It's not even a word."

"Well, I think it should be," he replied, but slowly—like he was focused on something else. He wasn't looking me in the eye anymore, his gaze traveling from my head to my toes. The beads of sweat on my upper lip began to sting.

"Do you want to play?" I asked, my body humming—telling me I needed to move; I needed to play. "I'll grab my extra stick?"

Five minutes later, Marco had kicked off his flip-flops and pulled off his T-shirt so he didn't sweat through it. Two years ago, my high school field hockey team rolled our eyes at the girls who'd hang out in the bleachers after school, all to catch a glimpse of Marco's invincible abs at soccer practice.

It should've been a ticketed event, I thought, blood thickening in my veins.

Marco's stickwork wasn't disastrous by any means, but by the time I'd scored my fifth goal in a row, he abandoned any semblance of rules entirely. "Obstruction!" I called when he stopped and stood in my path, blatantly preventing me from dribbling farther down the field. "Major obstruction!"

"I didn't hear a whistle. The refs think it's fair." He gestured to the porch, where Arthur and Francine were once again passed out asleep.

I couldn't help but let out a laugh. "Move."

He didn't, standing as strong and steady as a stone statue, so I backed up a bit and swerved to dodge him...

But before I could, his arm swung out and wrapped itself around my waist. It was sticky with sweat, but warm from the sun. I wanted to protest when he hoisted me up over his shoulder, but any and all words stayed on the tip of my tongue. I clung to him, feeling his back muscles flex under his smooth skin. Afraid of falling, my heart bounced with my body as he attempted to run toward the goal, knocking the ball forward with his free hand. "This...doesn't...count," I managed to say right before he scored, but he took me on a victory lap anyway.

"Field hockey," he declared once he'd slowed to a stop, "is an *amazing* sport."

"That," I said, my limbs entirely entwined around his upper body, holding on for dear life, "was *not* field hockey."

Marco laughed, his heartbeat hammering against my thigh. Despite the heat, a sharp shiver shot through me. "Then I guess we've developed some sort of hybrid," he said breathlessly. "We can workshop names later."

"Sure." I sighed, eyes closed and my cheek resting against his back. "May I please be released now?"

"You were never being held captive," Marco said, but when he started to flip me over his back, I yelped and clung to him like a koala all over again. He didn't say anything, but I could almost see the corners of his mouth tip up in a smile.

"Put me down," I commanded. "Or you can forget about being offered lemonade."

"Lemonade?" he asked as he worked on ungluing my forearm from his collarbone. "Are we talking Minute Maid? Or homemade?"

I snorted. "Do you even know my parents?"

Da made the *best* freshly squeezed lemonade, usually for Dad's signature blackberry whiskey lemonade cocktail.

In response, Marco promptly placed me back on the ground, but I still felt the heat radiating between us. "Would you like to stay for dinner?" I blurted. "Da's doing shish kebabs on the grill, and Samira is in town." I gestured toward the McCallisters' house, obscured by acreage and tall pine trees. "Connor and his family are coming over too…" I trailed off, shifting from one foot to the other. "I mean, no pressure. I get it if you already have plans."

Marco smiled and shook his head. "I have no plans." He took a step closer and teasingly zapped my waist.

Paralyzed by the strange electric current, I just barely heard him add:

"And I'd cancel them if I did."

Marco sucked down three glasses of Da's lemonade before he told me that he should head home to shower before dinner. "I'm really sorry, Mads," he said before climbing into the Bumper Car. "I shouldn't have left TI with Shelly that night when I suspected you'd be left alone, and I shouldn't have later apologized on her behalf. That was up to her to do, not me."

I smirked. "I'll die if I hold my breath for that. I blocked her number, too."

Marco chuckled. "Are we okay?"

"Yes." I nodded. "We're okay."

And truthfully, we were, but that didn't mean my family was one hundred percent forgiving. I texted the Fisher-Michaels group chat—named Good Genes—that I'd invited Marco to tonight's cookout, and Austin was the first to respond: I thought we were Mad Mads at him.

Me too, Dad seconded.

Me three, Da said. (And didn't you block his number? Or was that all talk?)

I lovingly rolled my eyes. They were ganging up on me. We WERE, I typed, but he came over today to repent.

Although Dad got straight to the point that evening. "Marco Álvarez," he said after picking Samira up at the train station. "You let our underage daughter's glorified tour guide abandon her at her first college party."

"First?" I asked.

Dad gave me a look. "I'm sure this was the first of many, Mads."

Da further embarrassed Marco, adding, "All to get some action." He glanced between the two of us, eyes narrowed inquisitively. "Do the kids still say that these days?"

"Yes, I did." Marco flushed. "It was far from my finest hour, and I'm truly sorry." He shifted from one foot to the other. "I've regretted it every day since then, but I thought it was better if someone else apologized first."

"Mmm," my parents hummed, knowing he meant Shelly.

"I procrastinated doing it myself," Marco continued. "And by the time I finally got the guts, your daughter had taken drastic measures to make sure she wouldn't read it. I am, to quote Mads, a 'dickhead.'"

"Duh, but thank you for walking her to Katie's house," Austin said, walking into the kitchen out of nowhere. He had an overnight bag slung over his shoulder and haphazardly deposited it on the floor so he could hug Samira. I watched her squeeze him back tightly, as if they were reuniting after being kept apart for years.

"Katie make a detour to visit the horses?" Da carefully ventured several seconds later.

"No," Austin said. "She bailed." He ran a hand through his hair. "We kind of got in a fight."

About what? I wondered, but Dad put his hand over my mouth before I could ask.

"So, I'm gonna stay here tonight." Austin gestured to his discarded duffel. "If that's alright."

"Of course it's alright," Da replied, with Dad adding, "You *do* still have our house listed as your permanent address."

I tried not to giggle. It was true; Austin got more mail than I did. Capital One was practically begging my brother to apply for a credit card with them.

Austin half smiled. "When are the McCallisters coming over?"

"Anytime now," Da said, then turned to Marco. "Would you mind helping me finish prepping the appetizers?"

"Just tell me what to do, Chef," Marco answered, and once he followed Da into the kitchen—his famous watermelon salad with feta, blueberries, and mint was on the menu—and after Samira and Dad disappeared to ready the bar, I hauled ass upstairs to Austin's room.

"Hey," I said, walking through his open door in time to catch him collapse face down on his bed. "Is everything okay?"

"Yeah," he said into his pillow. "Fine."

I waited.

My brother groaned. "Katie is so ridiculous sometimes."

Well, yeah, I thought, then asked what happened.

"We had a tasting at Bedens Brook this afternoon," he said. "You know, for the wedding food."

"A wedding should definitely have some," I remarked.

Austin laughed, but it sounded forced. "It's customary for the country club to cater receptions, but Katie hated everything. Literally, *everything*. The hors d'oeuvres, salads, entrées…" He trailed off and shook his head. "She didn't even try hiding it, either. She kept flipping her hair."

I nodded, having noticed Katie did that when unimpressed. "What did *you* think about the food?"

"I thought it was pretty good," Austin said. "Better than most of the weddings I've been to, actually." He shrugged. "Honestly, I don't expect a dinner for two hundred to be the most magical meal of my life."

My pulse jumped. "Two hundred?"

Austin didn't appear to hear me. "Now Katie and her parents want to hire outside caterers."

"Uh, is that allowed?"

"Not technically, but the Gallants are going to *make* it allowed," he said. "Katie's mom already has a list of potential prospects, and of course the Álvarez family is at the top even though they are *invited* to the wedding."

Marco's invited? I thought.

Austin sighed. "I'm embarrassed, Mads. Commissioning the cake from a specialty bakery is one thing, but I think it's an insult to Bedens Brook if we don't serve their food. I mean, this is already going to be beyond expensive, but why are we even having the reception there if we're not taking advantage of that?" He grumbled. "She's the one who wanted the full-on country club wedding."

I bit my lip. "I'm guessing you aired these grievances to her?"

"Yep." He inhaled, then exhaled. "She asked me why I cared so much. I'm only the groom—which I guess means my only part in this whole thing is showing up for the ceremony—and it's not like I'm footing the final bill, so what does it matter to me?"

"Oh my god." I didn't want to believe it. "Talk about a bridezilla!"

My brother didn't say anything. I took that to mean he didn't disagree with me.

"Austin, that's terrible," I said. "Terrible, and super unfair. You should…"

Break up with her, the voice in the back of my head whispered.

"Please don't tell Dad and Da," he murmured after a moment. "I'm going to tell them we argued about whether or not we should go to Katie's business school friend's wedding in October. They aren't that close, and it's in Cabo."

"But—"

"I've never really felt the need to visit Cabo," he said. "I wouldn't be lying."

"You wouldn't be telling the truth, either," I quickly countered.

Austin's eyes were heavy with exhaustion. "Mads…"

"Where are you?!" someone shouted from downstairs. It was Liam, Connor's thirteen-year-old brother. The McCallisters had arrived. "I need you to back me up! Lauren doesn't think Shawn Mendes is hot!"

"Uh…" Austin's brow furrowed. "Who's Lauren?"

"Someone from school." I tried not to wince. "Lauren Bitterman plays lacrosse."

"Okay, cool," he said slowly, still confused. "But why is Lauren Bitterman *here*?"

I groaned. "I'm assuming because she's finally clawed her way into Connor's heart."

Once again, it appeared I wasn't enough for him.

We ate outside on the front porch, crowded together around the glass-topped table. Da's food was incredible, and our ceaseless laughter drifted up into the twilit sky. Austin and Samira were the first to call it a night. "We're going to Fable," they announced after we'd devoured the decadent olive oil and salted chocolate brownies Samira had made.

"You're never going to get a table..." Marco warned. Fable was his family's whimsical dessert and cocktail lounge. It was almost like a speakeasy in the sense that there was no sign of its existence beyond a brassy gold plaque with a quill on it. Seconds after knocking on the nondescript front door of a side-street rowhouse, the host opened one of the wooden panes and asked for your name. Inside, it was like a magical library with gleaming wood walls, flickering candles, cozy velvet and leather chairs, and bookcases upon bookcases.

There was always a waitlist.

"Then we'll squeeze in at the bar," Austin responded. His eyes darted to Samira. "I need a nightcap."

"The seasonal mocktails are very popular," Marco noted. "I recommend the s'more martini. It's mixed with a liquor substitute."

"A *s'more martini*?" Connor and I said simultaneously, and I felt myself flush as he asked: "How can that possibly taste good?"

"Because I invented it," Marco said.

My parents and the McCallisters laughed, the sound crackling like a campfire. I rolled my eyes when Marco smiled smugly and straightened up in his seat. "Boom, *toasted*," Mr. McCallister said with a wink.

"Oh, jeez, Dad..." Connor groaned as Da and Mr. McCallister shared a fist bump for a Dad Joke well-done.

Marco and I went to hang out in what my family called the "Garden" after the McCallisters headed home (Connor and Lauren hand in hand!). Years ago, Da and Austin had ambitiously planted a large vegetable patch, which was now flanked by flourishing herb and flower gardens. Dad had been the architect of a split-rail fence complete with wire mesh, in order to keep deer and other critters from trespassing. It outlined a square, and in the center of the Garden was a brick patio with an inlaid koi pond and wrought-iron summer furniture. After slipping through the garden gate, I flicked on the market lights I'd strung up overhead and then flung myself onto the couch's red cushions. "Graceful," Marco commented.

"And beautiful," I quipped. "You can't forget beautiful."

She is beauty and she is grace, I remembered him joking after I'd tripped down the stairs at Austin and Katie's engagement party.

Ugh, *Katie*.

I couldn't even think about her right now, because if I did, I'd either focus on the off chance that she and Austin might not recover from this fight and I would get Austin back...or we'd get Austin back, but he'd be devastated without Katie.

Why was there this tug-of-war?

"Did you have fun?" I asked Marco after he'd settled in the chair across from me.

Because I'd barely spent any time with him tonight. He'd cooked dinner with Da and then talked about everything under the sun with Dad during appetizers. He and Samira had even been whispering back and forth earlier.

"Yes." Marco grinned. "A lot of fun."

"Good," I said, grinning back. "I think it's safe to say that if you showed up out of the blue, no one would be particularly mad about it."

"Well, your dad—Harry—and I did talk about me working here," Marco replied. "Every now and again, I need a change of scenery to write."

"Wait, *write*?" I asked.

"I'm working at Ember & Ash a few nights a week," Marco said, "but one of my lit professors asked me to be his research assistant this summer. He writes historical fiction, in the same vein as Amor Towles."

I gave him a blank look.

Marco gave me an incredulous one. "You don't know who Amor Towles is?"

"I've never been a big reader," I admitted, intrigued that he seemed to be. "Only when we're at the beach."

"Fair enough," Marco said. "But *A Gentleman in Moscow*? You really haven't heard—"

"Okay, yes." I snapped my fingers. "It's on Dad's bookshelf.

Someone gave it to him for Christmas one year."

Katie, I realized. *Freaking Katie.*

"How is this fitting in with summer soccer training?" I asked.

"It's not." Marco shifted in his seat. "Soccer and I have parted ways."

I gasped. "What? You quit?"

He nodded.

"*Why?*"

"Because playing a Division One sport is a huge time commitment," Marco said, "and while I'll always love soccer, Princeton has broadened my horizon. I've discovered some new interests and opportunities, and so I've decided to hang up my cleats to see what else is out there." He paused. "I'm researching World War One this summer for my professor, but I'm also trying my hand at writing a book. Simon convinced me to take a fiction-writing course with him this past spring, and I loved it."

I smiled and launched a throw pillow at him. "Who are you and what have you done with Marco Álvarez?"

Marco easily caught the pillow and shrugged. "This *is* Marco Álvarez, Mads. I feel like I'm finally him."

I was quiet for a moment, thinking of Marco in his hoodies in high school—always carrying a soccer ball (or sometimes actually dribbling in the hallways), fist-bumping his teammates while carrying on conversations with a gaggle of girls, and being voted Homecoming King his senior year. He was, as in every story, The Man.

He looks so different, I noted. From his lightweight summer button-down shirt to his tortoiseshell glasses and fresh haircut to the fact that he was a reader and even writing a book! It struck me that Marco now seemed more present, calmer. We'd chatted after sports when we were in school together, but I doubted Marco really remembered those conversations. He never made it seem like he wanted to leave, but he still always ended up racing off somewhere, late for something. Things were different now. We were getting closer. I somehow knew in my bones that he'd truly heard every word we'd exchanged in the past several months.

We were really friends.

I shifted on the couch. "What is your book about?"

Marco smiled but shook his head. "Nobody knows." He thought for moment. "Sometimes I'm not even sure I do yet."

"Well," I said, "as long as there's a spirited and sweet field hockey player in it, I think you have a winner."

Marco raised a single eyebrow. "Did you just refer to yourself as *sweet*?"

Heat rushed to my cheeks. "A lot of people tell me I'm sweet," I said, then challenged him. "Are they wrong?"

"No, because opinions are subjective," he answered. "I don't find you sweet, though. You aren't sweet to me."

I felt pinpricks at the corners of my eyes. What was I then? Sour?

"You are kind," he continued. "You are caring, you are

respectful, you are polite." He paused. "But you're also sarcastic, clever, flirty—"

My pulse leapt. *Flirty?* I thought. *Did he just say* flirty?

"Intimidating, loud, and easy to rile up."

I gave him a look. "Easy to rile up?"

"Yes." He nodded. "You have certain buttons that are really fun to push."

I opened my mouth, then closed it. What was I supposed to say to that? *Pushing buttons.* He sounded like a fourth grader on the playground, so I responded in the same manner.

"Well, you're annoying. Of course I get irked."

Marco tipped back his head to laugh. I tried to scowl, but it was impossible. I might not have been sweet, but the sound of his laughter was. Stars twinkled up in the sky, the soft breeze swirled around us, and the crickets stopped chirping, as if wanting to listen. "How is your dating scheme going?" he asked a few beats later. "Are the bridesmaids still setting you up with guys?"

I snorted. "Setups have been suspended until I decide otherwise," I said, and then told him about my ice-skating date with Chad and the blowup at Katie's bridal shower.

He winced. "Okay, I feel like I should tell you…I was at the rink the same day you went out with Chad. My aunt had been threatening to murder my little cousins, so I offered to take them off her hands for the afternoon." He took a breath. "I spotted you across the snack bar while I was waiting for the twelve courses of crap we'd ordered, and you looked really uncomfortable." He ran a hand through his hair. "I recognized Chad from a study group last fall and did make the connection between him and his brother, but Chad's a good kid. It seemed like you realized that." He smiled a bit. "Plus, you had a weapon."

"Yes, I did," I said, knowing he meant my skates' sharp blades. "And he *was* a nice guy, but..." I trailed off and shrugged. "The ridiculous resemblance was too weird."

Was it also weird that Marco had been at the rink, too?

Not nearly, but talk about a coincidence!

I appreciated that he'd let me handle Chad on my own, though. I didn't need someone swooping in to save me.

"When do you think this moratorium will end?" Marco asked.

"I don't know," I said. "Meredith—one of the bridesmaids—wonders if I've already met the right guy but haven't realized it yet."

"Ah..." Marco took off his glasses to clean their lenses. "Connor."

My stomach dropped. "You think so too?!"

Because the Monnor (or Cads?) ship was gaining speed. Austin, Samira, the bridesmaids, Natalie, and I doubted my dads would ever oppose...

"I don't *think*." Marco gave me a *cut the bullshit* look. "I *see*. You were staring at him all night tonight."

"I was?" I asked, even though I knew he was right—the supercut began to play in my head. Connor glancing up from the bowl of chips and salsa to smile at me, Connor running a mindless hand through his fair hair, Connor backing his brother up when Liam claimed that Taylor Swift would ultimately fix the United States economy, Connor's elbow brushing mine while we chowed down on Da's grilled corn on the cob.

But then there was also Connor…and *Lauren*. Connor holding Lauren's hand as she smiled and said it was great to see me. Connor laughing when Lauren confessed to Austin, future DMD, that she never flossed. Connor introducing Lauren as his "girlfriend" to my parents.

You idiot, the voice in my head berated. *You blew it!*

I should've known better. Connor had a reputation with girls. He wasn't a man-slut or anything; he genuinely liked having a girlfriend and Lauren had been campaigning for months. *Why* had I procrastinated so long about asking him out? Connor wasn't expecting me to, he had no idea it was coming—or, *supposed* to come. Why the hell had I thought he would wait for me to get my shit together?

"It's too late," I whispered, to both Marco and the moon. "I'm too late."

"Maybe," Marco whispered back. "Maybe not."

"Listen, I'm *not* going to break them up," I said. "I would never do that to Connor."

"I wasn't remotely suggesting that," Marco replied. "And I'm a bit insulted you thought otherwise."

I laughed. "You're right; I'm not that sweet to you."

"Nah, you are." Marco grinned. "You're just more of a sweet tart than a sweetheart."

"Connor goes for sweethearts," I grumbled.

Because Lauren Bitterman? She might've gotten on my nerves, but everyone at school thought she was nice. Like Connor, she'd unanimously been voted next spring's lacrosse captain.

"Connor's only seventeen," Marco said. "He doesn't know anything."

"Oh, and you do?" I asked airily. "Has Princeton already taught you everything?"

"Not *everything*," he answered, tossing the throw pillow back at me. I hugged it to my chest after catching it. "But yes, sweet tart, I like to think I know some stuff."

"Like what?" I teased, but when he only winked at me, I felt the sudden and strange urge to hide my face in the pillow and scream.

He was exasperating.

FOURTEEN

Little did I know that while I'd been away at Penn's field hockey camp the following week, Marco had pretty much made himself at home. I slept in the day after getting back, and once I'd finally summoned the energy to drag my aching body downstairs, I spotted him through a window. He was out on the front porch, working at his laptop and surrounded by books. "She rises!" he said when I joined him at the table with a plate of scrambled eggs, bacon, and toast slathered in raspberry jam. "Like a phoenix from the ashes!"

"Mmm," was my muttered response.

Marco chuckled. "How was camp?"

"Completely and utterly—*shit*!" I spotted the time on my Apple Watch. "I'll be right back! Make sure the dogs don't get my breakfast!"

(Because Arthur and Francine? They couldn't be trusted around unsupervised food.)

Even though my muscles screamed, I leapt out of my chair

and ran back into the house. "What's wrong?" Da asked as I raced up the stairs, my pulse also pounding.

"I have a conference call!" I shouted.

"You sound like your father!" he shouted back.

I only exhaled when I'd grabbed my MacBook and rejoined Marco. In all honesty, I probably should've taken the call in my room, but my stomach rumbled for food. Plus, I hadn't seen Marco in a while. We'd texted a lot while I was away, but it wasn't the same. I hadn't been able to see the expressions on his face. I'm not a FaceTime guy, he'd said.

Why not? I'd asked. You were blessed with such a gorgeous face.

Stop making me blush, he responded.

And I admit, I *really* wanted to see if he was actually blushing. Marco *had* called me flirty, and maybe if I strengthened my supposed skills now, I'd have more confidence putting myself out there if/when Ready-Set-Date resumed.

Now that Connor was taken, I was thinking about it.

"You don't need to put in headphones," he said now, as I started untangling an ancient pair (my AirPods were currently MIA). "I'm not a big eavesdropper."

"Hmm." I gave him a skeptical look. "I don't totally believe you…"

I navigated to my Gmail and tapped on a Zoom link from Amanda Gallant, the subject line reading: Katie's Bachelorette!

Hopefully no one minds watching me annihilate my breakfast,

I thought as I hung out in the virtual waiting room. *Sorry not sorry.*

Personally, I thought a Zoom was unnecessary. This all could've been coordinated over email. Text was apparently too tedious, because for the last few months, there had been two group chats. One that included Katie, and another that was solely the bridesmaids. Amanda had told us that all details of Katie's bachelorette weekend were to stay in the latter thread, so the bride had no idea where we were off to party for three days.

But then Paige had accidentally sent a Charleston Airbnb link to the chat with Katie.

After that epic fail, Reese had proposed the Finger Lakes in upstate New York. We can rent a house on the lake, follow a wine trail, maybe even rent a pontoon boat...

"Welcome, everyone," Amanda said now, as if commencing a corporate America meeting. "I hope you are all doing well!"

"I promise I'm listening," Paige replied. The screen switched to her; she was looking down at her tablet. "But I have to finalize this romance cover. It's due tomorrow."

I had to swallow a giggle when I caught Amanda roll her eyes. But she didn't outright comment. "We're about a month out from the Finger Lakes, so I wanted to touch base on logistics."

Logistics, I thought. *This definitely could've been an email.*

"You'll be getting an email," Amanda said, "with all this information, but I thought it would be best to discuss it together..."

"Keep talking, Amanda," a male voice said when she trailed off. "I'm on the edge of my seat."

"Stephen!" Meredith exclaimed as the bridesmaids broke into laughter. "You said you were going food shopping."

"You haven't texted me the list," her husband replied smoothly.

"You could've texted me to text you the list," Meredith countered.

"Well, I wanted to say hello." Wit appeared onscreen, impossibly turquoise eyes sparkling and sandy hair wind whipped. "Hi, ladies."

Across the table, Marco waved his arm to get my attention. *Should I say hello, too?* he mouthed as everyone warmly chorused, "Hi, Wit!"

I gave Marco the middle finger.

So much for not eavesdropping!

"Okay, I've secured the house," Reese said once Meredith had kicked Wit out of the room. "It's right on Seneca Lake, and absolutely gorgeous."

"How much is it going to be per person?" Yasmin asked.

"Six-fifty," Reese answered.

It took everything in me not to balk. Six-fifty? *Six hundred and fifty* dollars? Who could freaking afford that?

Well, I guess my fellow bridesmaids could. Except for Paige—who was frowning at her tablet—the others nodded like it was no big deal.

Out of the corner of my eye, I saw Marco quickly scribble something in his spiral notebook. *You okay?* it read.

I wanted to shake my head, but the best I could do was gulp. These women were adults with jobs; I was seventeen going on eighteen and had *never* had a job. Austin had been our town's go-to babysitter, but while I liked kids, I didn't *love* spending hours with them. And I was always too busy with field hockey to fold clothes at Lululemon or waitress. I made money over the summer by following Da's laughably long list of household chores or completing miscellaneous tasks for the Cheval Collective.

I needed that money for the school year, but thanks to the bridesmaid dress, shoes, and my cut of the Airbnb, I could forget it. Not to mention whatever else I spent on the bachelorette trip. Amanda was now talking about each person bringing food and making a meal?

"Breathe," Marco said when the Zoom finally ended. I slammed my laptop shut so hard that I worried I'd broken it for a second. "You haven't let out a breath in ten minutes." He paused to recalculate. "Actually, closer to fifteen."

"Why do I have to pay for all this?!" I exhale-exclaimed. "Katie asked *me* to be a bridesmaid! I didn't ask *her* if I could be one. I didn't realize that accepting meant offering up all the money I have to my name!"

Marco chuckled. "Ah, Mads, there's no shame in declaring bankruptcy."

I groaned. "Marco!"

"What?" he said, smiling. "You're being overdramatic."

"But true!" I countered.

He didn't argue. "Listen, this is the way it is these days," he said calmly. "My sister has been in four weddings, and they've all been an investment."

"Are you sure you don't mean a bill?" I grumbled, even though I'd caught his drift. Carina Álvarez was invested in her friendships; she didn't consider them a cost.

But wasn't asking people to spend over a thousand dollars kind of too much?

"I hate this!" I announced to the world. "I hate this, I hate this, I hate—"

"Excuse me, what do we hate?" Dad pushed through the front door. "Hopefully today's list isn't too long yet."

I made an unintelligible noise.

"We just logged off a bridesmaid Zoom call," Marco translated. "They went over details for Katie's bachelorette weekend. A follow-up email is imminent."

"And how did that go?" Dad asked me.

"Do you think Nana will write me an early birthday check?" I answered. "September isn't *that* far away..."

"Ah." He easily picked up what I was putting down, retracing his steps over to the doorway. "Lee!"

Marco packed up his laptop and books. "I'm going to do some reading in the Garden," he said as Da joined the party on the porch.

"I suspect I know what this is about," Dad said once Marco was gone. He, Da, and I sat together at the table. "But humor us."

I did, and didn't give my parents a chance to respond before adding, "Do I really need to go on the trip? I mean, I can't drink and Amanda talked about this whole wine crawl."

"Trail," Dad corrected, amused. "It's wine *trail*."

"And pub *crawl*," Da said, then cleared his throat. "If you don't want to go, Mads, we aren't going to stop you from bowing out. This is your decision."

Dad nodded. "Conflicts happen."

Guilt seeped into my skin. Conflicts *did* happen, but for once, I didn't have one. Katie's bachelorette was in mid-August, which was usually when we took our family vacation. By that time, I was finished with camps, my club team training was way more relaxed, and high school preseason didn't start until the week after we got home. I'd be lying if I said I was unexpectedly busy. My dads were going to visit my great-aunt Penny in Rhode Island, but Austin would see right through that if I asked to tag along.

Austin also will be disappointed, I thought. *He won't be angry, but he'll be really disappointed in me if I don't go.*

And my brother had been in the best mood lately. He was now in his final year of dental school, determined to be a pediatric dentist, plus he and Katie had smoothed things over... pretty much thanks to Da. Since Austin's lying days were far, far behind him, he *had* told our parents about the less-than-terrific tasting at Bedens Brook and the Gallants' plan for outside caterers. "Why don't you do another one just to be sure?" Da had suggested. "I'd love to come with you, if you want another opinion."

(The second tasting had gone much better.)

Now, they gave me a look. "Mads, it's admirable—and adorable, truthfully—that you believe you need to cover your bridesmaid expenses," Dad said. "But there's no way that's happening."

Thank god, I thought, my sigh of relief embarrassingly audible. *Thank god, thank god, thank god!*

"We'll take care of everything," Da told me. "It'll be up to you when your field hockey friends inevitably ask you to be in their weddings someday, but your situation will be different then. You'll have graduated college and be working." He shook his head. "You cleaning the grout in the bathrooms this summer is not the equivalent to earning a salary."

"Helping stage houses and reviewing inspection reports is closer," Dad said. "Although still not the same."

The corners of my eyes smarted with tears. "I'll go on the trip," I said. "I'll go to the Finger Lakes."

"Well, would you look at that!" Da exclaimed. "Harry, the second she finds out she's not paying her tab, she's no longer such a hater."

"No, no," I said as Dad laughed. "I'll go, but that doesn't mean I *want* to." I folded my arms across my chest. "Haters gonna hate."

"Do you think Austin's best man has something like this for Montana?" I asked. Marco and I were both on the Garden's couch, sitting close enough that I could smell his sunscreen, its coconut scent now so familiar. We were reading through the Google Doc that Amanda had shared. It detailed everything from the Airbnb mansion to the scheduled vineyard visits to meal planning. My cooking skills were so limited that I'd quickly signed up to make breakfast one day. Coffee, muffins, yogurt, and fruit salad would work, right?

Marco shook his head in disbelief.

I giggled. Austin's bachelor weekend wasn't until September. "We invited Wit," Austin had said on the phone the other day. "He's not a groomsman, but who cares? The guy is a ton of fun…"

Marco scrolled past the decorations section, which had a bullet-pointed list but also an all-capitals comment: PAIGE, YOU ARE IN CHARGE OF THIS!

"Holy crap," Marco said. "There are *games* on here."

"Games? What kind of games?"

I imagined playing truth or dare again and resolved that I had no problem being dared to dive into lake butt-naked. If eleven-year-old Annie could do it in *The Parent Trap*, so could I!

"Mmm…" Marco scanned the list. "Something called Prosecco Pong. With a note that reads: *Mer, bring your dad and uncle Brad's beer pong table. Not the crappy one Wit made.*"

I sighed. "Meredith's family sounds fascinating."

"How Well Do You Know the Bride," he continued. "The Newlywed Game, some type of wedding-themed Mad Libs, and—"

"What?" I asked when he dropped off. "What else?"

Marco's only response was pressing his lips together, as if trying not to laugh.

Part of me wanted him to break; I loved seeing him burst into laughter—the sight was so palpable that sometimes I could feel the sound reverberate against my cheek.

With no such luck, I glanced back at the laptop screen and noticed the cursor hovering above three words: The Panty Game.

My spine straightened, and Marco took that as his cue. "*For this game,*" he read, "*each bridesmaid should bring a pair of unwrapped panties that reflects their personality. All panties should be hung on a clothesline, and the bride must guess which bridesmaid gave her which pair.* Reese suggests Katie should drink every time she gets one wrong. Amanda agreed."

I disregarded that, too focused on the game itself. "What the actual fuck?" I said. "Panties"—I grimaced, for some reason always despising that word—"that show off my *personality*?" My face was ablaze. "That's beyond humiliating!"

"Why?" he asked, totally deadpan. "Are the contents of your top dresser drawer humiliating?"

"No! Lots of black and lace and various shades of blue. Maybe one pair of purple…" I trailed off, my body freezing but lungs fluttering frantically. "Oh my god, why I am talking about this with you?!"

Marco smiled. "Because I don't think you think I'm such a dickhead anymore," he said. "I think you like me." He tilted his head, bemused. "I think you trust me."

Something white-hot crackled in my core.

I think you like me.

I think you trust me.

"Stop smirking at me!" I snapped as someone called out, "Hey!"

Marco and I turned to see Connor and Lauren heading toward us, both with lacrosse sticks in hand. As captains of our school boys' and girls' teams, they never went anywhere without them—or, for the last few weeks, each other. "Hey!" I called back, grateful to Marco for hiding my computer under a couch cushion. The last thing I needed was Connor or Lauren seeing the scandalous Google Doc.

"What's up?" Connor asked once he'd unlatched the gate and gestured for Lauren to pass through first. Connor was a gentleman, but I resisted the urge to roll my eyes when Lauren settled on his lap instead of sitting in her own chair. She used to mostly annoy me, but now I just didn't like her; she was clingy and manipulative. Whenever Connor had plans with me or his other friends, she laid a major guilt trip on him. I'd gotten used to third-wheeling them so he could avoid her wrath.

"Not much," Marco answered. "Mads got home from camp yesterday, so we're just hanging."

"I know," Connor said as his girlfriend wrapped his arms around her waist. "She, Lauren, and I grabbed pizza and water ice last night." He caught my eye. "It looks like you're doing *more* than just hanging…"

My heart jolted. Did Connor think Marco and I were—

"Something serious was *definitely* being discussed," Lauren emphasized, raising an inquisitive eyebrow.

Okay, no, they just think we're keeping something hush-hush, I thought, relieved, but still inwardly groaning. Connor was joking, but Lauren was nosy.

"Well, yes," I caved. "We were talking about a seriously serious subject." I paused for dramatic effect. "Katie's bachelorette weekend."

Lauren squealed. "Everything's finalized?!"

"You bet," Marco said. "Date, time, location—"

I elbowed him before he could add *activities*.

"Mads, I'm so jealous," Lauren said. "You must be psyched."

I made a noncommittal *mm-hmm* noise.

"You are lying through your teeth." Connor smiled. "You aren't excited, are you?"

"I guess." I shrugged. "I probably sound like a spoiled brat, but this isn't *really* a vacation. It's Katie's vacation; for me, it's a business trip."

"You don't sound like a brat," Connor said. "You sound like *yourself*." He chuckled. "I've known you forever, Mads, and knowing you forever means I know that you love going on vacation." He turned to Lauren. "She always has a hundred tabs open on her computer, and at least half of them are travel blogs. She has an impressive bucket list."

"And I suspect Stone Harbor isn't at the top," Marco said, knocking his knuckles against my knee. "But what do you think about it?"

I looked at him blankly. I had no idea what he was talking about.

"Oh, you invited her to the house?" Connor asked Marco.

And one, two, three: it *clicked*. The Álvarezes owned a house on the Jersey Shore. According to Dad, they usually rented it out for most of the summer, but…

"Yeah," Marco said. "My parents have been down there for the last couple weeks, and I'm driving down on Friday. I was hoping Mads would come." He paused. "You too, McCallister."

"That's awesome!" Lauren replied, unaware that the invitation had not been extended to her. "I love Stone Harbor. There's this one ice cream place—"

"Don't you have club practice?" Connor asked me.

"Yes…" I said slowly. "I do." I felt my lips twist in a smile. Marco was a genius, helping me spend time with Connor sans Lauren. "But if you want to go, Con, I'll skip it."

FIFTEEN

Marco had offered Connor and me a ride to Stone Harbor, but Connor had an afternoon allergist appointment he couldn't reschedule, so I volunteered to stay behind and leave a few hours later with him. As an extrovert, Connor didn't love long solo drives, and being alone with him today was *thrilling*. Finally, no Lauren.

"She's still upset I didn't invite her," he said while turning out of our neighborhood. "Pretty pissed off."

"It's not your invite to extend," I pointed out. "We're going to *Marco's* house."

"My words exactly." Connor chuckled. "Marco actually told me I could bring her, but…" He trailed off and shook his head.

But what? I wondered. *But she's super clingy and you need a break from her?*

Nevertheless, I smiled and punched him on the arm. Because for once, Connor McCallister realized not every get-together needed to be "the more, the merrier."

On the drive down, we moaned and groaned about our summer reading list, even though Connor loved audiobooks and I'd been reading a lot more lately. Both of us cheered when we crossed Stone Harbor's causeway and drove through town. I'd been there before, so I smiled when we passed Bill's Pancake House, the (bougie) Reeds hotel, and Hoy's, the famous five-and-dime store. My mouth watered when I spotted kids licking giant ice cream cones.

Soon enough, Connor slowed to a stop at the Álvarezes. Their house was simple, its shingles painted a pale sea-glass green with white shutters that matched their white picket fence. A detached garage sat at the end of the crushed seashell driveway, and instead of a grassy front lawn, the yard was covered with beige pebbles. It was a quaint Jersey Shore cape built in the 1950s set amid grand new homes, but I knew if Marco's parents decided to sell it, they could get *millions*. Marco had mentioned the cottage was less than a block from the beach, and now, I could see his family owned a double lot. Someone would pay a king's ransom to tear down their house and build some massive mansion in its place.

"Welcome!" Mrs. Álvarez called to us, the cottage's screen door slamming shut behind her. I didn't know her well but hugged her back when she pulled me into one. "Marco and my husband are out grabbing some lobsters for dinner," she said after hugging Connor, "but they'll be back soon." She gestured to the house. "Let's get you all set up!"

I immediately felt at home upon walking through the front door into the family room. Eclectic paintings hung on the white shiplap walls, in between framed family photographs and wreaths made of seashells. Built-in bookshelves showed off worn paperbacks and jars of sand. Somewhere, a wind chime started singing. Connor and I made eye contact.

I love this place, I mouthed.

"My sister's family is here, too," Marco's mom said as she led us down the hall, "but we've shoved her kids in the back bunk room." She stopped outside two doors across from each other. "Connor, you can take Marco's other twin bed." She pointed to the right, then the left. "And Mads, Carina's room is all yours."

"Thank you, Mrs. Álvarez," I said. "We're so excited."

"Oh, please, call me Rose." She smiled and waved a hand. "I'll let you get settled. Dinner will be around seven."

Connor and I exchanged a look once she was gone, and I couldn't help but laugh when he said: "When should I tell her I'm allergic to shellfish?"

We hit the beach at practically the crack of dawn. "We've got to," Marco insisted, somehow carrying two beach chairs and a red-and-yellow-striped umbrella, while also pulling a wagon loaded with beach towels, shovels, and his cousins' sandcastle-making equipment. "Otherwise, we won't get a prime spot."

Connor nodded midyawn. He'd never been an early riser.

Marco had walked to the beach barefoot, but Connor and I kicked off our flip-flops in the dunes before we claimed our territory. The white sand felt like soft sugar. Our "prime spot" included an unobstructed view of the blue-as-could-be Atlantic Ocean and was only ten yards away from the tall white wooden lifeguard stand. "Morning, Marco!" one lifeguard called, sporting a pair of aviators with a whistle around her neck. She looked familiar, her golden-brown curls in a carefree messy bun.

"Hey, Grace!" Marco waved. "Everett stationed somewhere else today?"

Ah, I realized as Marco wandered over to talk to her. *Grace Barbour.*

I'd forgotten how many kids from our town spent the summer on the Jersey Shore.

After I put on sunscreen, I tossed the Sun Bum to Connor. "You missed a spot," I commented when he didn't bother doing his back.

He sighed and handed over the sunscreen. "Will you? Please?"

"It would be an honor." I smirked and squeezed some lotion into my palm, but hesitated before rubbing it in, as if I were afraid of Connor's skin scorching my hands. My heart thudded once, twice, three times before I blinked and went to work.

"Mmm, that's nice," Connor murmured. "I didn't realize I would also be getting a massage…"

Heat rushed to my cheeks, and I was glad Connor couldn't see me. I hadn't meant to give him a full-on massage. It was just—well, running my hands over his shoulder muscles felt good.

"We have to wait twenty minutes for it to soak in," I said, swallowing hard. "Then we can go in the water."

"That won't be a problem," he yawned for the umpteenth time as he unrolled his blue towel. "I'm gonna take a nap."

"You do that." I nodded, then wasted no time in taking a picture of him passed out to post on my Instagram story. I geotagged Stone Harbor.

Classic, Austin commented a minute later.

Meredith heart-eyed the photo and wrote: Beach days are the best days!

I liked her message before tucking my phone in my tote bag and pulling out a book. Marco did a double take when he returned to our setup. "*A Gentleman in Moscow?*" he asked. "You're reading it?"

"I'm about to," I said as he dropped down into the beach chair next to mine. "I'm not exactly dying to read *Wuthering Heights* for school, and you said this was good, so…"

Marco grinned. "Amor Towles did no prior research before writing it," he said, eyes shining. "He'd never been to Russia and never took any Russian history courses in school. It was only after he finished the first draft that he visited Moscow. He moved into the Metropole Hotel to revise—" He grimaced. "Sorry, I'm nerding out."

"A bit." I fought a smile. "But as long as you don't spoil anything, nerd away."

"No guarantees," Marco joked, and when he laughed, it was like the sun took the sound as its cue to shine brighter—the rays now sizzling against my skin. I watched Marco lean back in his chair and run a slow hand through his hair. "Swim after a few chapters?" he asked after cracking open his own book. "We'll be hot by then."

"I'm already hot," I murmured as I skimmed the book's dedication.

"I agree," Marco said smoothly, and it wasn't until he'd pulled out his own book and started reading that I suddenly wondered whether he agreed with me—that it was hot today—or if he was in agreement about something else. My pulse quickened.

I had to read *A Gentleman in Moscow*'s first page three times before it made any sense.

―――

After dinner that night, it was time to make what the Álvarez family called the "Pilgrimage." Marco's dad and cousins hopped on their bikes and sped off toward town, determined to reach Springer's Homemade Ice Cream before the line grew out of control. "What would you two like?" Marco asked his mom before we followed on foot. She and her sister were relaxing with sangria on the screened-in porch. "Coffee? Maple walnut? Peanut butter cup?"

"We'll split two scoops of maple walnut with marshmallow sauce." Rose smiled and blew her son a kiss. "Please and thank you."

Springer's had been the most popular ice cream place on the Jersey Shore since Prohibition. Marco warned us that the line of people stretched down the block and turned the corner once the sun set, but it was mind-boggling to see it in real life. There were even aspiring musicians entertaining the crowd; the atmosphere felt like a block party. As we searched for Marco's cousins, I took a video for Samira—the biggest ice cream lover I knew. It was only after I texted it to her that I remembered she and Austin used to spend a day in Stone Harbor to celebrate their anniversary every year. She'd once told me their first kiss had been after a game of miniature golf.

Oops, I thought, then shook the embarrassment away. It wasn't like Samira was still in love with my brother. The last time we saw each other, she'd mentioned dating someone.

"Oh, jeez," Connor said a few minutes after we found Marco's family in line (if the people behind thought we were cutting, they didn't say anything). He pulled his phone from his pocket, the screen reading: Lauren B.

"Lauren B?" Marco said, seemingly amused.

"I have four or five Laurens in my phone," Connor said, and I bit the inside of my cheek when he let his girlfriend's call go to voicemail. It'd have been terrible if I smiled.

"How're things going with her?" Marco asked.

"Pretty well," Connor said as we took a few steps forward in line. "She's cute and funny, and obsessed with lacrosse. We never run out of stuff to talk about." He laughed, as if remembering a joke Lauren had made the other day. "We have a lot of fun together."

"So much fun you blew her off?" Marco teased.

Yes, I thought, heat rising to my cheeks. *Why?*

Connor shrugged. "It's loud here. I'll call her back later." He looked at me and gestured ahead of us, to the white-and-brown-shingled two-story Victorian house. Inside was a whirlwind of bright colors and controlled chaos. "What're you gonna get?"

"Oh," I squinted at the menu board, mounted on Springer's wide front porch. We were still a little too far away to see it clearly, so I turned to Marco. My guess was he had the flavors memorized. "What do you recommend?"

"Hmm." He stroked his chin, as if in deep contemplation. "Let me think…"

Connor ended up getting black raspberry while I took Marco's recommendation and ordered something called Drunken Cherry, but I wasn't the drunken one later. There had been plenty of sangria left when we got back to the Álvarez cottage, and once everyone else had gone to bed and Marco's lips turned scarlet, he suggested the three of us go for a late-night stroll. "There's nothing like the midnight stars and salt air," he insisted, dreamy and wide-eyed. "And the streets are empty, so we can hear the waves crashing on the beach." He shook his head in wonder. "There's also a blood moon tonight."

Connor glanced at his phone, then tossed it across the porch's couch. He still hadn't called Lauren back. "I'm in." He took a sip of his Miller Lite. Connor accepted any beer offered, but rarely finished them, tricking his friends into thinking he could really hold his alcohol. "Mads?"

I drained my ginger-lime soda and grinned. "Let me get a sweatshirt."

The temperature had dropped during our walk back from Springer's, so I went into Carina's room to grab my favorite Champion crewneck. I glanced at myself in the mirror; I looked happy after a perfect day on the beach with my sun-kissed face and salt-water-stiff hair weaved into two braids. To pass the time in the Springer's line, Marco's cousin had twisted them into silly little buns.

Marco still had his sangria in hand when I returned to the living room, and Connor nursed his Miller Lite. "Come on, guys," I told them. "No roadies."

"Right," Marco said. "Open container law."

"And the liquor law." Connor set down his beer and nodded at Marco. "Ditch the fruit juice, Álvarez. We're not twenty-one yet."

Marco showed us his cup; only sliced orange, apple, and lemon remained, the red wine punch gone. Part of me didn't blame him; I'd taken a sip and it'd been delicious.

The other part shook my head. He'd pay for it in the morning. Marco clapped his hands together. "Shall we promenade?"

―――

"Hey," I heard someone distantly whisper. "Hey, sweet tart, wake up."

"Mmm?" I mumbled before blinking until I clocked Marco crouched by the side of my bed. "What…time…is…it?"

"Five thirty," he answered. "I thought—"

I groaned. Five thirty meant I'd only been asleep for three hours. Connor went to bed after our walk, but Marco and I'd hung out a while longer. "Why are you here?"

"I thought you might want to see the sun rise. I tried waking Connor, but…"

"There *is* no waking Connor," I told him. "Only Connor wakes Connor." I glanced over at Carina's window and saw starlight slipping through her blinds. "But yeah, I'll come." I sat up in bed. "Give me two minutes."

There were several other people and some dogs on the beach when Marco spread out a towel for us to sit on, but they seemingly disappeared the moment the sun broke on the horizon. Blazes of red, orange, and yellow streaked across the sky, giving the clouds a heavenly glow. The ocean had never looked so blue. Marco whistled. "Best one this summer."

"This feels like a dream," I said.

"It's not," he said, flashing me a smile.

I would've taken a picture if his grin hadn't been so quick; instead, I settled for a photo of the sunrise.

"How do you not have a hangover?" I asked Marco on the walk home, sun now bright in the blue sky.

"My mom has a pineapple juice–based witch's brew that wards them off," he said. "I drank some before bed."

I wrinkled my nose. Pineapples were *not* my favorite.

Marco chuckled, and I blinked when we ran into Connor in the driveway. Red-blond hair tousled from the morning breeze, he was holding a white bakery box. BREAD AND CHEESE CUPBOARD, its orange sticker read.

"I was first in line," Connor said. "Yesterday you said you haven't had a sticky bun in a while."

I could barely do more than nod, amazed that he'd set such an early alarm. Bakery hours were not Connor waking hours.

He winked and held up the box.

I felt something blossom in my heart, and in that moment, I realized no one knew me better. Connor and me? Why had I been hesitating? We weren't Austin-and-Samira; we were Connor-and-Mads. It was so obvious, so *right*.

Do it, I told myself. *Shoot your shot!*

"I hope a dozen frosted is acceptable—shit." Connor handed the box of pastries to Marco so he could dig his chiming phone out of his pocket. "It's Lauren. I'm sorry. I should talk to her." He accepted the call, smiling a little. "Morning, Laur…"

And just as quickly as my heart leapt, it sunk and hit me all over again: I'd totally and truly blown it by procrastinating. Connor and I couldn't be together.

Because he had a freaking girlfriend.

SIXTEEN

After getting home from Stone Harbor, I texted Katie and the bridesmaids that I was ready to resume Ready-Set-Date, and they couldn't have been happier. Okay, I'm game, I'd texted our chat. Bring on the boys!

Because I needed to stop thinking about Connor.

Amanda replied first: Let's find you love!

She and her boyfriend must be doing well, I surmised.

Paige: Amazing!!!!

Courtney: I'm on the phone with a client, but I have ideas...

Yasmin: YAY

Reese: Should we have the next guy take a lie detector test and a personality assessment?

I couldn't help but laugh. I knew she was being snarky, but as someone who leaned toward the sardonic end of the spectrum, I found it part of Reese's charm.

Meredith didn't respond for a few hours, although when she did, the message read: I really think it should be the boy next door.

I sighed. He has a girlfriend right now.

Connor had literally dropped me at home before speeding off to see Lauren.

Ah, Meredith replied, like she could hear the glumness in my words. I see.

Fantastic, I thought. *She knows I like him.*

Katie's response was weirdly delayed. Could she tell I liked Connor too? She weighed in only when we moved on to other possible candidates. Courtney's dermatologist's son was a rising freshman at Villanova? He was moving into his dorm next week for football preseason, but campus wasn't that far away from me, right?

No college guys, Katie wrote, and I somehow knew she wasn't thinking of my ice-skating date with Chad, but my weekend at Princeton. She didn't want me disturbing her sleep at 2 a.m. again. Villanova was right outside Philly; if something went wrong, she knew Austin would be my first call.

It was Reese who suggested I create a profile on a dating app, and she was very quickly backed by the others. Don't use Tinder, Amanda said. These days, it's all about hookups (and there are a lot of weirdos).

Amanda, every app has weirdos, Reese pointed out.

I met my fiancé on Bumble, Courtney said. It's nice because when you match, the girl has to message the guy first. We hold all the cards.

I'm mostly on Hinge, Yasmin told me. It's geared toward people looking for a serious relationship.

Paige, Meredith, and Katie remained silent. I could picture workaholic Paige curled up on her couch, answering emails and drawing on her tablet—did that thing's battery ever die?—but were Katie and Meredith busy? I wanted their hot takes.

They were the ones who really bolstered me.

My phone buzzing brought me back to the conversation. Paige, this time. I vote Bumble, she said. Sometimes it's awkward to DM matches you like, but it helps filter out the ones you don't.

Okay, thank you! I texted when neither Katie nor Meredith chimed in, stomach a little unsettled. I'll keep you updated.

BUMBLE, Courtney emphasized.

"Bumble?" Dad said at lunch. He was sitting at the island, inhaling a BLT on sourdough toast before his 1:30 showing (Aaron and Sophie Zankman, who couldn't decide between midcentury modern or urban farmhouse). "Nope, no way." He shook his head. "Forget it."

"Why?" I asked. "I'm almost eighteen."

"Yes." Dad gave me a look. "Keyword: *almost*."

"When did this desire to date start?" Da asked casually. "You've never seemed particularly interested."

"Which is fine!" Dad quickly added. "We're just curious."

"I don't know," I said, feeling a little keyed up. "I guess..." I trailed off, unsure what to say. I didn't want to tell them the truth—my arrangement with the bridesmaids—so that left me with the *truth*-truth. "I think it'd be nice to have a boyfriend." I shrugged. "Someone to dance with at Austin's wedding."

My parents exchanged a look.

"Does our school still have that dating app?" Marco piped up from the kitchen table. He was working here today, researching something for his professor. "This girl developed it for a class, and it was really popular my senior year. Everyone was swiping on it. You need to have a Council Rock school district email address to create a profile."

Dad swallowed the last of his sandwich. "I like that. I'd much rather you bring home a high schooler than a thirty-seven-year-old from Bumble."

"Hilarious, Dad." I rolled my eyes. "Yes, it's still active," I told Marco. "I mean, I don't know how many people really use it anymore, but I can make an account."

Marco sat up straighter in his chair. "You want to do that later? I had one for a while."

Really? I thought, surprised. Marco Álvarez, who'd had girls surrounding him left and right in high school, had an online dating profile?

And wait, was he on what Reese referred to as "the apps" *now*? Would he tell me if he was hooking up with someone from Tinder? Or had met the girl of his dreams on Hinge?

As Marco's friend, I was learning that he was pretty private.

"No, thank you," I said, because I could also be private. I might've shown him Katie's bachelorette weekend dossier and revealed what color underwear I wore, but somehow this felt *more* personal than that. I winked at him, though. "I think I can handle it."

But, as it turned out, I could *not* handle it. I got about as far as entering my name before a profile picture stumped me and I decided I needed a wingman—or wingwoman. Hey, are you around today? I texted Natalie.

Tell me when and where! she replied, and I laughed. We texted regularly but hadn't seen each other in a while. Her summer had been swamped, too.

An hour later, we were camped out on Little Sunflower Bakery's patio with iced coffees and almond croissants. "Wow, holy crap," Natalie said after I filled her in on my quest for true love (or however the bridesmaids liked to frame it). Next to Marco, she was now the only person I'd told. "So that's how you and Davis happened?"

"Yes," I said. "His cousin Reese is one of Katie's bridesmaids, so she set us up."

Then I recapped my date with Chad, which involved telling her about partying at Princeton with Derek. "What a fucking creep!" she exclaimed, loud enough that coffee addicts and pastry lovers at nearby tables glanced over at us.

Both of us blushed, but soon started giggling. Natalie took my hand and squeezed it. "I'm sorry that happened to you, Mads."

"Thanks," I smiled at her. We'd become friends in the weirdest way, but somehow, it was easy between us. "It was awful, but I'm okay and have moved past it."

"Good." Natalie nodded. "Now, before we make you the best profile ever, I need to know where we stand with Connor."

"Just friends," I reported. "He's still with Lauren, and she's gotten sick of me third-wheeling them." I rolled my eyes. "But if Marco's over, we all hang out together."

Natalie slightly raised an eyebrow.

"Connor and I still hang out at night, though," I said. "Lately we've been ordering cheap Chinese and watching whatever his brother recommends on Netflix. We're starting *Emily in Paris* tonight."

"Alright, I'm not going to comment on *Emily in Paris*," Natalie said. "I don't want to spoil anything, but is it safe to say you're still pining after Connor?"

I hesitated, but eventually nodded. "I can't shake the feeling that we'd be good together, and I know it's not going to go away unless we try."

"Uh-huh." Natalie pulled off a piece of flaky croissant and popped it in her mouth. "So then let me ask you this…" She gave me a look. "If you can't stop daydreaming about Connor, why are we signing you up for this student dating app?"

Feeling my pulse speed up, I avoided answering by taking a sip of coffee.

"Is it an effort to get over Connor?" she pressed. "Or is it…?"

"Is it what?" I asked, trying to keep my voice light.

Natalie didn't buy it. "Ah, so we are pulling a Davis."

"No!" I blurted, then amended, "Yes—no. I don't know. I mean, it worked, right?"

"Yes, it got us to talk and ultimately brought us back together," Natalie agreed. "But it was messy, painful, immature, and overall, *yikes*."

"I'm not trying to make him jealous the way Davis made you jealous," I said. "I just want to see if it'll get him to notice me."

"I think the only way he's gonna notice you in a new way is if you show *direct* interest in him," Natalie said. "You've already gone out with two guys."

"I know," I said, a lump forming in my throat, "but he didn't *know* them. If I go out with someone from school, I think it'll be different."

Madeline Fisher-Michaels, you are a terrible person, the voice in the back of my head said, and I couldn't disagree. I was being pretty devious.

Natalie groaned. "Why am I helping you do this?"

"Because you love me, Nat," I said. "You also love the idea of Connor and me as a couple." I paused. "And if you don't help me, I'll end up choosing a field hockey action shot as my profile picture and not get any interest from anyone."

She laughed. "You do make some valid points," she said, reaching across the table for my phone. "Let's see what you've got…"

I ADORE THIS, Meredith commented later, once I'd sent screenshots of my dating profile to the bridesmaid group chat.

Your pictures are beautiful, and I love your answers to the icebreaker prompts. They sound just like you.

My friend helped A LOT, I texted after the others had echoed her. Because Natalie had chosen the (required) three photos that represented me best.

"Who took this?" she'd asked as she cropped a recent picture of me. "You look ridiculously happy."

"Connor, actually." I smiled at the photo of my glowing grin.

Natalie swoon-sighed. "Okay, I fully support this endeavor now. You should be together. He really brings you to life."

"Yeah, he does," I said, because it was true...even if it wasn't the case in this particular snapshot. Connor wasn't the one who'd nearly had me in tears. He'd only shouted my name so I'd turn and look at the camera. No, it was Marco who was goofing around right then. Happily drunk on his mother's sangria, he'd been singing and dancing barefoot under a Stone Harbor streetlight in an old T-shirt and cuffed jeans. Connor and I'd laughed so hard our lungs had almost given out.

Now, Yasmin texted: Katie, have you passed the Cards Against Humanity test???

I sucked in a breath. One of the prompts Natalie and I'd chosen was I'll Brag About You to My Family If...

My answer?

You beat me in Cards Against Humanity.

Not yet, Katie texted back, and then had the sheer *audacity* to add: Harry's too clever for his own good.

Come on, give me some credit! I thought, frowning at my phone screen. Granted, Dad *did* always win our games, but I usually came in second!

I exited out of Messages and swiped across my home screen to the dating app's icon. After polishing my profile, Natalie and I'd swiped together for a while; I hadn't opened up the app since. But now, I was greeted by a pop-up message: SNATCH YOUR MATCH!

My pulse leapt. Someone had liked me!

I tapped to see who it was.

Okay, I thought, smiling a little. *I can work with this.*

With Lauren constantly hanging around, there was no casual time to tell Connor my news. I didn't want it to interrupt our nightly Netflix binges, so I waited until the day of my date to give him a heads-up. We were riding Chip and Chop bareback in the far field; along with shellfish, Connor was technically allergic to horses, but he loved them too much to stay away. Zyrtec, jeans, and long-sleeve shirts mostly kept his hives at bay. "Just an FYI, I can't watch *Emily in Paris* tonight," he told me. "Lauren's been dying to go to Six Flags, so we're heading there later."

"Okay, no problem," I said, trying to keep a straight face. Because, to put it gently, amusement parks were something straight out of Connor's nightmares. After getting trapped at the top of a roller coaster for two hours when he was ten (a freak technical difficulty), he'd developed a serious fear of heights, and he hated waterslides. "I don't know what it is about chlorine..." he once said. "But it makes me so nauseous."

Our seventh-grade field trip to Six Flags water park? He lasted five minutes in the wave pool before profusely vomiting in the lazy river.

"I actually can't do tonight, either," I added. "I'm going to the movies."

"Oh," Connor said. "With the girls?"

I shook my head. Most were still on vacation.

His brow furrowed. "I thought Marco had friends from Princeton in town?"

"He does," I confirmed, then cleared my throat. "I have a date."

"Wait, a date?" Connor asked. "You have a *date*?"

I played it cool. "Yes, tonight."

"With who?"

"Jacob Bluestein."

Connor slowed Chip to a stop, and I did the same with Chop. He gave me a blank look. "I'm confused. I didn't even know you knew Blue."

"*Of course* I know Blue," I said. "He's on the wrestling team."

"Well, yeah," Connor said. "But like, you don't *know him*-know him."

"Yes, I do." I straightened my shoulders. "We matched on that dating app Isa Cruz invented and have been chatting for a week. He asked me out a few days ago."

Connor opened his mouth, then closed it. "What have you been talking about?" he eventually asked.

"Just stuff," I replied. "Our summers, sports, movies, families, how we'd never want a bird as a pet." I shrugged. "Randomness."

He slowly nodded. "That sounds good."

I smiled. "I think so."

The expression on Connor's face had twisted, making him look half perplexed, half pissed off.

Something on your mind? I wanted to say but didn't. *Are puzzle pieces fitting into place?*

Instead, I laid it on thicker. "I'm really excited."

And truthfully, I *was* excited.

"He's here!" Da called up the stairs just as I was finishing my makeup and pulling my hair into a high ponytail. I glanced out my window to see Jacob's Silverado truck park where my car usually was. He's picking you up, right? Meredith had asked, and after I'd said no, that we'd agreed to meet at the theater, Katie wrote: Unacceptable. Get him to pick you up. Tell him your car is in the shop so you need a ride.

I agree with Katie, Natalie said as my secondary consultant. Davis should've picked you up for our JProm. Show some manners, dudes.

No worries! Jacob texted back after I'd messaged him about car issues. *I'll swing by and grab you!*

He was a big fan of exclamation points.

And he was also pretty cute. Stocky and strong from wrestling, he had curly brown hair and kind hazel eyes. I liked that he'd pseudo-dressed up for tonight, wearing a short-sleeve button-down and khakis. He came to the front door, and even though his knock set off Arthur and Francine, he took it in stride—letting them push up against him for pets while my parents welcomed him. "It was really great to meet you both," he said after we talked for a few minutes. The movie started in a half hour. "I'll have her home by—"

"Ten," Da said at the same time Dad went, "Eleven."

"Twelve!" I joked.

"*Before* the clock strikes twelve," Da amended with an air of finality.

Dad shot me a look that said, *You're fairly confident in this date, aren't you?*

My stomach swished. Yes, I was, but I also had a feeling Connor would show up after he dropped Lauren off after their Six Flags date.

And I admit, I didn't want to be home.

"Ready, Mads?" Jacob asked.

"Yep." I clapped my hands together as Da grabbed the dogs' collars and tugged them away from Jacob. "Let's go!"

I blinked when we walked into the movie theater's lobby. "Tim?" I called to the guy wearing a light blue polo with a needlepointed lobster belt waiting at concessions. "Timothy Hobson-Kirby the Fourth?"

He turned toward us. His face, freckled from spending the summer on Nantucket, broke into a grin. "Hey, Mads! How've you been?"

Oh my god, I thought. *The Princetonians are here?*

"Who's that?" Jacob asked when we walked toward the snack line.

"Timothy Hobson-Kirby the Fourth," Marco's friend introduced himself, offering Jacob his hand to shake. "Pleasure to meet you."

"Jacob," he said as they shook. "Bluestein."

"Tim is a friend of Marco Álvarez's from Princeton," I explained.

"Ah, right, Marco Álvarez…" Jacob said distantly, like Marco was someone that could be forgotten. "Good guy."

"Yes, a good guy with a questionable palate," Timothy Hobson-Kirby IV said. "He plans to mix Milk Duds with his popcorn."

That sounds seriously delectable, my sweet tooth sang. *Like chocolate caramel corn.*

I glanced at the snacks that had accumulated on the counter.

A medium popcorn, Milk Duds, Sour Patch Kids, and two water bottles. "Are all four of you here?"

Timothy Hobson-Kirby IV shook his head. "No, only Marco and me. We left Simon cosplaying F. Scott at Fable—he's literally writing longhand at the bar—and Zach's not due in until the day before we leave for Stone Harbor. He's still in Florida with NASA."

I nodded. Marco had mentioned that he'd invited a bunch of Princeton people to the shore next week to celebrate the end of summer. Meanwhile, I'd be up in the Finger Lakes celebrating the future Mrs. Austin Fisher-Michaels.

But it was cool. I'd bought my pair of personality panties.

"Are you guys seeing the new Christopher Nolan?" Jacob asked, and I didn't realize how worried I was about it being the same movie until Timothy Hobson-Kirby IV confirmed it wasn't.

"I should get back in there," he said after finally paying for his food. "The trailers kicked off twenty minutes ago, so the actual film should start soon." He smiled at me. "I'll tell Marco you said hello."

"Great, thanks." I gritted my teeth. Granted, we lived near each other, but why was Marco always in the right place at the wrong time? Or the right place at the right time? These cameos of his were becoming more than a charming coincidence.

Forget about it, I told myself, listening as Jacob ordered us two separate popcorns. It felt automatic to just share a bucket like I did with Connor, but no problem. Not everyone liked sharing their food.

"I can get it," I said after ordering some peanut M&M's, and my heart warmed when Jacob shook his head.

"*I* asked *you* out," he said. "Tonight's on me."

"Thank you." I smiled but had barely glanced away before I heard Jacob swear under his breath.

"Actually, do you mind?" he asked me, motioning to the register. "I forgot my wallet."

"Oh, sure." I opened Apple Pay on my phone and tapped it against the PIN pad. "The wonders of technology," I joked awkwardly.

Jacob blushed. "I'll Venmo you."

Less than a minute later, my phone made a *cha-ching* noise.

My stomach twisted. I was cool with paying, but being immediately reimbursed didn't feel very romantic.

In the theater, we reclined our cushy chairs and talked about school being less than a month away until the lights dimmed and the trailers began. I dug into my popcorn and candy and mentally assigned each movie to a family member. Trailer one, the new Marvel? Austin. Trailer two, a family crime drama (with a luxury home as headquarters)? Dad. Trailer three, an underdog sports story? Da. Trailer four, a high-octane femme-fatale espionage flick with star-crossed lovers?

"Is everything okay?" Jacob asked as I unlocked my phone, screen glowing in the darkened theater.

"Yes, it's fine," I said, quickly tapping out a text with no hey-hi-hello whatsoever. Just: Check out the trailer for The Antihero. Looks good, right?

Maybe Ready-Set-Date wasn't the only way I could try to bridge the gap with Katie. Maybe it could be the little things, too.

I smiled at Jacob after switching my phone to the little-known "theater mode," and then casually positioned my arm on the armrest between us.

But either my date was clueless, or he wasn't interested in holding hands. Because for the first third of the movie—or halfway, I was barely paying attention—he took *zero* notice. He didn't even glance over at me!

This is painful. I ached inside as my entire right arm gradually lost all sense of feeling. It went from healthy blood flow to pins-and-needles pricks to cold and numb, completely and utterly lifeless. *Can't he take my hand before we need to amputate?*

It wasn't until a jump scare happened onscreen (I guess Christopher Nolan dabbled in horror now) that Jacob jolted and clamped his hand down on mine. Heart rate spiking, I chanced flipping my dead lobster hand over so our palms pressed together. Jacob wasted no time in lacing our fingers. "Your hand is ice-cold," he whispered.

I couldn't help but laugh. "I'm sorry."

"Don't apologize." Jacob squeezed my hand. "I'll warm it up."

┠─┼─┨

Per most Christopher Nolan films, the movie lasted around three hours. Jacob and I left our theater holding hands, but I stopped short when I saw Marco and Timothy Hobson-Kirby IV sitting on a bench nearby.

They hadn't been waiting for us, had they?

"How was it?" Marco asked once he and Jacob had nodded at each other. I swore I caught a muscle in Marco's jaw twitch.

"Mind expanding," I answered smoothly, because it sounded better than: *I already don't remember how it ended.*

"Nice," Timothy Hobson-Kirby IV said. "We're waiting for the midnight showing."

"I bet you are," Jacob muttered.

"Well, have fun!" I said brightly. "My parents love a good curfew, so we've gotta go…"

I suggested we play some music on the ride home, but Jacob asked what Marco was up to these days. "He looks like a jock pretending to be an intellectual." He shook his head. "I mean, why did he get those glasses?"

"Because he's nearsighted," I said.

Seriously, I'd die on a hill for those tortoiseshell specs.

"And he *is* an intellectual," I added, feeling a little defensive. "Even on the soccer field, he's always been smart."

"He's also always liked you," Jacob said matter-of-factly.

Something surged up my spine. "What?"

"Yeah." He chuckled and made a left-hand turn. "You never saw that?"

"Um, no," I sputtered. "The only thing to see was the harem of girls surrounding him in the cafeteria." I rolled my eyes. "And don't even get me started on this one girl at Princeton…"

Jacob, bless him, listened to me wage war on Shelly Freeman all the way home. It wasn't until we reached my neighborhood that I stopped to breathe, and that was only because he shifted his truck into park by our mailbox.

"Keep going, Blue," I joked, gesturing up my long driveway. "We still have some ground to cover."

"So you aren't interested in Marco?" Jacob asked.

I laughed. He should've been asking about Connor, not Marco! "God, no," I said. "Marco Álvarez is just a friend."

No, he's one of your best friends, I realized, and felt a swift swirl of sweetness in my core. If something happened, Marco was one of the people I wanted to tell most. Just like Austin and Connor.

"Well, good." Jacob unbuckled his seat belt. "Because I had a really great time tonight, Mads."

"Me too…" I murmured, all musings on Marco evaporating into oblivion. Jacob was leaning across the truck's center console, my heart hammering relentlessly.

This is it, I thought. *Finally, my first kiss.*

Jacob's lips were warm when they brushed mine, but before I could make a valiant attempt at kissing him back, his slick tongue slipped into my mouth so he could snake it all the way down my throat.

I hoped it would get better, but once *his* drool started spilling down *my* chin, all I could think was: *Ew.*

Ew, ew, ew.

And, for good measure, *EW!!!*

So much for a sparkling first kiss.

SEVENTEEN

With Da and Dad in Newport visiting Great-Aunt Penny, it was Austin and Connor who helped me pack the car for the Finger Lakes. Yesterday my brother had dropped Katie off at Hotel Gallant before coming home to find Connor and me marathoning the latest season of *Emily in Paris*. Connor had ended up crashing with the dogs on the couch. "Hold on there, sis," Austin said now, as I heaved my full-on I'm-ready-for-Europe-sized suitcase into the trunk (Amanda's packing list was no joke). "We need to put the cooler in first; then we'll play Tetris around it."

"Smart call," Connor said. "I think we should add one more layer of ice, though." He looked at me, hair still sleep-rumpled. "Just to top things off?"

"No, let's wait a little longer." I shook my head, then glanced down the driveway. You could see the heat burning off the pavement, but other than that, nothing. "Marco said he'd be here."

Today was Friday, and I was in charge of breakfast tomorrow—a.k.a., day one of Katie's bachelorette weekend!

Originally, I'd planned to wake up super early and make a quick run to the grocery store, but then I'd mapped our rental house and found out that the closest supermarket was an unfamiliar half-hour away. I didn't want to get up at the crack of dawn, so Austin had dreamt up a solution: Connor and I would go into town to get everything I needed for Saturday's breakfast spread. Then I would pack it all into the YETI for the trip.

The final piece of my breakfast would be a couple of quiches Marco had volunteered his mom to bake. The bridesmaids had loved them so much at the bridal shower that I thought they'd be a nice touch. He'd promised to deliver them this morning, but there was no sign of the Bumper Car.

Come on, Marco, I thought. *Please hurry.*

Because after everything was loaded into the Defender, I had to drive to Princeton to fetch the bride. You don't mind, do you? Amanda had texted me after the car pool assignments had gone live on the Google Doc. I would drive her myself, but the rest of us need to get there early to decorate…

"Mads, forget about the quiche," Austin said after a few minutes. "Kates is expecting you soon. She texted me to ask about your ETA."

Frustrated with Marco, I took it out on my brother. "Why didn't she just stay here last night?" I asked. "It's stupid that I need to drive to Princeton to get her."

Austin kept his cool. "It was easier for her to spend the

night there," he said. "There was wedding stuff to go over with her parents—"

"And you didn't need to be part of that conversation?" I gave him a look. This didn't sound like Katie and Austin's argument over my brother's say in the wedding had been resolved; it sounded like he'd just accepted that his thoughts didn't matter.

"No, not really." He shook his head. "I don't have a strong opinion on hairstylists and makeup artists for the bridal suite."

Connor cringed. "Dude, I wouldn't either."

I sighed, but my ears perked up when I heard the *hum* of a car. "I'm sorry I'm late!" Marco basically sprang out of the Bumper Car. "There was an accident, then a ton of traffic..."

"Wait, you drove up from the shore?" I asked as Connor accepted two white boxes and went to arrange them in the YETI. "You drove two hours—plus traffic—back here? Just to deliver a couple quiches?"

Marco nodded. "Yeah."

Austin whistled, impressed. "Álvarez, that's commitment."

"Believe me, I don't mind," he said, scratching his neck. I squinted to see what looked like some type of reddish-purplish blemish. "It's only been twelve hours, but the house is about to combust from so many bodies." He shook his head. "Everyone's telling war stories about their internships."

Oh, right, I realized. *Princeton Week has kicked off in Stone Harbor.*

I felt my phone buzz in my pocket—a message from Katie: Why does your location show that you're still at your house?

I rolled my eyes. Amanda had request-required everyone to sync up on Find My Friends. I'm leaving in a minute, I texted back. Is lunch packed? Or should I plan a pit stop at Burger King?

Because, after all, she'd offered to cover lunch. Katie didn't know how to drive stick, so I'd be driving the entire six hours to Seneca Lake.

My mother made us sandwiches, she replied. We also have potato chips, homemade brownies, and San Pellegrino.

Is this all packaged in a picnic basket? I joked.

Of course, she immediately responded. With china plates and cloth napkins.

I inwardly laughed a little—Katie and I'd been texting one-on-one more lately, ever since I'd sent her that female spy movie trailer. A real scheme? she'd responded. Or is it all a dream?

Connor hefted the YETI into the trunk, and then Austin shoved it to the left so they could get my luggage inside, too. Meanwhile, Marco was looking at me bemusedly.

"What?" I asked.

He shrugged. "Nothing."

"Please tell your mom thank you for the quiches," I said, sunshine scorching the back of my neck. "And thank you for being their courier."

"You're welcome," Marco said, then opened his mouth to say more, but Austin cut in between us to shake my shoulders.

"You're all set," he said. "Go grab Kates!"

"And gas," Connor added. "You need gas, remember?"

Austin groaned. "Are you serious?"

Connor's eyes flashed to mine and held my conspiratorial gaze for a moment before we dissolved into laughter. "Oh, lighten up," I told my brother as he rubbed his temples. "Don't you know me?"

I never let my gas gauge dip below a quarter of a tank.

Austin tugged my braid by way of a goodbye. "Drive safely. Stick to the speed limit."

"I'll follow the flow of traffic," I assured him, then braced myself for a football tackle from Connor.

But instead, he wrapped his arms around me and squeezed me gently—still tightly, but also, well, *tenderly*. I let myself relax into it, swallowed up by the aroma of Dove soap and laundry detergent mixed with two overly affectionate Newfoundlands as I hugged him back.

He's a good hugger, I thought. *When he wants to be, he's a* really *good hugger.*

"I'll see you in a couple days," he said quietly.

"Yeah, a couple days," I whispered, wondering if I was imagining his heart rate hurrying. "I'll be back on Monday." I pulled back, a lump in my throat. "Have a good weekend with Lauren."

He nodded, his lips twitching like he couldn't decide whether to smile or frown—like he didn't know what to think. Out of the corner of my eye, I caught Austin raise an eyebrow.

Interesting... it said.

I turned to Marco. The sun was beating down, but I swear the air grew even thicker with heat. I folded my arms across my chest, suddenly feeling awkward.

He's always liked you, Jacob Bluestein's words echoed in my ear.

Honestly, I doubted it—Marco and I'd barely known each other in high school—but he had become one of my closest friends, so I took a breath and several steps forward to wrap him in a hug, whether he was awaiting one or not.

"Thanks again," I said, smelling salt water, sand, and sunshine on his skin. *Stone Harbor*, I thought, if it were a scent. All we were missing was that magic midnight air. I closed my eyes to picture Marco drunkenly dancing under that corner streetlamp. In hindsight, that night felt like some type of fever dream. "I hope you live it up this week!"

"It's safe to say some of us will," he replied, squeezing me back. The blood pumping through my veins amplified when he touched his lips to the tip of my ear. "Don't let them rile you up," he whispered. "Just have fun."

I distantly heard myself murmur that I'd try to keep my cool.

Although with a line of sweat trickling down my spine, I suspected it wouldn't be so simple.

⊢—⊢—⊣

Driving Miss Katie.

What could I say about driving Miss Katie?

Of course, the in-person conversation was never scintillating, but I knew I had to shoot for some small talk before I proposed a playlist, podcast, or audiobook. "Are you excited?" was my riveting opening line once we were on the road (which took a hot minute, because Katie had two suitcases and a trio of tote bags).

She grimaced when we popped over a pothole. "Would you mind keeping both hands on the wheel?"

"Oh, yeah, sure." I repositioned my hands at ten and two. Driving the Defender was second nature to me, so I usually just drove with my left hand while my right played with a fidget toy from my cupholder. But I admit, as I caught Katie reach for the car's safety strap, riding in the Defender was an *experience*. My history professor grandfather used to say that it could be as bumpy as a World War II B-17 bomber plane. "You've been in this car before, haven't you?" I asked.

"Only once," she answered. "Austin took me for a short ride a few years ago, when you were in Florida for a showcase. He's very respectful about this being your car."

Warmth filled my heart. "He wasn't too thrilled when Grandpa gave it to me. I didn't even have my license yet, only my permit."

"He mentioned that."

She didn't elaborate.

"There are a pair of sea bands in the glove compartment," I said when Katie didn't look any more comfortable. "They really help with car sickness."

"I'm not carsick," she said, but rifled around for the wristbands anyway. "You're just driving too aggressively."

I tried not to sigh. We'd been on the highway all of fifteen minutes.

"Do you want to listen to something?" I asked after a while of nothing but wishing I hadn't put the Defender's soft top back on this morning. It was a beautiful summer day, and I wanted to feel the wind in my face and whip through my hair while I blasted my pump-up playlist. "You can scroll through my Spotify, or I have *Rules of Civility* on Audible. It's by the same author as *A Gentleman In Moscow*—"

"No thanks," she cut in. "I've read *Rules of Civility* twice."

"Okay," I said quietly.

Why was this so hard?

"Yes, I'm excited," Katie said, as if starting our conversation over. "I've been to three bachelorettes this summer, and they've all been absurdly over-the-top in cities that never sleep. I mean, we had to do this ridiculous scavenger hunt in Nashville for my one friend..." She trailed off. "Anyway, I'm glad this weekend is going to be more relaxed."

"Amanda said it's going to be super chill," I confirmed, even though the Google Doc didn't make it seem that way. Everything, right down to our outfits, was planned.

Katie nodded, but before I could resume staring dead eyed out the windshield, she asked how things were going with online dating. "Are you still talking to Jacob?"

I tried not to make a face. Katie wanted to know how my journey to true love was going? It truly seemed like her interest and enthusiasm had timed out of Ready-Set-Date, which honestly felt like a cut each time she ignored updates. She hadn't commented when I'd texted the bridesmaids after the movies. This just in… I'd written, eager to entertain. We had a really great time!

Yasmin responded first: Did you guys kiss?!

I teased them with a smirking emoji.

Meredith's message stuck out among the cheering others. How was it? she asked. Swiftian?

If only, I wrote, having discovered ages ago that Meredith was a Swiftie. We'd traded friendship bracelets.

I wouldn't worry, Paige said after I'd elaborated. My first boyfriend wasn't a good kisser at first either. It takes some practice!

Paige Cavanaugh, did you even read her message? Reese texted. She compared kissing him to a St. Bernard slobbering on her! She used the word "drool."

We've all been there… Courtney wrote.

The consensus was that first kisses weren't everything, and that if I'd genuinely had fun with Jacob, I should dismiss our kiss as a fluke and give him another shot. "Yeah, we're still talking," I told Katie now. "He asked me out again for this weekend, but obviously I said no. I think I'll ask him to get pizza and ice cream or something when I'm back. I just don't..." I trailed off to ease up on the Defender's clutch pedal and grab the gear stick so I could shift.

"You just don't what?" she asked when I had both hands back on the wheel.

I shrugged. "I just don't know if I like him enough to kiss him again. Okay, sure, first kisses aren't like the ones in the movies, but this was seriously gross."

"I'd friend-zone him then," Katie said, unscrewing the cap of her water bottle. She took a sip. "What's the point of going on another date if you know he's your frog and not your prince?"

Because Connor hasn't cut ties with Lauren yet, my Machiavellian mind thought. I wasn't actively trying to break them up, but if Lauren got frustrated with Connor when he included me in their plans—her pout–silent treatment combo was right on point—or if Connor kept making a face whenever he asked who I was texting, then fine.

Fine, fine—totally fine!

"Friend-zone him," Katie repeated, "and match with someone else until Connor figures out you swimming around in the dating pool bothers him."

My eyes widened, and not because anything was happening on the road. "What?" I blurted. "How do you know about Connor and me?"

The answer was the most obvious answer in the world, but

it didn't fully connect until Katie said my brother's name. "He thinks you guys could be amazing together," she said as my face reddened. I couldn't be upset with Austin; Katie was his fiancée, the peanut butter to his jelly, the star to his burst. Why wouldn't he tell her his hopes and dreams and fears and family updates?

Plus, he hadn't violated my trust in any way. Wanting Connor and me to be together wasn't the same as saying that I had a crush on Connor.

But it was a little embarrassing.

"Austin's a huge fan of friends-to-lovers," Katie continued. "He told Paige it's his favorite trope."

Her voice had quieted a little, and I wondered if she was thinking of Samira—of Austin and Samira, and their friends-to-lovers-to-friends relationship. I knew Katie didn't like Samira, but did she feel *threatened* by her? Was she, too, secretly wondering if Austin would wake up one day and realize he wanted to be with his best friend again?

No, I blinked the thought away. No, there was no way. She was the one with the ring on her finger.

"Hey, you want to hear something weird?" I asked, to change the subject.

Katie agreed, but out of the corner of my eye, I saw her admiring her French manicure. I was losing her. A podcast was imminent if this didn't pique her interest.

"Okay, get this," I said. "Besides none of my dates advancing to a second date, they've all had something else in common…"

"Mmm? What's that?"

I licked my lips, the two ready-and-waiting words almost ticklish, then said: "Marco Álvarez."

Katie's eyes snapped up from assessing her nails. Finally, I'd hooked her! "Wait, what?" she asked. "You talk about Marco on every date?"

"No." I shook my head. "Marco has *been* on every date."

Finally, after two bathroom breaks, spurts of inexplicable traffic, a missed exit, *and* a wrong turn, Waze told me to turn onto a private paved road leading into the woods. It went uphill, so I shifted into first gear while Katie basically pressed her face against the window like a little kid. "Wow," she breathed when the thick trees opened up to reveal a rambling mansion, three stories of beige stucco, soaring white columns, and every window style imaginable. "What would you list this as?" I'd asked Dad after showing my parents the house online. "It looks vaguely French country meets Craftsman? Right?"

Da had spoken first. "I don't know, but I'd market it as *The Great Gatsby* meets lake life."

Katie burst from the Defender the second I put it in park and didn't bother waiting for me. "No worries!" I said once she'd slammed the passenger door shut and taken off for the house. "I'll get the luggage…"

Big balloons had been arranged on the front porch, metallic gold letters spelling out WELCOME KATIE! along with the ubiquitous diamond ring mylar balloon. Determined to carry a hundred things all at once, I gritted my teeth and pushed through the strings of pearlescent beads that had been hung in the front doorway. "Oh, Mads, perfect!" Amanda said after I literally tripped into the enormous foyer. "These are Katie's things, right?"

I nodded slowly, too busy taking in the cathedral ceiling, arched windows, and crystal chandelier.

"I'll take them," Amanda continued, gesturing to the gleaming wood staircase. "I sent her up to find her room and so she can change."

Katie had multiple outfits for this weekend, all of them predictably white. Tonight's was a simple athleisure two-piece set that the bridesmaids had chipped in on as a surprise gift.

"You should hurry and change too," Amanda told me. "The chips-and-salsa spread is almost ready. Courtney is making her famous guac and Reese is gonna mix margs."

"Sounds good," I said. Just like Katie, the bridesmaids had assigned outfits for the weekend—or coordinating outfits. Tonight, I was supposed to wear black and pink.

Upstairs, a silver star with my name in metallic purple puffy paint had been posted on a door that opened into a small cozy bedroom. My custom T-shirt was waiting for me.

And the T-shirt wasn't the only welcome gift left on the

room's twin bed. "This is no joke," I murmured, spotting a shiny gold-sequined fanny pack. SQUAD was stitched across the front in black lettering. I unzipped it to find what I assumed was this weekend's survival kit, which included everything from Altoids to throwback soda–flavored lip balm to packets of Liquid IV powder to a pair of heart-shaped red sunglasses.

After changing into black gym shorts and my light pink KATIE'S LAST SPLASH shirt, I followed the chorus of voices downstairs to the kitchen. The bridesmaids were gathered around the marble waterfall island, everyone in their matching bachelorette T-shirts and chipping-and-dipping while sipping margaritas.

"You are so specific about your salt rims!" Reese said to Katie, who was sitting on the island and glowing in her crop top and biker shorts with a BRIDE-TO-BE sash and tiara. "Mads!" Reese called. "How serious do you want your salt rim?" She held up the bride's glass, whose rim was heavily coated with pink Himalayan salt. "On a scale from one to Katie?"

I swallowed. My parents had told me I could drink a little this weekend, but I wasn't really feeling it tonight. "Give her a chance to hydrate first, Reese!" Meredith said, as if reading my mind. She appeared out of nowhere, wearing what looked like an XL T-shirt. The hemline almost reached her knees. I'd learned that Austin affectionately called her "Tink," and I couldn't say he was off base. She did look like a little fairy with her sun-streaked hair in a topknot and gold ankle bracelets.

"How strong are Reese's margaritas?" I asked after she handed me a bottle of water.

"Strong enough that I'll confiscate your keys if you drink one," she replied, then shifted from one foot to the other. "Actually, I'm going to confiscate your keys no matter what."

I almost laughed. *Where am I going to go? We're in the middle of nowhere!*

"I'll go grab them," I told Meredith. "They're upstairs in my backpack."

"I appreciate it," she said kindly, but her expression was solemn. Remembering Austin telling me about Meredith's sister dying in a drunk driving accident, I suddenly was overcome with the urge to hug her. She squeezed me back when I did. "Just chuck them with everyone else's in Yaz's and my room…"

Later, Paige was properly booed as she preheated the double ovens for the six frozen pizzas she'd supplied for dinner. She took it in stride. "What do you want from me? You guys know I don't cook!"

We brought our dinner and a couple bottles of rosé out back to eat, and the second I stepped onto the deck, I understood why we'd splurged on this house. The property was idyllic, with a grassy-green lawn and pebbled beachfront, and beyond that was nothing but the seemingly endless and stunning Seneca Lake. A dock stretched out into the glistening blue-green water, complete with lounge chairs, kayaks, and paddleboards. My heart leapt. I'd always wanted to try paddleboarding.

Everyone was a little tipsy by the time the sun set and the pizza had been polished off, so there was a lot of giggling as Amanda directed us toward another patio across the lawn. It had a sheltered outdoor kitchen, where Paige was redeeming herself by setting up a make-your-own-ice-cream-sundae station. A white tarp had been mysteriously strung up, but it made more sense when Amanda flicked on a projector. "This weekend is all about our sweet Katie," she said once we'd settled on the couches with our sundaes. "Tonight, we're relaxing with some of her favorites…" She took a bite of her banana split. "And tomorrow evening, we'll get down to business." She wiggled her eyebrows suggestively as Meredith whistled and Reese went, "Ow, ow!"

A wave of relief washed through me. Dinner had been fun, but I wasn't prepared for any games tonight. It had been a long day of driving, and the one glass of rosé I'd been nursing hadn't exactly loosened me up enough to find out Katie and Austin's favorite sex position.

Ew, I cringed, even though my salted caramel sundae was delicious. Details about my brother's sex life were pieces of knowledge I *never* needed to acquire.

Amanda soon hit play on Katie's favorite wedding-themed movie: *The Hangover*. Courtney groaned. "Katie, you are so *weird*. This is so not a wedding movie!"

"I told her the same thing," Amanda said after Katie shushed her cousin. "I made her agree to a double feature. The next pick is way better."

Bleh, I thought, predicting something like *Wedding Crashers* or *Bridesmaids* was on deck. I'd never seen Katie watch an honest-to-god romantic comedy. They weren't my favorite, either, but sometimes I wanted a guaranteed happily ever after.

Especially when it came to weddings.

I remembered Meredith taking the video and later texting it to me, but I must've been so tired that I didn't really recall sending it to other people. Per its 12:13 a.m. timestamp, I'd dropped it like a bomb in several text threads, and when my alarm went off the next morning, I saw a handful of notifications. Mortified, I felt my cheeks burst into flame.

YOU ARE AMAZING, Natalie had replied, and Connor: How drunk are you?

My club field hockey group chat—twenty girls total—was going absolutely wild with emojis and GIFs, so I didn't do more than skim their messages. Instead, I tapped into the Good Genes thread. Funny, Dad had written, I was under the impression you were celebrating Katie's bachelorette?

Dad had the most acerbic texts.

A girl only has a brief window to connect to this song, Da said. I forgive you.

I tapped on the video, only to be treated to thirty seconds of myself singing and dancing along to ABBA's "Dancing Queen."

Katie's second movie selection had surprisingly been *Mamma Mia!* Her fake rhinestone-encrusted tiara had somehow ended up on my head, and there I was, standing on the outdoor kitchen's island and showing off my moves. Shimmying my shoulders, shaking my hips, and even attempting some gymnastics.

It was quality content, but...

Why the hell did I send this to my family?! I thought while watching myself inappropriately running my hands along my body.

I promise I wasn't drunk! I quickly texted my parents. Ice cream sundae sober. Literally.

Oh, we know, Dad replied. You never would've pulled off that handstand otherwise.

Just be careful, Da added. No more attempts to steal Katie's thunder...

"I wasn't—" I grumbled but cut myself off when I glanced at the nightstand's alarm clock. Shit, 8:30. I had to roll out my breakfast spread.

Meredith, thankfully, was the only one awake. She stood at the counter, not eating but dumping Italian dressing into a gallon-sized ziplock bag. "Good morning," I said.

"Good morning, dancing queen!" She smirked when I rolled my eyes. "I'll be out of your way in a second. I'm just marinating the London broil for tonight." She nodded at the huge slab of steak on the counter as she added some salt, pepper, and herbs to the marinade. Dijon mustard for the finishing touch.

"Isn't Reese a vegetarian?" I asked after she'd sealed the meat in the bag and stored it in the fridge. There had been a DIETARY RESTRICTIONS section in the dossier. Someone—Courtney?—had a peanut allergy.

"She'll be fine," Meredith said. "I'm making a salad, and there are plenty of side dishes on tonight's menu." She clapped her hands. "What can I do to help with breakfast?"

I shook my head. I wanted to channel my inner host; I wanted to channel Da. "Nothing," I told her. "I've got this."

First, I preheated the oven to warm up the Álvarez quiches and then queued up the coffee maker to brew twelve cups before washing the berries for my fruit salad. By the time Katie and the others wandered downstairs, the quiches were cooling and I'd finished setting up the bagel station. "Oh, Mads, this looks amazing!" Yasmin exclaimed.

Paige winced, clearly hungover.

"Doesn't it?" Amanda said, slathering strawberry cream cheese on a poppy seed bagel. "It'll totally fortify us for the day."

I noticed Katie hadn't said anything and didn't seem interested in any of the food. She'd grabbed a plain Chobani and a small plate of fruit before joining Meredith in the breakfast nook. Everyone else had said thank you; she didn't.

Is Katie mad at me? I texted Austin after reporting to Good Genes that breakfast hadn't been an epic failure. For my dance last night?

Because if she was, that honestly wasn't fair. I remembered

her bequeathing me her tiara, thus giving her blessing to dance my ass off. She might've even *smiled* at me.

Austin: All she said was you guys had a fun night!

Somewhat relieved, I sent back a thumbs-up emoji and told myself I would chill today. Taking a back seat would be easier since we were scheduled to visit five vineyards, all of which would take one look at my driver's license and shake their heads.

The uniform for the wine trail was a "classy bustier top and jeans," so I pulled on those along with sandals and my new bridesmaid swag. As if scripted, the seven of us gathered in the foyer before Katie descended the staircase. She was a vision in a lacy white sundress and wedges. She too had a fanny pack, except hers was white sequins and said BRIDE in gold stitching. Her pair of heart-shaped sunglasses was also white. Her bright cherry lipstick coordinated with our red glasses. "How do I look?" she asked.

Our cheers bounced off the foyer's walls, and from there, we piled into our rented party bus. Our fearless driver had decorated it with streamers and immediately offered Amanda full control of the aux cord. The "Bachelorette Bangerz" Spotify playlist we'd collaborated on was blasting before we'd even made it out of the driveway.

People settled in their seats after the first couple of songs. From my spot in the way back, I fished my phone out of my fanny pack to look at my text thread with yet another "Dancing

Queen" video recipient. I only had one glass of rosé, I'd written, but this movie makes me feel some type of way...

You're cruel, Marco had replied.

That's it.

You're cruel.

Two words.

Two words, and I had no idea what he meant by them. Did he also think I was stealing Katie's spotlight? Or that my dancing was so terrible that I was disrespecting ABBA?

I didn't realize how long I'd been contemplating a response until Amanda silenced Beyoncé and shouted, "We're here!"

The sun blazed in the sky, and Courtney reminded us that we had travel-sized sunscreen in our SQUAD packs. I was impressed; they'd really thought of everything.

"Mads, why don't you save us a table over there?" Amanda suggested, gesturing to Rose Hill Vineyard's flagstone patio. "While we go in and get flights?"

"Oh, okay," I said, wondering a.) what a "flight" was, and b.) if they were embarrassed to have me with them. The house was one place, but a drinking establishment was another. It wasn't like I was going to scandalize them by trying to flash my ID!

"I'll help Mads hold down the fort," Meredith announced. "Katie, I'll have whatever you're having." She looked to Yasmin. "Order some pitchers of water, too."

"Absolutely, Mom," Amanda deadpanned, and I had to

swallow a laugh when Meredith flipped her the bird after she led the rest of the group inside the building.

"I love Amanda," Meredith told me. She laughed. "I really do, but she has to realize this is a marathon, not a sprint."

We chose an oblong wood table under an umbrella, and before I knew it, I asked Meredith if Katie was upset with me. "She didn't talk to me at breakfast," I said. "Was my dance last night too much?"

"No, don't worry." Meredith shook her head and smiled. "She told me before bed that she thought the dance was hilarious." She paused. "She's just worn out, Mads. She's working really hard for a promotion at work, gone on multiple bachelorette trips this summer, which are honestly exhausting, and wedding planning is *a lot*." She laughed. "Part of why I eloped was because I didn't need that kind of stress."

Oh, wow, I thought. I'd had no idea Katie had so much on her plate. Could that explain why she wasn't a regular participant in Ready-Set-Date conversations?

Meredith sighed. "I hope she unwinds this weekend."

"Yeah, me too," I whispered before asking where she and Wit planned to move in the fall.

Fifteen minutes later, Katie and the bridesmaids emerged outside carrying individual trays of wine. They had two Rose Hill staff members in tow with two icy pitchers and water glasses. "Thank you so much," Katie said graciously, and slipped them both tips.

It turned out a "flight" was basically a selection of wine samples. Each tray had six mini stemless wine glasses; three were filled with white wine, and three filled with red. Reese proposed filming our first and last drinks of the day, to compile into an Instagram Reel.

Reese was above TikTok.

Katie volunteered to go first. "I'm Katie, the bride," she said luminously, and held up her baby glass of sauvignon blanc. "And this is my first drink of the day!"

"To Katie!" the table toasted as she took a sip.

When it was my turn, Reese offered me a little glass of red. I accepted.

"I'm Mads," I said, "I'm a bridesmaid, and this is my first drink of the day…"

EIGHTEEN

Everyone had a nice buzz going by the time our bus dropped us off, five wineries and a wine slushie stand later, at 5:00. Well, everyone but me. Reese's wine had been the only time alcohol had touched my lips today. During our formal wine tasting at the gorgeous chateau Domaine LeSeurre—*Dad would love this place*, I kept thinking—I'd stood with the group, but was not served anything but sparkling water. Katie had left with an extremely expensive case of Riesling. "Mom's sixtieth is coming up, remember?" she'd told her sister.

Amanda sent a mostly sobered-up Katie upstairs to take a leisurely bath while the rest of us were given fifteen minutes to change into our assigned animal-print pajamas. Ironically, my PJs were tiger striped. "Fucking Princeton," I muttered before snapping a selfie. I'd texted Connor a couple pictures throughout the day, but all he'd done was heart them; I felt a pang in my chest, knowing he was busy with Lauren.

I sent the tiger pajama selfie of myself to the Princetonians, and Simon, Zach, and Timothy Hobson-Kirby IV all liked the photo. Marco didn't acknowledge it. Savage! Zach wrote. Who picked those for you?

Truthfully, I didn't know.

Downstairs, everyone had been put to work. The family room had been decorated when Katie and I'd arrived yesterday: gold, silver, and white streamers artfully arranged with signs that said things like SHE FOUND HER LOVER (KATIE'S VERSION) and I CAN'T TALK RIGHT NOW, I'M DOING BACHELORETTE SHIT and POP THE BUBBLY, SHE'S GETTING A HUBBY!

(The last one mystified me; I'd read it so many times yet still didn't understand how it even remotely rhymed.)

Paige was sprucing up the family room with embarrassing-bordering-on-blackmail photos of Katie asleep through the years while Reese and Yasmin strung up a clothesline to hang up our personality panties. In the end, I'd gone a sardonic route with pink boy shorts featuring a "Little Miss" meme: LITTLE MISS CRIES OVER SOMEONE SHE NEVER DATED.

Even I had to admit it was on point.

In the kitchen, Meredith was prepping dinner in a sleep set covered in foxes and a zebra-print Courtney was pouring predinner cocktails. "Would you like something?" she asked after handing Meredith an Aperol spritz.

"Yes, please," I said, because to be honest, I'd really felt the FOMO today. I couldn't do anything about only being seventeen (nearly eighteen!), but now we were back at the house. No one was going to card me, and my parents said I could indulge. Everything would be fine.

"Pick your poison," Courtney said. "I bartended in grad school."

"Whiskey sour," I said. It was one of Dad's favorites.

Courtney nodded. "Coming right up!"

I waited, excited, and grinned when Courtney garnished the cocktail with an orange wheel and cherry. The first sip of the caramel-colored drink was glorious, refreshing and punch-packing. It tasted like the last sunset of summer: wonderfully bittersweet.

Meredith's dinner was freaking delicious. Not only was the London broil marinated and grilled to perfection, but she'd also tossed a green salad and made a huge tomato and mozzarella platter with basil and balsamic dressing drizzled on top. And then, there was her corn salad with sliced radishes and jalapeños—simple, but *incredible*. "I wish I could marry you, Meredith," Paige said. "Do you cook for Wit like this every night?"

Meredith smirked, eyes shining. "Cooking is one of my love languages."

The rest of us groaned, partly because we were in food comas and partly because we were super jealous of Meredith's husband.

We'd switched to red wine for dinner, but cocktails and rosé from our seemingly endless supply returned for the festivities. I still felt totally with it, but an unfamiliar sense of warmth had spread through my entire body. "Okay, ladies!" Amanda said once we'd all gathered in the living room. Meredith had set up a cute dessert spread on the coffee table. "Tonight, we are going to start with a game from Katie's past!"

"Yes, I will jump into the lake naked," I said through a cupcake.

Amanda laughed. "I appreciate your enthusiasm, Mads, but this isn't truth or dare." She turned to her sister, dressed in a swan-print nightgown with white feather boa and sleeping mask. "Katie, do you remember Kiss-Marry-Kill?"

Katie took a sip of Whispering Angel. "I always wanted to marry Nick Jonas."

"Can we change it to *Fuck*-Marry-Kill?" Reese asked. "We're adults now."

The maid of honor had us vote. Surprisingly, Kiss-Marry-Kill won. "Katie, you're up first." Amanda smiled mischievously, then waved to the girls. "Three names."

"Austin," Yasmin said.

Katie beamed.

"Nick Jonas," Paige added.

Everyone laughed as Katie blushed.

"And Charlie Carmichael," Reese said.

"Well, the last one is easy," Katie said. "I would kill Charlie Carmichael."

Amanda and Meredith groaned. "Here we go…" Amanda muttered before taking a long sip of her gin-and-tonic.

"Who's Charlie Carmichael?" I asked.

"One of my friends from boarding school," Reese answered. "Katie met him at a party our junior year. He's that lethal combination of charismatic flirt meets excellent listener. He asked for Katie's number then ghosted her."

Rude! I thought.

"Kiss?" Courtney prompted.

Katie hesitated, caught between her future husband and her celebrity crush. "Kiss Nick," she eventually said. "And marry Austin."

We toasted her.

"Okay, Mer, you're up," Amanda said.

Meredith went *bang, bang, bang* once we threw three names at her. Kiss? Timothée Chalamet. Marry? Seth Meyers. Kill? Tamlin, High Lord of the Spring Court.

Then it was my turn.

"Girls, I've got this." Reese put up a hand before turning to me. "The kid who drooled all over you, the boy next door, and the hot guy washing dishes at the engagement party."

"Marco," Katie translated.

My stomach swished. "Where's my celebrity option?"

Reese shook her head. "Not a requirement."

"Umm," I said. "I'd kill Jacob, but no hard feelings."

The group nodded in agreement, and Yasmin quickly pressed for my one-time kiss.

A name flashed in front of my eyes…but it wasn't Connor

McCallister's. Blood thumped through my ears, so intensely that I could barely hear myself think. *Marco*, my mind murmured. *Marco, Marco, Marco.*

Holy shit.

Did I *like* Marco Álvarez? As more than a friend? Or, like, whatever we were?

Friend suddenly sounded wrong.

The bridesmaids squealed after I said I'd marry Connor.

"We'll help you!" Amanda exclaimed. I noticed her speaking voice grew louder and more enthusiastic with every drink. "Oh my god, we can totally make this happen—"

Katie cleared her throat. "Paige, your turn," she said before draining her drink and gesturing at her empty glass. Yasmin dutifully poured her more rosé.

I had selective listening for the rest of the game, and by *selective listening*, I meant I did no listening whatsoever. Instead, I stared at the stone fireplace and replayed this summer in my head. Marco and me, both slick with sweat as we played field hockey on my front lawn—the way he'd tossed me over his shoulder and how fast my heart had raced as I clung to him, the way my body had buzzed. Marco and me, sitting on the porch—him working on his cryptic novel while I read *This Side of Paradise*. Marco and me in Stone Harbor, the two of us waking up before the stars stopped twinkling so we could watch the sunrise on the beach.

And all the hours we had spent together in the Garden.

More writing, more reading, but so much talking and laughing. I closed my eyes to imagine what things would be like if our relationship was different. Marco slipping through the garden gate, but instead of just zapping my waist hello before settling in his usual chair, I'd stick out my foot so he'd trip over and I could catch him for a kiss. *You're cruel*, I imagined him whispering before taking my face in his hands and kissing me back.

The daydream made me ache.

"Hey, are you okay?" Someone waved their hand in front of my face. "Mads?"

I blinked to see Meredith. "Yes," I blurted. "Yes, I'm fine!"

"Good, because it's time for Prosecco Pong," Reese said. "Are you in or out?"

"Totally in," I said. "I'm just gonna run to the bathroom…"

Is Marco alive?! I texted the Princetonians after locking the powder room door behind me.

Yes, alive and thriving, Marco replied, and I felt like a moron for forgetting that he himself was in this chat. What's up?

What's up? I thought. *WHAT'S UP?!*

"You've been ignoring me all day," I muttered as Timothy Hobson-Kirby IV texted: Can we get a play-by-play of the panty game?

Sorry, Marco told us, Zach said.

Simon: But he was under duress.

Their words blurred together a little, so I had to really focus when typing back: We're about to play beer pong, but with champers. Any and all tips appreciated...

Marco privately texted me as the Princetonians poured pointers into our chat: You okay?

I didn't respond; I didn't know what to say.

A few minutes later, he tried again: How is it?

Miserable, I told him, then changed my mind. Magical.

I wanted to scream, I wanted to cry, I wanted to throw up. But most of all, I wanted to hear his voice.

Never had I ever imagined Amanda Gallant and I would have a signature handshake, but we made one up about a half hour into Prosecco Pong (it ended with our fists exploding into fireworks). We trounced Yasmin and Meredith, and now were pretty much decimating Katie and Reese. "Drink!" Amanda shouted after I elegantly landed a hot pink Ping-Pong ball into a plastic champagne glass. Reese gave us the middle finger while steadying the bride so Katie could down the prosecco. I'd noticed she was starting to sway.

"New partners!" Courtney said in a crisp British accent after Amanda and I had bested everyone. (Apparently, she adopted a different nationality every time she got drunk.)

And like the ultracompetitive jock I was, I shouted Paige's name, but giggly Yasmin grabbed my arm before Katie's cousin and I could make confirmative eye contact.

That's when I tasted revenge. "Do you have *any* hand-eye coordination?" I asked Yasmin.

"Nope, none." She smiled. "My law firm's softball team cut me!"

We fell into a fit of laughter; I soon felt tears pricking the corner of my eyes.

Across the pong table, Katie snickered. She and Paige were beating us so badly that she'd taken to drinking a non-gameplay glass of rosé. It was her move. "It ends here," she said. "Right here, right *now*."

She sunk the ball at center court.

I picked up the plastic glass and let the bubbles burn down my throat, then fizzle in my stomach. Yasmin hugged me for my service.

Katie made eye contact with me. "Next round?"

"Totally." I nodded, then pointed at Paige. "Partners?"

The Bride folded her arms over her chest, but didn't say anything.

Once Amanda had been crowned Prosecco Pong Champion of the Lake, it was time for Katie to guess whose panties were whose. "Hey." Meredith lightly touched my arm as the others moved toward the clothesline. "How are you?"

"Thriving," I told her. "Why?"

She gave me a look. "I know I'm not Harry or Lee," she said quietly, "and I know I'm not Austin." She paused. "But I *am* looking out for you, Mads, and I think you should call it a night."

I stared at her, incredulous. "Call it a night? Like, go to bed?"

"No, I mean with the drinking." She gestured to the frozen daiquiri Reese had handed me. Courtney had the blender going in the kitchen. "You've had *a lot* to drink."

"Yeah, so has everyone," I said, the back of my neck warming. "Katie's drunk like ten times her weight in Whispering Angel and Summer Water and Bouquet of Roses and whatever other rosé we have."

"I know," Meredith said calmly. "But you're—"

"God, what is the problem?" someone asked, and I turned to see Katie behind us. Her face was bright pink and her lips pursed; she looked pissed.

"Mads and I were just talking, Katie," Meredith answered smoothly. "There's no problem."

"Yes, there is," she said, but was looking at me instead of Meredith. Or *glaring* at me, more like. "What is *wrong* with you?"

"Me?" My eyebrows knitted together. Maybe Meredith was right; maybe it *was* time to tap out, because I had no idea what Katie was referencing. Had I been too intense during Prosecco Pong?

"This is *my* bachelorette," Katie said, a catch in her voice. "And you are talking to literally everyone except me."

Oh my god, I thought. *She's jealous I'm stealing her spotlight?*

I knew the right thing to do was apologize. "Okay, I'm so sorry, I didn't realize I was being an attention whore."

"No, it's not that." She shook her head, and her expression twisted like she couldn't articulate what she meant. I glanced at Meredith, but not only had she backed away; she'd also shuttled the other bridesmaids into the kitchen, knowing they didn't belong in whatever this "conversation" was. "These are my friends," Katie said. "And you're bonding with them."

"I'm trying my best, yeah," I told her. "Being a high schooler in a group of twentysomethings isn't my natural environment, but I'm trying, Katie."

"Well, you're not trying hard enough!" Katie screeched, and it felt like she'd slapped me in the fucking face.

So I bit back; in fact, I might've even sunken my teeth into her. "I could say the same about you," I said, trying to keep my voice somewhat level. "You don't make me feel welcome or included at all—you barely spoke to me on the drive up here, you spoke to me even less today—even though you asked me to be your freaking bridesmaid!"

Tears swam in Katie's eyes, but her lips didn't quiver. They curled into a sneer. "I don't regret asking you to be a bridesmaid," she said. "You're Austin's sister."

"And I don't regret accepting," I said, even though I totally did right now. "It was the right thing to do, but I never should've let myself sink so deep to please you." I folded my arms across my chest. "I agreed to Ready-Set-Date because I naively thought that even if no guy grew to like me, the bride would." I forced myself to laugh. "My mistake."

"And mine," Katie said, her face as white as her nightdress. "Because I thought asking Marco to keep an eye on you would have a happier ending."

Wait, what? I froze. *Did Katie ask Marco to* chaperone *me this summer?*

She'd seemed shocked yesterday when I'd told her about his guest appearances in my dating life.

But it was too late to clarify; in the span of five seconds, Katie had dry-heaved before spinning around and fleeing for the bathroom.

Heart suddenly hammering and alcohol twisting and twirling through my veins, I *needed* to get out of the house. No one chased after me, too busy crowded outside the bathroom, where Meredith was probably holding Katie's long hair back as she purged her soul of all her sins. My guess was it would be a while.

We'd been having too much fun to notice the downpour happening outside, but I let myself get soaked as I unlatched the Defender's trunk and climbed into the back of the car. Heavy raindrops pounded against the soft roof, and I was woozy after heaving myself over the back seat. *You are drunk*, I thought. *Soooooo drunk.*

Hands shaking, I pulled my phone from my pocket and fumbled to unlock it. I had several messages from Marco, but he'd accidentally switched to his Spanish keyboard.

Spanish wasn't my top subject, and I didn't have enough control over my fingers to tap a text back, so I called him. "Hello?"

he picked up on the fourth ring, voice breathless like he'd raced to catch me. "Mads?"

I opened my mouth; not even a hiccup came out.

"Mads, are you there?" he asked, and when I didn't respond, he said, "I don't know if you've seen my texts or been on Instagram tonight, but—"

"It's you!" I shouted over the rain. "Marco, it's *you*!"

And…nothing.

Nothing.

Nothing.

The line was silent long enough for salty tears to spill from my eyes.

"It's me?" Marco eventually whispered, and I could hear the wince in his voice—a wince that told me he understood. I had a crush on him, one so massive it amazingly hadn't hit me until now.

"Yes," I said, then tried swallowing the sudden lump in my throat, wishing I could take the words back.

Because my confession had sealed our fate.

NINETEEN

I woke up early the next morning, convinced that an anvil had fallen on my head because it hurt so badly. My eyes were red-rimmed and puffy from crying myself to sleep, and it felt like someone was stirring sludge in my stomach.

I decided to pack up my stuff and head home, using my spare set of keys since Meredith still had mine. About an hour into the drive, I felt so nauseous that I had to pull over on the side of the highway to blow some chunks. Where was Rose Álvarez's magic preventive hangover potion when I needed it?

Then, I called my parents. They were furious that I'd left with such a hangover.

And somehow, they beat me home from Newport. "We're going to discuss this *at length*," Dad emphasized. "But first, you need to drink about a gallon of Gatorade and then get to bed…"

I slept for fourteen hours but felt sick all over again when Reese sent the bridesmaid chat a compiled video of everyone's first and last Saturday drink. I watched myself, all sunshine and smiles, take a sip of wine before the clip cut to that night. Reese had caught me in the kitchen, soaked from the rain. I looked *rough*. "Yeah, I'm Mads," I said, tipping melted daiquiri over the sink. "You know I'm a bridesmaid, and I'm *dumping* my final drink of this super enlightening evening."

Meredith had texted me to ask if I was okay, and I told her I was alive but not exactly thriving. You were right. I overdid it.

It seemed like everyone needed a break from one another, because the chat went silent for a while. Amanda wrote to say our bridesmaid dresses had arrived at long last, but that was it.

I *did* miss the group a little; in a way, the bridesmaids felt like another team I'd played for this year, but high school field hockey started in a few days. It would fill the void.

⊢—⊢—⊣

I didn't block Marco again, but I declined his calls and ignored his texts, so either he would get the message and stop trying to contact me, or he'd get the message and show up in person to have it out. Because that's what I planned on doing if/when he eventually knocked on my door. The whole drive home from the Finger Lakes, I'd kept replaying our conversation.

Marco: *It's me?*

Me: *Yes.*

Marco, after the most awkward pause in existence: *Mads, it's not that I don't care for you, but—*

I hadn't listened to the *but*. Instead, I hung up on him. It was a reflex; I was too scared to know what he'd been about to say. *Mads, it's not that I don't care for you, but...*

You're just a kid.

You're like my little sister.

You're not enough for me.

The possibilities were endless, and it wasn't until I'd emerged from hangover hibernation that I learned part of the truth. Hi, friend, Natalie had texted. Do you follow Shelly on IG?

Hell, no, I replied. Natalie somehow knew Shelly through family friends. She's blocked.

Okay, Natalie said.

Nat? I asked when she didn't say more.

I'm going to send you something, she wrote after a couple minutes. I feel shitty for doing it, but I think you should see it.

Alright... I wrote and stared at my phone until a screenshot appeared in our chat. It was an Instagram post by @seashelly, whose caption read: living for these waves and whispers.

I blinked once, twice, three times, but the photo didn't disappear like I wished it would. In ripped jeans and a black PRINCETON FIELD HOCKEY sweatshirt, she, Marco, and a couple others had squeezed together onto one of the beach's lifeguard stands. It was twilight and Shelly was sitting on Marco's lap with her arms around his neck, hugging him close while she laughed. He had a Miller Lite in one hand, the other resting on Shelly's knee, and he was smiling as he whispered something in her ear.

Stone Harbor? I thought. *Shelly had been invited to Stone Harbor?* Marco *had invited her to Stone Harbor?!*

But he cut ties with her!!! I texted Natalie, eyes welling up with tears.

I guess she stitched them back up? she texted back. I'm so sorry, Mads. I know we never talked about it, but I could tell you had a thing for him.

That makes one of us, I said before locking my phone and changing for a run. Not only did I need to sweat out a bunch of alcohol, but I also needed to sweat out Marco Álvarez.

Who, in fact, *did* stop by to touch base on life; I spotted the Bumper Car through the keeping room window a week after I got home. "Marco is here," I informed Dad and Da. "I'm probably going to yell at him, okay?"

They both nodded—I'd told them *everything*, right down to me drunkenly professing my feelings for him. "Jacob—Bluestein—was—wrong," I had sobbed into Dad's shoulder as Da offered me warm brownies. "Marco—hasn't—always—liked—me."

My parents had looked at each other, as if to say, *Remind me who Jacob Bluestein is?*

"By all means, verbally tear him to pieces," Dad said now. "Should we have a code word in case you want backup?"

"Yes," I said. "*August*."

Since it was turning out to be the *worst* month.

I took a deep breath, then marched out the front door.

"Hey," Marco said, stopping at the bottom of the porch

steps. I stood at the top with my arms folded, physically and psychologically wanting to be a level above him.

"Hey," I said back, along with a disinterested, "What's up?"

He ran a hand through his dark hair. "I was hoping we could talk."

I shrugged. "Sure."

Marco gestured toward the Garden, but there was no way we were "talking" in there. It was a special space, full of special memories. Sweet moments with Marco, yes, but also with Connor, Samira, and my family.

I would not violate it.

But I wasn't evil enough to stay on the porch, where my parents could obviously eavesdrop on us, so I led him toward the Christmas trees and slowed between two tagged Douglas firs. "Okay," I said to Marco. "Would you like to make the opening statement?"

He did. "Mads, about that phone call—"

"Forget the phone call," I said, because we were *not* unpacking that. For all he knew, that could've been a glitch, my brain a broken system thanks to my many, many (*many*) drinks. "How about the fact that you *lied* to me all summer?"

His Adam's apple bobbed.

He's not sure, I thought. *He isn't sure whether I'm referencing spying for Katie or Shelly's social-media hard launch.*

"You told me you'd ended things with Shelly," I said. "You told me it was over." I tried to keep my voice cool. "You *never* mentioned that you guys still talked."

"We didn't!" Marco said. "I mean, sometimes she'd send me a meme on Instagram or I occasionally sent her one, but that was it." His tilted his head. "Why does that matter to you?"

I felt a twinge in my ribs, knowing he was baiting me. He wanted to circle back to the phone call.

"Because she's terrible!" I exclaimed, refusing. "Didn't we agree on that? Maybe she's not the *worst* person in the world, but come on, Marco! You said you didn't want anything serious with her, yet you invited her to Stone Harbor?"

"It would've been rude not to," he said. "We have the same circle of friends."

I rolled my eyes. "Yeah, like Tim, Simon, and Zach think she's *so* great…"

Do we love Shelly? Timothy Hobson-Kirby IV had responded after I'd sent the Princetonians (minus Marco) Natalie's screenshot.

Do we even like Shelly? Zach texted.

No, Simon confirmed.

"You know it was a bigger group than that," Marco said. "You saw the photos."

"No, I saw the *photo*," I told him with a bitter taste in my mouth. "What were you whispering in her ear, pray tell?"

Marco was silent for a moment, then said, "You sound incredibly jealous."

The corners of my eyes stung, threatening tears.

Marco sighed. "Mads, I thought about you all summer. I dreamt about you and only you."

A wonderstruck wave went through my veins. "You did?"

"Yes—god, yes." He nodded. "All summer long, but you made it clear you weren't interested in being more than…" He trailed off to find the right word. "Well, whatever we were."

Whatever we were.

Friends really didn't cover it.

"I spent pretty much every day here," he continued. "But you always found a way to bring up Connor—"

"He's my best friend!" I argued. "It's not my fault that most of my anecdotes involve him."

"And you were going on all these dates."

"You know, it's interesting you bring those up," I said. "Because while I thought it was a star-aligned coincidence that you appeared out of nowhere, Katie told me otherwise. She said she told you to spy on me."

Marco raised an eyebrow. "*Spy* on you?" He shook his head. "Mads, no."

"Oh, please!" My hands went to my hips. "The first time I met Davis? For coffee? You were at Crescent Moon."

"Yeah, because I study there," he said. "Religiously."

But you walked me back to my car afterward, I wanted to say.

"You were also at Davis's pre-prom dinner at Ember & Ash," I added. "Not at the table next to us, but you were *there*."

"Again, entirely coincidental," Marco said. "I go to school

in Princeton, and Carina runs that restaurant—hell, my family *owns* that restaurant. Of course I eat there!"

"Stop lying!" I shouted. "I go ice-skating with Chad? You bring your cousins skating. Jacob invites me to the movies? You and Tim ditch Simon to see whatever." My heart hammered. "Always the same place, same-ish time. And the only person who knew those details was Katie." I swallowed hard. "How do you even know Katie, anyway?"

Marco adjusted his glasses, the ones I loved so much. "She used to babysit me," he admitted. "When Carina started waitressing in high school, Katie babysat me a couple nights a week."

Hold up, I thought. *Katie? A babysitter?*

I couldn't see it.

"And you never thought to mention that?" I asked. "Even as a fun fact?"

Marco shrugged. "I was more saving it for a trivia question." He smiled a little. "Plus, I can't exactly give her a ringing endorsement. She never let me eat junk food."

My hands balled into fists. "Get serious."

"Only if you get serious. Katie—"

"She's laughing at me," I said. "You being Katie's eyes and ears…" I shook my head. "She's laughing at me, and even if they *do* want to help, so are the other bridesmaids." I turned away to wipe off some escaped tears.

"*I'm* not laughing," Marco murmured.

"Maybe not," I said. "But you don't trust me. You don't trust me to make my own decisions."

"What are you talking about?" he asked. "You've made your own decisions with these guys, and they've been the right ones!"

"No, I haven't," I said, looking him dead in the eye. "Not *all* of them have been right."

Marco tried to take my arm, but I dodged him. "Mads, wait!" he called when I started back toward the house.

"Go fuck yourself, Marco!" I called back, and then sobbed myself to sleep that night, knowing he wouldn't have to.

He had Shelly.

AUTUMN

TWENTY

September was, by far, my favorite month of the year. There was just something about it I especially loved. Maybe it was the fact that the weather was still summery but the air was crisper when I woke up and met Connor to run through the Christmas tree farm every morning. Maybe it was because high school field hockey season somehow felt more relaxed than my club team. Or maybe it was because of my birthday.

I turned eighteen on September 10. My parents surprised me by renting out a private room at an Italian place I loved; when we'd walked in, Connor, Natalie, Davis, a couple of my teammates, and even Samira popped up from behind the table and shouted, "Surprise!"

It had been a great night, even though Austin hadn't been there. He was battling bronchitis, which we all suspected he'd caught from one of his patients. Katie was, of course, also invited, but she didn't come. I wasn't going to lie—it hurt, but I couldn't say I was heartbroken. We hadn't spoken much since I ditched everyone at the Finger Lakes last month. "It was really fun!" I'd told Austin when he'd asked about the weekend, and Katie must've corroborated my version of the truth.

I shifted my focus entirely to my future and field hockey. I knocked out my Penn application forty-eight hours after college applications went live, and asked Mrs. McCallister—an English tutor—to proof my essays before I hit submit. There, done.

Natalie was convinced the only way for me to get over Marco was a rebound. "I know you guys never *actually* went out," she said, "but you fell for him like an elevator."

"Thank you very much for that image," I said dryly. "Really, Nat, I won't think of it at all the next time I use one."

"Sorry." She giggled from her spot on my bed. I was in the bathroom, changing into my bridesmaid dress. Dad had stopped by the Gallants' house to pick it up the other day. "Maybe you don't need a rebound, per se," she amended as I slipped on the cranberry-colored velvet gown. "Maybe you just need someone to make out with; I think that might be good for you."

I made a face. "In what way?"

"Well, first, you should kiss someone else, for practice and peace of mind. It'll make you forget about that Jacob guy's saliva dripping all over you."

She has a point, I thought. Not wanting to kiss Jacob again, I'd made up excuse after excuse to dodge dates until he said he didn't think things were going to work out between us. I'd been more relieved than upset.

"Connor is still with Lauren," I reminded her.

"Good," she replied. "Connor *cannot* be your next kiss."

I zipped up the dress. "Why not?"

Marco aside, I had never wanted to kiss Connor so much. For my birthday, he'd gotten me a new field hockey stick, one I'd been lusting after for *months*. Black with a red handle and white skulls and crossbones all over it. "Lady Death," he'd nicknamed it.

Natalie snorted. "Because he's *Connor*, Mads. Kissing him would mean something."

I didn't respond, distracted by myself in the mirror—horrified by reflection. The dress was all wrong. Nana had taken my measurements, and there was no way in hell they translated to this! The gown looked about five sizes too big, its waist not hugging mine whatsoever and with the sleeves falling off my shoulders and the scoop neckline sagging below my chest. I was even wearing my bridesmaid heels, but the fabric still pooled at my feet. *Text the chat*, I thought. *Ask if anyone else's dress is a disaster...*

But the last thing I wanted was for bridezilla Katie to get wind of anything being amiss. Instead, I called Nana, and when she didn't answer, I called her salon and asked for her. "Hello, darling!" she said. "I'm about to do a cut and color—"

"My bridesmaid dress is a nightmare," I said, suddenly all choked up. *Why did this have to happen?!* "I'm swimming in it, Nana. You can full-on see my boobs."

Nana laughed before assuring me that she'd be home by 6:30 if I wanted to come over that night. (She did some seamstress work on the side.)

Phew, I thought later, after leaving an extremely pinned gown in my grandmother's capable hands. That was one less thing to worry about, so I started obsessing over Natalie's suggestion to casually hook up with someone. When I mentioned it to my club teammates, they agreed with her. "A one-time thing can be fun," our goalie said. "I think you should go for it…"

So that's how I found myself dancing with Robbie Nielson at Council Rock North's September semiformal. "You never go to Friday-night dances," Connor had commented when I offered him a ride. For whatever reason, he and Lauren were driving separately.

"I know," I'd told him. "But it's senior year, so I think that should change, don't you?"

Robbie and I had been chatting over the app for a couple weeks, and we shared several classes, so I didn't mind his hands moving along my body or when he whispered Dad Jokes in my ear instead of sweet nothings. It was so much better than State Night with Derek at Princeton. I felt safe (partly because I knew I could beat him up if necessary), and I didn't hesitate when a song ended and he asked if I wanted to get some air. "Sure," I said, anticipation and excitement rippling down my back.

Five minutes later, he had one hand on my waist and the other tangled in my braid as we frantically kissed under a maple tree. And oh, wow, it was the *perfect* amount of saliva being exchanged. "You are such a good kisser," Robbie murmured. "Really good."

"You are, too," I murmured, but wondered why we couldn't slow down a little. We had the whole night; we didn't need to rush. What was wrong with wanting a slow and steady but spark-filled kiss? Or was that too Swiftian?

At least I'm not thinking of anyone else, I thought, now trying to keep up with Robbie. My hands were on his shoulders, squeezing them tightly. *Not thinking of him at all…*

TWENTY-ONE

The day before Austin left for his bachelor weekend, he, Katie, and her parents came for dinner. "Please be pleasant," Dad told me before they arrived. "I know things with Katie…"

Are horseshit? I almost suggested.

"Dad, forget about pleasant," I said. "I'll be *nice*."

Da raised an eyebrow.

I shrugged. "*The* Stacy Gallant will be here. You know it's impossible to be anything but nice in front of Stace."

Because really, Katie's mother might've had hard opinions on food and home décor, but she was also the sweetest.

"Mm-hmm," my parents said, as if they didn't *quite* believe me.

I responded with my most dazzling forced grin and did play nice for the first half of the evening—if only because no one really spoke to me. It was the Katie-and-Austin show, and it wasn't a great episode. "Are you all packed?" Da asked him.

Austin nodded. "I've been ready to go for a week!"

Dad and I exchanged a look. Austin, for as long as I could

remember, was a six-hours-before-departure type of packer. The only thing that took him a week was *un*packing.

"He's also *checking* a bag," Katie said with the hint of an eye roll. "He brought a carry-on to Paris, but he needs a *suitcase* for a long weekend in Jackson Hole."

"Kates, I can't fit a tent in a carry-on," Austin responded as I thought about the pot calling the kettle black. Katie had brought ten times more stuff to the Finger Lakes! "I also need my waders for fly-fishing."

"Oh, you're going fly-fishing?" Mr. Gallant whistled. "Damn…"

"You're welcome to join, Marc," my brother said. "The more, the merrier."

"Dad, no," Katie said before her dad could even pretend to entertain the idea. "The Devils have their first preseason game on Saturday." She shook her head. "No."

Mr. Gallant chuckled. "Relax, I'm only joking, Catherine." His eyes twinkled. "I was actually going to ask if you wanted to join me at the game?"

Katie kissed her dad's cheek.

"Madeline!" Mrs. Gallant exclaimed. "How is your bridesmaid dress?"

"Oh, it's good," I said casually. "It's gorgeous."

"Yes, it is, isn't it?" Katie's mom beamed. "Amanda looks sensational in hers." She took a sip of wine. "Is there any chance you'd give Katie and me a sneak peek after dinner?"

"I'd love to," I said, stomach starting to swish. "But I, um—it's actually missing from my closet right now."

Nana was still performing intensive surgery on the gown.

Austin, who knew about the dress's seriously screwed-up condition, gave me a look that said: *Bad wording, Mads.*

"Excuse me?" Mrs. Gallant's eyes widened. "It's *missing*?"

"She's joking, Stacy," Da quickly said. "Mads tried it on and it was evident that a few alterations were necessary."

"Well, that's nothing to worry about..." Katie said disinterestedly.

Her dad nodded just as disinterestedly.

"You took it back to Petal & Lace, I hope?" Mrs. Gallant asked. "Because bridal salons know the designers and styles intimately; other tailors won't be familiar with it."

"Yes," I lied. "Yes, Nana and I went back so they could fit me. Just a few nips and tucks here and there." I smiled. "It's so beautiful, though. *Stunning* for a Christmas wedding."

"Seasonal," Katie muttered. "December fourteenth is *seasonal*, not Christmas."

Austin covered his laugh with a cough, then raised his napkin to hide his smile. "It's totally a Christmas wedding," he'd said recently. "Everyone who has RSVP'd with regrets notes that they're either traveling or had holiday parties that weekend."

"And *why* did Katie pick that date again?" I asked. "Didn't you tell her it's Grandma's birthday?"

"Mrs. Gallant actually picked the date," he said. "Probably because St. Paul's and Bedens Brook were available, but she thought it might be a sweet tribute, too."

"Oh," I said. Because it was. It was a sweet tribute to our grandmother.

Just like Austin proposing with her ruby would've been a sweet tribute, I thought.

I felt a little bad about the 'tis-the-season teasing, but dinner was going twenty-five miles per hour and wasn't speeding up anytime soon. It was so boring that I nearly jumped for joy when my phone started pinging incessantly in my pocket.

Connor!!! the screen read.

"Hey," I said after Da had given me permission to leave the table. "What's up?"

"Do you think I should rewatch *Emily in Paris*?" Connor asked. "Or start *The Marvelous Mrs. Maisel*?"

"You aren't allowed to start *The Marvelous Mrs. Maisel* without me," I said, smiling. "In fact, you *promised*."

"Then will you come over so we can watch it?" Connor asked—no, *whined*. "I need to become overly invested in someone else's drama." He went silent for a second. "So I can forget about my own."

I gripped my phone tighter. "Wait, what do you mean?"

Connor sighed. "Lauren and I broke up."

Oh my god, I thought, suddenly unsteady on my feet.

"Oh my god!" I blurted. "Con, are you okay?"

"I'm considering rewatching *Emily in* freaking *Paris*," he replied. "Do *you* think I'm okay?"

I smirked. "I mean, it's not *that* bad a show..."

"*That* bad?" Connor smiled; I could hear it in his voice, and it honestly gave me butterflies. "Mads, it's a melodramatic masterpiece." He started shaking his head—again, I could tell because I knew him so well. "*Allons-y, allons-y, allons-y!*" he teased.

"Start assembling the snacks," I told him, pulse picking up. "I'll be over in ten minutes."

The McCallister household had always been a safe space to express your feelings. Both Connor and Liam had never been afraid to share anything with their family. I'd been sitting at their kitchen island the day Liam came home from sixth grade and announced that he had a crush on a guy from his math class. "What's his name?" Mr. McCallister asked, not fazed in the slightest. Connor was like that, too. He'd outright told his mother about losing his virginity only hours after it'd happened. "What?" he said when I'd gawked at him. "She asked what I did this afternoon!"

So, neither effort nor tact was required to get him to tell me about Lauren. He already had Netflix queued up on the basement's gigantic seventy-four-inch flat-screen; I simply flopped down next to him on the couch, grabbed some peanut-butter pretzels, and then crunched and munched for a few seconds before he said, "I can't really pinpoint who broke up with who, but we're definitely done."

"I'm sorry," I half lied.

"Nice try," he replied, then affectionately elbowed me. "You hated her, but sure, we can pretend otherwise."

I laughed. "Did something happen? Or did things just run their course?"

"Both." He sighed. "I found out she's been cheating on me—"

"What?!" I gasped.

"Yep." He nodded. "For a couple weeks now."

"With who?" I asked, incredulous. Connor McCallister was *Connor McCallister*. No girl in her right mind would risk wrecking that relationship.

"Robbie Nielson, funnily enough," Connor said. "The guy you wouldn't stop sucking face with outside the gym."

"Huh." I comically scratched my head. "That name doesn't really ring a bell…"

Connor smirked. That night, Robbie and I'd only jumped apart when we heard a chorus of laughter, whistles, and catcalls. We'd turned to see people pouring out of the gym. My face had gone up in flames, and I'd contemplated making a run for it until Connor had pushed out of his pack of lacrosse guys and walked over to offer Robbie a fist bump. "Dude, Mads Fisher-Michaels? Well done!"

They pounded, and as if on cue, his teammates erupted into applause. It had been beyond sexist, but I'd thanked Connor for defusing the situation.

"Anyway, I'm sorry," he said now. "He and Lauren pretty much started hooking up right after you guys…"

"No, it's fine." I shook my head. "He told me that it was a casual thing. He said he thought I was cool, but he liked someone else."

"Well, that's shitty." Connor's brow furrowed. "Were you upset?"

I shrugged. "Not really. I thought he was a nice guy—until now, obviously—but I wasn't bummed or anything." I dropped my voice to a whisper, as if we weren't the only two in the basement. "I also needed to get Jacob Bluestein out of my system."

"You guys kissed?" he asked.

I nodded.

"How was it?"

"Wet," I said. "Imagine making out with Arthur or Francine."

Connor scrunched up his face, and I laughed.

"So basically, you and Lauren broke up because of her cheating?" I asked after we'd snuggled up under one of Mrs. McCallister's chunky knitted blankets. The AC had kicked on, and it always turned the basement into a meat locker.

"I guess," he said. "I mean, of course. I never want to be a sidepiece or turn into someone's sidepiece; I want to be the light of her life." He winked.

My heart twinged, then twisted. *Maybe you could be the light of my life*, I thought.

Because even through his high-maintenance girlfriends, Connor had always been there for me. He made me smile, he made me laugh, and he made me feel seen, heard, and safe.

"I think I would've called it with her anyway," he continued. "Things have been off for a while. I can't actually explain it, but I've been feeling antsy. Like I was with Lauren because I'm waiting for something that's just not coming. I thought maybe if I broke up with her, whatever I'm waiting for would finally happen." He rubbed his eyes, suddenly looking so tired. "I know that makes no sense."

"No, it does," I said softly. "I get it."

"You usually do," he murmured, and then it was silent between us for a couple beats.

Do it, I told myself, heart speeding up. *Say something*.

"Can I ask you a question...?" I eventually said, because I had to. I had to know.

He nodded.

I took a breath. "Did you ever—" I stopped short, pulse pounding too hard to speak. "I mean, have you ever, maybe, thought about what it would be like if we were together?"

Connor slowly reacted. "Yeah," he said, lips spreading into a smile. "Yeah, I've thought about it a lot."

My stomach somersaulted. "Oh."

"You're surprised?" he asked.

"A little," I answered. "You've never made a move…"

"Neither have you," he pointed out.

We looked at each other and laughed.

"You also never seemed interested," he added.

"You never gave me the chance," I countered. "You haven't been single since freshman year!"

Connor chuckled. "I meant you've never seemed interested in dating *period*."

I shrugged. "Field hockey remains my first love."

He dramatically sighed. "And Olivia Lupo was mine."

"Fair," I said. "Although you are the boy next door."

"And you are the girl next door."

"Yes," I joked. "I think it's required we date at some point."

"Strongly suggested," he agreed. "I'd rather date you because you're my best friend, though."

"Same." I grinned. "Same here."

"Good." Connor grinned back. "Now can I ask *you* a question?"

My smile was stuck on my face. "Shoot!"

Connor's was not; his expression turned solemn before he said: "Marco…"

Marco is some dickhead guy, I thought, resisting the urge to roll my eyes.

"Just a friend," I told Connor, the technical truth. "He was always just a friend."

"That's it?" he asked.

"That's it," I confirmed, wishing I didn't feel like I was lying. Why tell him I once had a crush on Marco? Nothing had ever come of it. If anything, I had Marco to *thank*. He'd been something similar to a learning experience; flirting and confessing my crush on him and our fight this summer had actually given me the confidence to go for it tonight. No matter what, I could go after anything I wanted.

Connor nodded, and I suddenly worried he was rethinking everything. When he took my hand, my breath caught. "I want to give things a try between us, Mads," he said.

"Me too," I agreed.

His smile reappeared. "But I'd like to wait a few days if that's okay. I don't want this associated with my breakup with Lauren."

"I understand," I said, then gestured to the flatscreen. "Shall we?"

"Yes." He squeezed my fingers before letting go. "We shall."

My club team was thrilled when Connor made an appearance at our scrimmage on Saturday, and spent warmups checking him out. "Mads, does he have a girlfriend right now?" one of my teammates finally asked during shuttles.

"Yes," I said matter-of-factly. "Me."

And even though their hopes were dashed, they squealed like fangirls...which was *exactly* how Austin had reacted before his Jackson Hole flight took off yesterday. "Jeez, Austin!" I'd pulled my phone away from my ear. "You just gave me some serious heart palpitations."

"Sorry. I'm sorry," he quickly said. "But this is so great, sis. He's your *best friend*."

"*I know*," I mimicked him.

"I have to go," Austin said. "My zone is boarding now." He sighed. "I'm so happy for you, Mads. This is the way it should be."

Samira echoed him in her texts; funnily enough, she was also about to fly somewhere. That's amazing, she'd written. I can't wait to see you two together!

Meanwhile, Da and Dad had spent half the drive to my game explaining new guidelines now that Connor's and my relationship had shifted from friends to more than friends. "No sleeping over unless you are in the guest room," Dad said, "or on the couch with the dogs."

"And if you're in Mads's room, Connor, her door must be at least halfway open," Da added. "No more closed-door movie nights."

Our first official date was that night; Natalie had invited Connor and me to her hockey game, and he asked if I'd like to get dinner nearby. The only reason I hesitated was because Natalie's game was at Princeton's ice rink. *There are so many restaurants*, I reminded myself as I tried on a third sweater. *You aren't going to run into him.*

Slime suddenly coated the roof of my mouth. I hated that I worried about seeing Marco. Who cared? Who freaking cared? Connor and I had finally had our "You Belong with Me" moment. Even Marco himself had said that he thought we'd be good together. At least, I think he had.

Maybe.

I was also *happy*; I was happier than I'd been in a while.

We went to Winberie's Tavern for burgers, and it was close quarters with all the Princeton students crowded around us. We were practically dining with the couple next to us. "Are you two freshmen?" a burly guy asked us.

Connor and I shared a silent snicker. "Yes," he said, taking my hand. His palm was warm against mine.

"Cool, cool," the guy said and then introduced himself and his girlfriend. They were juniors. "Where're you living?"

"We're both in Forbes," I answered as Connor excused himself to go to the bathroom. I reluctantly let go of his hand, using it to ward away the midnight memory of me at Wawa—refusing to let Marco walk me back to Shelly's room.

"Oh, yeah, Forbes," he said. "That's…" He dropped off, bursting into laughter at something over my shoulder. "Dude!" he called out. "What the hell?"

"Seriously!" an excruciatingly familiar voice called back. "Bit early in the night, don't you think?"

My stomach soured hearing Marco's footsteps come closer. "What's the deal?" his friend asked when he'd reached their table.

But Marco didn't answer; instead, his face slowly drained of color, which made the burgundy stain on his shirt even more startling. Had someone spilled their drink on him? It reminded me of Stone Harbor this summer; his mother's sangria had left him flushed, his face scarlet. *You are my favorite person, you know?* he'd said after Connor had gone to bed. We were stretched out on the screened-in porch's ropey rug, listening to the ocean waves crash against the beach. My feet were on his lap, and I'd gently kick him every time he made me laugh. He was still kind of drunk. *I mean it, Mads. Not only my closest friend, but honestly, my* favorite *person...*

I was so obliviously obsessed, I thought. *So obliviously obsessed with him to see how obsessed he was with me.*

Now, I wanted to get up and leave, but my stomach growled in protest. Connor and I hadn't gotten our food yet.

"Long story," Marco said, snapping back to attention. "I'll tell you at Tower later."

"I'm gonna hold you to that," his friend said, and Marco clapped him on the shoulder before making his exit.

Five seconds later, my phone buzzed with a text.

Please tell Connor hello for me, it said. I'm really, really happy for you.

"This is weird," I said, unable to stop myself from giggling a little.

"I know," Connor chuckled, too. "It's definitely weird."

We were standing on my front porch, procrastinating our good-night. It was ten minutes past my curfew, but I knew my parents had heard Connor's Jeep pull into the driveway earlier. "Are you a first-date kisser?" I word-vomited. "Because I feel like we should probably kiss."

"Well, I know *you're* a first-date kisser," Connor said, then faux coughed, "Jacob…"

"Okay, *rude!*" I shoved him, then braced myself for a good-natured shove back.

But rather than friendly roughhousing, Connor wrapped me in a half-hug, half-straitjacket situation. I smiled and settled into it. "Sometimes I'm a first-date kisser," he said, his heart beating steadily against mine. "Sometimes I'm not. It depends on the vibe."

I arched an eyebrow. "What vibe are you getting now?"

"Clown," he said. "Clown vibe."

I pulled back and stuck my tongue out at him.

He laughed and hugged me close again. "I'd rather not be clowning around when we kiss," he whispered.

"Yes." I nodded. "I want to be swept up."

"Oh, I'll sweep you up." He lightly kissed my forehead. "You wait."

"I will," I told him. "But you know I'm not known for my patience."

Connor winked. "Night, Mads."

I winked back. "Night, Con."

I slept extremely but luxuriously late on Sunday, only to wake up to a text from Connor. Morning! he'd written. Let me know when you're up! We can do HW at Little Sunflower and then something fun?

I'm awake... I texted back, my timestamp reading 12:27 p.m. That sounds great!

"Hey!" I called once I started down the stairs. I could hear someone moving around the kitchen. "Do you guys want anything from the bakery? Connor and I—"

"No, it's alright, it's okay!" I heard Dad say in a firm voice that made my heart plummet. It was the cadence he employed whenever Austin was anxiously amped. "Relax, take a deep breath."

I leapt the last five steps and turned to see Dad with his phone pressed to his ear, listening to whatever my brother was saying on the other end.

"I know you do, kid," Dad said, "but going after her isn't going to help."

Wait, what? I thought, alarmed. *What's going on? Who's her?*

Had something happened with Katie?

"Austin, take your scheduled flight home," Dad said. "We'll talk more here, okay?"

They hung up a minute later. "What happened?" I squeaked. "Is Austin hurt?"

"No." Dad rubbed his eyes. "He is physically fine, but mentally shaken." He sighed. "Samira told him she's in love with him."

TWENTY-TWO

Austin's flight didn't land until that evening, so Connor and I went to Little Sunflower Bakery with our overloaded backpacks. But after ordering pumpkin spice lattes (the season was upon us!), we didn't even crack a textbook. I told Connor all I knew was that Austin's groomsmen had surprised him by inviting Samira on the bachelor trip, which ended with her confessing unresolved feelings for him. "Katie went out of town this weekend, too," I added, "so Dad's grabbing Austin and bringing him home. He doesn't think this conversation is meant to happen outside Terminal B."

"Where's Katie?" Connor asked.

"She and Amanda went to visit their cousins in New York." I thought for a moment. "It's funny how whenever one of them goes on a trip, the other leaves Philly, too. Austin came home when Katie went on all those bachelorette trips this summer, and when Austin's gone, she goes to her parents' or stays with friends. That's strange, right?"

Connor shook his head. "I don't think so," he said after a sip of his latte. "I don't think they like being apart. They did long distance for what? Five years?"

I shrugged.

"Yeah, so now that they're finally living together, I bet it's really tough when one of them is gone. They like being *together* together. Plus, it doesn't seem like either person is a fan of being alone."

Hmm, I thought, chewing some muffin. *Is that why Katie was rude the night before Austin left for Jackson Hole? Because she was going to miss him so much?*

Connor sighed. "I knew this thing with Samira was going to shatter at some point."

My brows knitted together. "You did?"

"Haven't you noticed her staring at Austin when he isn't looking? It's like she's always swallowing a secret when they're together."

"Then she should've spoken up sooner," I said, finding myself frustrated with her. "The wedding is only three months away. She's had plenty of time."

Connor was silent for a beat. "Do you think Austin feels the same way?"

"I don't know. He didn't tell Dad much on the phone, but he's definitely stunned." I rose from my seat and pointed to the bakery case. "I'm gonna buy some chocolate-peanut butter cupcakes to bring home."

They were my brother's favorite.

The vibe was most certainly *not* romantic when Connor dropped me off later. Even though he hopped out of his Jeep and ran to open the passenger door for me, always chivalrous. "Let me know how it goes," he said as we hugged.

Dad's Lexus cruised up the driveway around 6:00. Da and I were ready and waiting in the kitchen. "Hello!" Dad called when the mudroom door opened. "We're home!" He entered the kitchen and mouthed, *Buckle up.*

Austin looked *rough*. He wore an inside-out sweatshirt with old jeans, and under his baseball cap, his hair was matted down with grease. The stormy sea-colored bags under his eyes told me he hadn't slept. "Could I please have some tomato soup and grilled cheese?" he asked.

I opened the oven, where we'd been keeping his sandwiches warm, and Da popped the lid off the pot on the stove. He ladled thick red soup into a big bowl.

"Thank you." Austin took a seat at the island, and we watched him eat in silence. After devouring three grilled cheeses and basically licking his soup bowl clean, he said he was going to take a shower. "Then I'll tell you everything," he said.

Half an hour later, we congregated in the family room with the cupcakes. "Okay, so what happened?" I not-so-delicately asked when no one said anything.

Dad and Da shot me sharp looks.

"You can't let me enjoy my cupcake first?" Austin laughed, but it sounded hollow. He took one final colossal bite, swallowed, then spoke. "It started out great. No one's flight was delayed, we hung out at the cabin until they surprised me with Sam, and then we hit some bars in town…"

He summarized their adventures on Saturday, right down to cooking the fish they'd caught for dinner. It couldn't have been more different than Katie's Last Splash.

Until.

"Earlier in the day, Wit and Sam struck a deal that whoever caught the least fish had to camp out in a tent that night. And well…" He sighed. "I'm embarrassed to say that ended up being me." He gave us a sad smile, as if the fish tally were the most important thing in the world. "After dinner, I made a big show of setting up the tent while everyone else was around the campfire. We were playing Cards Against Humanity—Wit brought like every expansion pack in existence—and the s'mores stuff was long gone, so someone broke out the beer, bourbon, and even fucking Fireball." He groaned. "Full-on drinking."

"Were you drinking?" Da asked.

Austin shook his head. "I did a celebratory shot on Friday night, but no. I stuck to nonalcoholic beer on Saturday."

We nodded. Austin described nonalcoholic beer as "juiced bread," but I knew it made him feel included among his friends.

"Things were rowdy," he continued, "but not *too* rowdy. We

were having a great time. Then Katie called around midnight, so I went up to the cabin to talk to her for about an hour."

An hour? They'd talked for an *hour*? Even though Austin was on his bachelor trip?

But then I remembered Katie disappearing for a while our first night on Seneca Lake, and realized she'd probably been in her room on the phone with Austin.

Connor's right, I thought, shifting on the couch. *They really don't like being apart.*

"Wit was the only one who wasn't plastered when I came back out," Austin said. "Sam was…" He trailed off. "Sam was drinking the Fireball straight from the handle. Wit helped her inside when we called it a night. They went into the house while I retired to my tent."

"Then what happened?" I gently prompted after he was quiet for a while.

Austin ran a hand through his hair. "I texted Kates that I loved her, but before I fell asleep, I heard footsteps and someone say my name. It was Sam, so I unzipped my tent and saw that she'd brought out a sleeping bag. She didn't want me to be alone."

Dad, Da, and I all leaned forward in our seats. *Keep going*, I thought, my heart pounding. *Keep going, keep going!*

He did. He said that he'd welcomed Samira into his tent because she was still super drunk and he didn't want her to hurt herself walking back up to the cabin in the dark. And then they talked. They talked about middle school field trips, being voted "Cutest Couple" in high school, and breaking up at Johns Hopkins. They talked about their friendship...and Samira talked about how she wanted it to be *more*. "I didn't get what she was saying at first," Austin said. "She just said, 'I love you, Austin,' and I thought she meant it in the normal best-friend way, so I told her I loved her, too."

"Alright, that's not terrible," Da said. "You can always—"

"Lee." Dad put a hand on Da's knee. "Let him finish."

My insides twisted as Austin took a breath. "After I said I loved her, she asked me to run away with her. Leave Katie and be with her."

"How did you respond?" Da asked carefully.

"I told her I loved her again," he said, growing frazzled. "I didn't know what else to say! She was snoring ten seconds later, so I thought things would be okay. I thought she'd forget the whole conversation." He groaned. "But I *knew* I had to ask for the truth when she sobered up. Otherwise, it would eat me alive—it was *already* eating me alive. I didn't sleep at all."

He said he'd left the tent before Samira woke up to make breakfast, and he'd gotten her alone on the deck later. She'd surprisingly remembered her confession and told him she meant every word. Austin was the love of her life. She wanted him to call off the wedding—

"And what did you say?!" I blurted.

"Nothing," he answered. "I said absolutely fucking *nothing*. I stood there, and when it was clear I didn't have the guts to say anything, she avoided me the rest of the trip." He held up his phone. "She sent me a text at the airport, saying that she'd give me time to think, but asked me not to contact her until I had an answer." He exhaled. "That's it. That's all she wrote."

Dad covered my mouth with his hand when I opened it again. "Okay, now that we have all the information," Da said, "let's just sit here and breathe before we unpack it…"

The devious, diabolical, downright villainous part of me thought, *If there's ever a time to talk him out of marrying Katie, this is it.*

But then the rest of me wondered: *Is that what I really want?*

We weren't on the best of terms now, but Austin looked heartsick, and I realized that deep down, I wanted to apologize to Katie for our bachelorette weekend blowup.

Maybe that meant something.

"First thing's first." Dad folded his hands together. "What does Katie know?"

"Nothing," Austin said. "Just that my plane landed and I'm here. She's on the train home from New York now."

"Are you going to tell her?" I asked.

"Well, that depends on what he decides," Da said before my brother could. "If he wants to be with Samira, then he'll have no choice but to tell Katie."

Austin cocked his head, suddenly looking at us like we were strangers. "I'm not choosing Sam," he said, an edge to his voice. "What makes you think I'd *ever* leave Katie for her?"

"Because you and Samira are best friends," I answered. "And for the last several months, all you and she have been saying is that best friends make for the best romance." I quoted Samira. "You should be with the person you never stop laughing with, the person who always has your back, the person who knows you inside and out." I held up my hands. "When I told you about my crush on Connor, you and Samira both thought it was amazing that my best friend might become my *favorite person*."

I tried to ignore the ache in my rib cage, remembering Marco calling me his favorite person this summer.

Austin shook his head. "Sam isn't my favorite person, guys." He shrugged. "I thought she was once, but we are *just* best friends." He paused. "We share this unbreakable bond, and while it was romantic at times, it wasn't meant to stay that way forever. Timing ideal or not ideal, we would've been together if it were written in the stars." He paused. "If I ever thought of Sam while Katie and I were long distance in college, it was because I missed Kates so much, not because I still had feelings for Sam." He shook his head. "There was nothing like picking up Katie from the airport when she visited for the weekend, with her overstuffed tote bag and pink rolling suitcase. Or when I went to Hamilton—she, Meredith, and Yasmin always met me outside baggage claim. They screamed my name and waved around the most obnoxious welcome sign. No matter where we were, Maryland or New York, I felt like I was coming home." Austin made eye contact with me. "Does that make more sense?"

Yes, I thought, feeling a tight twist of sadness. *But it doesn't explain why Katie is so special. I still don't understand what makes her so special.*

Special enough that he really wouldn't give things with Samira a true shot.

Austin half read my mind. "Mads, you know how I met Katie."

"Yeah, you used your fake ID to get into Triumph and went up to her at the bar to work whatever magic I still don't totally believe you have on her."

Dad and Da chuckled before Austin spoke. "We talked for a bit. She was quiet at first, so I couldn't quite tell if she was interested, but after I made her laugh, I offered to buy her a drink. She nodded and told the bartender—who'd made me a soda with lime earlier—that she wanted exactly what I was drinking." He let out a long breath, like he had disappeared into the memory. "I got really nervous then, because I knew she was expecting vodka or tequila. It *looked* like I was drinking one or the other, and I thought she'd be turned off when she discovered it was *neither*. I'm not embarrassed by my sobriety, but I did get teased about it now and again."

Da leaned forward in his chair. "Who teased you?"

Austin shrugged, as if to say it didn't matter.

"But Katie showed no surprise when the bartender raised the soda nozzle and filled her glass and added the lime. She just took a sip, smiled at me, and said, 'This is *really* refreshing.'"

He shrugged. "I knew right then and there. I *knew* this girl was special, and that the clock had finally chimed—the timing was right. Nothing was in the way of me falling in love with her. I didn't see how *anything* could get in the way of falling in love with her." He smiled to himself. "Katie has this irresistible quality of making me feel like I can take on the world, and she's the best partner and teammate, always right there with me. I love how we build each other up." He paused. "Did I ever tell you about the time she surprised me at Hopkins junior year?"

I shook my head.

"She showed up at my door out of the blue, with tomato soup and grilled cheese, when she should've been leaving for the DR with Mer and Yasmin. She was on spring break, but knew I had midterms." He laughed. "Funnily enough, I'd arranged for flowers and champagne in her hotel room…" He trailed off. "She's my favorite person who has also become my best friend."

A lump formed in my throat. I hadn't known any of this. We knew that Katie was supportive of Austin's drinking habits (or lack thereof), and despite the fact that she could drink a bottle of rosé with a straw, I remembered she and Austin didn't keep any alcohol in their apartment. And she skipped her vacation?!

"I think Samira is the coolest person on the planet," I said. "If I didn't have all these *totally unbiased* people"—I gestured around the room—"telling me I was an icon, I'd aspire to be her when I grew up."

My family laughed.

"If I'm being honest, I still don't know Katie as well yet," I continued. "But I do know *you*, and if you say she's your favorite person…" I shrugged. "There's no contest. I understand, and I support you to the moon and back."

Because I did. Austin loved Katie; he wanted to marry Katie.

I just wish I'd known these stories earlier. Maybe then I wouldn't have misjudged Katie so badly. She was deeply in love with my brother, and with such unconditional support, I could see why Austin loved her back.

"And she's really cute," Austin added, starry-eyed. "You should see her in—"

"Okay!" Dad interrupted, smiling. "We get the picture, kid."

"He's not going to tell her," I told Connor. We were waiting in the Chick-fil-A drive-through line after football and field hockey practice. It was a gridlock, packed with soccer moms in loaded SUVs and minivans. "He doesn't think it's a good idea."

"Interesting," Connor said. "Because, from my extensive movie-watching experience, when this type of thing happens, the secrecy almost always sets off a bomb, and we learn that *honesty* is the best policy."

"I know, I know," I agreed. "But Austin wants to try to save his friendship with Samira, and the chances of that are pretty low if Katie knows all."

"Katie still hates Samira, huh?"

"Technically, yes," I said. "Though I have a theory she's actually intimidated by Samira; she doesn't hate her." I paused. "Although she would *definitely* hate her if she found out what happened this weekend…"

We pulled up to the drive-through window, and while Connor placed our massive order, I snapped a photo of him; he looked cute in profile, with his postpractice unkempt hair and flushed face. I loved that he was wearing a PENN FIELD HOCKEY T-shirt. It had warmed my heart after he'd first shown it to me. I smiled at the picture before posting it on my Instagram story.

By the time we'd rounded the curve to the pickup window, the bridesmaid chat had blown up with messages. Aww!!! Yasmin had texted with a screenshot of my story.

He's hot and cute at the same time, Reese texted.

You guys… Amanda wrote with heart-eye emojis.

Childhood-friends-to-lovers trope for the win! Paige said.

Katie hearted the screenshot, and then so did Meredith. They weren't remotely in the same place, but I pictured them sitting together at a coffee shop. I wondered if Meredith knew Katie had dispatched Marco to chaperone my dates.

She couldn't have, right?

Too hungry to wait until we got home, Connor parked and we ate our food in the car. "I'm not convinced it's the right call," Connor said through a mouthful of fries. "Katie should know."

"Well, I trust Austin," I replied. "He said if his gut tells him to change his mind, he'll follow it. I think it's valid for him to keep it close to the vest for a bit." I glanced at Connor and laughed. There was a smear of Polynesian sauce above his upper lip. "Hold on, you've got…" I reached over to wipe away the red sauce.

Connor stared at me as I licked its sweetness off my fingertip. "Mads…"

I snorted. "What?"

An odd expression crossed his face, but a blink later, he was laughing with me. "Maybe honey mustard is more my color?"

It wasn't until he dropped me home that I realized that might've been a perfect moment for our first kiss.

It also didn't strike me until I sent him a good-night text later that neither of us had lingered after our hug goodbye. "See ya!" we'd said simultaneously, so in sync.

When is the romance coming? I wondered.

TWENTY-THREE

My high school teammates thought it was weird at first when the Princetonians started regularly attending our home games. "Wait, how do you know them?" my co-captain asked the first time Zach, Simon, and Timothy Hobson-Kirby IV claimed front-row seats in the stands, but by their third appearance, she was inquiring if Simon was single.

"As far as I know…" I said, so happy they'd come to see me play. "Have you read *This Side of Paradise*?"

She looked at me blankly.

"By F. Scott Fitzgerald?" I tried. Little did they know, Marco and his friends had turned me into a reader. "Based on his days at Princeton?"

"Oh, no," she said. "We read *The Great Gatsby* in English lit, though." She wrinkled her nose. "Not my favorite."

I smiled. "Then trust me when I say Simon's not your type."

We always caught up after my games ended. I heard about their classes, eating club antics, and how the food was getting better.

I even sometimes found myself hopeful about spotting Marco in the crowd. Then I remembered that I did *not* want to see him, especially after those awkward few moments at Winberie's. I'd never responded to his text about Connor and me getting together. *I'm really, really happy for you.*

Thanks, I'd thought about writing. *Would you like our date night calendar?*

But I worried a text wouldn't convey my deadpan well enough. (Plus, it would've been super immature.)

I never asked about him, and the Princetonians somehow knew not to tell…until, one day, they did. "We thought you'd want to know that Marco and Shelly broke up," Zach said tentatively.

My body reacted like a roller coaster, stomach dropping before rising back up and twisting in a corkscrew motion. "Oh?" I managed to say. "How come?"

They all spoke at once; all I could decipher was that Marco had ended things.

"Well, hopefully being dumped doesn't affect Shelly's game too much," I said. Princeton wasn't having a stellar season so far.

"It shouldn't," Simon said. "I suspect she knew that Marco was never hers to lose."

I felt the blood in my veins thicken. "What?"

But Simon didn't repeat himself; Zach's phone had pinged. "Ride's here," he announced, gesturing to the parking lot. "Misha's driving a blue Kia Soul…"

I walked them to their Uber, where we said goodbye. Then I booked it over to the Defender, feeling electricity pulsing in my fingers. *Just breathe, just relax*, I told myself. *It'll be okay.*

Marco and Shelly were over.

"Hey," Natalie answered. I'd called her as soon as I'd parked in my driveway. "How'd your game go?"

"We lost four-two, but it was a fun game." I rubbed my forehead. "Do you want to hang out later? Nana brought my bridesmaid dress back the other day..."

"Sure!" Natalie said. "Will I miss dinner if I leave now?"

I laughed. My friend loved Da's cooking.

Tonight was chicken piccata over an arugula salad, and we mostly talked about the current drama on Natalie's hockey team.

We sequestered ourselves in my room after loading the dishwasher. "What's Connor up to tonight?" Natalie asked as I shuffled through hangers in my closet. I'd hung the bridesmaid dress in the back since it wouldn't be called to duty for a few more months.

"SAT tutoring," I said. Connor had a great GPA, but he was about to take the test for the third time. *I am far from dumb*, he liked to say, *but man, can that exam* humble *a person...*

"Gotcha," Natalie said. "Things are still going well between you two?"

"Yeah." I nodded. "Of course. We're best friends."

She nodded back. "I know, and that's what I love about you guys." She raised an eyebrow. "Have you kissed yet?"

I hesitated, then released a sigh. "No," I said. "The vibe hasn't been right yet."

"Ah, yes," Natalie said. "Your *first kiss* vibe."

"Hey, you thought it was cute!"

"I do!" She giggled. "I totally do, but it's been like three weeks. Why hasn't the mood struck?"

"Because we've both been really busy," I said, the back of my neck flushing a little. "Sports and homework after school, and club field hockey and club lacrosse on the weekends, so we've pretty much been hanging at each other's houses. Nothing really romantic." I spotted the wood hanger that held the plastic garment bag. "But"—I snatched the hanger—"we're going to Grey on Saturday, so I'm excited!"

Grey was the recently renovated restaurant just outside town, a stylish upscale steakhouse that sprawled across the ground floor of the historic Greystone Manor. Dad had gotten a gift certificate from clients and had regifted it to me. "You and Connor have been working hard this fall," he said. "Enjoy yourselves!"

Ironically, my parents had also chosen it for Austin and Katie's rehearsal dinner. It would be classic, but with a twist of modernism.

"Ooh, that sounds amazing!" Natalie grinned, then pointed to my dress. "Now go try that on, please."

Nana had truly performed some type of witchcraft. Instead of being swallowed up by the fabric, I now looked like I'd been poured into the cabernet gown. It hugged me in all the right places, and the neckline scooped tastefully low while the cap sleeves fluttered. Natalie gasped as I did a glam-cam twirl for her. "Do you mind taking a picture?" I asked, handing over my phone. "I should send one to Katie's mom to prove that I haven't accidentally set it on fire."

Natalie gave me a quizzical look but relished her photographer role. Madeline, you look absolutely gorgeous!!! Mrs. Gallant immediately replied to my photo. Have you thought about hair and makeup yet? Text Amanda and ask her to share her Pinterest board.

I sent the shot to Katie, too.

Great, was all she texted back. I waited for more, my eyes prickling when more did not come.

"Okay, what's her deal?" Natalie asked as she unzipped my dress for me. "I know texts don't always convey tone well, but would it kill her to add an exclamation point? She sounds like she couldn't care less."

"Yeah, she always comes off that way whenever wedding stuff comes up over text. Completely detached, or sometimes even miserable. Like she doesn't even want to marry Austin." I shrugged. "She's probably still pissed at me for the whole Finger Lakes fight, too. I texted her an apology, and she accepted it, but nothing has gotten better."

Natalie grimaced. "Does Austin know about that?"

"Not unless she told him," I said, realizing that Katie and

my brother were both keeping secrets from each other. Katie was keeping our post–Prosecco Pong duel on the down-low, and Austin was hiding Samira's ultimatum.

"Hmm," Natalie said. "May I see their wedding invitation again? I looked up Lily Hopper—the artist—on Instagram, and her portfolio is *magical*."

Now wearing cozy joggers and a retro zigzag-patterned Patagonia, I grabbed the envelope from my desk drawer and joined Natalie on my bed. *Miss Madeline Fisher-Michaels* was handwritten across the navy-blue envelope in gold calligraphy. Mrs. Gallant must've proofed the guest list, since Katie always misspelled my name: *Madeleine*.

Other than that, the invitation was intriguing. It didn't vibe with their overall Christmas-at-the-country-club theme. It was—well, it had more character. Inside the envelope was a custom insert, a watercolor of a frozen pond surrounded by snow-dusted pine trees, with one of those really rare winter sunsets: a misty blue-gray and amber sky that somehow glowed gold. "I've never been to Bedens Brook," I told Natalie, "but I guess this scene is somewhere on the property?"

"Nothing gets past you, Mads," Natalie said sarcastically before admiring the invitation itself. The same cream card stock and navy border, along with the formal wedding invitation language, but it was made interesting by an interlocking *A* and *C* at the top. Katie's *C* in gold, and Austin's *A* in icy blue. The letters were wreathed by greenery, a playful crest of sorts. Their names leapt out of the matrimonial summons, too, in whimsical navy script:

Catherine Marie
to
Austin Frederick

It was traditional but, at the same time, so *not* traditional. It was, honestly, kind of fun. Freshly cut blue spruce and balsam fir trees leaned against the red barn that had been painted on the back of the little RSVP card. Again, Bedens Brook must've been more than the photo gallery on its website. "Shit, I still need to send this," I said. "What should I have to eat? There's herb-roasted chicken, but Austin said the maple-glazed salmon is really good."

Natalie snorted. "You haven't submitted your RSVP yet?"

"Well, it's obvious I'm coming," I said. "The deadline also isn't until next week." I checked the box for the salmon, then drew a line through the space for my plus-one's name and his meal preference.

"Mads, you have a date," Natalie reminded me. "Connor?"

I waved my hand. "He has his own RSVP. He's invited to the wedding."

She smirked. "I bet Katie and the bridesmaids would still *love* for you to write his name down!"

"Oh, would they ever…" I smiled and stuffed the little

card in its little envelope, prestamped and addressed to Hotel Gallant.

Natalie's voice softened after I sealed it with saliva. "Mads, you do know these invitations…"

"More or less cost five thousand dollars?"

"I would hope so!" Natalie said. "Lily Hopper works *wonders*, my friend." She shook her head. "But no, I meant…you know every piece of this invitation is a love letter to your home, right?"

I gave her a look. "Wait, what?"

Natalie nodded. "All of this, Mads, is for your family." She pointed to the RSVP missive. "The barn on the back of your dinner order? It's your Christmas tree farm." She rifled around for Austin and Katie's watercolor save-the-date and pointed to the chestnut mare outside the Bedens Brook clubhouse. "That's Tally-Ho!"

My heart slowed, seeing our horse in her holiday tartan blanket. *Oh…*

Natalie got right in my face with the envelope's winter watercolor insert. "And this scene isn't at Bedens Brook!" she said. "It's based on a photo that's framed downstairs." She swept her arm toward my window, as if pointing all the way down to our pond. "It's right over there."

"Austin," I whispered, eyes smarting with realization. "This was all Austin's idea. Katie…" I rubbed my forehead. "She let Austin design the invitations."

"Well, I think Lily deserves at least *a little* credit." Natalie poked me. "But yeah, it looks like it. You've been saying Katie hasn't wanted any of his opinions."

"Except this one." I picked up the invitation, as if to look at it for the first time. Austin's and my childhood flashed in front of my eyes. "It's timeless."

"Yes," Natalie agreed. "It's timeless."

A few hours after Natalie left, I called it a night. "I'm going to Bedfordshire," I yawned, snapping shut my copy of *Emma* before giving my dads hugs.

But once I'd changed into pajamas, brushed my teeth, and exchanged good night texts with Connor, I found myself restless. I tossed and turned in bed for a while, then threw back my covers to pace my room. Moonlight slipped through my closed blinds. *We thought you'd want to know that Marco and Shelly broke up*, I heard Zach's voice in my head, followed by Simon: *I suspect she knew that Marco was never hers to lose.*

In the end, I had to dare myself to do it. *I dare you*, I thought. *I dare you to text Marco.*

Hey, I typed, trying to tune out the voice in my head: *Why are you doing this when you have Connor?* I hated myself for it, but after hearing Austin talk about Katie, I'd started wondering if Connor truly *was* my Samira...and *only* my Samira.

Which meant I had a Katie out there.

I closed my eyes when I hit send, knowing the conversation could go wrong. Or, even worse—he could ignore me exactly like I'd ignored him.

But his reply was almost immediate.

Hi, it read. Long time...

No see, I finished for him. No chat.

And whose fault is that? he wrote.

My cheeks warmed. I don't know. You never come to my games.

Only because I have class. In addition to the very minute detail that you don't want to see me.

That's not true, I thought. *It once was, but not now.*

I also joined the club soccer team, he added when I didn't respond. Significantly lower commitment than varsity, less pressure, and much more fun. Everyone has pure love for the game.

I smiled a little. You're still playing soccer?

Yes, he said. It turns out it wasn't that easy to give up.

Suddenly, I wanted to ask him a thousand questions. I wanted to know what he found interesting about his classes this semester, his family, and if he'd finished his manuscript. I wanted to hear about something that had recently made him laugh.

I wanted to know why he'd agreed to play Katie's reconnoiter.

They told you, he texted. Right?

Shelly. He was talking about Shelly.

I gulped and did my best to dodge the question. Do you want to call and catch up? I asked. I'm wide-awake.

Gray typing dots appeared, then disappeared.

Appeared.

Disappeared.

Appeared again.

No, Marco messaged.

My stomach sank, but I still had the guts to challenge him. Why not?

Because, he wrote, if I hear your voice, I'm never going to hang up the phone.

I swallowed hard, a lump in my throat. *This isn't platonic*, I thought after leaving him on read. *And I can't ever pretend it is.*

Mr. and Mrs. Gallant had invited my parents to a Devils game on Saturday night, so I had the house to myself while I got ready for dinner with Connor. Grey was a fancy restaurant, so I went all out in a little black dress, silver heels, and the diamond earrings my late grandmother had left me. The studs sparkled in the mirror, and I remembered her ruby engagement ring just sitting in our basement's safe instead of on Katie's finger. Part of me still couldn't believe she didn't want a family heirloom. It was unique, but if she was Austin's favorite person, it belonged to her.

The doorbell rang.

This is going to be a spectacular evening, Connor McCallister! I thought, a thrill racing through my veins.

But by the time I'd quelled Arthur and Francine's barking with treats and opened the door to see Connor looking so handsome in a suit and tie, my excitement had turned to anxiety.

This was it; this was The Moment. We were alone in the porch light glow with the sun slipping down in the sky. The crisp autumn breeze reminded me that I needed a coat, but I quickly forgot about grabbing one. "Hello," I said to Connor.

"Hello," he said back and took a step closer to me.

I smiled while my lungs kicked and screamed, begging me to breathe. Goose bumps burst when Connor put a hand on my waist, and when he leaned in…

Laughter bubbled out of my mouth.

"I'm sorry." I tried pulling myself together, but I couldn't stop giggling. "I'm so sorry…"

Connor cocked his head. "About?"

My stomach sank when he stepped back, knowing I needed to face the facts. I couldn't lie to myself, and I definitely couldn't lie to him.

I shifted from one high heel to the other. "I know everything is perfect," I started. "*You're* perfect, but…" I shook my head. "I can't do it, Con. I can't kiss you."

Connor didn't respond; he didn't even *move*. He stood on the porch, stunned, as I grimaced, bracing myself for the worst. Not only our relationship ending, but also our *friendship*. It was only when I caught his shoulders relax that I realized they'd been tensed since I'd opened the door. "Okay, wow," he finally said. "Thank you for telling me." He squeezed my side, but not in a flirty way. It felt like reassurance. "Because I can't kiss you, either, Mads. I love you—"

"I love you, too!" I quickly said.

Connor half smiled. "You don't feel that *pull*, though, right?"

I shook my head, mind flashing to Marco.

"I don't, either," he said. "You are the smartest, funniest, and most beautiful girl I've dated, which makes this pretty confusing..." he trailed off. "But for some reason, I'm never going to fall *in* love with you. No matter how much I wish I could."

"Me too," I said, now thinking of Austin and Samira. They were best friends, and best friends only. "You're my oldest friend, Connor, but if we were destined to be a certified power couple, it would've happened by now. I mean, we live less than a half mile from each other. There was never any distance between us, and honestly, I've never been jealous of your girlfriends. Just annoyed if they treated you terribly or hijacked our plans."

He nodded. "I know I acted jealous, but I wasn't actually begrudging of the guys you went out with," he admitted. "I thought you were wasting your time, because none of them were good enough for you. You deserve someone incredible."

"So do you," I said. "And her name is *not* Lauren Bitterman."

Connor smirked. "This should be way more awkward than it is, right?"

"Probably." I smiled. "But we don't have time for awkward." I hip checked him toward his car. "Our reservation is in ten minutes."

"You'll always be my best friend," he told me as we drove to the restaurant.

"Why, thank you," I said and reached over the center console to give his knee a good old grandmotherly pat. "If you're lucky, you'll always be mine."

When Connor glanced over at me, I winked.

And he winked back.

TWENTY-FOUR

I found myself *alone*-alone again the next weekend. Despite their running joke that they wanted to spend their thirtieth anniversary in Paris, my parents had decided to fly to wine country in California for a long weekend in October. "No parties," they warned me before leaving for the airport Thursday morning, to which I responded, "But Connor already ordered the kegs!"

Austin usually stayed with me while Dad and Da were out of town, but he too had plans. Samira had invited him to Baltimore so they could talk in person. "I told Katie," he said when he called from the road. "I told Katie everything."

I'd winced. "How many mugs did she throw at you?"

After all, there were plenty to spare from their cabinet.

"None," Austin said. "She was actually *calm* about the whole thing, like she'd been expecting it." He sighed. "She was honest and said that she doesn't fully trust Samira, but she trusts me implicitly and understands why I want to try to work out our relationship."

Hmm, I thought. *Either he's downplaying things or that was very anticlimactic…*

I wondered if Samira would be able to fall out of love with my brother, and instead just love him the way he loved her.

Connor and his family were also out of town, celebrating his grandfather's birthday, so I ordered Chinese takeout for dinner. It was date night for Natalie and Davis, and I wasn't in the mood to go to the huge party one of my teammates was throwing. We were headed to the state playoffs, and apparently the perfect way to prepare was a ton of alcohol paired with her heated pool. *Someone is going to hurt themselves*, I worried. *Someone is going to show up to practice on Monday with crutches.*

Which was all to say that my only human interaction that evening was a Zoom with the bridesmaids. Katie had not been included, since the main item on the agenda was rehearsal dinner speeches, but my recent breakup ended up taking top priority. "You were only together three weeks," Yasmin said. "Are you sure that was enough time?"

"Yaz, she couldn't even kiss him," Meredith said. "I'm pretty sure it was enough time."

"Says the person who fell in love with her husband in *one week*," Amanda deadpanned.

"I still think you should've kissed him," Paige told me. "Just to make one hundred percent sure you weren't attracted to him."

Meredith shook her head. "You should never feel pressure to kiss anyone."

"Listen, a kiss wasn't going to change anything," I said. "I'm not attracted to Connor, he's not attracted to me, and we never will be. I know what it feels like to be attracted to someone!"

Onscreen, the bridesmaids all gave me inquisitive looks. "Who have you been attracted to, Mads?" Reese asked sweetly.

Marco... my heart singsonged. Marco, Marco, and...oh, did I mention Marco?

We now texted every couple days, keeping things light and casual.

And by *light and casual*, I meant that I composed an unprompted, lengthy text about why Connor and I didn't fit into a romance novel, yet I still didn't know why Marco had broken up with Shelly. Maybe he hoped I would forget about it.

Neither of us ever mentioned hanging out together. The lack of communication between us was more than eye-roll-inducing, but I didn't want to risk losing him by trying to communicate better.

"It doesn't matter," I grumbled, then focused on Amanda. "Now I vaguely remember you mentioning something about rehearsal dinner speeches?"

The Zoom ended around 10:30—a lot had been brainstormed from scratch—so I yawned as I shucked on a coat and whistled for Arthur and Francine. They needed to go out one last time before I locked the doors and closed up shop for the night.

I followed the Newfoundlands out into the chilly air. It

wasn't cold enough to see my breath, but we were getting there. The sky was overcast, no moon or stars in sight, so it grew *dark* as I wandered away from the house and into the back field. The dogs were almost invisible; I could only see their silhouettes darting between pine trees and hear their barking or heavy breathing. *Creepy*, I thought, but before I could switch on my phone flashlight, the iPhone started chiming with a call.

Bridesmaid Meredith, the screen read.

"Hello?" I answered.

"Hey," Meredith said. "Am I interrupting anything?"

"Nope," I told her. "My dogs and I are just conducting a late-night perimeter check of the property. We're heading toward the barn."

Meredith laughed. "The Cheval Collective's headquarters?"

"Nah, the back barn," I said. "It's where we keep everything for tree season."

It also needed to be renovated within the next couple of years. My parents wanted to pour a concrete floor so that groundhogs would stop burrowing through the dirt one.

"Right," Meredith said. "Pearl's Christmas Trees."

"My grandmother started it," I explained. "And unapologetically christened it after herself." I sighed. "She died when I was ten, but lived with us ever since Austin was little. Christmastime was her favorite season."

I could hear the smile in Meredith's voice. "That's exactly how Austin tells it. I think she and my grandmother would have been fast friends…" She trailed off. "Anyway, I wanted to talk to you about something."

"Okay, I meant what I said," I told her. "I *don't* need a date for the wedding. My family's going to be there, Connor's going to be there, other Gallant-approved friends are going to be there; it's not like I'm going to feel left out or embarrassed."

"I'm glad to hear that," Meredith said. Our earlier Zoom had *shockingly* circled back to my lack of a wedding date. "Really glad, Mads. I was once in your shoes, and while my mental health wasn't in a great place, you'd think it was the end of the world that I didn't have a plus-one to my cousin's wedding."

"But that's when you met Wit, right? Katie said you guys met at a wedding."

"Yes, and that's who I want to talk to you about," she said.

"Wit?"

"No, Katie."

Okay, I thought, kicking the ground with my boot. *If we must.*

"I know there was a spectrum of stories told while discussing speeches tonight," Meredith said. "Some teasing was more innocent than others, so I need you to know that Katie is one of the most special people you will ever meet. I feel so lucky to call her my best friend, and you are even luckier that she's about to be your sister-in-law."

Unable to think of a response, I used Francine's barking as an excuse to keep my mouth shut. "What do you love about her so much?" I asked once she quieted.

"Well, I don't want to spoil my speech," she answered coyly. "But one thing I really love and admire is how fiercely protective she is of the people she cares about."

Fiercely protective? My eyebrows knitted together as I randomly twirled around the left side of the barn. That sounded like Austin, not Katie.

"Yes," Meredith said. "You probably know that my older sister died in a drunk driving accident? Maybe Austin told you?"

I winced. "I'm so sorry—so, so sorry."

"Thank you," Meredith said, and it went quiet for a moment. "I told Katie about Claire our first week in college, and she has been overwhelmingly caring and considerate of it ever since. She suggested we have a 'sober soldier' whenever our friends went out, and orchestrated games like rock paper scissors to randomly draft one. We also had the buddy system at bigger parties—and she always, *always* wrote her phone number on our arms in case of an emergency." She paused. "My parents were local, so my mom and I attended MADD weekly meetings—Mothers Against Drunk Driving—and when I studied abroad my junior year, Katie went to them with my mom. She wasn't trying to be me or my sister; she was just being herself and thought my mom could use the company. She is so supportive of her friends and everything important in their lives. She keeps us safe and makes us better."

"Oh, wow..." I took a step backward, sort of stunned. "Meredith, wow, I—*shit*!"

Pain sliced through my ankle, and I swear I heard a *snap*.

"What?!" Meredith sounded alarmed. "What is it? What happened?"

"No, nothing," I said, pinpricks at my eyes. "I accidentally stepped in a groundhog hole. They're burrowing around the barn."

"Yikes." She sucked in a breath. "You're okay, though?"

"Yeah, I'm fine." I crouched down and looked longingly toward my warm house. "I'll ice it before bed. I probably rolled it." I let out a long breath. "I never knew any of that about Katie."

"You wouldn't," Meredith said. "She's stealthy."

I laughed, but god—it somehow made my ankle scream. "I should go," I said through gritted teeth. "Arthur and Francine have gotten into something…"

"Ahhh, I've been there so many times with our Jack Russell," she said. "Have a good night, Mads."

"Good night, Meredith," I said, and after hanging up, I whistled for the dogs and hopped home.

I woke up in the middle of the night feeling like I'd spent the last week baking in the sun with no water. My mouth as dry as tortilla chips without salsa, I pushed back my covers and got out of bed…only to collapse when I tried to stand. Burning pain seared all the way up my leg, and I yelped the second I hit the wood floor. The old pine groaned under the sudden drop of weight.

My phone was plugged in on my nightstand, so I stretched to grab it. *Please*, I thought, fumbling to turn on its flashlight. *Please let it be okay...*

It was *not* okay. The ice pack I'd strapped to my ankle before bed had slipped off while I'd been sleeping, and now the flashlight's beam showed me the most grotesque thing I'd ever seen. My ankle was so majorly swollen, at least twice its normal size, and bruised red and purple. The *snap* I'd heard earlier hadn't been my imagination; I'd broken something. Whatever bone or bones that made sure my foot faced forward. Now, it was crooked, my foot awkwardly pointing to the right.

I vomited. Kung pao chicken, brown rice, and the various sweet treats I'd snacked on after dinner spewed across my bedroom floor. Then, at the sight of the vomit, I puked up whatever was left in my stomach.

Slowly but surely, I hefted myself back into bed. My lock screen said it was 4:37, and I broke out in tears. I was completely and utterly alone in my house with no one to help me. All of my emergency contacts were unavailable. My parents were in California, and the McCallisters also were out of town. Austin was in Maryland, and I knew Nana silenced her phone at night. She wouldn't hear her ringtone if I called.

One other option came to mind, an option I *never* would've considered this time last year. I tried to pull myself together as the phone rang. But I caved as soon as I heard her voice. "Mmm, hello?" Katie said groggily. "Mads?"

"Katie, I'm sorry it's so late," I said, sobbing. "But I need your help."

Her voice changed, like a switch had been flipped. "Where are you? What happened?"

"I'm home alone," I told her. "I think I broke my ankle. I was outside with the dogs tonight, and I tripped on a groundhog hole..." I squeezed my eyes shut, more tears threatening to spill. "I iced it, but now it's so swollen and it *really* hurts... I can't walk, Katie."

"Okay," Katie said calmly, and I heard some rustling in the background. "Okay, breathe—just breathe."

I did—or *tried* to, at least. My exhalations came out as wails.

"I'm in Princeton," Katie said. "I need to wake my dad, because I won't be able to carry you down the stairs, but we're coming, alright?"

I nodded even though she couldn't see.

"Elevate your ankle with a pillow and put your ice pack back on," she said. "I know it's no longer cold, but do it anyway. We'll be there soon."

Everything was a blur once Katie and Mr. Gallant got to my house. Katie charged into my room, blond hair in a messy topknot and wearing ancient Ugg boots. Her dad and the dogs were at her heels. A huge lump formed in my throat. "Hey, hey, hey," she whispered. "Don't worry, I've got you."

Mr. Gallant carefully lifted me into his arms, and then suddenly I was in the back seat of their car with a sneaker on my left foot and nothing on my right. Katie sat next to me and let me squeeze her hand.

Every pothole in the road to the hospital nearly made me faint until finally Mr. Gallant was carrying me into the emergency room. A nurse helped me into a wheelchair, but we were basically told to take a number and wait. "Can we at least get a bag of ice?" I heard Katie snap, my eyes drifting shut.

I woke up in a hospital bed, my ankle wrapped and raised. Katie had pulled her chair right up to my bedside and was slumped over, face down against the starchy white sheets. Instead of saying anything, I playfully batted her bun a few times like a cat.

"Hi," she said, sitting up and yawning. "How do you feel?"

"Did you call Austin?" I croaked.

She nodded. "He's on his way, and I called your parents. They're trying to get on the earliest flight back home, but Lee is on the phone with the doctor now."

Classic, I thought. As a retired surgeon, Da had always been a little bit of a helicopter parent whenever his children needed medical attention.

"Your nana is in the bathroom," Katie continued. "My dad went home, but he'll be back with breakfast. My mom is cooking as we speak."

"Do you know how bad it is?" I whispered.

Katie shook her head. "They wouldn't tell me particulars since I'm not family." She raised her hand to show off her bling. "This didn't do the trick."

"That's bullshit," was the only comeback I could think of.

Katie's lips lifted in a small smile, and about forty-five minutes later, I was wheeled out of my room for X-rays. I tried to meditate during them so I wouldn't start crying. "Yikes," I'd heard a nurse mutter while unwrapping my bandage. My heart beat to the rhythm of: *This is not good, not good, so not good...*

Hurt ankles and field hockey did not play well together. In fact, they didn't play *at all*. My eyes welled up. What if this was more serious than missing a few practices?

Mr. and Mrs. Gallant had arrived with cranberry-orange scones for everyone by the time I was brought back to my room. Austin was there, too. I didn't ask how fast he'd driven, worried his answer would involve the phrase *outraced a state trooper*.

"Hi there, sis," he said after everyone had cleared out of the room. "I'm sorry I'm late, but I had three state troopers on my tail, and it took a detour to lose them."

I couldn't laugh; it would hurt to laugh.

My brother squeezed my shoulder. "Don't worry. Everything is going to be okay."

"What if I can't play?" I whispered. "Austin, what if this is the end?"

"Mads, I'm an almost dentist. Not an orthopedist." He waited for me to smile, but I didn't. "But even so, I'm fairly confident you won't be scoring the game-winning goal in the state championship. This…" He sighed. "I don't think this is a twisted ankle."

Tears slipped down my face. *No*, I thought. *What if this is the end end? What if Penn field hockey is now a pipe dream?*

An actual orthopedic surgeon walked into the room. X-ray films were tucked under his arm, and he held an iPad with my dads on FaceTime. Whatever strings Da had here, he'd pulled them. "Good morning, Madeline," the surgeon said. "I'm Dr. Lambert." He turned to Austin. "Good morning, Dr. Fisher-Michaels."

Dad's voice was tinny from the iPad, but I heard him loud and clear. "That's my kid!"

Austin's cheeks flushed with embarrassment while I smiled. Even though he technically had seven more months until graduation, he did treat patients at school. Our family was beyond proud of him.

"What's it looking like, Noel?" Da asked.

"Well…" Dr. Lambert put my X-rays up on the board and flicked on its light. "Not great."

I knew I was supposed to pay attention to what he was pointing out on the screen, but my stomach was churning so badly that I needed to close my eyes. Austin would look; I would listen. Not only had I seriously sprained my ankle, but I'd also fractured a bone. When Dr. Lambert got around to mentioning torn ligaments and a severed tendon, I retched.

"Here!" Katie exclaimed, and I opened my eyes right as she handed off a bedpan to Austin, who caught my puke just in time.

"But can I play field hockey?" I asked after wiping my face. "Will I still be able to play?"

"Madeline, you *really* mashed up your ankle," was Dr. Lambert's delicate response.

Fuck, why doesn't anyone get it? I thought. *Why doesn't anyone understand what I'm asking?!*

"She doesn't mean *now*," Katie said as she squeezed my shoulder. "She means by next year. She committed to the University of Pennsylvania back in the spring."

"That depends on her recovery," Dr. Lambert said. "Now let's discuss surgery. I'd like it to happen as soon as possible, but we need to wait a few hours for an OR to open up..."

Da and Dad were at my bedside postsurgery. "It went well," Da assured me as Dad leaned down to kiss my forehead. "Dr. Lambert said no complications whatsoever."

"You have some impressive hardware," Dad said, trying to sound upbeat. "A titanium plate, a handful of screws, and an anchor for the tendon."

"Yes, it's a shame no one will ever see," I deadpanned.

"Fear not," Da said. "I've insisted on a copy of the X-ray."

Dad winked. "We can bring it out at parties."

I smiled weakly. "When can we go home?"

"Soon," Da told me. "They want you to rest a little longer, and then you'll be discharged."

I nodded, exhausted.

"We're so sorry we weren't home," Da said, running a hand through my hair. "And we shouldn't have left you alone, especially with Austin and the McCallisters also gone."

"Probably not," I said. "I'm clearly ill-equipped." My eyes welled up. "But Katie came."

"Yes," they said. "Katie came."

I wasn't the most delightful patient. For the first two weeks after surgery, I wore a splint that was so tightly wrapped it felt like there was no blood circulating below my knee. After many a complaint, Da unwrapped and rewrapped the bandage to make me more comfortable, and I started sleeping on the family room couch so I wouldn't need to be carried upstairs every night. Arthur, who loved the couch, looked absolutely affronted when he realized there was no space for him. He settled for his monogrammed dog bed in the corner.

School did not happen the first week. I stayed home and binged *One Day* on Netflix, which depressed me. The original *Sex and the City* series boosted my spirits, but calling my field hockey coaches made me miserable. "Here's my dad," I said like a little kid, handing the phone to Da when their questions got super specific.

I received so many texts and FaceTimed with teammates.

Connor brought my homework every day. He unpacked his backpack, and we worked together until dinnertime.

Natalie and Davis visited. She painted my nails while Davis played some hidden gems he'd discovered on Spotify.

Meredith and Wit sent me a box of sympathy fudge a couple days after the bridesmaid chat blew up from the news. OMFG, Amanda wrote one day, like she'd just had an epiphany. Will you be in a boot for the wedding?! Or still on crutches?!

I skimmed it in silence, but then openly performed my best imitation of Amanda. No one would hear me; today was unseasonably warm and sunny, so Da had moved my camp into the Garden.

"Respond that you'll be in boot, but you'll need a scooter to go down the aisle," someone said, his smooth voice a stranger for so long. "You won't be able to put any weight on it yet."

A ripple rolled up my spine, I looked up from my phone to see Marco at the garden gate. Tousled brown hair, burgundy sweater, navy pants, and Chelsea boots. His eyes gleamed behind his glasses. Here he was, finally, in the flesh.

"What are you doing here?" I choked out.

"My afternoon classes were canceled today," he replied, settling on the edge of the koi fishpond. "Or, in other words, I had a scheduling conflict and could not attend them."

He skipped, I thought, pulse quickening. *He skipped class to see me.*

"My mother has requested I be home for dinner," Marco said as I resisted the urge to touch him. He was so close, close enough for me to reach out and rest my hand on his knee. "But I'm yours until then. We can do whatever you'd like."

"Twenty questions?" I asked. "Can we play twenty questions?"

He smiled. "Sure."

"Great," I said, fire flaring in my heart. "My version, though."

"What's your version?"

I went in for the kill. "There are only three questions, not twenty, and I will be the one asking them."

"Ah." Marco rubbed the back of his neck. "I walked into that, didn't I?"

I tried to keep my composure. "Sometimes I feel like we're so close," I said. "Last-thought-at-night, first-thought-in-the-morning *close*." I thought about everything he'd shared, from how happy he was to shed his high school hoodies and prom king persona when he got to Princeton, to his dream of writing a book, to inviting me to Stone Harbor. "But then suddenly you're drifting away, like you've changed your mind—you'd rather be nothing more than a guy I used to know." I swallowed. "You can't have it both ways, Marco. It's not fair."

Marco was silent for a moment, then caught my eyes and held them. I felt like I was standing on the edge of a cliff, right about to fall. "What's the first question?"

I cleared my throat. "Why did you break up with Shelly again?"

"Because she's toxic," he said. "She's arrogant, narcissistic, and manipulative." He paused. "She also stole my laptop to email herself my manuscript." He made a face as my eyes widened. "Apparently, she wanted to see if it was any good."

I wished I could sew my mouth shut.

Marco smirked. "If you ask what it's about, it counts as a question."

I rolled my eyes.

"Maybe someday." He winked, then prompted, "Next question?"

"Why did you get back together with Shelly when…?" I trailed off, leaving the rest unsaid. *Why did you get back together with Shelly when you were thinking about me?*

"Because I'm only twenty, Mads." He sighed. "I'm a dickhead who doesn't know anything."

"No," I said. "That's not a good enough answer."

"What would make it better?"

"The truth. Tell me the truth."

Silence. Silence for one, two, three, four, five minutes. His voice actually made my heart leap a little in surprise when he spoke. "I suspected something was going to happen between you and Connor, and I was jealous—*really* jealous—because I could tell how badly you wanted it to happen. Shelly begged to get back together in Stone Harbor, so I said yes."

I folded my arms across my chest. "You couldn't have turned her down?"

Marco shook his head, at a loss for words. He raised his hands in surrender. "I was..." He trailed off in thought. "I was scared of how hard I was falling for you, Mads. I have always been drawn to you—ever since high school—but it felt like treading water in the ocean this year." He took a deep breath. "And just when I found out you felt something too, you and Connor decided to give things a shot—which I feel like you guys needed to do. Shelly was there, and I knew where I stood with her." He grimaced. "What I did was terrible. Playing cat and mouse with you was wrong, and I'm sorry. You overwhelm me. You overwhelm me in the most amazing way, but I wasn't ready to embrace that—it would've been dangerous to embrace that, because I was keeping an eye on you for Katie."

"Why?" I said over my pounding pulse. "Why did you agree to spy?"

Marco mimed zipping his lips.

"It's my third question," I said. "Answer, please."

"Because she knew you weren't comfortable with Ready-Set-Date. She knew you were game, and that it would be good for you in a sense, but she knew you weren't fully comfortable."

She is so supportive of her friends and everything important in their lives, I remembered Meredith saying. *She keeps us safe and makes us better.*

"She called me that night you were at Princeton," Marco

said gently. "It wasn't a coincidence that we ran into each other at Wawa. After you told Austin you were all alone, she called me and told me to get my ass over there to make sure you were okay. She didn't want anything or anyone to hurt you."

My heart ached. Oh, Katie—*freaking* Katie. "Holy crap," I murmured. "She cares. She did it because she cares about me."

"Yeah." Marco nodded. "She cares a hell of a lot, Mads."

We slipped into silence again. I noticed that during this intimate interrogation, Marco had migrated across the brick patio, and was now kneeling by the couch. "May I ask one more question?"

"No," Marco replied. "You said only three questions, and you've asked three questions."

"Marco…"

Marco moved to rest his elbows on the edge of the couch cushion. "Sorry, but you made the rules."

"Which means I can amend them!" I said. "One bonus question, okay?"

He agreed.

"Do you miss me?" I asked.

"Every second," he answered, then asked his own question. "Do you forgive me?"

I put a finger to my mouth, to dramatically contemplate.

Did I forgive him?

Marco leaned in close, nose brushing mine. Golden cords tightened around my heart. "I love you, Mads," he whispered. "For whatever it's worth."

"It's worth quite a lot," I whispered back. "Because I love you too, Marco."

Then, heart hammering, I pressed my lips to his.

Marco's response was instant, both hands coming up to cup my face before he teasingly tugged my braid. Some type of spellbinding magic shot through my veins when he gently tilted my head to deepen our kiss. My body hummed, and he laughed after I moved to tangle my fingers in his soft sweater and pulled him closer. The sound reverberated against my chest.

This is it, I thought, heart about to burst. *This is a* kiss.

One that left me wonderstruck.

Marco left me wonderstruck.

TWENTY-FIVE

I was on crutches when I returned to school, so every day, one of my field hockey teammates was assigned to help me to class. "Out of the way!" my co-captain shamelessly shouted in the congested hallways. "Mads is on the move!"

It would've been nice if the building's elevator wasn't in an entirely different wing, and it was harder than I thought it'd be watching my games from the sidelines. "Stop bouncing your knee," Da instructed. My right knee, which was part of my right leg, which was attached to my right ankle—my *bad* ankle. "Keep still."

"I want to be out there," I whispered.

"You *will* be out there," he whispered back, knowing we were actually talking about Penn next year. He leaned over to kiss the top of my head. "It's just going to take time, patience, and physical therapy."

My orthopedic surgeon inspected my ankle two weeks post-op. "Very nice," Dr. Lambert said, impressed enough to promote me from my splint to a boot. I still wasn't allowed to put any weight on my ankle, so Da ordered a scooter off Amazon. It looked like a tricycle, complete with handlebars and brakes, but instead of me sitting on the padded seat, my knee rested on it.

Austin jokingly bought me a kid's purple bike helmet with gold stars, while Marco gifted me an old-fashioned bell, the same one his mom had for her beach cruiser. "For you to ring in the hallways," he explained. "You don't want to run anyone over on your way to calculus."

"What if they deserve it?" I'd quipped.

"Then you'll wipe out half the school," he'd quipped back.

My parents had another Intimidating Dads conversation with Marco after I'd announced that he, the dark horse, was now the last suitor standing. It started with *We thought this might happen*, and ended with *You will be answering to us if you break her heart*.

"I understand." Marco nodded solemnly. "And if it helps, I'm highly confident that if it comes to that, *Mads* will break *my* heart."

Dad clapped him on the shoulder. "No wonder you're a Princeton man!"

Because I wasn't very mobile, and for a million other reasons, Marco and I agreed to take things slow. He came home from school a couple nights a week to study and watch Rangers games even though he knew nothing about hockey. And Connor, who for once was enjoying the single life, lost it after game three. "For the love of god, Álvarez, if you're going to watch a hockey game, at least *learn* your hockey..."

Once I mastered my scooter, we ventured into town. Marco drove and then insisted on walking on the street side of the sidewalk. "You're the only guy I know who does that," I remarked after he soundlessly ducked to the left. "Even before my ankle, you always made sure I was nowhere near the road."

I remembered our first walk in Princeton; whenever I got too close to the curb, Marco smoothly nudged me toward the storefronts.

Marco smiled. "It's a tale as old as time," he said. "Men would stroll street-side so passing carriages wouldn't ruin women's dresses by splashing mud or water on them." He paused. "Horse shit, too. Horse shit was everywhere."

I laughed, and in response, Marco took my hand and threaded our fingers together. Smiling, I squeezed as he knocked on Fable's discreet front door. The hostess opened the top left mahogany pane, exchanged a nod with Marco, and then opened the door and led us to a secluded, smoky-mirrored nook in the back. Marco helped me into the cushy velvet banquette and carefully propped my boot up on the chair across from us before joining me. We ordered almost every appetizer and drink off the mocktail list. It was then that I discovered that Marco was adorably affectionate by nature, and that I was, too. We only let go of each other's hands to eat, and every so often, I leaned over to drop a kiss on his warm shoulder.

By the time Fable's famous butterscotch pudding arrived, Marco had wrapped an arm around my shoulders and we were kissing. Silently, slowly, dreamily kissing. "Marco Álvarez, what would your mother say?" our server asked.

"Something encouraging," Marco replied as I blushed. "She's wanted this"—he gestured between us—"to happen for a while."

In mid-November, Marco invited me to Stone Harbor for the night. My parents asked me to close up the house for the winter, he texted me, and I'd like some company.

Company sounds spectacular! I'd said, pulse twisting and turning with pleasure. But I don't know if my parents will be cool with it.

I'll ask them, he texted.

I had no idea what Marco ended up saying to my dads, but amazingly, they gave us the green light. I suspected they knew Marco wasn't going to try anything; my boot-and-scooter combo was an effective chaperone.

Marco knew how to drive stick, so after some begging and pleading on his part, I let him drive the Defender to the shore. I liked the way he drove, with one hand on the wheel and the other on my knee between gear shifts. He looked completely at ease, and I kept not-so-sneakily snapping photos of him. "They're for my own personal consumption," I said.

I hadn't told the bridesmaids about Marco and me yet. Katie knew, but I didn't want her friends to act like Marco had won a contest. I mean, I'd joked that he had, and his grin said he knew it, but this was different. I wanted it to be just the two of us for a little while.

It felt good to see the Álvarez cottage again with its light green shingles, pebbled yard, and picket fence. Marco helped me inside—my scooter wasn't meant for such rocky terrain, so I'd packed my crutches—and he brought our stuff in after I sank into the den's deep couch. We watched an episode of that creepy stalker show *You*, but while curled into Marco's side, his body as warm and cozy as a crackling fire, my eyelids fluttered shut.

I must've slept for an hour, maybe longer. The TV was off when I woke up, and Marco gone. I found him in the kitchen, humming as he stirred something on the stove. We'd picked up groceries on the way here. "Hello…" I said, my delivery perfectly Penn Badgley. "*YOU*."

Marco jumped and spun to face me. "Never do that again," he said, dead serious. "Please."

I smirked. "Dinner smells incredible."

"Paella," he said, which was like a Spanish stir-fry with rice, saffron, vegetables, chicken, and shrimp. "It'll be ready in a few minutes."

"Okay." I leaned my crutches against the wall and then hopped over to hug him from behind. He laughed when I nuzzled the back of his neck.

Later, we waited for our food comas to subside by watching

a movie, and afterward I took a shower and changed into a sweatshirt and pajama pants. "Hey, sweet tart!" I heard Marco shout as I carefully strapped up my boot. "Guess what?"

"What?" I shouted back.

"It's snowing!" he said from outside his sister's door. "Come on, I have your coat."

Marco gave me a piggyback ride to the beach, his breath visible in the night air. I could feel my wet hair starting to freeze. Both of us had beach towels around our necks and I held a lantern to light our way.

"I've never seen anything like this," I whispered once we'd settled on our towels. We'd duct-taped a garbage bag over my boot so no sand would get in it. "Snow on the beach." I turned to Marco, white flakes soundlessly falling around us and calming waves washing ashore. "I feel like I'm in a dream."

He nodded before breaking into a wide grin, one that suggested his soul shined brightly within him. When I looked at Marco, the rest of the world blurred. "But it's not," he pointed out, then smiled and murmured, "I've never been so happy to be awake."

His words sent a shimmer through me, one that rippled deep into my core and swirled into a long ache. "Yes." I smiled and snuggled into his side. "You took the words right out of my mouth."

I thought of that night a couple weeks later, at the dining room table on Thanksgiving. Marco and I'd walked back to his house around midnight, and after he helped me into Carina's bed, I'd convinced him to climb in so we could sleep together. The next morning, the snow had vanished—it hadn't been cold enough to stick—and after French toast for breakfast, I cleaned up, and Marco shut off the water and did whatever other chores needed to be done to winterize the cottage. We'd hit the road around noon.

Most Novembers, my family drove up to Rhode Island to spend the holiday with Da's side of the family. But this year, those relatives had decided to celebrate Thanksgiving on a Disney cruise. "No," Dad said before the rest of our family got any ideas. "I am not having Mickey Mouse carve my turkey. No, thank you."

"Trust me, Harry," Da said. "We are in total alignment."

This year's group was small. Nana brought her Man Friend, and because she and Austin were less than a month away from getting married, Katie came, too. She and Austin had never spent Thanksgiving together before; it was the one holiday they refused to sacrifice.

I wouldn't mind being in Boca right about now... I thought, glancing at the downpour outside. Rain, rain, freaking nonstop rain. From the trying-not-to-pout-but-totally-pouting pout on Katie's face, you could tell she was missing her grandparents' house.

Austin's fiancée was *miserable*.

"The mashed potatoes are really good, Katie," I said, to break the silence. Our dinner table conversation topics had all led to dead ends so far. "Where did you get them?"

"I didn't get them anywhere," she replied evenly. "I made them."

"Oh." I flushed. It wasn't that I thought Katie couldn't cook, but these potatoes looked and tasted like the product of a professional caterer. They were whipped to perfection.

"It's her mom's recipe," Austin said quickly, "but Katie took over making them when she was sixteen."

"Lucky us," Dad said. "Lee knows everything about turkey and stuffing, but his potatoes have *never* been this good."

"They're better than yours, Harry," Da countered.

The table laughed, but Katie smiled blandly before taking a sip of water. My heart wound into a knot. *What's wrong?* I wanted to ask, because now that I knew Katie cared so hard, *I* cared so hard. *If you miss your family, tell us you miss your family! We'll understand!*

Nana's Man Friend brought up the wedding while the pumpkin pie was being sliced. "Are you having a band or DJ?"

"Band," Katie replied. "We're having a twelve-piece band."

"It's going to be fabulous," Nana said. "Austin's played me samples from their website."

"Yeah." Katie nodded. "They're great…"

Nana's Man Friend smiled. "What's your song, if you don't mind me asking?"

"It's called 'Garden,'" Austin said, smiling. "It's by this indie-folk band we love."

"The band's rendition is astronomically different than the original song," Katie said. "But that's how it is, so…" She trailed off into the distance.

"It's still going to be incredible, Kates," Austin said, then grinned like a lovestruck idiot. "We practice dancing in our kitchen every night. Neither of us is a good dancer, so we don't want to completely embarrass ourselves."

"Ah, yes…" Dad mused as I dove into my slice of pumpkin paradise. "You never did have a natural rhythm."

I caught Katie roll her eyes.

And that, combined with the fact that she hadn't touched her slice of Nana's delightful pie, was the final straw.

"What's bothering you?!" I blurted, and my family went silent. I took another bite of pie for a boost of confidence. "Seriously, Katie," I said after swallowing. "What's your deal?"

"*Mads*," Austin hissed.

I shook my head. "I want to know, Austin. She's been sulking since you guys got here, and anytime anyone brings up the wedding, it's like she couldn't care less or would rather walk Captain Hook's plank than go through with it." I looked at Katie. Her eyes were glassy. "You are my brother's *favorite person*, Catherine, but these days, I'm having a tough time believing he's yours." I brandished my fork like a sword. "I mean, call it off if that's what you want!"

Everyone sat there. Austin was glaring at me while our parents exchanged a look that screamed: *Didn't we raise our daughter to have manners?*

Out of the corner of my eye, I saw Nana diplomatically rise from her chair, pick up her plate of pie, and gesture for her Man Friend to follow her out of the room.

"No," Katie said, expression accusatory. "But that's exactly what *you* want, Madeline, don't you?" She looked at my dads. "That's what *all* of you want, right? For me to call off the wedding?"

None of us got the chance to answer; Katie was too quick to detonate.

"I know none of you like me!" Her voice went up several octaves. "You've always been polite, but I know for a fact that you don't like me or think I'm good enough for Austin!"

"Well, we don't see you!" I shouted at the same time Dad said, "Excuse me? You know for a *fact*?"

Katie opened her mouth, but no words came out. She didn't know which question to answer first.

I overpowered my dad. "Katie, you are physically present," I continued, "but we don't *see* you. You don't show us who you are, or *even* part of who you are. It's been years and I still can't name any of your interests beyond reading, watching hockey, and writing detailed Yelp reviews for brunch places." I swallowed. "Your mom told me you played field hockey in high school— why haven't you *ever* told me that? Is it now a taboo subject or something?" I laughed. "Who cares if you didn't play in college?" I held up my hands. "And music, it seems like you're into music? I *love* music."

"Mads, lay off," Austin said when the last part came out a bit sarcastic. "Stop grilling her. She's…"

"Shy," Katie filled in the blank. "I'm shy, I'm an introvert, so you have no idea how intimidating it is to meet and connect with such an extroverted family. Especially one who loves each other as much as you guys do, who enjoys talking and genuinely *being* with each other as much as you do. It *has* been five years, yet I *still* feel like an outsider. I try, I really do, but I don't even *feel* like myself when I'm here sometimes. And whatever version of me that is?" She shook her head. "She's tired of trying to prove herself."

Da kept his voice calm. "Katie, you don't need to prove yourself—"

"Yes, I fucking do!" she exclaimed. "Or I was supposed to and failed miserably!" She wiped her eyes. "You tolerate me because Austin loves me, but you don't approve."

"What makes you say that?" Dad asked.

"I'm not Samira!"

Something grew thick in my throat. Katie—oh, Katie.

I'm not Samira.

"I know you all wish Austin was with her," she continued. "I heard you say it." She looked at my parents and me. "The first time I came to your Memorial Day cookout, I overheard you guys say how I was nothing like Samira, and how much you *missed* Samira, and then Mads said it didn't matter if you didn't like me because you all knew that they'd be together in the end."

I gulped. My parents and I *had* said that. Memorial Day four years ago had been the first occasion we'd ever spent any *real* time with Katie, and we'd been so excited—maybe *too* excited. Because while we'd met Katie before, she was pretty quiet, and we were hoping a party would unleash the fun and loving person Austin wouldn't shut up about. I remembered how my dads and I'd powwowed at the horse pasture when that hadn't been the case.

"Katie, all of that is true," Da said gently. "And on behalf of everyone"—he glanced at Dad and me—"I'm sorry." He sighed. "We just weren't sure what to expect, since the only girl Austin had ever seriously dated was Samira. We were presumptuous in thinking he might have"—he rolled his eyes—"a *type*. It turned out we didn't know his type yet, because his type was *you*."

"And when we said we missed Samira," Dad added, "we meant that we missed her that *evening*. She was studying abroad that semester, so it'd been several months since we'd seen her. We missed her as a dear friend." He turned to me.

"I meant what I said," I admitted, blood thumping in my ears. "I missed Samira in our lives, and I wanted her to *stay* in our lives, and I wasn't sure if that was possible if she and Austin weren't a couple. And you're right, I didn't give you a fair chance because of it." I closed my eyes. "I'm so sorry, Katie."

Katie nodded, but she didn't say it was okay; instead, she held up her left hand. The gleaming ice cube looked heavy on her finger. "This is a *gorgeous* ring," she said. "But it's not the ruby. Austin has told me so many stories about his grandmother, including how much she loved that ring. My heart dropped when he proposed because the ruby wasn't in the box." She shook her head. "You didn't give it to him. Maybe you accepted that I'm not Samira, but I must still not be special enough."

"Austin, why don't you take this one?" Dad suggested.

"Katie, they have nothing to do with the ruby," Austin said. "The ruby is mine." He scratched the back of his head a little sheepishly. "Grandma left it to me to give to the woman I wanted to marry—and that has *always* been you." He paused. "But you never asked to see it, and it's a little out there, so I was worried you'd hate it. Your ring"—he pointed to the diamond—"was something I knew you'd love."

"And I do love it, Austin," Katie said. "Because it's from *you*." Her voice cracked. "But I suppose I wanted a piece of it to be from your family, too."

We failed her, I thought, stomach sinking. *We absolutely failed her.*

"Catherine Marie Gallant," I said, "the only person you need to be 'special enough' for is Austin, but you're special to me, too. You *did* try to open yourself up to us, but I didn't try to see you—or I didn't try my best. Even when you asked me to be one of your bridesmaids. When we played truth or dare at our sleepover, and I heard about the midnight Wawa Icees, I thought that was the coolest thing ever, and I should've told you that." I took a breath. "You also care so much about the people in your life. Thank you for picking up the phone at four a.m. and taking me to the hospital—you yelling at that nurse for ice will go down in history as one of the greatest moments in my life." I smiled when she laughed a little. "And I know you meant well when you asked Marco to be my shadow. I'm sorry it took me so long to realize that you just wanted to protect me."

Katie reached up to wipe her eyes.

"Katie, you give me a novel every year for Christmas," Dad said. "I have grown to adore your insightful and pithy annotations in the margins—they feel like secrets between us." He smiled. "I also told every single client of mine that my future daughter-in-law graduated from UChicago with her MBA."

"And I have always had a soft spot for you," Da said. "You remind me of my mother. Pearl was a colorful character." He nodded out the window. "She would take polar plunges in the pond whenever she thought autumn had officially turned to winter." He smiled. "But she was also reserved and quietly remarkable with her innate kindness and cleverness." He reached to squeeze Katie's hands. "You are more than special enough, Katie. You are *family*."

Katie dissolved into tears. "I want to marry Austin," she said, choked up. "I want to marry Austin more than anything, but I *hate* this wedding. That's why I've been so upset about it, and horrible to you, Austin. It isn't me at all."

"Then who is it?" I asked.

"My parents," Katie answered. "Mostly my mom. She and I used to pretend-plan my dream wedding when I was little, and she refuses to accept that what I wanted then—Christmas at the country club with a million guests—is not what I want now. Even my dress…"

Uh-oh, I worried. *Looks like a pastry?*

"What would you like now?" Austin asked, as if the Gallants hadn't already spent like a hundred thousand dollars on this blessed event. "What is your dream wedding today?"

Katie smiled sadly. "You know."

My brother smiled back, nodding. "The invitations."

"Yeah," she whispered, then looked at my parents and me. "I commissioned and helped design the wedding invitations behind my parents' backs—"

"Wait, that was you?" I asked. "Tally-Ho in her tartan blanket, the Christmas tree barn, and the frozen pond watercolor? I thought *Austin* gave the artist the vision for the invitations."

"Nope," my brother said proudly. "That was all Katie."

"I love your home," she said. "Connecting with you was challenging, but I immediately felt wrapped into this magical, timeless place. It always feels like a warm hug every time I pull up the driveway." She sighed. "I really wanted the wedding to be that way, too."

"I think it still can be," I said, excitedly sitting up in my chair. "Or, at least, a piece of it can." I turned to my parents. "Is it too late to get the deposit back on the rehearsal dinner venue?"

"Yes," Dad said, then waved his hand. "But by all means, speak now."

I grinned and did.

WINTER

TWENTY-SIX

I was still in a boot by December, but I could officially put weight on my ankle again. "No, don't even think about it," Marco said when I tried to help Austin and him move Dad's antique rolltop desk. "You aren't allowed to lift high-impact, heavy stuff yet."

"Then what am I supposed to do?" I asked. "Everything here is high-impact."

"Supervise!" Da called. "Visualize!"

It was December 13, and everything in the Cheval Collective's barn was either being moved upstairs or stored in our garage. We had other plans for the office tonight.

"Should we take the current listings down?" Amanda asked, eyeing one Realtor's FOR SALE board on the wall. "And leave the artwork?"

"Definitely." I nodded. Dad had an impressive art collection, all classic oil paintings featuring what else? Horses. "I think the art will go well with the wreaths."

Amanda smiled. "Mom made so many."

"They're stunning," I said. It had taken a hot second to get Mrs. Gallant on board with the new plan for Katie and Austin's rehearsal dinner. But Mr. Gallant, who'd deemed this the best idea ever, had dropped Katie and his wife off at a spa for the morning. "This is your show," he'd told my family. "Stacy and I want to help, but I don't think she needs to necessarily be on the premises…"

Once the office was all cleared out, Amanda and Nana hung Mrs. Gallant's handmade wreaths on the warm wood-paneled walls. Fresh pine and boxwood were mixed with magnolia leaves and cypress, and Mrs. Gallant had adorned each wreath with perfect bows in blue, amber, and gold. Dad and Nana strung green garlands and fairy lights around the barn's wood beams.

Then came the rugs. Mr. Gallant and Da hauled in Persian rugs, which we unrolled to create a patchwork quilt across the floor. "The guys are here!" Austin announced when the groomsmen arrived that afternoon, and we immediately put them to work, arranging the round teak farmhouse tables and chairs. Carina Álvarez brought over the sound system while Rose Álvarez and her crew marched into the barn's kitchen, because who else was catering tonight?

Ember & Ash.

"Fear not, friends!" a voice called later. "I've arrived!"

I glanced up from arranging the table centerpieces (a trio of white candles arranged among more greenery and pine cones) to see Wit walking into the barn. The groomsmen basically lost their minds, whooping and whistling. "Okay, but he's not even a groomsman," I told Austin.

"No, he's not," my brother said. "But I still asked him to give a speech tonight..."

"Samira's coming tomorrow, right?" I asked quietly.

Austin nodded. "She promised she'd be there. After, though..." He sighed. "We're not going to talk for a while. She said she wants some time."

To fall out of love with you, I knew. *She needs to fall out of love with you.*

It would be bittersweet, but their silence wouldn't last forever. "You can't lose her, Austin," I'd overheard Katie gracefully tell my brother. "She's a once-in-a-lifetime friend."

"Ay!" Wit pointed out the barn doors. "The bridesmaids are here, too!"

"That's my cue." I clapped my hands. "Time to herd some cats."

Austin smiled. "You know you're the best, right?"

"The best what?" I asked. "The best sister? The best friend? The best future college field hockey player?"

Penn had emailed me my acceptance letter yesterday. Tears had streaked down my face as Austin shook my shoulders in celebration. I was in—*officially* in. And fuck it, I knew I was going to kick ass on Franklin Field next year.

"Yes, as long as you kick ass at physical therapy," my brother said now. "But really, just *the best*, Mads."

I smiled. "Austin…"

We hugged, and when I hurried out of the barn to welcome the bridesmaids, everyone shouted, "Don't run!"

Compared to tomorrow's two hundred guests, the rehearsal dinner was super exclusive—only immediate family and the wedding party (and Wit). We would caravan to St. Paul's in Princeton for a late-afternoon ceremony rehearsal, and I'd tried to turn my room into a bridal suite for Katie and the bridesmaids. There was an assortment of snacks and a cooler of water bottles, sodas, and little bottles of prosecco (that Dad had bought because I wasn't twenty-one).

Katie looked fresh-faced from her spa day, and she beamed while presenting us each with a garment bag. "Tomorrow's gowns are so elegant," she said. "My mother has beautiful taste, but I *really* love these…"

All the dresses were whimsical and jewel-toned; Meredith's was a luxurious turquoise, while Reese's was a warm amber and mine a deep purple. All silk, the dresses wouldn't withstand the December chill, so we gasped when Katie gave us cable knit sweaters to wear on top. They were cream and cropped. "I'm obsessed," I said, the others agreeing. "I'm *obsessed*, Katie!"

"Thank you!" she said. "I know it's unconventional, but I

hoped you might wear them tonight. My dress is white, and I have a gold sweater to go with it."

"Do we owe you anything?" Paige asked, and it was then that I realized I hadn't been the only one who'd thought the bridesmaid life wasn't cheap.

Katie shook her head. "You've all given me so many gifts, so this is my gift to you."

We changed into our dresses—Amanda insisted my boot tied the whole look together—before starting on hair and makeup. "So, Mads," Reese said as I weaved Katie's long blond hair into a braid crown. "Who would you give your First Impression Rose to?"

I sighed as the others laughed. In the mirror, Katie smiled slyly at me. Of course we would come full circle with my *Bachelorette* spin-off. "Easy," I said. "First Impression Rose goes to Davis, especially since he's now a really great friend."

"Front-runner?" Yasmin asked.

I grinned. "Connor."

I loved Connor McCallister with everything I had. It just wasn't wonderstruck love.

"Yes!" the group cheered before the subject switched. No one wanted to talk about "Here for the Wrong Reasons."

"Okay, Amanda," Paige said. "Smoky eye: yes or no?"

Katie coughed. "Excuse me, ladies, but you didn't ask Mads about her Final Rose."

The bridesmaids all cocked their heads. It had been a little over a month, but I still hadn't mentioned Marco. "Hold on!" Meredith suddenly started bouncing on her tiptoes. "Hold the hell on—is it your ridiculously handsome Princeton friend? Whose family has a monopoly on all the best restaurants in town? Marco something?"

I glanced away to grin.

"Katie!" Meredith exclaimed after I coyly suggested they check out his boutonniere tomorrow. "I can't believe you didn't tell me!"

Katie shrugged. "It wasn't my news to tell."

"I only knew because they kept staring starry-eyed at each other during setup earlier," Amanda said. "It'll be so obvious once you see them together."

"Yes, yes, yes." I smirked after the squealing stopped. "It seems I've ended up with a promising plus-one, after all…"

Mrs. Gallant started crying the second she walked into the barn after our successful ceremony rehearsal. Luckily, we had plenty of tissues on hand. "I don't know what to say," she told my parents. "Thank you so much." She shook her head. "This is absolutely enchanting."

"It took a village!" I smiled, feeling Da squeeze my shoulders at the same time Dad said, "It was all Mads."

I couldn't help but glow with pride as I asked Nana's

Man Friend, tonight's bartender, for a flute of sparkling cider. Afterward, I went to find my seat at the center table and smiled to myself. **Madeline**, my place card read, in Katie's neat handwriting.

No longer was I *Madeleine*.

Da took the mic to announce it was time to dish up dinner. Everything was family style tonight, tables laden with Ember & Ash's interpretation of "elevated comfort food." Buttery brioche burgers, lobster mac and cheese, vegetarian chili, corn bread soufflés, Caesar salad, and the world's crispiest truffle fries!

Marco and the few other servers circulating were barraged with compliments. "I need to talk to your mother, young man," I overheard Nana say to Marco. "She needs to tell me *what* is in this chili..."

Katie and Austin, like they always did, ate off each other's plates. They kept smiling and laughing at each other. I had never seen Katie look so happy and relaxed. Even though we had a professional photographer around, I took a photo when they weren't looking. Katie was whispering something in Austin's ear; Grandma Pearl's ruby ring glittered in the candlelight.

My brother had reproposed to Katie in the horse pasture several weeks ago. They were both in heavy coats and muddy boots, but Tally-Ho had never neighed or flicked her tail so enthusiastically. She'd started headbutting Katie as soon as Austin had gotten down on his knee.

Paris, who?

I went to the bathroom between dinner and dessert, and by that I meant I went and looked for Marco. "I'm on my smoke break," he explained when I found him outside on the barn's kitchen doorstep. He took a puff from an invisible cigarette.

"You're such a dork," I said, shaking my head. "Have you ever even smoked?"

"No, but Simon has an antique pipe that I want to try at some point." His smile rivaled the stars in the sky. "Come here."

Making sure not to run, I impatiently walked into his arms and burrowed my face into his chest when he hugged me close. "You smell delicious," I murmured.

I felt his lungs expand and contract as he laughed. "Well, I *did* just finish prepping the peanut butter pie..."

"Mmm," I hummed before tilting my head back to smirk at him. "Like I said, you are delicious."

Marco smirked back before pulling me back in to kiss my neck. Light and little kisses that made the backs of my knees go numb.

All too soon, we were making out against the back of the barn. Marco had slipped his hands under my sweater, and I could feel them burning through my thin silk dress. When I took it off later, I swore I would see his handprints tattooed on either side of my rib cage. "I don't want to say goodbye," I said after an aching kiss. My heart wanted to beat its way out of my chest, pulled toward Marco like a magnet. "But I need to get back." I ran my fingers through his hair. "I can't miss the speeches."

"Then don't say goodbye," Marco told me. "I'm not leaving anytime soon."

"Okay," I said, then kissed him deeply enough to fog up his glasses.

"*My god!*" he breathed. "*You're fun to kiss!*"

I laughed, recognizing the *Tender Is the Night* quote. Simon and F. Scott had me hooked. "I'll see you later," I said.

Da gave an eloquent and heartfelt welcome speech, and then Wit rose from his chair, removing a folded piece of paper from his black velvet jacket's breast pocket. Meredith stood up, too. "Hello, everyone," he said. "I'm Wit, and you all know my *beguiling* wife, Meredith." He grinned crookedly at her. "We've known Katie and Austin for far, far too long now, so we've decided to spare you all the tiny details and instead paint you the big picture in a poem…"

After Wit and Meredith brought the barn down in belly laughs, Reese took the mic and talked about her two-decade friendship with Katie, which spanned from their childhood to adulthood. Katie was the one person who knew Reese through and through, who knew her even better than Reese's therapist. "It's true," Katie told our table. "So naturally, I don't agree with her therapist!"

I'd requested to give my speech at tomorrow's reception, so

I sat back and listened as the evening proceeded. Groomsmen spoke; more bridesmaids spoke; family members fought over the mic. The love in the room was palpable, the warm hug Katie and Austin so deserved. I swore my brother's smile was stuck on his face, and Katie's eyes sparkled with tears. "I wish we could do it," I heard her whisper after Meredith's solo speech received a standing ovation. "Tonight is perfect, everything is perfect. I wish we could get married now."

Something zipped through me.

I wish we could get married now.

"Me too, Kates," Austin whispered back. "But we have St. Paul's and Bedens Brook tomorrow."

"It doesn't matter," Katie said, excitedly shaking her head. "We can get married twice. Tomorrow, with everyone, and tonight, with the people who love us most. We can do it, Austin. Let's do it."

"You don't have anyone to officiate," I said, forgetting that I was an eavesdropper and not a participant in this conversation. "Who is going to marry you guys?"

Austin sighed. "We should've invited Father Powell."

Katie didn't say anything; instead, I watched her try to flip her hair before she remembered she had an updo tonight.

She flips her hair when she's deep in thought, I realized after years of thinking otherwise. *Not when she's unimpressed.*

Austin and I shared a sudden look. We knew someone ordained. "Dad!" we said at the exact same time.

Katie's brow crinkled. "Harry?"

"Yes," Austin said, laughing and smiling. "He's ordained. He married two friends like a decade ago."

"And this *is* his place of worship." I gestured around the barn.

Austin quickly kissed Katie. "Let's ask."

"Okay," she agreed. She touched Austin's cheek. "I want to do it myself."

And then she pushed back her chair, smoothed her dress, and approached the bar, where Dad and Da were both waiting for more champagne.

"Do you think he'll say yes?" I asked as we stared at them. Their backs were turned, so there were zero indicators beyond body language. Katie's hands were clasped, nervous.

"Mads, what kind of question is that?" Austin said. "*Of course* he'll say yes."

After a couple minutes, our parents both hugged Austin's fiancée fiercely. I grinned as they walked together toward our table. Dad looked poised and professional, but Katie looked like she was floating on air. "Austin, would you mind joining Katie and me upstairs for a moment?" he asked. "I think it's truly important to get a sense of the couple so I can perform their marriage ceremony accordingly."

A shit-eating grin spread across my brother's face. "You mean you don't want to just wing it?"

Dad laughed. "No thanks. This is an incredible night, but

now we're going to make it an even better one, which is going to take at least two minutes of preparation." He put an arm around Katie. "You and my soon-to-be daughter-in-law deserve to be timeless."

The rehearsal dinner turned into a wedding, and after that, a reception. Tables were quickly rearranged so Mr. and Mrs. Austin Fisher-Michaels could have their first dance as husband and wife with the help of Spotify. I cheered louder than anyone else when they kissed.

Field hockey games had given my lungs plenty of practice.

Then Dad got ahold of the aux cord to put on one of his throwback playlists. Earth, Wind & Fire's "September" came through the speakers, and the bridesmaids screamed when "Dancing Queen" followed.

I rolled my eyes, but it was nice to know my performance at the Finger Lakes had not been lost on them—or on Marco, who Katie was pushing toward me. I burst into a smile when he offered me his hand. I took it, and he immediately twirled me. "Be careful," I told him. "I'm in a boot, remember?"

"Oh, trust me, I remember," he said. "You've stepped on my foot enough times that I doubt I'll ever forget!"

Our dancing was careful and controlled for the classics, and then we swayed together to the slow songs. The barn was so full of laughter, love, and life that I found it easy to slip out of sight when Marco and I made eye contact and both thought, *Let's run away now.*

We kissed outside, immediately breathless in the December night air. "Are you sure?" Marco asked.

"About what?" I deadpanned.

He laughed. "You know what I mean."

I did. I'd already taken his hand and was leading him toward the farmhouse. "Yes," I told him, desperately wanting to break into a sprint. "I'm sure."

"Alright." Marco squeezed my hand. I could feel his pulse pounding in his palm, and he stayed quiet until we were inside and climbing the tight staircase to the attic guest room. My room was technically still the bridal suite. "It's probably going to hurt," he said, voice gravelly. "I'm sorry. You might not like it at first."

I stopped on the staircase and turned to look at him with an arched eyebrow. "Are you seriously mansplaining a woman losing her virginity to me right now?"

"No!" Marco flushed. "I mean, yes—that's what it sounds like, but I don't mean it that way. I'm just…"

"Nervous?" I asked.

He flushed harder.

"Why? You've had sex before."

"Yes," he said. "But never with you."

"You mean with a virgin?"

Because I knew that couldn't be true.

Marco shook his head and took a couple steps up, so that we were now only one stair away from each other. I felt the back of my neck heat. "No," he murmured. "I meant I've never had sex with my favorite person before."

Favorite person.

The words felt as precious and rare as the shimmer of a shooting star.

"Well..." I ventured. "If we ever get to the Fantasy Suite, I'd really love for you to experience what that's like." I swung our entwined hands and kissed his fingers. "Even if it means I have to endure excruciating pain."

Marco tipped back his head and groaned. "Mads!"

I giggled and tugged him upstairs and into the bedroom. He spun me into his arms after I'd locked the door, and I let him hold me for a moment before I hooked my fingers into his belt loops and kissed him. "Don't ask if I'm sure again," I said once our clothes and a foil wrapper were on the floor. My boot, too. "I'm sure, okay?"

"Okay." Marco lowered himself on top of me and began a trail of sweet kisses up my neck. His skin hummed against mine, heat radiating between us. "But how are you *sure* you're sure?" he asked as I ran my hands over his shoulders.

"Because I trust you," I whispered back. "I trust you, Marco, and I love you."

"I trust you too," he told me as our hips started to move

together. Slow—slowly, so we could find a rhythm. Marco kissed me. "Mads, I love you so much."

"And because you are my favorite person," I told him later, after it had hurt like hell. We were tangled together under the covers. "You will always be my favorite person."

Marco smiled. "This feels like a dream."

I smiled back. "It's not."

―――――

The final thing I did that night, after kissing Marco for the millionth time and saying goodbye to guests, was button up my wool coat and head out to the horse pasture with a lantern and some carrots. The frozen ground crunched under my boots, and I heard voices still drifting out from the barn. "Tally-Ho!" I called as I weaved through pine trees. "Tally, I have treats!"

I stopped in my tracks when I saw someone already at the split-rail fence, feeding our chestnut mare an apple. "Katie," I breathed. "Hey."

She turned and smiled at me. "Hi."

"What are you doing here?" I asked. "Back in the barn, it sounded like your mom was going over tomorrow's marching orders."

"She is," Katie said. "But I wanted some peace and quiet for a minute." She sighed contentedly. "It's been such a big night."

I smiled. "You mean an *unforgettable* night."

"Yes." She nodded as I joined her at the fence. "Or more like an unforgettable *year*."

An unforgettable year.

My breath caught, the past twelve months suddenly playing like a movie in my mind. Austin's Paris proposal, my meltdown over Katie asking me to be a bridesmaid, all the Ready-Set-Date drama, unexpectedly making new friends, and getting into my dream college—and falling in love. There had been bumps along the way, but I realized now that I wouldn't change any of it (except breaking my ankle). *You might not have Marco*, I thought, my heart igniting. *If you'd done anything differently, you might not have Marco, and you might not have…*

"Katie," I said.

"Yeah?" She turned from nuzzling Tally.

I swallowed and said, "I'm so happy you're my sister."

Her lips spread into a smile. "I'm so happy you're my sister too," she whispered after wrapping me in a hug. "Because Amanda can be *so annoying* sometimes."

"Right?" I joked. "Lucky for you, I'm *never* annoying."

We both laughed, the sound echoing into the starry night.

READ ON FOR AN EXCERPT OF
WHAT HAPPENS AFTER MIDNIGHT

ONE

Fears are meant to be faced. I just didn't expect to be facing one of mine this early in the morning. Perhaps later in the day, but before 8:00 a.m.? I could barely keep my eyes open as I yawned my way down the stairs and found my mom in the kitchen. She was eyeing the far corner cautiously, as if in a standoff with the espresso machine that sat on the soapstone countertop. "It's time." She glanced at me. Her mouth was almost a straight line, but one corner had tugged up with optimism. "We have to try."

"No, we don't," I quickly said. "We don't have to *try* anything."

My mom turned and held up the Tupperware of biscotti Mrs. DeLuca had gifted us yesterday. Our neighbor was the one who'd passed down the espresso machine in the first place; she'd bought a bigger one but hadn't wanted to get rid of the original. It was still in perfect working condition—supposedly. We'd never used it. "Lily, we must," she said. "Mrs. DeLuca specifically said that the biscotti is best when dipped in a cappuccino."

I considered the golden-brown almond biscuits. Truthfully,

they did look magnifico...and I *was* hungry. "Ah, okay," I conceded. "Let's give it a go."

Grinning, my mom hugged the Tupperware and pointed to our stainless-steel Starbucks situation. "I think the directions are somewhere in the lower cabinet."

That was my cue. My mom's strengths included storing leftovers inside the refrigerator, using the microwave, and switching on the teakettle. We'd both agreed it was best if she stuck with those. This was *my* kitchen, so naturally the cappuccinos were to be my area of expertise.

I found the car manual-sized instructions and the unopened bag of coffee beans before moving to the machinery. *A cappuccino is two-thirds milk*, I reminded myself, examining the steam wand. *A shot of espresso and then steamed milk with a frothy finish.*

Barely coffee!

Because the thing was, my mom and I didn't like coffee. We didn't like it *at all*.

My mom had disappeared upstairs to change out of her pajamas but was back by the time I had finished grinding the beans. The kitchen had been engulfed by the smell of espresso, and I gestured at her outfit through the pungent smog. "It'll never be fair that you get to wear that."

While I was stuck in a sundress and my school blazer, she sported purple camo leggings and a breezy lilac shirt. The perfect model for Lululemon, especially when she dramatically jutted out her hip. "Well, you know I'm hopping on my Peloton after first period," she teased and gave her long hair a nice fluff. I absentmindedly did the same to mine, only it was wavy and shockingly red instead of curly blond. You could spot me from a mile away. My guess was I'd gotten it from my father, but I'd never asked. He had no idea I existed, which was fine by me. He wasn't *missing* from my life; he just wasn't a part of it. And I didn't imagine I would ever need him to be. I had my mom.

"Nice nail polish," I added dryly. My mom's flip-flops showed off ten periwinkle-painted toes. Why students had a firm dress code but faculty did not was something I would never understand. "Where'd you get it?"

"Oh, from my favorite little boutique," she replied with a wink and a smile. "It's not very far from here. Just upstairs, actually…"

I rolled my eyes but maintained my barista bravado. The espresso brewed without incident, and after grabbing the milk from the fridge, I successfully steamed it into a puffy white cloud.

"Do we dunk first?" she asked after I'd poured the cappuccinos into two mugs. "Or sip?"

We decided to sip.

"Pinkies up," my mom said, and on an unspoken count of three, we raised the mugs to our lips.

"Coffee…" I soon rasped with a burnt tongue. "It's *still* coffee!"

Nose wrinkled, my mom dumped her cappuccino in the sink and waved me over to do the same. "Tea," she finally said. "We'll make tea tonight and soak the biscotti in that?"

"Deal." I nodded. "Now how about an *actual* breakfast?" I crossed the kitchen and opened the refrigerator, where two mason jars sat front and center. "I made overnight oats for us last night," I said. "I think my maple syrup-peanut butter-banana slice ratio is really coming along, and I added chia seeds this time too."

My mother considered. "I'm more in the mood for a short stack today," she admitted. "May I take those for a snack later?"

I sighed and shook my head as I handed her a jar but smirked when I raced upstairs to grab my backpack. If she wanted pancakes, we had to hurry.

Half a minute later, we hustled out the door, both weighed down by schoolwork. The sound of the sea said good morning, and I couldn't help but close my eyes and inhale the briny scent. Our house—a white clapboard cottage with dark-green shutters—might've been on the very edge of the faculty neighborhood, but it had its perks. My backyard being a beach was one of them. I had been falling asleep to the Atlantic Ocean's rolling waves for sixteen years now, ever since I was two. I'd practically lived my whole life on the Rhode Island coast. Or more specifically, I had always lived *here*, at the Ames School.

"Hello, Hopper ladies!" someone called as we speed walked through the neighborhood, my mom's flip-flops slapping against the pavement and my ballet flats warning me my day would end with blisters. "Beautiful morning, isn't it?"

"Gorgeous!" my mom called back to Penny Bickford, who

was walking toward the main campus in one of her chic power suits. I caught her assessing my mother's athleisure wear, but Ames's head of school said nothing. She never did because my mom was the most beloved teacher in the English department—maybe even the whole school since the yearbook's superlatives did not lie. Favorite teacher? That title wasn't up for grabs. Ames's Almanacs hadn't come out yet, but with only twelve days left before graduation, they would soon and everyone knew Leda Hopper was a lock.

And as her daughter, I was fortunate to be a student here. If tuition wasn't free for faculty members' children—or "fac brats" as most people called us—we never could've afforded a prep school like Ames.

"Congratulations again, Lily," my headmaster said with a proud smile. She'd known me so long that she treated me like a granddaughter. "I'm sure your speech will be marvelous."

"Thank you." I smiled back but felt my cheeks warm. Last week at our all-school meeting, I had been announced as this year's salutatorian. It was an honor, but I was also dreading it. Because while the valedictorian had the main stage at graduation, the salutatorian spoke at the senior class dinner the night before and was supposed to give a humorous address instead of a serious speech. The goal was to make your fellow alumni-to-be *laugh*.

I wasn't exactly known for my stand-up comedy routines.

"Okay, be cool, be cool," my mom stage-whispered once

we'd crossed the covered bridge that led to campus. We slowed our pace to a casual walk. Beautiful brick, clapboard, and cedar-shingled academic buildings and dormitories rose in front of us, and students were everywhere. Some were on their morning runs while others had clearly just rolled out of bed to drag themselves over to the dining hall for breakfast. I overheard a group of girls giggling about their upcoming freshman formal.

"Yeah, Ross asked me last night," one girl said. "It was super sweet. He asked for help on our math homework, and under the final question, he wrote 'Will you go to formal with me?'"

"Good for you, Ross," my mom murmured, smiling. Her students didn't just talk to her about grammar and *The Great Gatsby*. She had a way with them, a way that encouraged them to truly open up to her. Insisting they call her by her first name instead of "Ms. Hopper" was always an effective first step. She was a beyond-tough grader, but they adored her.

The freshmen soon noticed us. "Leda, guess what?!" they shrieked, and while she got all the exciting details, I pretended to listen along but really thought back to my own freshman formal. He'd called me, introduced himself as if we weren't already acquainted, and then asked if I wanted to go with him in a nervous rush of words. "Yes, that would be nice," I'd replied, and several weeks later, my gold dress had been splashed with salt water and sand by the end of the night. While walking me home, he'd raced me barefoot along the beach and I'd kissed him as soon as he'd caught me up in his arms. His lips had been warm despite the wind. "Tag," I remembered whispering afterward, my smile so wide. Both of us were breathless.

"You're it," he finished for me, then laughed before I kissed him again and took off into the darkness, hoping he would follow.

I wish we could go back, I thought, the words a murmur in my mind. *I wish we could go back to the very first night...*

"Lily?" I blinked to see my mom looking at me. The freshmen were gone; they must've migrated toward the dining hall, but we hadn't strayed from our route to the historic Hubbard Hall. My mom held the door open and ruffled my hair as I walked through it.

With soaring white columns, distinguished brick chimneys, and innumerable windows, Hubbard Hall looked like a mansion that once belonged to the last great American dynasty. It had a rooftop balcony and housed the Alumni Relations, Financial Aid, and College Counseling departments on the upper floors, but Ames's student center ruled the ground floor. Leather couches and wing-backed armchairs and an array of Persian rugs created a lounge-like lobby, and every time you looked at the cream walls, you noticed something new. There was a rotating gallery of student artwork and Ames memorabilia from the library's archives: old newspaper articles, photographs, and even antique school flags.

Beyond the lounge, the hall's huge limestone fireplace was flanked by built-in bookcases and study nooks. To the left were the newspaper and yearbook offices and the mail room, and to the right was what everyone simply called "the Hub." The little restaurant was the student center's main attraction. Vintage nautical lanterns hung over each booth, and the white beadboard walls held an impressive collection of black-and-white photos featuring generations of fishermen showing off their catches.

Oh, and the mouthwatering diner food. Everyone was always trying to squeeze in a quick bite between classes or during their free periods.

But only seniors and faculty were allowed to eat breakfast here. We pushed through the door to find the place packed. "Well, it's a good thing I made special arrangements," my mom said, leading me to a table in the back. I'd wager it was only empty because of a folded piece of paper that read, RESERVED!

My mother plucked it off the warm wooden table and slipped it in her tote bag, but the Hub's head honcho was on us the second we got comfortable in our teak chairs. "Reservations are not allowed," Josh said, all deadpan with a pencil tucked behind his ear.

"I will have cinnamon roll pancakes," my mother replied brightly. "Please do not skimp on the vanilla frosting."

Josh gave her a look. "Leda."

She tilted her head and smiled. "Josh."

I glanced around the Hub, not interested in listening to my mother and her boyfriend flirt today. It would sound like bickering to anyone else, but Leda was the ray of sunshine to

Josh's seriousness. Any true romantic would agree that they were a perfect match.

Half the boys' lacrosse team had jammed themselves into a booth and were rehashing their recent playoff loss, cradling invisible balls in their invisible sticks. At the next table over, Zoe Wright caught my eye and threw up her arms. *You lost!* she mouthed. *Get over it!*

I smiled and shook my head, then spotted Tag Swell and Alex Nguyen sitting together at the counter. Alex was talking a mile a minute and taking colossal bites of his waffles while Tag strategically squirted ketchup all over his scrambled eggs.

Gross, I thought but continued to watch him with a pang in my stomach. He liked putting ketchup on everything.

"But like, are you *sure*?" Alex said. "Because…"

I rolled my eyes. They were most likely talking about Tag's latest breakup. He and Blair Greenberg had gotten together last year, and their relationship had been a feast for the hypothetical tabloids. One second, they were stupidly in love, and the next, they were a hot mess, shouting at each other during Saturday night dances. The student body had been pretty much over the whole song and dance until Tag broke things off with Blair yesterday. "Who cares anymore?" we'd mumbled to ourselves, but the truth was, everyone cared. We all wanted to know what went down between them. Would this be the last time? The final time they went their separate ways? Or would they get back together in a couple days?

Because again, it was the tail end of Ames's "senior spring." With less than two weeks left in the term, we upperclassmen cared about approximately three things.

The prom was one of them.

And Tag Swell had dumped his girlfriend right beforehand, with no apparent rhyme or reason. "Yes, I'm sure," he told Alex now. "I want to go with someone else."

Who? I wondered at the same time as Alex said, "Who?"

Tag finally put down the ketchup bottle. "Well, isn't it obvious?" He smirked at his best friend. "You, Alexander."

Alex didn't miss a beat; he raised his water glass in a toast. "It'd be my pleasure, Taggart. How do you feel about matching boutonnieres?"

A small lump formed in my throat. Tag and Alex's bromance was one for the books; they were so close that sometimes they seemed like the same person. "We met in freshman algebra and just *knew*," Alex once told me. "Whoever marries him is marrying me too."

I'd punched him in the arm. "And she shall be the *un*luckiest of ladies!"

God, that had been ages ago.

Soon, I heard Josh sigh in defeat. My mom had worn him down for the morning. "Okay, Lily," he said to me. "What would you like for breakfast? Your mom"—he looked at her with revulsion—"is having cinnamon roll pancakes."

"I'll take an orange juice, please," I said as I unzipped my backpack and began digging around inside. "With a spoon on the side." I emerged victorious with my jar of overnight oats. "I brought my own today."

"Yes!" Josh snapped his fingers. It was ironic he ran the Hub because he was really a health nut. "This is what I'm talking about, Lil. I love to see it." He faced my mom. "You should try eating something off your daughter's menu."

My mom folded her hands on the table. "For your information, she made a lovely chicken stir-fry last night. I helped with the prep work."

Josh turned to me for confirmation, and I nodded. "But cinnamon roll pancakes *do* sound amazing," I added. "May I get a fork with my spoon? That way, I can steal some bites?"

We laughed when Josh groaned. "Exasperating," he said. "You two are endlessly *exasperating*. First, reservations. And now this?" He shook his head.

"Excuse me, but endlessly exasperating?" my mom said once her boyfriend had disappeared into the kitchen. "I'd say he finds us endlessly *fascinating*."

"Yes," I agreed. I loved these breakfasts with her. "Endlessly fascinating, for sure."

READ ON FOR AN EXCERPT OF
MAYBE MEANT TO BE

CHAPTER 1
SAGE

There were cigarettes wedged in the cracks of my windowsill, and my mom noticed right away. "Those aren't mine!" I blurted when she held up two of them, tips browned and singed. This was a given, because I'd lived in this room for all of ten minutes. My sheets weren't even on the bed yet.

She frowned and shook her head. "Use an ashtray next time."

"Maybe it's in here," my dad joked, pulling out one of my desk drawers. I was surprised the cleaning crew hadn't caught the butts. My mom had opened the window because the smell of Clorox was so strong.

"Who lived here last year?" she asked.

"Schuyler Cole," I said, and couldn't help but laugh as she dug out another stub. I almost told her to stop, since I kind of wanted to show the girls later. Up on the third floor, my friend Reese had already texted us that her room's last occupant left her prom dress hanging in the closet.

Not a night to remember? I'd written back.

"Schuyler Cole..." my mom mused. "Isn't she...?"

"Yeah, Charlie's ex."

She nodded. "Will he be coming by to say hello later? And help, since we all know how much you *love* unpacking?"

"We wish." I smiled. "He's still in rehearsal." Charlie had gotten a weeklong head start here at Bexley, moving into school early for the musical's "preseason." This year's show was *Into the Woods*, and he was playing none other than Prince Charming.

My mom sighed. "What about Nicky?"

I shook my head. "Soccer."

"Andrea," my dad said, chuckling. "We don't need the extra labor. This is Sage's senior year. We've got this."

I smiled. My parents were divorced, but I loved that they always moved me in together. "Oh, that's a relief." I faked a yawn. "Because I'm a little woozy from this smell." I flopped down on my mattress and shut my eyes. "Please wake me when the people from Pottery Barn Teen arrive for the photo shoot."

I went to boarding school, but I didn't grow up *thinking* I'd go to boarding school. When I was in third grade, I'd fantasized about someday wearing blue and white at Darien High School's football games and maybe being voted homecoming queen. But all that had gone out the window in eighth grade. Holding court from the back of the bus, Charlie told me he couldn't come over and binge on ice cream and Netflix because he needed to go home and work on his Bexley application. "Mom wants Nick and me to start them today," he'd explained. "She doesn't want us to get behind."

"Wait, Bexley?" I'd said. "*The* Bexley School? Like where Kitsey went? You guys are going to go?"

"Well, yeah." Charlie shrugged. "We all go. My grandfather, my dad, Kitsey… Of course, Nicky and I are gonna go."

So naturally, I started my own application as soon as I'd gotten home and finished an episode of *Gossip Girl* and a bowl of Ben & Jerry's Half Baked. If Charlie was going to Bexley, then I was too. I wasn't going to let us be separated.

I smiled as I tacked a picture of us up over my bed. One of me wearing Charlie's spare hockey jersey with black paint under my eyes and standing on his skates as he danced us around outside the locker room. It went next to a fifth-grade snapshot, taken after our school's production of *Charlie and the Chocolate Factory*. We both held huge flower bouquets.

My parents were gone, my mom en route back to Connecticut and my dad to New York, and the girls and I were about to head over to the Pearson Arts Center for Move-In Day's school meeting. "Okay, enough pictures," Reese said, and waved her phone around. "Jennie sent the scouting report."

"Oh, yes!" Nina hopped up from my desk chair. "Anyone British?"

I laughed. "You're not still hung up on Jamie, are you?"

Nina blushed. "Listen, he was *really* nice."

"But he had that *posh* girlfriend back home, Miss Davies," Reese reminded her, nodding her head toward my door. Nina and I followed her out of the room, down the hall and stairs, and once outside, we were swept up in the sea of students. Bexley had rolled out the welcome wagon: the auditorium had our black-and-blue school flags streaming down from the windows, and odds were, Headmaster Griswold, with his retro handlebar mustache, was greeting people as they passed through the front doors. It was the same way every year, and though I'd been so excited on the drive here, I suddenly felt something in me deflate, like I was secretly hoping that this time would be different.

But all signs pointed to same old, same old.

"Okay, Jennie's list," I prompted as we walked, arms linked. Jennie Chu was our fourth musketeer, and as student council president, she'd scored a lineup of this year's postgraduate guys. They were the new kids in the senior class, and most of them came to Bexley for sports after graduating from their own high schools. They were known to everyone as the PGs. Nina's beloved Jamie had been a soccer PG last year.

Reese scanned her phone. "No Brits," she concluded. "But there're two football guys, both from Texas, a lax bro from Long Island..." She glanced up and smirked at me. "Sage, you're *so* lucky."

"Why?" I asked. "Is Shawn Mendes here this year?"

My friend shook her head. "No, but someone named Luke Morrissey is, and you'll get to meet him very soon."

Luke Morrissey, I thought. *Why does that ring a bell?*

"Oh my god," Nina said. "You're going to sit next to each other at the meeting. Morgan and Morrissey. Alphabetical order!"

"I recognize his name for some reason," I said. "What's he here for?"

"Cross-country," Reese answered. "He's from someplace in Michigan called Grosse Pointe."

"It's right outside Detroit," Nina informed us after consulting Google Maps on her phone. She looked at me.

I shrugged. "Grosse Pointe sounds kind of familiar."

But why?

"Find his Insta," Reese said. That was her answer to everything. Instagram.

I laughed. "Okay, no. I don't want to know that his family has a goldendoodle named Waffle before we actually meet."

She raised an eyebrow. "Waffle?"

"Yeah! How cute would that be?"

"So cu—" Nina started, but then the mob of students surged forward, so we surged with it, getting torn apart by the time we made it into the PAC's lobby. A thousand voices bounced off the white walls as I elbowed my way through a horde of junior boys in striped polo shirts, suddenly excited to find my new auditorium seat.

Because after nearly getting tripped up in the balloons out front, I'd figured out who Luke Morrissey was. A conversation in May with Charlie had started: "My aunt Caroline called last night and said the kid who babysits my cousins is coming to Bexley next year. The one Tater Tot is in love with…"

"You're the Carmichael twins' cousins' babysitter!" I exclaimed the second I turned into my row, and at that, a head turned…

An *adorable* head.

But an adorable head that also looked like I'd just slapped him in the face. I saw his cheeks heat, and when I dropped into my seat next to him, he reached up and ran a hand through his jet-black hair. ("The kind of hair you want to run your hands through," I'd tell the girls later). His eyes darted around behind tortoiseshell glasses. "Uh, pardon?" he asked.

"You're the Carmichael twins' cousins' babysitter," I repeated.

"Or Luke." The guy nodded. "I go by Luke too. Less of a mouthful."

I smiled and held out my hand. "I'm Sage."

We shook. "Nice to meet you," Luke said, and then he was quiet. Not awkward-quiet, but definitely shy-quiet.

That didn't faze me.

"So, why are you at Bexley?" I asked, even though I already knew he ran cross-country. I also wanted to pinch myself at how enthusiastic I sounded. *But at least Charlie isn't here.* "You and Charlie freak people out," Nick once told me. "You guys are like sunshine on steroids."

"Oh," Luke said. "My indecision."

I blinked. "What?"

Luke smirked, and I felt a flutter in my chest. "My indecision."

My eyebrows knitted together. "You *aren't* here for cross-country?"

"No." He shook his head. "I mean yes, I *do* run cross-country, but that's not why I'm here. I graduated from my high school last year, but with zero idea what I wanted to do for college." He hesitated. "This, uh, also might sound stupid, but I didn't feel ready for it."

"Well, no offense," I said with a laugh, "but you certainly don't *look* ready for it."

Luke smiled and rolled his eyes. "Yes, I'm aware I look fourteen. My sister, Becca, who *is* fourteen, looks older than I do."

"Did you apply anywhere else? Or just here?"

"No, also Lawrenceville, Taft, and Kent. But this was my first choice."

I nodded. "So you've met Charlie and Nick?"

Another head shake. "Not yet. You know them well?"

"You could say that." I grinned. "We took baths together back in the day."

"What're they like?"

"Oh, well, Charlie's the best!" I said, but then the PAC's lights dimmed, and the giant projection screen lowered in front of the stage's blue velvet curtain. I smiled and got comfortable in my seat. *This* was the reason for the stampede inside; it was tradition for the student council to emcee school meetings, and they always made an *entrance* for the very first one.

"Get ready," I whispered to Luke. "You're going to *love* this."

This was a ten-minute video of Bexley meets *The Office*, and I wanted to nominate it for an Emmy. The skit was a mock student council meeting, with each member playing up their title. President Jennie was banging the oval-shaped Harkness table in frustration over how Bexley was a good school, but this year, it was their job to make it a *great* one!

"I appreciate Jennie's passion," VP Samir Khan said in a confessional, "but in order to make this a great school, she needs to support my ideas for a stronger peer tutoring system, instead of just focusing on the athletic and theater departments…"

Then the camera panned to a shot of Jennie in the library, with the redheaded Carmichael twins waiting on her hand and foot. "You're really tense, Madam President," Nick, in his hockey jersey, told Jennie as he massaged her shoulders.

"Oh, Nick, I *know*. Feel free to dig in *harder*…" She sighed happily as Charlie held up a chocolate from the enormous box on his lap. He was decked out in his Prince Charming costume and totally grinning. ("That boy could set off fireworks with his smile," my mom always said.)

"And this one, dearest Jen, has a raspberry *cream* filling." He took a slow, seductive bite of the candy and licked his lips before popping the rest into Jennie's mouth.

"That's them," I whispered to Luke.

Luke nodded, but didn't say anything. He just watched, and then listened as Jennie came onstage and welcomed everyone to the new school year before introducing the rest of her cabinet. "And last but not least, this is your Arts Representative, Charlie Carmichael," she told us. "His favorite color is blue, he loves Cool Ranch Doritos, and before you ask, *no*, he is not a paid model for Vineyard Vines!"

Out of the corner of my eye, I saw Luke lean forward in his seat.

ACKNOWLEDGMENTS

"It's been a long time coming…"

Because it has! I wrote this book in 2023! Two years ago!

A First Time for Everything might've taken the scenic route to publication, but words cannot describe how happy I am that readers finally have it in their hands. I'm extremely fond of this one.

Eva Scalzo, thank you for responding to my fast and furious and totally stream-of-consciousness texts (most of which were sent while I hid in Barnes & Noble's philosophy section). Whenever I brainstorm a new book concept, I love nothing more than fleshing it out with you. If I'm remembering correctly, I had a map for Mads before my lunch break that day. Our partnership is, to quote a very niche singer-songwriter named Taylor Swift, "so productive, it's an art."

Cheers to the team at Sourcebooks! Annie, Gabbi, Delaney, Karen, Thea, and Aimee. Thank you for being so supportive and patient when the manuscript I was supposed to be writing turned into something else entirely. You have given me the freedom to write four books of my heart, and I am incredibly grateful.

Shout-out to Monique Aimee, for another stunning cover—I can't help but feel all the warm and fuzzies because it hits so close to my home.

Kelly Townsend, one of the reasons I get so excited when I finish a draft is because it means I can finally send it to you. I truly hit the beta-reader jackpot.

Thank you to Anthony, for your artistic eye and renovating my website pro bono. Squarespace will never defeat you!

To Michael, because you are still the best.

Nell Webber, retired Division 1 field hockey superstar (and beloved cousin): thank you so much for outlining the college recruiting process, creating a mock practice plan, and answering all my random questions. Not everything made it into this book, but hopefully I made you proud!

Scout Webber, I adore you for sharing your dating shenanigans. You keep me young.

And the rest of the Webbers! I am so obsessed with and in love with and proud of our family; I would never be able to do this without you. Stone Harbor summers will always hold a special place in my heart.

I want to extend an apology to Ross Webber and the other Princetonians in my life: I am sorry I took creative liberties with your eating clubs; I know you don't "bicker" until your sophomore year, but I really wanted Marco in Tower. Forgive me, won't you?

Thank you to everyone with ties to the unforgettable Palmer-Schenker wedding. Not only was it a hell of a party, but it was also so wonderful to see all the love, light, and joy that surrounds Madison and Chris. Suzanne, my mouth waters when I daydream about your bridal shower spread, and Delaney, I still think about our Dragonfly Landing weekend and giggle to myself. You successfully herded cats. #Mad4Chris

Madison: I have so loved growing up together, because it means I've gotten to watch you become the incredible woman you are today. Whenever you do something extraordinary, I think to myself, *That's my best friend!*

A hundred tugs on the sleeve of Josh Walther, the wittiest and coolest and most cherished uncle in all the land (Play with us, play with us, play with us!!!). Thank you for introducing me to NOLA, helping me decide which credit card to apply for, and always making me laugh. I'm glad you agree that the barn would've made an excellent office space.

Tibbles. Timmy, you were the best personal assistant an author could ever have; I am so grateful to you for running errands upon errands last year, chauffeuring me all over the place, and cooking dinner every night. And Tommy, thank you for every single piece of financial advice. I feel so unconditionally supported by you both and hope you know the feeling is mutual.

Christopher: I started drafting this book after the stars finally aligned in 2022, and it was a huge challenge...because you made writing a romantic lead nearly impossible. How was any love interest ever going to make me swoon when I had this devastatingly handsome man creating his own algorithm to track my sales? Tell me, how?! I'll admit Marco managed to make me blush (multiple times), but you are the book boyfriend of my dreams and my absolute favorite person.

The biggest thank-you to my parents, this time for buying a white farmhouse with black shutters and a red door in 2005. Despite the list of renovation projects (the kitchen would've been beautiful, had it come to fruition), 6 Old Barn Court (or Sarah's "Camp Ralph Lauren") was nothing short of an idyllic backdrop for childhood. The cookouts, campouts, personality-plus dogs, Halloween festivities, street hockey, snow days, sweet treats, lacrosse sticks, laughter, and so much love—thank you, for all of it.

And finally, a love note to my readers: your enthusiasm—or, dare I say, passion—for my characters and their stories truly helps me soar. You have made the KLW Universe possible, and I'm in awe of every single one of you. XO

ABOUT THE AUTHOR

K. L. Walther was born and raised in the rolling hills of Bucks County, Pennsylvania, surrounded by family, dogs, and books. Her childhood was spent traveling the northeastern seaboard to play ice hockey. She attended a boarding school in New Jersey and went on to earn a BA in English from the University of Virginia. She is happiest on the beach with a book, cheering for the New York Rangers, or enjoying a rom-com while digging into a big bowl of popcorn and M&Ms. She is also the author of *Maybe Meant to Be*, *The Summer of Broken Rules*, and *What Happens After Midnight*. Visit her online at klwalther.com.

sourcebooks fire

Home of the hottest trends in YA!

Visit us online and
sign up for our newsletter at
FIREreads.com

....

Follow
@sourcebooksfire
online